*b*

## PRAISE FOR CHERYL ANNE PORTER

### MAD ABOUT MADDIE

"A frothy romantic confection . . . energetic prose and snappy dialogue." — *Publishers Weekly*

"A cute, funny story . . . Cheryl Anne Porter makes a great splash with her first single title contemporary release." — *Interludes*

"Filled with humor and sexual tension . . . *Mad About Maddie* is a quirky love story that will make readers smile." — *Writers Club Romance*

"Ms. Porter is better known for her historical romance, but readers will be delighted with her humorous take on modern day romance . . . Guaranteed to have the reader laughing." — *Romancereviewstoday.com*

"Readers will be mad about Cheryl Anne Porter's delectably humorous contemporary romance." — *Reviewers Book Watch*

*J*

# POPPING THE QUESTION

## CHERYL ANNE PORTER

St. Martin's Paperbacks

POPPING THE QUESTION

Copyright © 2002 by Cheryl Anne Porter.

ISBN: 0-312-98282-8

Printed in the United States of America

St. Martin's Paperbacks edition / September 2002

St. Martin's Paperbacks are published by St. Martin's Press, 175 Fifth Avenue, New York, NY 10010.

10 9 8 7 6 5 4 3 2 1

*To Nick and Paul and Mark and Jim, four very mono-syllabic men—for popping the question to, and bringing into our family, Tara and Sarah and Diane and Dianna, four equally rhyming women . . . well, almost.*

# POPPING THE
# QUESTION

# CHAPTER 1

"Will you marry me?"

"God, no."

"Ah, for the—I give up. What'd I do wrong *this* time?"

"Everything." Closeted in the private salon of her shop with the nightmare boy-next-door from her youth who had tormented her from diapers to senior prom, and who was now her inept client, Dianna West engaged in a staring contest of clashing wills with Lenny Daschowitz. No way, she vowed, was he going to make her lose her poise. Because if he did, she feared she would—and much too cheerfully—strangle him.

Lenny stood in front of her, no taller than five-feet-seven and almost as round. Dressed all in black, he bore an unfortunate resemblance to a total eclipse. A stubborn pout claimed his full-moon face. "Oh, I did *everything* wrong? Like what? I spoke in hieroglyphics or something?"

Dianna ignored that. "You're supposed to be down on one knee when you propose."

"Says who?"

"I do." . . . *you whiny little shit.* Though her smile was bright, she offered it through gritted teeth. "And so does tradition. You said you wanted tradition."

With a flick of his wrist, Lenny waved this away. "Tradition, schmadition. Besides, you just said 'I do.' So that's a 'yes,' and we're done here."

*God, he will never get this right.* But if he didn't, Dianna vowed it wouldn't be for lack of trying on her part. She pointed to the carpeted floor. "Bended knee, Lenny. Now."

He grumbled and muttered, but Dianna held to her resolve, punctuating it with an avenging-genie stance . . . arms folded together, eyes narrowed in warning. Still, she hated how being around Lenny brought out the worst in her. But he'd messed with her so much when they were kids. Stupid things. Throwing water balloons, pushing her down, following her everywhere, taking her lunch money, tattling on her, hitting her, obnoxious things like that. The memories and resentments remained, and they were enough to make her teeth itch just being in the same room with him.

But childhood irritations, she reminded herself, were not the point here. Instead, the points were these: She and Lenny were now grown-ups; she was a successful business owner; and Lenny was an idiot. But a paying idiot. So, she should be nice to him, if for no other reason than that. However, there was a better reason. One word: Mom. That sweet, oblivious, little traitor. This was all her idea. *"Now, you help Lenny, honey,"* she'd said. *"It would be a nice thing to do."* There was no human way to say no to the woman's gray-haired, apple-cheeked appeal.

Bottom line? If Dianna were mean to Lenny, he would tell *his* mother. And then that impossible woman would run next door to *Dianna's* mother and tattle on her. Next scene? Her mother on the phone to her, dealing out guilt. See? Complete and total hell to pay and for years to come.

Dianna forced her attention back to Lenny. Surprise! Though his bottom lip still poked out sulkily, he was actually complying with her on-bended-knee command. Basking in her victory, Dianna magnanimously offered him encouragement as he awkwardly eased himself down to the carpet. "Careful now. Take it easy." Going one huge step farther, she gave his icky Lenny-shoulder a congratulatory pat. "Good, Lenny. Like that. So, are you comfortable?"

"Do I look comfortable?" The man's cranky tone of voice underscored his question, which he went on to answer. "No, I'm not comfortable. It hurts like hell."

Exasperation ate at the edges of her patience. "Why does it hurt, Lenny? What's wrong?"

"I had surgery on this knee."

Dianna's heart nearly stopped. "Surgery? Why didn't you say so? Get up, you"—she struggled for control of her tongue—"big silly man, you." Grabbing his arm, she pulled upward on him. But gravity proved stronger. She could not levitate him one inch. "When did you have surgery? I don't remember that."

"Five years ago."

"Five *years* ago?" Dianna let go of Lenny with a vengeance. "Lenny, I could just—five *years* ago?"

"Is there an echo in here or what? I keep hearing 'five years ago,' 'five years ago.' "

Stepping back, fists punched to her waist, Dianna glared at the man and inhaled deeply . . . slowly . . . very calmly . . . held her breath a therapeutic length of time . . . and then gently exhaled. Relaxation technique, followed by thinking good thoughts. *Okay, good thoughts. It's Friday; it's springtime in Baltimore, trees are in bloom, the air is sweet; and my time with Lenny won't last forever because I am not stuck with him for all of eternity in the ninth ring of Dante's vision of Hell.*

Feeling much refreshed now, Dianna forced a helpful note into her voice. "Okay, look, can you get down on your other knee, maybe? I don't want you to do it if you really can't. But it is more romantic for the guy to be on bended knee when he pops the question."

"So I keep paying to hear you say. But if it's what I gotta do to get you off my back, then I'm gonna do it." Having said that, Lenny set about switching knees. Overweight and graceless, he rolled about, much like an off-balance sumo wrestler.

Dianna's eyes widened. Maybe this on-bended-knee thing was a bad idea after all. She made a feint in Lenny's direction to steady him—but stopped just as suddenly. Holding her in place was the realization that to help Lenny at this point might shame him. And she really didn't want to do that. *Great. Now I'm a nice person, and Lenny really isn't all that bad; is that it?* Maybe. And maybe she didn't even dislike him all that much. *Fine.* This left her with no other choice than to stand there and hope for the best.

Alas, hope died a quick, hard death. Lenny fell. Yelping his shock, he landed heavily on all fours . . . and glared at Dianna. She stood frozen in place, her hands clapped over her mouth. Lenny sent her a look that signaled this was clearly her fault. "What are you doing just standing there? You can't see I need help getting up, or what?"

"Right." Dianna jumped into the fray—it was all right now; she had his permission—struggling right along with him and his ungainly bulk. Many moments of teeth-gritting effort followed until she finally—*finally!*—got him into an acceptable marriage-proposal position. "There. Whew." She backed away, again planting her hands at her waist and offering encouragement. "Say, you look pretty good down there, Lenny."

"Ha. Tell me that when I'm at Tamborello's Ristorante Italiano tonight"—the man's voice was a grating sneer—"and can't get back up. I'll be a living fat joke. Everyone will be laughing, and I'll have to crawl out on all fours."

"Oh, stop that, Lenny. We're trying to get you happily on the road to marriage, remember? So, come on, try it again. Ask me."

Lenny muttered a particularly pungent curse word that had Dianna widening her eyes. Though impressed with his eloquence, she pressed on with her own point. "Remember, we need heartfelt here. Make me *feel* it."

"The only thing I *feel* is excruciating pain in my good kneecap now."

Life would be so much better, Dianna decided, if she could just pummel Lenny silly. Without repercussions, of course. Instead, she smiled. "There's one way to get it to quit hurting, and that's to actually propose so you can get up."

Lenny poked out his thick bottom lip. "Who knew it would be this hard?"

"Me, Lenny. I knew it would be this hard because I knew you'd make it hard. Now, ask me to marry you, dammit, and quit stalling around."

Down on his good knee, looking pained and with his chubby thigh straining against his slacks, curly-haired mama's boy Lenny Daschowitz simulated holding up a diamond engagement ring. He gazed into Dianna's eyes and tried again. "Will you marry me?"

"No, Lenny, I will not. I mean, come on—am I the only one here? Have you not heard anything I've said? Heart. Love. Feelings. Where are they? This is a *big* moment, Lenny. The-rest-of-your-life big."

Dianna paused, rubbing absently at her temple as she stared at Lenny and tried to come up with another way to get through to him. "Look, here's the thing: Tonight is the only time when you're in control of the whole 'getting married' experience. Once you pop the question, Lenny, it's out of your hands. Your bride-to-be, her mother, and your mother take over from there. Trust me, the little guy on top of the wedding cake will have more say than you do after tonight. So you have to play it for all it's worth."

"I will. But, jeez, Dianna, you're busting my balls here."

Dianna looked deeply, threateningly, into Lenny's eyes and spoke very slowly. "That can be arranged, my friend, so don't give me any ideas." When Lenny's eyes widened satisfactorily, she pointedly checked her wristwatch. *Yes. Nearly three o'clock.* Joy that her allotted hour with Lenny was nearly up brought a bright smile to Dianna's face. "We don't have much time left. We'll have to hurry."

Lenny puckered his mouth into a pout. "Too late. My foot's gone to sleep, and I'm about to fall over like a beached whale."

Well, he'd forced that unflattering image onto her consciousness, now hadn't he? Lenny's pale body washed up in the surf; a water brigade tossing little Styrofoam cups of sea water on him; the crowd exhorting him to live. No more than he deserved. "*Anyway,* and before that happens, Lenny, one last try. Heart and soul. Give it all you've got."

"Maybe I could if you'd help me get in the mood. Maybe if you did something romantic. Like French-kiss me."

"Sure," Dianna sang cheerfully. "When the headlines read 'Pigs Fly Out of a Frozen Hell.' That's the very same day I'll French-kiss you, Lenny. Look forward to it."

This was lost on Lenny. A Little Boy Naughty expression on his face, he brought himself ever nearer the brink of disaster. "Then maybe you could sit on my lap, and we could talk about the first thing that pops up. Get it? Pop up?"

"You're the one who's going to get it." Dianna shook a scolding finger at him. "Do not provoke me into being physical, Lenny. If I have to smack you, I will. And I will *still* send you a bill. Don't think I won't."

He shrugged as if that were of no consequence to him. "It was worth a try. After all, I'll be a married man soon. I need to sow my wild oats while I can."

"Wild oats. Right. You have less than five minutes left, Lenny, and then I have another client coming in."

Without any warning, Lenny's entire demeanor changed to pathetic, his heart in his eyes. "It's no use pretending. I can't do this, Dianna."

Daunted by this show of a real, live, human emotion on Lenny's part, Dianna proceeded with caution. "Sure you can."

His face reddening, beads of sweat dewing his upper lip, Lenny shook his head. "No, I can't. I never, you know, sowed oats in my whole life. I don't know what to do . . . after the wedding, I mean. Well, I know *what* to do. I just don't know *how* to do it. I mean, how to do it right, so it's good for—"

"Aaah! Stop! Enough said, I get it, I get it, shut up!" Dianna had her hands clapped over her ears until she felt certain Lenny understood he was not to say one single word more. Only then did she sit down heavily on the padded seat of the white wrought-iron chair that was, luckily, right behind her. "Lenny, look at me. We—you and I—cannot have this conversation. If you don't know what to do, you get that information like other guys do. And I mean from dirty videos and magazines. You got that?"

His expression very hangdog, very pathetic, Lenny nodded that he did.

"Good." Crossing her arms atop her knees, Dianna leaned in toward the distraught man. He might be exasperating as hell, but apparently she did care a tiny, little bit about his feelings. "Are you telling me you don't want to get married, Lenny? Because if that's true, then why are we putting ourselves through all *this*?"

She accompanied her words with a sweeping gesture that included her shop and implied her time, the cost, the musician with the violin, the flowers, the rented tux, reservations at Tamborello's restaurant . . . everything that she'd arranged to make this night special for Lenny and his intended. "Did you actually read the sign out front? It says POPPING THE QUESTION. See, we help guys like you come up with romantic scenarios so you can ask your girlfriends, in unforgettable ways, to marry you. You knew that when you came in here."

Like a scolded little boy, though he was thirty years old, Lenny lowered his gaze and picked at his bitten-off fingernails.

Dianna stared in total dismay at the top of the man's

curly-haired head. Yes, he was a mess, and yes, she could sympathize with him. But, on another level, she simply could *not* believe that it was Lenny Daschowitz, of all people, who might ruin her business's perfect score. After one year of being open, she and her associates owned a one-hundred-percent track record. Meaning that every client who'd come to them seeking their help had received a yes from his or her—mostly his—sweetheart. Sweet success. And a totally killer advertising campaign, already in the works, would soon debut around that very fact. That, and a lot of publicity. Television. Newspapers. Magazines.

Now, wouldn't she look foolish and have a lot of explaining to do if that statistic were no longer true by the time the ad spots aired? Okay, so it wouldn't be the end of the world. But her business could lose credibility. And *that* could mean the end of her business. Which, in turn, *could* be the end of the world because her elderly parents had loaned her their entire life's savings to get Popping the Question up and running. They believed in her. And she had yet to repay them. So no freakin' way was Lenny Daschowitz going to be the spoiler for her and her family. No. Just wasn't going to happen. Lenny *would* marry Olivia if it was the last thing she, Dianna Joan West, ever did. End of discussion.

Thus resolved, Dianna tucked her hair behind her ears and poked a finger at Lenny's shoulder. "So talk to me. What are you doing here if you don't want to get married?"

Lenny sighed heavily. "I *have* to get married."

Dianna smacked his arm. "Oh, shut up. You do not. You just said you haven't ever—"

"And I haven't," he whined, rubbing his arm where Dianna had cuffed him. "I didn't mean like that. I meant Mother said I have to. She said it's time, and she's paying for everything. She wants grandchildren."

Fear seized Dianna. *Little Daschowitzes everywhere? No. Please.* Then she thought of Lenny's girlfriend.

Sweet, timid Olivia Goldman, who was going to be surprised and swept off her feet—if there was a God—by Lenny tonight. The woman had been waiting years for this moment, and Dianna was determined that it would come to pass. "And what about Olivia? She deserves better than this, don't you think? She deserves a man who wants her and loves her."

Looking defeated, with actual tears standing in his eyes, Lenny nodded. "I shouldn't have said all that because I do love Olivia, and I do want to marry her."

*Here we go.* How many times in the past year, in her professional capacity as a proposal planner, Dianna wondered, had she—though only twenty-six herself—turned into counselor and surrogate mother? "All right, Lenny, this is good. If you love her, it will be all right. I mean that. You both deserve happiness."

His expression remained woeful. "We're going to live with Mother."

Alarmed, Dianna clutched at Lenny's arm and shook it as she spoke. "No. Do you hear me, Lenny? *No.* Do not do that. Run. Grab up Olivia and skip town. Get your own apartment. Or live in a refrigerator box under a bridge. Anything but with your mother." *Who lives next door to mine, so I'd have to see you and your X-File offspring every time I visit. Yikes.* Dianna's next thought, though, had her releasing his arm and sitting up straight. "Wait. Why aren't you moving into Olivia's place?"

"Her lease is up, and the landlord raised the rent. We can't afford it now. And Mother won't give me the money for it. Then Olivia's employer moved his business out of state to the Sun Belt, and she didn't want to go. So she doesn't have a job now. And Mother has never let me work."

"I know. That's what makes you special, Lenny." Dianna stared at the man and rubbed absently at her temples. Nutshell conclusion? The wheels were coming off this whole affair. "So . . . Lenny, your mother. The three of you. Together. Does she at least get along with Olivia?

I mean, well enough for them to be in the same room together. You know, like in the winter and without physical violence. That kind of thing."

Again, Lenny shrugged. "I guess. She's a nice girl. Olivia, I mean. Not Mother. Well, I guess she was, too, at one time. My poor departed father had to have seen *something* in her."

"No doubt." Dianna knew that story. Lenny's poor father wasn't departed in the conventional sense. No, the man had apparently, one sunny day, decided he'd had enough of his wealthy but shrewish and penny-pinching wife. So off to the store he'd gone, never to return. No one was surprised. Dianna stood, assuming a brisk but cheery businesslike manner. "All right, you love Olivia and your mother can't live forever—Oh, sorry, no offense meant. Anyway, this could still have a happy ending. So let's do this, Lenny. Take my hand, pretend you have the ring, and ask me to marry you."

Lenny fidgeted about. "My whole leg is asleep now."

"Then hurry. And use Olivia's name, not mine."

Though still a bit crestfallen, Lenny took Dianna's offered hand and breathed in noisily through his nose, while with his free hand he made big loops in the air, as if gathering to him the moment and the ambience. "So we've got violin music. A darkened restaurant. Flowers. Et cetera. Very romantic. A couple of drinks. The ring. I can feel it now . . . and here it is." His expression dramatically earnest, Lenny turned his doe's eyes up to Dianna. "Olivia, I love you. And you would make me the happiest man alive if you would be my wife. Will you marry me?"

Elation filled Dianna and spilled over into her grinning expression. "*Very* good, Lenny. Exactly like that. Olivia will be so happy. And so will your mother."

Lenny's grip on Dianna's hand tightened painfully. "Oh, God, a cramp in my leg. I can't get up. Help me."

The joy fled Dianna's heart. She extricated her hand

from his grip, gamely clutched him under his doughy arm, and pushed up with all her strength. So did Lenny. Bracing his hand against Dianna's just-vacated chair, using it for leverage, he grunted and shoved upward. Not one blessed thing happened. Embarrassed for him, Dianna once again stepped back, planting her hands at her waist. "Maybe you should try it on your own. Maybe I'm in the way."

"It's my good knee. It's locked."

"Then how good can it be, Lenny?"

His eyes widened suddenly. "I think something just popped." Panic claimed his expression. "Don't just stand there. Get me some help!"

Dianna started, then stopped, then cried out, "What kind of help? You mean like 911?"

"No," Lenny yelled back. "Just get someone with some meat on his bones. Anyone stronger than *you,* Spaghetti Arms."

Okay, now that particular taunt of his from their childhood did nothing but make Dianna want to smack him one. "You know what, Lenny? Insulting me right now is probably not what you want to do. Wait here." Lenny's sarcastic ha-ha look made her hear her own words. "Oh. Of course you'll wait here. You're stuck. Just hold on— I'm going for help."

Lenny's face reddened in earnest. "Then how about you shut up and go do it, huh?"

Good point. Dianna wheeled around and ran out of the salon, hurrying down the long hall to the front of her gracefully cluttered shop and calling out as she went. "Paula? Melanie? Mrs. Windhorst? Can you help me here a second?"

Much as if the two-story, renovated Victorian house that held the offices of Popping the Question were a child's pop-up book, and Dianna had just turned the page, three women zipped out of their offices, appearing to have sprung magically into the hall. They faced her, their questioning expressions, no doubt, in answer to the note of disaster in their boss's voice.

In the forefront, closest to Dianna, was Paula. As always, she was eating. This time it was the tag end of the day's doughnuts. It was amazing. The woman weighed about as much as a bird—a small bird who dressed retro, sported very short red hair, and wore funky blue, narrow-framed eyeglasses. A pencil was stuck behind one ear that boasted multiple piercings. "So. What's up, boss?"

Dianna leaned in toward her ace proposal consultant and whispered, "Lenny's stuck in the position."

This left Paula unmoved. "Lenny, huh? Good. Leave him there, the nasty little creep."

"My sentiments exactly. Only that would mean he would be here forever. With us, Paula. And nobody wants that."

"Gotcha. So what do you want me to do?"

"I want you to help me get him up."

Licking her fingers, Paula roved her placid gaze over Dianna's face. "You're serious, aren't you? No. Sorry. No way. I could tear something vital loose, like my pancreas, trying to get him up."

Dianna tsked. "You couldn't even point to your pancreas if you had to." She then turned, motioning to Melanie, her diametrically-opposed-to-Paula other proposal consultant, and Mrs. Windhorst, her post–middle-aged and tidily efficient receptionist and secretary. "Come here, please." Both women scurried to her. Her voice still lowered discreetly, Dianna said, "Mr. Daschowitz is stuck down on one knee, and I need your help getting him up."

To her surprise, immediate dissension in the ranks ensued. Employees backing up, shaking their heads, looking around for the quickest avenue of escape. Dismayed, Dianna advanced on them. "Oh, come on, help me. I can't leave him in there, and he can't get up by himself."

As if to prove what she'd said, a muted cry of "Help!" came from the salon. Her employees stopped. Dianna raised her eyebrows at them while jerking her thumb back in the direction of the plaintive bleat. "See? And I have another client due at any minute."

Mrs. Windhorst, God love her, adopted a brave face of helpfulness. She valiantly stuck her pen into her gray bouffant hairdo. "Why things like this always happen on Friday afternoons—and payday, to boot, when I'm at my most busy time of the week—I'll never know. However, Ms. West, your three o'clock isn't here yet, but all the same, count me in."

Relief coursed through Dianna. "Oh, good. Thank you."

Patting the secretary's arm, Melanie said, "You poor thing, Mrs. Windhorst. Always so busy. You work too hard, honey." She turned to Dianna. "I'll come with you, too, Di. Poor Mr. Daschowitz. He can't help it."

Dianna beamed at her sentimentally maudlin, rich-as-Godiva-chocolate employee who worked only because she wanted to. "You are a blessing, Melanie."

The three united women—Dianna, Melanie, and Mrs. Windhorst—turned as one to the lone holdout . . . Paula. She raised her chin stubbornly, tried to stare them down, couldn't do it, and finally gave in, slouching where she stood. "Well, lovely. Just freakin'—"

"We've talked about this before, Ms. Capland." Mrs. Windhorst glared disapprovingly at Paula. "Young ladies—even those like yourself, twice-divorced and nearing thirty—do not use vulgarity at the office. I will not be subjected to such language. It creates an atmosphere of stress that I find—"

"Hey, easy there, Madam PC." Paula held up a placating hand, palm outward. All five of her slender fingers were adorned with silver rings. "Don't get your girdle in a wad."

"Paula, really," Dianna said, feeling it was her duty, as the boss, to intercede at this point. "And you, too, Mrs. Windhorst. Both of you should make more of an effort—"

"Hello? Excuse me?" This muted but irritable cry

came, again, from the salon. "Has everybody left or what? Can I get some help in here? I gotta go to the bathroom."

Dianna's eyes widened. "No, no, no. That is new carpet in there." She whirled around, her employees close on her heels, and tore for the salon. "You better cross your legs, Lenny Daschowitz."

"If I could cross my legs," he yelled irritably, "I wouldn't be needing any help, would I? And you better hurry, Spaghetti Arms. I don't think I can hold it for long."

Standing on the white-painted, wraparound porch with the overhanging eave, Chris Adams eyed Popping the Question's closed front door. According to the stickers attached to its glass, they took MasterCard and Visa and most other major credit cards. So, anyway, it was a nice door, as doors go. And it probably didn't warrant this much scrutiny, but he was in no hurry to go inside. What was the rush? *Wow. Popping the question. A big step. One giant leap for mankind.* Hence, this study of the wooden door with its inlaid oval of glass. Inside, the glass was curtained with a lacy sheer held tight at both ends and caught up in the middle by some sort of satiny tieback thing. It resembled a woman's waist but more accurately described how his guts felt, Chris decided.

Yet he had no one to blame but himself. After all, he'd purposely driven all the way across Baltimore to get here, hadn't he? And he'd parked his car out front, right? He pivoted to check. Yep. There it was in the business's small, private lot. A self-deprecating chuckle escaped Chris. As if the big Beemer were his mother and this was the first day of kindergarten and he feared it would leave him the moment his back was turned. But it hadn't, so that was good. Still trying to screw up his courage, Chris reminded himself that he had, uncoerced, exited his car and walked, under his own power, up the flower-lined walkway.

Then he'd climbed (trudged heavily, if he was being

honest) up the five broad, wooden steps that led to this porch. Sure, he'd mounted the steps much as if, at the top, an extremely close shave with a guillotine awaited him. But no such luck. So the upshot of all that deliberate action of his now found him standing here among the forest of wicker furniture and hanging baskets stuffed with green and leafy plants. Something totally masculine inside Chris made him wince. It was like he had shrunk, and this was a dollhouse. A Barbie dollhouse, and he was Ken.

He'd never really liked Ken. Never thought the guy was all that masculine, to tell the truth—

*Knock it off.* Stalling. Big time. *Man, it's just another business appointment.* Right. But not until three o'clock. He looked at his watch. Dismay filled him. *This can't be right. Damn thing says it's three o'clock already.* Chris tapped the crystal and waited. Still three o'clock. Then it was true: He needed a new watch. Desperate now, Chris turned, stepped to the porch's edge and searched the wide street that ran in front of the business. No brigade of buddies anywhere on the horizon come to save him. Chris narrowed his eyes. *Apparently I need new friends, too.*

It wasn't that he didn't want to get married—Chris continued to argue with himself as he returned to the front door—and it wasn't that he didn't want to ask Veronica in some spectacular way to marry him. It was just that, well, he had to go inside and admit to these women that he didn't have the first clue about how to pull off something like this on a grand scale. But what guy did, right? Hence, the existence of Popping the Question. Okay, so he wasn't alone, not by a long shot, in being romantically challenged. That brought to his mind Rick Hampton's grinning face. Chris spared a big, fat, insincere *Thanks, pal* for his newlywed friend. He'd used these ladies' services, was now happily married, and had insisted that Chris come here.

*So here I am. What the hell. Just go inside.*

Squaring his shoulders, he depressed the antique-brass lever that served as a handle, stepped over the threshold, and into a small, tiled square of foyer. An air-conditioned breeze kissed his face as he closed the door behind him and looked around. On his left was a closed door. To his right, a grand archway revealed a room furnished like an old-time parlor. A delicately carved wooden desk of ladylike proportions dominated the middle of the carpeted room. Plenty of overstuffed, unoccupied chairs sat around with nothing to do. Atop a few low tables, many magazines waited in vain to be read. And a big bulletin board crammed full of pictures of happy couples held court on one wall. Obviously the reception area.

But no real, live people, other than himself, seemed to be around. To Chris, this was adequate proof that there is indeed a benevolent god of second thoughts. He could just leave, and no one would be the wiser. Except Rick Hampton. Chris could already hear the teasing and the name-calling, all of which would end in "butt" or "head." Determination firmed Chris's jaw. No way. He was here, and he was toughing this out.

So, what do I do now? he wondered. Just call out? Maybe there was a little bell on the desk he was supposed to ding-ding to raise someone. He looked. Didn't see one. Well, maybe there was a bell pull somewhere for the butler. Wouldn't surprise him—not in this house. He peered harder into the office, but from where he was, he couldn't see a tasseled candidate. He wasn't about to go in there to look for one, either. No, he meant to stay exactly where he was. The foyer was now home base. King's X. Couldn't be tagged while he stood there.

Smug now, hands in his pants pockets, Chris rocked back on his heels, deciding this place was like going back a hundred years in time. Big, heavy, antique furniture. Lace curtains. Cherubs everywhere. Lots of feather accents and dried flowers. Big oversized vases sitting on the wood floor. Gilt-edged frames holding pastoral scenes of picnics and such.

Definitely not his taste. But he could see where they were going. It created a mood: Victorian, romantic . . .

totally unlike him. Which explained why he was here. Popping the Question. That whole "one giant leap for mankind" feeling all over again. Yeah, leap right out over the abyss that was married hell.

"Damn. If that's how I feel . . ." Chris jerked around, aiming for the closed front door to the marriage-proposal business. But then he heard them. The voices.

# CHAPTER 2

Increasingly loud voices, too. Thankfully, Chris assured himself, they weren't in his head. Nor were they telling him to pick up an axe and go do something decidedly unsavory. Intrigued despite his better judgment, Chris turned away from the door and peered down a long hard-wood-floored hall, trying to pinpoint exactly what he was hearing and where it was coming from.

He took a few tentative steps across the foyer. At the other end of the hall, he could see an impressive sweep of stairs that marched upward to the second floor. Apparently, the voices came from a room far, far down there by the stairs. Chris backed up. *No. Definitely out of the safety zone.*

Just then, the commotion escalated to grunting, cussing, gasps, and lots of feminine encouragement.

Chris's eyes widened, but he suspended judgment. Hey, these were modern times. He tried to think what he should do next. Intervene? Leave? Pay admission? But maybe someone was hurt and needed help. This thought overrode his other concerns, even his belief in his neutrality as long as he stayed put. Chris stalked down the hall, ever closer to the noise and the action. When he reached the open doorway, very cautiously he peeked in. It took a moment, but he suddenly realized what he was seeing . . . and froze, wide-eyed. Whatever he'd expected to see, it sure as hell wasn't this.

Three—no, four—fully clothed women surrounded some big Ninja-dressed guy who was down on all fours on the white carpet. So much was going on that Chris couldn't take it all in at once. He couldn't say if the guy wanted to be there or not, but the women clearly were not amused. An older, gray-haired lady, skirt hiked up, all but sat astride the man. And the other women, three of them, much younger than the lady on top, were tugging on the guy from all sides, including his backside. Just then, the guy began bucking and bellowing.

Chris remained shocked and speechless. At that moment, one of the combatants—a phenomenally good-looking woman, Chris's always alert libido noted—looked up and caught sight of him.

"Ohmigod." She relinquished her hold on the downed man, stepped around the main event, and hurried to stand in front of Chris. "This is not what it looks like."

"And yet it might be because I have no idea what's supposed to be happening here." Chris smiled down at her. When he did, some pleasant yet involuntary thing in his chest tightened. She was a really sharp-looking brunette with wavy shoulder-length hair and amazing eyes. Almost gold in color. She stood about five-foot-five. Great figure. Tailored yet feminine sky-blue blouse and slim black slacks. Nice. Really nice. And she smelled wonderful.

Since she stood at a three-quarter pose to him, she divided her attention between the ongoing brouhaha and occasional glances up at Chris. "Well, maybe it is what it looks like. I don't know. But can you help us, please?"

Innate caution kicked in. "Help you do what, exactly?"

"Get him on his feet, of course."

Chris considered her words while eyeing the action. The Ninja was losing, big-time. "And then what?"

"Send him on his way."

"In a good way? I mean 'still alive'?"

"Against all that's holy, but yes."

"I see." Capturing Chris's attention was the sight of the stout older woman in the thick-looking nylons. She was all over the big guy's back. She had the right attitude for the job. All she lacked were the black leather, a whip, and a German accent. Chris wagged his chin in the mounted man's direction. "So what's he doing down on all fours, anyway?"

"He was asking me to marry him."

Chris damn near gave himself whiplash, so abruptly did he jerk his head to stare down at the woman standing next to him. Speechless, he spent some time doing that, just staring at her . . . then finally at the guy. Her again. The guy. Her. "No, seriously. What's he doing down there on the floor? Is he an intruder? Or are you practicing some skit? I'd feel much better knowing that."

Over the downed guy's shouts of distress and the other women's of aggravation, the pretty woman sighed. "No skit. Not an intruder. Sorry. That's just Lenny. And he *was* asking me to marry him, but only as a practice exercise."

Much more cheered by this bit of news, Chris pointed at her. "That's more like it. I didn't think you were with him."

"Me? With Lenny?" She made a face, as if she'd just smelled fresh skunk. "No. Hardly. But this happened because he's scared. Tonight's the night, and he's going to ask his girlfriend for real."

Even as he nodded, Chris frowned his confusion. "So let me see if I have this straight . . . you ladies are beating him up for being scared?"

The seriously sexy woman chuckled. "No, but it wouldn't take much. The truth is he got down on his bad knee. No, wait. It was his good knee. Anyway, he can't get back up." She sent Chris a pleading look, all but drowning him in those gold-colored eyes of hers. "What we need is some muscle."

"And you mean mine, right?"

She nodded. "Lenny has to go to the bathroom. Bad."

Chris raised his eyebrows. "And my knowing that, you believe, will convince me to help?"

Her rich, throaty laugh went all over Chris. "You're funny."

"Looks aren't everything. A guy has to develop his personality." He grinned back at her, enjoying the hell out of this exchange with this excellent-looking female, even while across the room the cacophony continued unabated. In fact, it escalated, finally drawing their attention. Chris stared, amazed, at the scene. The women were on Lenny like a free-for-all at a playground. Pushing, shoving, smacking, tugging. Gouging. Very impressive. "With any luck," Chris felt compelled to say, "this ugly fight could turn into a pretty good rugby match at any moment."

At his side, the pretty woman nodded. "It could. But it gets worse."

"Than this? I don't see how, but don't feel you have to share."

"But I have to. That's new carpet. As you can see, new *white* carpet."

Chris sent her a mock dirty look. "You shared. But, hey, that settles it for me. Can't have the carpet ruined. That stuff doesn't just grow on floors, you know."

She brightened considerably. "Then you'll help?"

He nodded fatalistically. "Yeah, it's probably gone on long enough. One side, yours or his, needs some relief. But one thing, okay? When it comes to my turn for lessons in romance, I think we can leave out the older lady there riding my back and all that hitting and shoving. I have a perfectly good mother capable of doing that for me."

The woman's expression sobered. "Oh, no. Don't tell me. You're not a delivery guy or anything like that, are you? No, of course you're not. How stupid of me." Though she stuck her hand out for him to shake, her enthusiasm level was that of someone who expected her hand to be chopped off at the wrist. "You're Chris Adams, my three o'clock, aren't you?"

"That's me." Chris clasped her hand . . . small, warm. Electric. A jolt shot right up his arm, all the way through him, going straight to his . . . well, not exactly his heart. The truth was much lower and more flamboyant in its expressions of its likes and dislikes. And right now, it liked . . . especially when her grip almost spasmodically tightened around his hand. Had she felt the connection, too? "You're Dianna West, the owner, right? My friend Rick Hampton sent me."

She smiled. "I know. We love Rick."

"Everybody loves Rick. He's one of those guys."

"He is and he's great. He called me to say he'd referred you. Oh, and yes, I am Dianna West." Much as if contact with him were painful, she withdrew her hand from his and made an apologetic face. "I'm sorry you had to witness this. And I promise you that it's not how we normally operate. Anyway, I wouldn't blame you one bit if you turned around and walked away, never to return."

Chris recalled his earlier reticence about even coming inside. "Been there, had the chance, didn't do it. So, I'm in. Tell me how to help."

At that very second, the whole tableau—three shrieking women and one shouting man—fell in a cursing, howling heap to the floor. Pulling back, Chris made a face. "Whew. Now, that had to hurt."

Dianna West gasped and rushed into the room. Chris was right behind her. While she pulled the older woman, whose skirt was now immodestly over her head, off the guy, Chris latched onto a skinny spitfire with short red hair and blue eyeglasses askew. The tiny woman was cussing like a middle-school kid who'd been tossed out of the lunchroom line on pizza day.

"Easy now, champ," Chris told her, his arm locked around her waist.

"Let go of me, whoever the hell you are."

Chris didn't, so she fought his hold on her while at the

same time taking ineffectual roundhouse swings at the squashed-bug guy laid out on his belly. She also hurled threats and insults at him. "Lenny Daschowitz, you grabbed my breast, you little perv! I'll kick your ass!"

*Whoa.* Believing she could do it, too, Chris immediately shifted his arm, making certain that he touched nothing of hers not G-rated.

But Lenny, who apparently still hadn't learned when he was down, turned his big curly-haired head in their direction. "Did not, Paula. But someone touched my penis, and I'm going to sue."

"Oh, as totally *if,* you asshole. If one of us did touch your teeny little peeny, you'd thank us and pay us big time, you freakin'—"

"Okay, we're done here." Ms. West, boss lady, sounded as if she meant it, too. "That's enough, everyone, and I mean it."

Thinking she could use some backup, Chris put in his two cents' worth. "You heard the lady. No one's touching anyone's . . . anything else. And we're all going to calm down"—he purposely tightened his grip on the welterweight in his arms; her muttered "Oof" told him she'd gotten the message—"and then we'll allow your boss to straighten this all out. Okay, now, nice and easy, got it?"

Everyone stared silently at him. Dianna West had a steadying grip on the shaking older woman who was straightening her clothes. Lenny still stared up at him. The spitfire hung loosely, like a towel, over his arm. And the fourth woman . . . "Oh, my goodness, where'd you come from?" she said.

Chris had about one second to eye her. Instant impression: With a change of costume and seven dwarves flanking her, she could be Snow White. Very pale skin. Jet-black hair. Big dark eyes. Red mouth. Soft voice. "High maintenance" was written all over her.

"He's my three o'clock." Ms. Dianna West smiled uncertainly at Chris, perhaps begging him to understand. "This is Mr. Chris Adams, everyone. Mr. Adams, this is

Mrs. Windhorst, my secretary." The older woman next to Dianna nodded regally his way. Chris returned the gesture. "And this is Melanie O'Hara, one of my associates."

Snow White fluttered her hands, telling him, "Like in *Gone with the Wind*."

Chris raised his eyebrows in question. "Beg pardon?"

"My name. Melanie. She married Ashley Wilkes. And O'Hara—"

"Gotcha. Scarlett's last name."

"I see you know your literature." She actually simpered.

Chris feared a case of the vapors was not far behind. *Where was Rhett Butler when you needed him?*

"And that"—Dianna West pointed to the woman Chris had all but forgotten he still held in a death grip—"is Paula Capland, another of my associates."

Chris looked down at the rag doll he held. With her narrow behind pressed against his hip, she swung her upper body until she could see him and raised a hand in greeting. "Pleased to meet you. And, my, what a strong grip you have, Grandma."

*Smart-ass.* Chris liked her immediately. "Hi, yourself. You still intending to take a swing at the guy there on the floor?"

"Maybe. Depends."

"Oh, I'm sorry," Dianna cut in, sounding much as if this were a cocktail party and not the equivalent of a WWF smackdown. "Chris Adams, meet Lenny Daschowitz. Lenny, say hello."

Lenny raised a thick-fingered hand in greeting. "How you doin'? I'd get up, but you know how it is. Lost a contact. Damned white carpet."

Chris chuckled. Lenny was pretty okay, too. "I understand. Need some help, buddy?"

Somehow managing to look totally dignified, he nodded. "That would be nice. But just you. I've had all the female help I can take."

Alarm bells went off inside Chris. "You know what,

Lenny? In your current situation here, I'd say ix-nay on the female bashing."

Chris followed this with releasing the combatant he held, steadying her on her feet before he faced the four women together. "If you ladies will excuse us? Lenny and I have some manly business to conduct."

"If you don't mind," Dianna West said, "I'd like to stay. My place of business. My liability. You understand."

He did. "Whatever you say. You're the boss."

Acknowledging this with a nod of her head, she then turned a frown on Lenny and pointed at him. "You hold on another minute, mister."

"I've been holding on. Whadda you want me to do— tie a knot in it? Hey, where you going?"

"Just outside here a second to talk to my employees."

With that, she herded the women past Chris. As they went by, they made apologetic noises, all except for Paula, and smiled up at him and straightened their clothing all around. The last one out the door, Dianna West, caught his attention. "I'll be right back."

He gave her his best smile. "I'll be counting the seconds."

"So will I." Lenny, again. "I still got to pee, only worse now."

Dianna whipped around. "Lenny, could you please *be* more crass?" Then she focused on Chris. "I've known him since I was a little girl."

Chris mimed a droll expression. "You have my condolences."

"Thank you. I won't be but a second out here."

Chris held the door, implying he would close it behind her. She nodded her thanks and walked past him. Chris indeed meant to shut the door, but a snippet of the women's parting conversation, containing his name and conducted in a loud stage whisper, stayed his hand.

"Could Mr. Chris Adams *be* better-looking? Mr. Tall, Dark, and Handsome is more like it. Why, I nearly swooned." That would be Miss Snow White O'Hara.

"Oh, shut up with the swooning. You swoon at guys on billboards." Paula.

"And you, young lady, flirt with every man who comes through the door." The secretary. Mrs. Wind-something. "And that's despite the fact that they're every one already in committed relationships when they arrive here. Very unprofessional."

"Now, stop it, all of you. Enough arguing." Dianna. "It's a wonder Mr. Adams hasn't already run out of here like rabid vampires were chasing him. He has to think we're all nuts."

"You mean we aren't?" Paula again.

"Not all of us." Dianna.

"But did you think he was good-looking, Di?"

Melanie's breathless question had Chris, though staring at Lenny, straining to hear Dianna's answer. Lenny smirked and eyed Chris knowingly from across the room. Chris chose to ignore this.

"Oh, God," Dianna said, "he is *gorgeous*. And *so* nice. I nearly died. I had to come out into the hall just to fan myself."

Across the way, Lenny sent Chris a thumbs-up sign. Chris answered with a nod of his head and a grin as, out in the hall, Dianna West kept talking.

". . . neither here nor there. Like Mrs. Windhorst said, he's here because he's a man in a committed relationship with a woman he wants to marry. And let me remind you: If we ever lose sight of that, ladies, if we ever give in to our attraction to one of our clients, it's called fraud and a breach of professional ethics—and this business and our livelihoods are history."

Chris had stopped listening after that "man in a committed relationship" thing. Who was she talking about? Lenny? No, probably not in the same breath with the word "*attraction.*" Then that left . . . him. *Damn.* Chris wondered what Dianna West would say, or do, if she knew exactly how *uncommitted* his relationship really was.

\*     \*     \*

About fifteen minutes later, and now behind the closed door in her office across the foyer from the reception area, Dianna sat with Mr. Chris Adams, prospective bridegroom, on the overstuffed rose-brocade sofa where she conducted her client interviews. They were alone . . . at last.

Dianna held in her hands her interview notebook and a pen. "I cannot thank you enough for coming to our rescue—and Lenny's. I don't know who was happier, us or him. And I know it's hard to believe, but he really is an old friend of mine. Well, hardly a friend. Tormentor is more like it. But his mother still lives next door to mine, which explains why I moved away. Lenny hasn't. Yes, he lives with his mother. The poor guy. Well, you saw him."

*You're babbling. Stop it right now.* Dianna did, reminding herself that Mr. Adams was here because he wanted her to help him ask his girlfriend—*that darned lucky, lucky woman*—to marry him. "So, anyway, you're a terrific sport. And I think I'll give you a big discount for being so nice, Mr. Adams."

"Call me Chris. And there's no need for a discount. It was nothing."

Dianna smiled. "Oh, but it was. It was a big something . . . Chris." For some reason, she felt shy saying his name, and so fell back on the familiar. "Poor Lenny." The words were a sigh. "Thank you for waiting while we got him dusted off and sent on his way."

"Again, not a problem."

Dianna nodded, just sitting there and grinning stupidly at the man. And he was watching her do it, too. She needed to say something. The first thing that came into her mind also came out of her mouth. "Why don't you call me Dianna?"

A playful light sparkled in his dark-chocolate eyes. "Mainly because you haven't asked me to before now."

"Oh, I get it." *Brilliant, Dianna. Scintillating. You've got him now, girl.*

Chris's sultry smile, coupled with his bold gaze, made

Dianna giddy. The man had no right to sit there so completely at ease, an ankle crossed atop his opposite knee and an arm draped along the sofa's carved-wood spine. His hand rested so close to her shoulder that, should a sudden insanity seize her, all she had to do was lean over the slightest bit to kiss his fingertips. Afraid she'd do exactly that, Dianna forced a businesslike smile to her face. "All right. So we're Chris and Dianna now. And you want to get married."

He raised his eyebrows. "Whoa. Slow down. I think we should date first. See how things go."

Totally confused, Dianna shook her head. "I'm sorry, I don't follow . . . ?"

"We went from first names to getting married in about two seconds."

"Oh, I get it. The way I said it. Sorry." Some stupid giggle left over from her teenage years erupted from her, leaving her unsettled, a bit off her game. "That would be silly. Me and you. Ha-ha."

"It would? Hmm. My mistake." He grinned big-time and just sat there.

He was flirting, and it was working. Dianna's heart raced with excitement. She wanted to kiss him . . . hard. Finally remembering to exhale, she reminded herself that Chris's flirting with her wasn't the first time she'd seen this phenomenon. Many of her male clients became self-conscious and seemed to feel a need to flirt and be macho, as if they needed to prove to themselves that they were still studly guys. Melanie and Paula reported the same experiences. Hence, that "breach of ethics and no jobs" reminder of hers. They were not to give in to their libidos' urgings where clients were concerned. But that was before Chris Adams, Dianna argued.

*Stop right there. Big problem. Before Chris Adams? Oh, girlfriend, do not make that mistake.* Sure, she was very attracted to him, and he was getting to her, but the rule remained: no dipping in the client pool allowed. Yet here she was, wanting to do just that. *God, this whole afternoon was designed to test me. First Lenny for being an idiot, and now this guy for being sexy. Get a grip, Dianna.* She did, putting on her best professional face and ending the silence between them that had stretched taut. "So, you're here because you want to ask your girlfriend or significant other—"

"Definitely girlfriend."

She smiled. "I figured. But that's not always the case in my business. So I try not to take anything for granted."

"Smart."

"Thanks. I think so." Dianna marveled that she could, somehow, hold this lucid conversation with Chris Adams. Inside, she was mush. It just wasn't fair. This man had taken her breath away the first moment she'd spied him standing in the doorway to the salon. And yet he was taboo. Just then, Chris firmed his lips together and ran his fingers over them. Dianna nearly swooned. His mouth. So sensually shaped. Generous. Prone to smiling. Was he just trying to make her lose control?

"So," he said, a bit too loudly, clearing his throat, "we were talking about getting married, right? Me to someone else." He suddenly frowned, much as if his own words had surprised him. Then he smiled, peering deep into Dianna's eyes and holding her gaze riveted to his. "Well, you know, I *thought* I wanted to get married. Until I came here, that is."

She knew exactly what he was doing, but she could barely swallow, so potent was his appeal. To save them both, she pretended she'd taken his meaning wrong and spoke fatalistically, even slumping her posture. "Oh no, I just knew it. That whole Lenny business, right? We put you completely off marriage. You poor man. And your girlfriend." *Remember her, Dianna?* "She'll be really happy with us here at Popping the Question, won't she?"

Chris blinked, shuttering his gaze from her. "I'm not sure. I really don't know how she would react."

"You don't? Seriously?" If he was her man and someone here had put him off marriage to her, Dianna knew she'd show up posthaste, prepared for some serious hair-pulling and name-calling.

"Oh, she might hunt you down and prosecute you," Chris cheerfully assured her. "Cite alienation of affection or something like that, I guess."

Dianna blinked. "Great. Let me guess. She's an attorney?"

Still smiling, he nodded. "A prosecuting attorney with the state, in fact."

Suddenly feeling ill, Dianna grimaced. "A prosecuting attorney. With the state." She tucked a stray lock of hair behind her ear. "So, she sounds like a lovely woman, your attorney. I mean your girlfriend. Of course, she would be, if *you're* involved with her."

Dianna froze. Had she really said that out loud?

"Well . . . thanks," Chris said, proving that, yes, she had. So he was wearing a Rolex watch and faded jeans and a blue oxford-style shirt tucked in and belted with a braided-leather belt. How could she have ever thought he might be a delivery guy? His shirt was open at the throat. Dark chest hair peeked over the top of the rounded crew-neck of his white T-shirt.

Not that she was checking him out. Dianna exhaled. "Is it warm in here to you? Because it seems awfully hot in here to me."

Not waiting for any answer he might give, she pushed up from the sofa and turned to the dainty, glass-topped end table that had been on her right when she was seated. Atop this she placed her pen and interview notebook before hurrying over to the thermostat. She stared accusingly at the seventy-five-degree reading on its digital face and tapped the cover. "I don't think this thing is working."

"If it's as old as this house, it probably isn't."

Dianna turned around to face her client. She repeated that word mentally. *Client, client, client. He's my client.* "You don't like the house?"

He shrugged. "Not my style, is all. Not what I expected, either."

"What did you expect?" Dianna started back toward him and the sofa. She had to fight a mental image of the two of them making out hot and heavy on its inviting cushions. By the time she sat down, she had him naked. Well, in her mind, anyway.

"Something more masculine, I guess, since you deal mostly with guys. You do, right?"

"Yes. Mostly. But you'd be surprised at the number of women who come in wanting to be the one to pop the question."

"Seriously? That's surprising. I mean, I thought that women had a lock on romantic. But, hey, women who take charge and ask the guy? Pretty cool."

Dianna smiled. "Glad you think so. And, on that note . . ."

She reached over to the glass-topped table and retrieved her pen and notebook. Resettling herself on the sofa cushions, she opened her ledger to a clean page. At the top of it, she wrote "Chris Adams." She stared at the two words and fought the urge to put a "Mrs." in front of his name and write it over and over, like some lovesick high school girl.

Dianna looked up, catching her client watching her. Sudden, palpable sexual attraction, like electrical currents, throbbed between them. Dianna had to fight its effects just to get her words out. "So, Chris. Right now we need to fill out a preliminary form and a contract. Then, today or during a subsequent meeting, whatever you prefer, we can talk about your likes and dislikes, what you want to have happen. Even things like music, location, flowers, any special needs you might have. And I'll also need some insights on your intended."

He'd been nodding along as she talked, but by the time she finished, he was frowning. "Intended? I have an— Oh, hell, I do. That makes it pretty official, doesn't it?"

"Almost." Dianna smiled at the brown-eyed, handsome man to her left. "Don't tell me you're going to do a Lenny and get cold feet?"

"Hell, no. Not after seeing what happened to him." Chris suddenly leaned in toward Dianna. His gaze dropped to her lips and then rose to her eyes. His face filled her vision. "Before we begin to get official here, I want to ask *you* something."

*The answer is yes.* "You do?" The sound of her own voice, all Marilyn Monroe breathy, snapped Dianna out of vamp mode. She abruptly sat back, but what she really wanted to do was jump on Chris Adams, wrap her legs around him and— She cleared her throat. "I'm sorry. What do you want to ask me?"

Not answering right off, he sat back and roved his gaze over . . . well, not her, but her office furnishings. How flattering was that? "How'd you get started doing something like this? It's really great. Very unique. Totally entrepreneurial. I'd bet there isn't another business like it in the whole country."

Dianna's chest expanded with pride. "And you'd win. There isn't, not that I know of. In fact, last Wednesday I was interviewed by a features reporter for *The Baltimore Sun* for an upcoming story. And *Baltimore Magazine* is featuring us, too. As if that weren't great enough, *People* magazine has already been here to do an article. Pictures and everything."

"Damn. You go, girl."

"I know. I can't believe it. Me. In *People* magazine."

"You're going to have more business than you and fifty employees can handle when that comes out. Are you ready for that? I mean, let's face it, men are pretty lame, for the most part, when it comes to romantic ideas for proposing."

"I hate to agree with you, especially since you put it like that, but that's exactly how I got started."

"Seriously?" He shifted his weight, settling himself on the sofa. "Tell me about it. I'd really like to hear this."

Obviously, he was genuinely interested, so Dianna happily obliged. "Well, you can thank—or curse, depending on how you feel about being here—my older brothers.

When they wanted to propose to their girlfriends, they turned to me, the resident girl in the house."

Chris nodded. "Makes sense. Go on."

"Well, they're guys, okay? Like you said: totally lame in the romantic vision department. Anyway, Tommy is thirty-two and a cop. And Edward is thirty-four. He's an accountant—"

"How old are you?"

"Me?" That stopped her. She didn't see how it was relevant.

Chris's smile was disarming. "Call me curious. Professionally speaking."

She had her doubts about that, but: "Okay. Well, I'm twenty-six."

He nodded. "I figured you had to be younger than your brothers."

"That was a compliment, right?"

"Right. You don't even look twenty-six, much less older than thirty-four. Are you married?"

Surprised, Dianna pulled back, but still managed to smile. "I don't see how that matters."

"I guess I'm prying, right? I don't mean to. I was just wondering if some guy had swept you off your feet already . . . you know, in the sense that if he had, then that would give you professional credentials. Meaning you personally know what works, et cetera." He stopped, frowned off into space, and then focused on Dianna again. "You know what? It doesn't matter. I'm just nervous about being here."

Dianna took pity on the man. "It's okay. Really. And no, I'm not married. But I do know what works."

Chris Adams grinned, reminding her of the big bad wolf. "I'll bet you do."

Highly flattered, and allowing herself one moment only of flirting right back, Dianna raised her eyebrows. "Did I tell you yet that one of my brothers is a cop?"

Chris laughed out loud . . . a gutsy masculine sound. "Point taken, Ms. West. So, two older brothers. No wonder you're not married. That's a lot for a guy to get past. But I take it *they're* married?"

"Yes. Happily. And I take some of the credit for that, speaking of professional credentials. I'm talking about my coaching and the romantic scenarios I set up for them, individually, when the time came. They were clueless. Turned out it was fun, and I loved it. And so did their girlfriends, who are now their wives, of course."

"I bet. So tell me what you set up for your brothers. Maybe I'll want something like what you did for them."

Dianna nodded and smiled. "Okay. Good point. For Tommy I put together a horse-drawn-carriage ride, string quartet, champagne, and a midnight-dinner-on-the-beach package."

"Sounds fabulous."

"It was. It was in Florida. And Edward—Mr. Traditional—popped the question on a weekend excursion up to Vermont. Sightseeing. Fall foliage. A bed-and-breakfast inn. Long walks. Antiques-shopping. Really shivery stuff to a woman's heart."

"I can imagine. Are you finding, though, that most people are sticking closer to home nowadays, not wanting to travel, that sort of thing?"

Dianna sobered and nodded. "Yes. But that's great, too. I mean, Baltimore isn't called 'Charm City' for nothing. And we do have a history of famous lovers here. Zelda and F. Scott. Clark Gable and Carole Lombard. Even Wallis Simpson and King Edward."

"Hey, so pretty much it's all going on right here in 'Marryland,' right?"

"Hey, 'Marryland.' I like that. Can I use it?"

"Sure. Just give me credit. So, anyway, what happened after your brothers got married? Don't leave me hanging."

Dianna chuckled at her own expense and tucked a stray curl behind her ear. "I don't know. It's kind of an embarrassing story, really."

Chris smiled evilly. "Even better."

He was teasing her—and Dianna loved it. "Oh, all

right. Let's just say I didn't catch on at first that I could do something like this for a living. There I was, just out of college—"

"What'd you major in?"

Dianna sent Chris an arch expression. "Still checking out my credentials?"

"No." He grinned that killer grin, one that liquefied her bones. "Just nosy. So what'd you major in?"

"Don't laugh. Philosophy."

He laughed. "I'm not laughing."

"You are. *But,* and as you seem to already know, my degree was completely useless in the real world. So I started on my master's degree—"

"In philosophy?"

Dianna raised her chin as if insulted, but knew the grin tugging at the corners of her mouth gave her away. "Yes. I'm a very slow learner. So, anyway, while I was toiling away in academia, I got started doing this on the side, totally for free. For friends. And friends of friends. For the love of the thing. But after a couple years of that—"

"A couple of *years*?"

"I said I was a slow learner. Anyway, my brother Edward—"

"The accountant. I think I see where this is going."

"Yes. The accountant. He's big on business and marketing. He suggested it. Tommy seconded it. And my parents loved it and gave me the seed money. Edward is my business manager now. And here I am, a year later and going strong. Thriving, even. I think that, given the times, people are wanting to commit. They seem to want stability now, something they can cling to, something that matters."

"Which explains why I'm here. But, hey, you're about to be on the cover of *People* magazine."

"Hardly the cover. Probably more of a footnote at the back of the thing."

" 'Where' won't matter. It's *People* magazine. You'll be swamped with clients once that comes out."

"Gee, that would be awful."

"Yeah, wouldn't it? Got a Web presence?"

"No, I don't."

"You need a Web presence."

"Why? You said I'd have more clients than I could handle with just the *People* thing."

"If you're on the Web, you can serve the country. The world."

"No, I couldn't. Think of all the different languages and customs."

"Not a problem. Get your brother to do his thing and then get in touch with a corporate attorney for the legal framework part. Then you could sell franchises all over the world."

"You sound like you know what you're talking about."

He nodded. "I do."

Dianna waited, but he didn't elaborate. So she frowned her doubts about his idea. "That sounds like a lot of work, worldwide franchises. Not to mention time and money and headaches."

"Only at first. But after that, you'd never have to work again. Just spend your time counting your money. Retire at twenty-six."

Visions of the lifestyles of the rich and famous danced through her head. "Well, that's not ugly, is it? But what would I do with my time? I mean, everyday stuff, my whole life left to live?"

Chris shrugged. "It'd be up to you, but that's the point. You'd go where you want. Do what you want. No one to answer to."

"God, that sounds totally seductive." She tried to envision it . . . couldn't. "No. I don't think I'd like that for long. A constant vacation would get boring. I wouldn't know what to do with myself. Or where to go." She was beginning to get upset. "I'd miss my family and friends and Baltimore. I love this city and the Orioles and Inner Harbor and Fell's Point and—"

Chris held his hands up, palms to her, to stop her.

"Hey, hold on. It's okay. I'm not the genie in the bottle granting you your wishes. I'm just talking. You don't have to go anywhere."

She felt foolish. "Well, thank God, because I don't think I could handle wealth on that rich and idle scale." Of course, she was only half-joking. "I mean, there'd be all those years with nothing to fill them. Too scary to think about."

"It's not as bleak as all that. You can move on to the next thing. Find what else it is you might love to do."

"But I love doing this."

"Good for you, then. You know what you want out of life. That's great. And also very rare."

"I guess it is." Something in Chris's manner, or maybe it was his suddenly subdued tone of voice, alerted Dianna. She thought maybe he wasn't talking about mere possibilities, not where he was concerned. Just exactly who was this Chris Adams sitting here so close to her and making her aware of every beat of her heart? "So, Chris, how do you know so much about being a jet-setter?"

He grinned . . . a lopsided, self-deprecating one. "I don't know the first thing about it. Not my style. I like to lie low."

Dianna pulled back. "Lie low? Are you wanted by the police?"

"No. I was talking personality-wise. Got the money, but not the desire to flaunt it."

Dianna sighed in relief. She'd seen a lot of suspicious characters come through her door. "Admirable. So you're independently wealthy, then? A man of infinite means, I take it?"

"A what? I think you've been in this Victorian house too long. What exactly *is* 'a man of infinite means'?"

Dianna felt her face heat up. Teach her to blurt personal questions that were none of her business. "Totally filthy stinking rich, I think."

"Oh. Then, yeah, that's me."

"Are you putting me on?"

He leaned in toward her. "If I did, do you think you'd fit?"

Dianna's cheeks burst into flames of embarrassed heat. She couldn't say a thing or even look away. Tears actually stung her eyes.

Instantly contrite, Chris put a hand on her arm. His grip was warm and firm. "Oh, hell, I'm sorry. I shouldn't have said that. I don't know what I was thinking. I forgot myself. Forgive me?"

Dianna swallowed, finally finding her voice. "Of course. But only if you'll forgive me. God, I've been sitting here grilling you about money. How rude is that?"

"From anyone else, completely. But from you?" He sat back and shrugged. "For some reason I'm not offended. It's like you have a right to know. And I don't know how else to explain it, so don't ask me."

"I won't, but I really don't have to . . . because I think I feel the same way." This was so odd. What was going on here? In another moment, they'd be in a serious liplock. Dianna realized she was staring at the man. Simply staring. Not talking. Just feeling the tug of his body for hers.

"And on that note," Chris announced loudly, "I think I'd better start taking care of official business here." Sitting back, settling again into his corner of the sofa, he began filling out a clipboarded client information form she'd given him, followed by the contract he needed to sign. Dianna sat quietly waiting, watching him. Without warning, he looked up. "Okay, I have to say this. You are one of the most interesting women I've met in a long time." He paused, his expression intensified. "A very long time."

"Oh. Thank you." Dianna barely kept the disappointment off her face until he returned his attention to the forms. She stared at his profile and wondered why, for her, it was never any different. He thought she was interesting. *Great. The kiss of death.* He couldn't know it, but every guy in her life thought of her that way. Interesting.

Easy to talk to. A friend. A little sister. Though she knew she was nice-looking enough and smart enough and, all right, funny sometimes, there just seemed to be something about her that didn't inspire lasting or long-term passion in men. Sure, they wanted to hang out with her, maybe date her and even sleep with her, or tell her all their problems with other women. But in the end, they didn't want to marry her.

Could she be in a more ironic business for her, then? Here she helped people merge onto the highway of love and marriage, but when it came to herself, she couldn't even find the on ramp. And neither could the three women who worked for her, none of whom was currently married. Mrs. Windhorst was a widow. Paula was twice divorced. And Melanie was single, like Dianna. Go figure.

So, what about this other woman, Dianna wondered, who had inspired Chris to want to marry her? What was she like? And what did that attorney have, darn it, that she did not? *Short answer? Chris.* Dianna focused on him, trying to decide what specifically about him was so appealing to her. Certainly, he was tall, dark, and handsome. Had the football shoulders and the winning smile. Was obviously intelligent. A sharp dresser. Great sense of humor. Everything there to like.

But what about the small things? Like the shape of his fingernails. Squared off nicely, neatly clipped. But his hands weren't soft. No, he was every inch the rugged male but with nothing coarse about him. His black hair was neatly trimmed. He wore it short on the sides and back, longer on top with a wave in front that fell forward when he had his head down, like now. Very attractive. He smelled of clean clothes and an expensive citrus aftershave. Nice.

And he was, right now, watching her watch him.

Embarrassed shock sent Dianna's stomach plummeting. She wanted to die. The man was clearly flattered and amused that he'd caught her, too. Dianna felt her face heat up to, no doubt, a flaming beet-red. Completely flustered, she leaned forward, all business now, to straighten up an already straightened stack of magazines on the coffee table in front of them. "So," she said briskly, sparing him but a glance, "are you ready?"

He chuckled. "I am, if you are. Just say the word."

# CHAPTER 3

"Oh, honey. 'The word,' boyfriend," Dianna said aloud, sounding bold yet breathy. All sexy and alluring.

Of course, her come-on would have been much more effective if she'd said it about six hours ago when the man was still around. But no, here she was at home alone on a Friday night in her condo. Nothing new there. And she was not happy with herself. That wasn't new, either. "Talk about your delayed reactions," she fussed, punching an innocent sofa cushion. "The perfect and obvious comeback, right? But did I say that? No."

Dianna puckered her expression. "God, I suck." This hung in the air a moment before she added: "And apparently I talk out loud to myself, too, like crazy Aunt Minerva, who is about three hundred miles down the road to Nuthood. The woman thinks she's Cleopatra. Why *do* all crazy women think they're some queen? How come they never think they're the handmaiden or the laundress?"

As if waiting for her tasteful yet decidedly inanimate furniture to answer, Dianna glared at it. Only a stubborn silence met her question. "Fine. And yet I'm *still* talking out loud to myself."

Sighing, she sank down into the cushions of her couch and thought about how the rest of the afternoon had gone. So there they'd been, she and Chris . . . and just as he'd told her to say the word, his pants had beeped. On the line had been Ms. Prosecuting Attorney for the State. So Chris had pretty much handed the signed contract back to her and left, telling her he had to go and he'd call her tomorrow for a follow-up appointment. In her mind, Dianna again heard her own response, all chirpy like a bird. *Okay. Talk to you then. No problem.*

Problem: Tomorrow was Saturday. She didn't work on Saturday. Neither did Mr. Filthy Stinking Rich, she'd just bet. So he'd probably spoken off the cuff, and she'd have to wait until Monday to talk to him again. Darn. Could she wait that long? Of course she could. She had to, if for no other reason than to prove to herself that she could. Feeling frustrated, Dianna ran her fingers through her hair, brushing it back around her shoulders. Maybe her gesture would wash that man right out of her hair. She whimpered, wanting to cry. This attraction she felt for Chris Adams was so *not* healthy, either emotionally or business-wise, and for the same reason: He was taken. His heart belonged to another woman.

Dianna narrowed her eyes. *There is always another woman.* He was probably with her right now. Someplace romantic. *And look where I am. Frozen pizza, popcorn, and the boob tube. Yippee. Another wild Friday night at home.* So she hadn't got to interview Chris Adams or talk to him about his ideas for music and flowers and such. But he had certainly interviewed her. She knew hardly anything at all about him, except for the short answers in a neat script that he'd supplied to the questions on the form. But he, without any printed questionnaire at all, knew almost all the basics about her.

She looked down at herself in disgust. *Basically, here I am, veged out in shorts and a too-big T-shirt.* Curled up at one end of her comfy sofa, Dianna dipped her hand into the plastic bowl in her lap and pinched up a little wad of popcorn. She got it about halfway to her open mouth before her next dreamy thought had her hand pausing in midair.

*Chris Adams.* She stared straight ahead, looking at but not really seeing the framed art print hanging on the wall opposite the sofa and above the TV. So, what did she know about Chris Adams? He was gorgeous. Rich. Single. Dianna grimaced at the final irony here: It was her job to help him relinquish that single status. Could it be worse? she wondered. She didn't see how. She was so attracted to the man. And yet too much that was important to her—business reputation, a sense of honor, integrity, and the fact that her parents had sunk their retirement fund in her business as a statement of trust in her, to name a few—would be lost, never to be recovered, if she acted on what she felt.

"Oh, God," she all but whimpered, shaking her head and knowing she couldn't live with herself if she betrayed her family, her ethics, and also her employees by doing the very thing she'd warned them against. Her next thought had her laughing at herself. "Oh, hell, look at me. I've already got myself in bed with Chris Adams. Who says he wants to go to bed with me?" Insulted now, Dianna's expression puckered in her own defense. "Why wouldn't he want to go to bed with me? What's wrong with me?

"Only everything, apparently," she assured herself, finally popping the corn into her mouth. Chewing absently, she focused on the TV screen—only to suddenly realize that the movie couple was in bed and seriously embracing. Dianna took it personally. "Is this a freakin' conspiracy, or what?"

She grabbed up and tossed a handful of popcorn at the TV. It fell woefully short, scattering here and there, much as if it had snowed in the living room. *Well, great. See what Chris Adams has done? Made me think about cheating, losing my business, becoming homeless—and now I'll have to vacuum. Worse, I've lost the thread of this movie.* And she'd really liked it, too. It was a period piece, set in Victorian times, about a female Pinkerton agent from Chicago who went to England because of a murder and then fell in love with the duke she suspected was the murderer. The hero was to die for. And the heroine was great. Totally kicked ass. A strong woman—

The phone rang right next to Dianna, startling her into yelping and jumping—and upsetting the big plastic bowl of popcorn balanced on her thighs. It went everywhere. "Ah, for—" The sentiment wasn't worth completing. Really irritated now, she shoved the bowl aside, reached for the TV remote, aimed it, hit the mute button, dropped the remote, grabbed up the cordless phone, cheered herself with the realization that this could be an Olympic event—synchronized couch-potato multitasking—pressed the talk button and put the phone to her ear. "Hello."

"Dianna? Dianna West?" It was a timid-sounding female voice.

And Dianna recognized it. Her heart sank. "Olivia, is that you? What's wrong? What did Lenny do?"

The woman was sniffling. Was she crying, or just congested as usual? "Dianna, I'm calling from Tamborello's. Lenny got down on one knee to ask me to marry him. It was so beautiful."

Dianna exhaled her relief and sank back against the plump sofa cushions. "Whew, Olivia. You're calling to thank me. Thank God." Popping the Question's success rate remained intact. Was she good or what? "I'm so glad it came off okay. Lenny and I rehearsed it this afternoon, but he was pretty nervous."

"With good reason, it turns out, Dianna. Perhaps you shouldn't have done that, making him get down on one knee."

Olivia's voice was so "little girl," so sweet, that a body never expected to hear bad things come out of her mouth. So it took Dianna a moment to absorb what she was hearing. But when she did, her smile faded as her body tensed. "Why not? What's happened, Olivia?"

"A lot, I'm afraid. You have to come, right now, to the restaurant."

"I do?"

"Yes. You see, Lenny got down on one knee, like you showed him. Everyone was watching. But then—and this is the bad part—he fell over and knocked into a table next to ours. He hit it hard with his head."

"No." Dianna's blood chilled. "Is he all right?"

"Well, he was . . . until the carafe of wine that this other couple were enjoying fell off their table—the one that Lenny knocked into—and it conked him on the head, too, and then spilled all over his rented tuxedo."

The rented tuxedo. "Shit."

"Actually, it looked more like blood all over his white shirt. I was so scared."

*Double shit.* "I'm sure you were."

"There's more."

"Good." It was a fatalistic pronouncement, chock full of irony.

"The carafe broke on the tiled floor."

"Well, there just isn't any good news here, is there, Olivia?" Dianna had this sudden mental image of herself jailed over this somehow and fighting for her shoes and food and virtue in a women's prison somewhere. "Let me guess. Lenny got cut, right?"

"Yes. Then, when he was almost up off the floor—three or four men were helping him—he overbalanced again and went to catch himself and fell again and his hand landed in a plate of four-cheese ravioli—"

"What in the name of Chef Boyardee was a plate of four-cheese ravioli doing on the floor?" Dianna rubbed at her suddenly throbbing temple.

"Oh, I see your confusion. I forgot to tell you that it had gone flying from yet another table when Lenny fell."

"Yet another table? I'm lost, Olivia."

"I'm sorry. I'll try to be clear. You see, when Lenny fell the second time, he went over backward and his feet flew out from under him. He accidentally kicked this *other* table leg and upset it . . . as well as the people sitting there, too."

"Oh, God." Innocent civilians were now involved.

"Upset how, Olivia? Are they upset angry or upset hurt?"

"Oh, um, the first one, I guess."

Upset angry. Whew. "Good." Totally numb, Dianna stared at the TV screen. She didn't know what to say, what even to ask, so her distraught mind latched on to the movie she'd been watching. There the half-dressed hero and heroine were, out in a long hallway and staring horrified at the huge butler who was holding an unconscious woman in his arms. Some errant corner of Dianna's otherwise freaked-out mind commented: *So the butler did it?* Just then she heard Olivia's voice in her ear. "I'm sorry, Olivia, but what did you say? What happened next?"

"I said Lenny got stabbed in the thigh with the violinist's bow."

Dianna jackknifed forward on the sofa. "Did you say 'stabbed'? With a violinist's bow? Is that even possible? Olivia, talk to me."

"I am." Her voice was tremulous. "When Lenny fell the second time, his one foot kicked the table leg and his other foot caught the poor little violinist behind the knees. He's a sweet old man, the violinist. He's very apologetic about stabbing Lenny. He said that had never happened before to him."

"I guess not." It was too much. Dianna's brain shut down. *No more incoming information will be processed at this time.* She slumped back on the sofa, knowing her evening, if not her entire business and her life, was a total wreck. All because of Lenny Daschowitz. If the gods were crazy, Chris Adams would somehow be mixed up in this and then the debacle would be complete. "So, what do you want me to do, Olivia? Why are you calling me, instead of, say . . . oh, an ambulance?"

"We did call an ambulance. They're sending two."

Dianna's hand tensed reflexively around the cordless phone she held. "Just to get Lenny?"

"No. The violinist, too."

A sudden urge to burst out in tears assailed Dianna. "Why the violinist, Olivia?"

"Because when Lenny accidentally knocked his legs out from under him, the poor little man fell and cut his hand really bad on the broken glass from the carafe. He fears that he will never be able to play again."

Instant anesthetized Jell-O. Cold and numb. That was Dianna. These events being relayed to her by Olivia had to be the most bizarre ones ever, outside of the plot of a Mel Brooks movie. Or maybe a Quentin Tarantino effort. This stuff just didn't happen in real life. And *that* was when it hit her. "Hey, are you putting me on, Olivia? Did Lenny put you up to this? None of that stuff happened, did it? It's a joke, right? Well, ha-ha, very funny. You crazy kids."

Dianna waited, hoped, prayed. But only silence, dotted by the sound of Olivia's congested breathing, greeted Dianna from the other end of the phone. She sobered. "This isn't a joke, is it?"

"No."

"Great." Because she had no other choice, Dianna plunged on. "Okay, tell me again why I have to come to the restaurant, Olivia."

"Mother Daschowitz said you do. She said this is all your fault. I don't think it is, Dianna. I really don't. But she's here, and she's very mad." Olivia sniffed.

Dianna sat very still and quiet until she could absorb this daunting bit of news. "Lenny's mother is there?"

"Yes. So is yours."

All right, now that was just bizarre. "*My* mother is there?"

"Yes. With your father."

"*Why?*"

"I suppose because she's married to him."

Dianna squeezed her eyes shut in a prayerful attitude. *Give me patience now.* She opened her eyes, resorting to speaking slowly and enunciating every word carefully. "Listen to me, Olivia. I'm asking you what are they all doing there on the night that Lenny is proposing to you?"

"Well, coincidence on the part of your parents, I think.

But I'm glad they're here. Your father is applying pressure to Lenny's leg wound. And your mother wrapped up the violinist's hand."

"I see." Tomorrow, no doubt, her sweet, sweet parents would cut her out of their wills. "And what about good old Mother"—Dianna mentally ran through her lexicon of every smutty word she could think of that could conceivably follow "mother," got them all out of her system and finished with—"Daschowitz? What about her, Olivia? Why exactly is she there?"

"Oh. Lenny brought her. Wasn't that sweet?"

And that comment on Olivia's part, Dianna affirmed for herself, was what made Olivia Goldman the perfect woman for Lenny Daschowitz and his mother.

"So what do I tell Mother Daschowitz? Will you come down here, Dianna?"

What could she say? "Of course, Olivia. I'll be right there."

Tamborello's was an Italian restaurant straight out of 1940s Hollywood. Intimate. Low lighting. Walls painted in earth tones. Little round tables with red and white checked tablecloths. Sitting in the middle of each table was a big, empty wine bottle plugged with a multicolored, dripping candle. Overhead, on the ceiling, a latticework trellis was woven with fake grape vines, meant to call to mind a vineyard. Rounded archways hinted at secluded alcoves for dining and romantic encounters. Murals depicting the Italian countryside graced the back wall. Very romantic. Again, very Italian.

So Dianna wasn't surprised that the scene inside resembled a Roman orgy gone awry. Police taking statements. EMTs taking pulses. Food spilled and blood spattered. Spilled wine. Whining people. Lots of patients to go around. And even more impatient waiters and busboys milling about. Nobody was eating. Nobody was getting tips. Nobody was happy.

Dianna could have died. This was a nightmare come

to life, and she was right in the thick of it. Dressed in jeans now, instead of her baggy shorts from earlier, and a pink cotton sweater, she'd already given condolences to the ancient violinist and to Lenny. Then she'd endured as much of a chewing-out from Mrs. Daschowitz as she intended to listen to before having consoled Olivia over this aborted Big Moment. And now here she was trying to tell the nice policeman why she really wasn't responsible for any of this, all while dodging the cleanup efforts of the restaurant's staff and fending off her hovering parents' unhelpful input.

"Uh, no, Officer. Not Olive. Olivia. She's the woman over there who saw everything. And not Pop*eye*. Pop*ping*," Dianna told the big, unamused cop who had lots of muscles and a huge gun. "Popping the Question. The name of my business." She watched him write it down in his notes.

"Your name?" He didn't even look up at her.

She swallowed. "Dianna West."

"Her middle name is Joan. After her grandmother on her father's side."

Yes, her parents flanked her, mom to the left, dad to the right. Dianna turned to pat her mother's arm. "Thank you, Mom, but right now that's totally irrelevant." Then she leaned over to whisper: "This is all *your* fault, by the way. 'Help Lenny,' you said. 'It would be a nice thing to do.' "

"I heard that. Don't be fresh with your mother, Dianna."

Stung, she pivoted to see her father's face. "Dad, this is a nightmare. And I wasn't being fresh." He raised an eyebrow. She thought about what she'd said. "Okay, I was. I'm sorry. But I—"

"Could you focus on me right now, miss?"

Dianna faced forward. "I'm sorry, Officer. They're my folks."

"I gathered. So what's your part in all this?"

Dianna thought about that, realizing there was no good,

easy, or quick answer to that. "That's a very good question. And it deserves an answer. But I really don't know how to give you one because it's hard to say how I'm involved."

The policeman eyed her. "Yeah? Well, I got time. Try me."

"Yes, sir." Dianna swallowed. "Actually, I have no part in this."

"Then why are you here, miss?"

"For the same reason you are, Officer. I was called."

"Say, do you know my son? He's a cop, too. Thomas West. We call him Tommy."

The cop sighted on Dianna's sweet little wispy-haired father in his red shirt, white golf sweater, and green-checked pants. "Yeah, I know a Tommy West. Out of Central Division?"

*Thank God, and bless you, Dad. A comrade in arms.* Dianna suffered no qualms over having family rank to pull. That was what it was for. If you had it, pull it.

"Yes, that's him." Her father was excited now, pointing and bright-eyed. "Tommy. Tommy West."

Dianna grinned and nodded, blurting the obvious. "He's my brother."

Dianna's mother tugged Dianna back so she could see her husband. "Now, calm down, Mel. Remember your heart."

"My heart's fine, Joy." Mel West benignly waved his wife off. "I'm talking to the officer here."

And that was apparently the officer's cue. "Yeah, I know Tommy." The policeman looked grim. "We don't get along too well." Which explained why he looked grim.

Dianna all but stomped her foot. *Damn that Tommy. See? He never played well with others.*

The West-family-hating uniformed officer turned to her. "Were you here with them when the incident happened?" He wagged his pen between her and her parents.

Now it was an incident. "No. They were here by themselves."

"No, we weren't. The Gundersens were with us."

Dianna stared for long moments at her father. "Dad. Honey. Nobody cares."

Her father got huffy. "The Gundersens do."

"Yes, I'm sure they do. But the nice *policeman* doesn't really care that you were here with them. He—"

"I can eat supper with whoever I want. It was a free country the last time I checked."

*Dear God.* "And it still is, Dad. But that's another thing. This is Friday, so I don't get what you're doing here at all. You're always at the Hufnagles' on Friday night."

Her mother answered. "Not anymore. Those people are dead to us." She was completely puffed up about it, too. Joy West held her purse tight against her little rounded body, as if she expected someone to make off with her oversized pocketbook. "We're not speaking to the Hufnagles."

"Oh, for God's sake, Mom, why not?"

"Mr. Hufnagle didn't return your father's garden hose."

Dianna narrowed her eyes in thought and then remembered. "The one he borrowed last summer? Ten months ago? *That* garden hose?"

Her mother raised her chin. "It came up again over bridge. We don't talk to those people anymore. You're not to, either."

"Mother, for—" Cutting her off was the sound of a not-so-stifled laugh that had come from the policeman. Dianna rounded on him. "What's so funny?"

Chuckling out loud, but not in a pleasant way, the man shook his head. "I see where Tommy gets it now."

"Gets what?" Insulted, Dianna raised a pointing finger at the big, armed cop, ready to go to battle for family pride. But she got no farther than that before her elbow was grabbed—and she was unceremoniously spun around, only to find herself staring up into Chris Adams's gorgeous, furious face.

Shock had Dianna drawing back, her mouth open. Surprise! Hadn't she said to herself at home, less than an hour ago, that the final straw would be if Chris Adams were here? And now, here he was.

"What are you doing here?" he hissed right into her face.

A bit taken aback, Dianna responded in kind. "I could ask you the same thing."

"I'm here having dinner with Veronica. And I don't want her to see you."

Dianna frowned. "And Veronica would be . . . ?"

"My girlfriend, Dianna."

Almost against her will, Dianna's eyes narrowed in jealousy. *So that's her name. Veronica.*

Chris was saying: "And if she sees you here—"

"But she doesn't even know me, so what do I have to do with anything?"

The policeman chose that moment to butt in by wagging his pencil at her, even as he spoke to Chris. "I been asking her that myself. She says she has nothing to do with this. Yet everyone here seems to know her."

"Not everyone," Dianna felt it incumbent on her to say. "For example"—she looked around, finally pointing to a knot of disgruntled-looking customers over at a corner table—"I don't know any of those people."

His hand still gripping Dianna's arm, Chris addressed the lawman. "Are you through with her, Officer?"

The man sworn to preserve the peace waved her away as if she were no more than a fly. "I'm done for now. Help yourself. And good luck."

Dianna bristled. "Good luck? What does that mean? I don't think you—"

"Never mind, Dianna." Chris's voice was singsong with caution. "May I speak to you over here, please? In private?"

"No. I'm not through—"

"Oh, but you are." With that, Chris set them in motion, essentially pulling her along behind him as he threaded them around tables, diners, and waiters.

Dianna didn't like this one bit. "Hey, let go of me! I will not be pulled along like this."

Her protests fell on deaf ears. She risked a glance back over her shoulder at her parents. Still standing with the policeman, they looked like elderly owls, so wide were their eyes. "Mom, Dad, it's okay. I know him. Get the Gundersens and go home. I'll call you tomorrow."

They seemed to understand. At least, they waved their good-byes. Dianna waved back at them and then concentrated on not knocking into the odd chair or table or diner as Chris rushed her out of the main dining room. He didn't stop until he had her off around a corner that revealed a short, narrow hallway containing a pay phone, under which sat a decrepit wooden chair. At the other end of the space were two facing restroom doors. Other than that, she and Chris were alone . . . but not in a good way.

Chris turned her to face him and finally let go of her arm. Fists at his waist, his feet spread, his stance was pure *The King and I.* The Jodie Foster version. "What are you doing here?" he demanded.

Dianna mimicked his stance. "Well, you know, and like I keep telling everyone, I was called here. There I was, sitting at home, minding my own business—" *Stop! Don't tell him you were home alone on a Friday night, no date or anything.* "Getting dressed to go out partying with my friends—"

Chris held up a hand to stop her. "Dianna. Never mind. You have to leave before Veronica sees you."

"No, actually, I don't. See, it's a free country. Just ask my dad."

"Dianna. Please. Veronica is right over there in one of those private alcoves. If she sees you, my surprise for her will be blown."

"Well, I don't see how, Chris. She doesn't know who I am." That being so—and this attorney being one woman Dianna really wanted to see—she turned, intending to peek out in the direction Chris had indicated.

He pulled her back. "Hey, stop that. She'll see you."

Dianna stared up at him, trying her best not to be affected by his nearness or his good looks. Like that was working. "Chris, it's okay. The only way your surprise will be blown is if you told her who I am. Did you?"

He shook his head. "Of course not. Right now you'd be the last person I'd introduce to her."

Stung, Dianna raised her eyebrows. "Thanks."

Chris exhaled, looking pretty ragged. "Oh, hell, I'm sorry. I didn't mean it like that. You know that."

She nodded that she did, but still . . . *Like I'm the tawdry little mistress who's shown up at the restaurant where my lover is having dinner with his wife, and I'm not good enough to be acknowledged, much less introduced.* "Anyway, I don't think you helped your own cause by grabbing me and hauling me back here. That's got to make your girlfriend curious."

Chris didn't say anything. He just stood there, staring intently at her, looking as if he had something momentous to say, something he couldn't get out, something that would be touching to her and—*No, Chris Adams. Don't you even do that,* Dianna wanted to rail at him. *Don't you dare look so handsome and vulnerable all at the same time.* She fought being caught up in him, but it was a losing battle. She wished he would say something. Anything. But he didn't. And so the silence between them deepened.

Outside their little corner of the world, though, could be heard the commingling noises of dishes clattering, the low buzz of several conversations, and someone's cell phone ringing. Dianna's hearing also picked up the familiar sound of Lenny's whining and of his mother's answering shrill voice. But none of it mattered. All she cared about, darn it, was how close Chris Adams was standing to her. And how he was looking at her. And how delicious he smelled. And how his nearness, without even touching her, made her body tingle. She wanted so badly for him to kiss her.

As if she'd made her request out loud, Chris reached

out to her and warmly clasped her arm. Dianna felt her heart surge and her pulse pick up. She had to stiffen her knees to keep from going to the floor. "Dianna," he said, "I don't know what to say. I mean, I don't even know what the heck I'm doing. And you're right: All I had to do was stay where I was. But I saw you, and I couldn't . . . I don't even know why I—"

"Excuse me. Am I interrupting something?"

Talk about your cold, arctic blasts of feminine outrage. Chris let go of Dianna as if she were hot to the touch and whipped around. "Veronica. What are you doing here?"

*Veronica.* The iceberg to their *Titanic.* Fear liquefied Dianna's bones. Now they were in big, fat trouble. The lawyer was here. And she and Chris did not have their story straight. Who could she say she was? Maybe Chris would think fast and say. Dianna vowed she'd go along with whatever he came up with. That settled, her curiosity won out. She leaned to one side until she could see around Chris's wide football shoulders. And there the woman was. *Dang.* Dianna's eyes widened. Veronica could have been a cover model. She was beautiful, and she oozed class. Blond, curvy, and every sleek hair in place. Even her casual outfit was major top dollar. She made a perfect picture—but of a pissed-off woman.

"What am I doing here, Chris?" she was saying. "I came with you, remember? Still, I hate to bother you here during your intimate moment—"

"This isn't an intimate moment, Veronica."

Dianna stared accusingly at the back of Chris's head. *It might've been if she hadn't interrupted.*

"If you say so." This was Veronica. "I just came to tell you that I got a call, and I have to leave. I have to go to the jail."

"What'd you do—kill someone?" Dianna clapped her hands over her mouth, absolutely not believing she'd blurted that. Embarrassed shock heated her cheeks. Now she'd done it. She'd drawn attention to herself.

Sure enough, Chris slowly turned to face her. He

looked mad. Dianna lowered her hands. Then Veronica stepped around her boyfriend to confront Dianna. The woman's features were set in lines as hard as diamonds. "No, whoever you are, I didn't kill anyone. At least"—dramatic pause—"not yet."

*Whoa.* Dianna's eyes widened. At this point, the blond attorney dismissed Dianna by turning to her boyfriend. Reduced now to silently watching the two together, Dianna was surprised to see the other woman's features soften. She looked almost human as she reached up to stroke Chris's cheek. Dianna wanted nothing more than to slap the woman's hand away. How rational was that?

When Chris and Veronica began talking to each other in low tones, Dianna found herself the dictionary definition, complete with picture, of a third wheel. Watching the couple in profile to her—trapped as she was in the narrow hall between their bodies in front of her and the bathroom doors behind her—Dianna didn't know what to do. This was too painful, and for many reasons. She needed to disappear. Her choices? Interrupt the lovers. Or hide in the powder room. Okay, she could have done that, but the doors—she sneaked a peek—were unhelpfully marked something like SIGNORE and SIGNORA. So which one was she?

She could just see herself making a huge mistake; some irate guy bellowing; the West-hating cop still here; he comes running. Thirty minutes later? Her having her mug shot taken downtown. No, being arrested as a pervert was not the topper she needed on this night. So, painful or not, she wasn't moving. Dianna crossed her arms and shifted her weight to one leg. May as well watch the show going on in front of her . . . and eat her heart out while she did.

"I'm so sorry," the blond Nordic goddess was saying, her voice intimate, apologetic, as she stared up into her lover's eyes. "I know this keeps happening, but I have to leave, Chris. I can't help it."

Chris covered his beloved's hand with his, kissing her fingers. Dianna's heart lurched painfully. Only this afternoon she'd wanted to do that to him. Still did, too. "Don't worry about it," Chris said. "The evening's ruined, anyway. I'll drive you over, if you want."

"No." The word was a sigh. Veronica moved back, pulling her hand away from Chris's touch. "You don't need to do that. Anyway, we came in my car."

"Oh, that's right. Then I guess I'm going with you."

"No, don't. This thing could take a while, and waiting all that time wouldn't be fair to you. Maybe your little friend here could give you a ride home?"

As one, they turned their attention to Dianna. She blinked, cocking her head much like a curious dog. *His little friend? Does she mean me?*

Chris turned to his girlfriend. "She's not my little friend, Veronica."

Dianna slowly raised an eyebrow. *I better not be.*

"Will you please be reasonable?"

Chris's raised voice popped Dianna back to the moment. He was talking to the ice queen, and Dianna realized that she'd missed something. The temperature had definitely chilled between the couple.

Sure enough, the blond lawyer retaliated. "Reasonable? Me? *You*"—she pointed a red-lacquered nail at his chest—"darted out of our booth and went directly to *this* woman"—that fingernail sought Dianna's chest; she drew back a safe distance—"and then hauled her off to this corner and left me sitting out there, Chris. I was humiliated. Then I come over here and find you looking as if you're about to kiss *her*."

Chris and Veronica both turned to Dianna and stared accusingly, silently at her. *As if this were all my fault.* Still, a hot thrill of embarrassment flitted along Dianna's nerves. Feeling defensive, she crossed her arms under her breasts and divided her challenging gaze between them. One more "little friend" out of either one of them, she determined, and someone was going to know exactly how she felt about being called that.

The moment of silent contemplation of Dianna broke,

and the argument recommenced, with Chris firing the first shot at his girlfriend. "I was *not* about to kiss her or anyone else, Ronnie. I was—"

"Please." Ronnie held up her long-fingered hand, palm toward Chris. "Can we talk about this later? I'm sorry, but I really have to go. I can't help it." As evidence, she held up her cell phone and sent him a pleading look.

For long moments, Chris stood there like that big dark monolith thing in *2001: A Space Odyssey*. But then he relaxed. Slumped. "I know you can't. Go. Don't worry about me. I'm a big boy. I can get myself home."

"You sure? I mean, about me going on?" The ice queen started to thaw out, maybe even melt a degree or two. "You know what? Never mind. I can call Joe. He'll cover—"

"No. Really. It's okay. You'll just fret and pace if you don't go yourself."

Suddenly the attorney was soft and feminine, her blue eyes beseeching. Dianna wanted to puke. "You know me so well. But are we okay, Chris? I mean really?"

Chris took the blond woman in his arms, hugged her to him, and kissed her forehead, all very tenderly. Dianna sniffed, almost moved to tears. Not because it was a beautiful sight, but because it wasn't her he held. She was so darned tired of being alone. Of being the onlooker. The bridesmaid. The loser. Big *L* on her forehead. The little friend.

Veronica the lawyer withdrew from Chris's embrace. The lovers stood there, staring into each other's eyes. Deciding this was where she'd come in, Dianna lowered her gaze. Then a rustle of fabric and the sound of feminine heels clicking on the tiled floor told her that the lawyer was leaving. Dianna looked up, expecting to see Chris's back as he perhaps escorted his beloved to the door or to her car.

But no. He was standing right there in front of her, staring at her. His hands were in his slacks pockets. He could not have been more handsome, more mesmerizing, despite everything. "Hi," he said simply enough.

"Hi, yourself."

"Look, I'm sorry for everything I said earlier, but mostly because you had to witness my . . . domestic upheaval, I guess you'd call it."

Dianna shrugged. "No need to apologize. But I wouldn't say 'upheaval.' It wasn't all that bad." In fact, it had been worse. More like a poke in the heart with a sharp stick.

"Good. So, little friend," Chris said conversationally, grinning at her, "can you give me a ride home?"

# CHAPTER 4

Late that next Monday afternoon, almost five o'clock, and as self-satisfied as if he'd fought some long and bloody battle to win a coveted prize—which he pretty much had—Chris triumphantly settled himself in one of the two well-padded chairs that fronted Dianna West's desk. Getting here had not been easy. Chris eyed the seriously somber Mrs. Windhorst, who just now was closing the office door behind her. The secretary had put up a good day-long fight. But Chris had hung tough through his many phone calls to her, and the means had certainly justified the ends because victory was his. Well, sort of.

Meaning, Dianna was studiously ignoring him. Chris wasn't worried. She had to talk to him. He was a paying client. Seated behind her desk, she busied herself fussing and flipping through a messy stack of manila file folders. Apparently she meant to locate a specific and elusive one. Watching her activity brought a reflective frown to Chris's face. *Now, why does her desk look odd? What's wrong? What's missing?* He concentrated on the question until the answer came to him. There was no computer. And now that he thought about it, he realized he hadn't seen any at all here.

Just then Chris's mind pulled forward his conversation last Friday with Dianna. He'd talked to her about being on the Internet, and she'd freaked. *Okay. Some kind of phobia working here?* Who knew? There was one way to find out. Ask the woman. God knows, he needed to say something neutral. And soon.

But Dianna glanced up at him and stole his moment. "Just give me a minute here to collect my thoughts, okay? I need to see where I am with your file. In the meantime, why don't you flip through this picture album"—she pushed a plush, satin-covered, three-ring binder toward him—"and see if anything in there gives you any ideas for your proposal? Those are all recent and successful scenarios we've done."

Ever the cooperative soul, Chris pulled the album off her desk and onto his lap. "All right. I'll take a look."

But he didn't. Chris ignored the album in favor of feasting his eyes on Dianna, whose attention was directed at her pile of work. No doubt about it: She looked great. All he could see of her now was her black jacket buttoned over a silver top. But when he'd come in a minute ago, she'd been standing at a filing cabinet. His reaction had been *Wow*. She had on a short black skirt with a slit up the thigh and black strappy sandals. His tongue had nearly hung out of his open mouth. Whoever made her outfit should have to pay her to wear it.

*Down, boy.* Chris shifted his gaze to more neutral territory . . . the picture window behind Dianna. Still the same gray and overcast spring day. It hadn't rained, but it needed to desperately. The barometric pressure was brutal, making the sky feel too heavy, like a fat balloon over-filled with water but not quite enough to make it burst. Chris had felt pretty much the same way—bursting to get here. He'd actually caught himself whistling at one point. How could it be that his excitement seemed to have more to do with the anticipation of seeing Dianna again than it did with proposing to Veronica?

That thought caught Chris up short. *Hey, come on, get over it. This is a simple thing. Dianna's a great-looking woman. Why wouldn't you get excited to see her? Who wouldn't? And you're not dead. Just about to get en-*

*gaged.* Feeling better for that bit of perspective, Chris broke the rather heavy silence between him and Dianna. "So," he said, making a show now of flipping through the album's pages and grinning at her to show he was just razzing her, "I can't believe you wouldn't give me a ride home last Friday night. That was cold."

Dianna's gold eyes held his gaze for one long, serious moment before she answered. "You deserved it. And don't tell me you really don't have any idea why I left you standing there at Tamborello's."

Chris chuckled. "Did it have anything to do with that 'little friend' remark?"

"Oh, yes. A lot." Dianna sat back in her chair, crossing her arms under her very fine breasts. She still wasn't grinning.

*All righty, then.* Chris sobered. Looked like he had some making up to do. "Hey, I didn't mean to insult you when I called you my little friend, Dianna."

"Veronica did."

"I know. I guess I was acknowledging that I also thought she was out of line with her comment." Chris waited, but in vain. Dianna's silence effectively lobbed the conversational tennis ball back into his court. "All right, look, I don't know what to tell you. She was just upset and jumped to conclusions."

"A pretty darned big one." Dianna tucked her shoulder-length hair behind her ears and leveled an accusatory stare on him.

Chris felt forced to defend Veronica. "Maybe. Maybe not. I don't know what she saw from where she was standing, but I did have my hand on your arm." *And things were about to heat up.* He managed not to say it out loud, but he knew the truth of it. He suspected Dianna did, too, even if she wouldn't admit it. "So, anyway, she went with that 'intimate moment' thing."

"Didn't she, though? You should be offended, too, by her implication. She as much as said she thinks you're cheating on her."

Chris nodded. "Yeah, I got that, and I was offended. I haven't given her any reason to doubt me." His conscience pricked him, saying that since he'd met Dianna, the possibility existed that he could very easily give Veronica many reasons to doubt him. Many.

"Well, I hope you haven't cheated." Dianna's chuckle was unexpected—and proved to be at his expense. "I mean, you are going to ask the woman to marry you. I'd hope you'd be over other women by now."

"Yeah. You'd think." For the life of him, Chris couldn't look away from her face, couldn't disguise what he was feeling.

Dianna stilled, her features softened. The very air seemed to thicken. Chris's chest tightened, and he could barely breathe. Dianna West was temptation personified. And he needed to get up and leave right now and never come back. Honor demanded it. Unfortunately, leaving was the last thing he wanted to do. Maybe if they got this thing between them out there, Chris reasoned, and talked about it, that would put it to bed. He suppressed a wince. *Poor choice of words.* Still, he'd come this far in his thinking. "Look, Dianna, there's something going on here between us that we both—"

"No. Stop." She held a hand up, palm toward him. "Don't say anything more. Let me talk first. Where you were headed right now, Chris, with what you were going to say, is a pretty common reaction. I've seen this a lot."

"I don't know what you mean. You make it sound like I have a rash."

She smiled. "No. It's more like an itch. See, too many times I end up being an amateur marriage counselor. Well, more like a relationship counselor. Guys get cold feet. Have second thoughts. And apparently get this far—to the point of popping the question—and then suddenly feel a need to flirt with me because I'm . . . I don't know . . . handy or safe or something. I think they feel a need to test themselves and what they feel for their girlfriends."

"I see. So I have a predictable itch and you're a convenient barometer. Attractive." She was denying this thing between them. Disappointing, but probably for the best. Stung, Chris cooled his jets and went for the light touch. "Okay, so maybe you're right. But it's your fault for being so easy to talk to and for being pretty darned cute, besides. I guess it's only natural I'd flirt with you."

Looking uncertain, Dianna peered at him from under her eyelashes. "Thank you for the compliment, but I hope I didn't hurt your feelings."

She had, but Chris shrugged. "Hey, I'm a big boy. But you probably just did me—and Veronica—a big favor."

"That was my sole intent, Chris." Her smile was shy, charming. "But I didn't like having to say it."

Talk about your mixed signals. Chris's body ignored the shy part and picked up on the come-hither. His nerve endings awakened, tingling and threatening to go erect. Striving for subtle, he gripped his chair's wooden arms and held on, anything to keep himself from vaulting right over the desk and taking Miss West to the floor.

"So, what'd you do—take a cab?"

"A cab? Oh, you mean last Friday." Chris relaxed his grip and chuckled. "Can't stand suspense, huh? But, yeah, as a matter of fact, I did have to take a cab."

"I'm sure the cabbie was glad for the business." Dianna's gold-colored eyes glinted with humor.

Chris grinned right back at her. "You're cute when you're sarcastic, you know that?"

"I've been told." Dianna folded her hands together atop her desk and became all pleasant and business. "So, what *are* you doing here today, Chris?"

And there it was, the question he had for himself, too. It went like this: Given how this woman seated across from him was playing hell with his daytime thoughts and nighttime dreams, what *was* he doing here and feeding them? How could he explain his need to be around her? She'd just told him to knock it off, essentially. But it was like a physical something driving him—

"Chris?"

He blinked back to the moment and to the woman seated on the opposite side of the desk from him. "You're still mad at me, aren't you?"

He'd surprised her with that. She sat back, raising her chin one proud notch. "No. Mad at myself. And surprised to see you. Your name isn't on my schedule for today."

"Blame Mrs. Windhorst. She gave me the appointment."

Dianna nodded. "That's how it usually happens."

"I'm a work-in."

"Okay."

They were treading water. Chris sat forward in his chair and plunked the mostly ignored album back onto her desk. "You just said you're mad at yourself. Tell me why. What'd you do?"

She shrugged, giving him that shy look again from under her eyelashes. "I didn't really *do* anything. It was what I *wanted* to do."

"Really? What did you want to do?" *And was I involved?* He knew he had no right to pursue her like this, but that look she was sending him had his pulse racing.

Her smile secretive, she exhaled. "Let's just say I broke a rule of my own making. A business rule regarding clients. And I'm not happy with me right now." She moved some papers around on her desk, in essence signaling a change in subject. "So, let's talk about you." Her direct stare was challenging. "Obviously there was a happy ending over the weekend? I mean, with you and Veronica— I'm sorry, what's her last name? We weren't formally introduced."

And there it was. "I would've introduced you, Dianna. But I didn't know who to say you were, remember? I couldn't think fast enough. Then it just didn't come up again. But, anyway, it's Alexander. Veronica Alexander."

She ignored everything else and said, "Alexander. Thanks. So you and Ms. Alexander made up after your fight, I take it?"

"There was no fight."

Dianna raised an eyebrow and her voice. "Oh? I guess I was mistaken. But . . . good. Great, in fact. So you still want to pop the question to her, I take it, or you wouldn't be here?"

Chris sat back in his chair, held Dianna's gaze with the weight of his own, and absently rubbed his knuckles over his lips. How to answer her question? Outside of her presence, the answer came easy. But the moment he was around her . . . not so easy. In the end, all he could say was: "Something like that."

Dianna nodded and stared at him . . . too long. She blinked and started talking rapidly. "Well, good, then. Let's see where we are here." She flipped through a folder with his name on it. "Okay. So we didn't get too far last Friday before you got beeped, did we?" She glanced up at him and smiled . . . polite, distant. "That means we need to start at the beginning and talk about how you see this coming off—the proposal itself, I mean."

She crossed her legs, folded her hands together, and then leaned over to rest an elbow against her chair's padded-leather arm. The professional in charge of the situation. "What do you want to happen here, Chris? Remember, this is *your* big moment." She pointed to the album he'd been charged with looking through. "Did you find anything in there that you liked? If not, we have others—"

"I didn't look through it."

"Oh. Why not?"

"I wasn't interested. I was watching you."

Dianna inhaled slowly and then exhaled. "Chris, we just went through this. If you're not here to talk about your proposal, then I don't know what to say."

She was right, too. If he didn't want to ask Ronnie to marry him, then he had no business here. The hell of it was, he couldn't honestly say that he *didn't* love Ronnie and *didn't* want to marry her, despite his obvious attraction to Dianna. Given that, he relented. "All right. You're right. Let's look through the books and talk about music and the ring and flowers and things like that."

Dianna instantly brightened. Obviously relieved. Chris suppressed a chuckle at his own expense. *Shot down. Rejected. All right, Adams. Keep it light. Keep it real. Time to be all business.* "So, what's first?" he said, getting up when she did. "Do we adjourn to the parlor or make a field trip, or what?"

"Adjourn to the parlor for now. The field trips come later when we're scouting locations."

"Sounds like fun."

"It is." She came around her desk and indicated the antique-looking sofa where they'd sat last Friday. "If you'll join me over here, I'll outline our various package deals for you, and then we'll go from there."

She sounded like an insurance salesperson. Or a funeral director. "Sure. But can you customize something?"

"Certainly. We do it all the time."

"Money is no object." Chris sat down exactly where he had last Friday.

Smiling, Dianna took up her position at the other end of the sofa. "I gathered."

Chris took the album she handed him, a different one from the first one he'd ignored. "These are recent pictures, taken on location, of happy couples who were our clients," she explained. "That's always a good place to start for ideas."

Chris nodded, positioning the album across his lap. He flipped through a few pages of snapshots, noticing the bright smiles and all that happiness and hugging. It was enough to make a guy sick. "Speaking of happy couples," he said, fixing his gaze on Dianna, "what's the latest on Lenny? You heard how he's doing?"

She rolled her eyes. "Oh, yes. From what my mother said, they've found mummies in Egypt in better shape."

"Ouch. Not the pretty picture, huh?"

Dianna laughed. "No, but he wasn't to begin with, either, the poor guy. My mother tells me that right now he looks enough like Frankenstein's monster to scare small dogs and little children. Apparently, he's on crutches and has stitches in his head and his leg. And lots of bandages all around everything."

"His head? What's wrong with his head?" Chris held up a hand to stop her from commenting. "Save it. I know the obvious answer to that. I mean specifically."

"You don't know? But you were there. I thought you saw everything happen."

"Apparently I didn't. I got up from the table at Tamborello's when the commotion began and saw the stabbing part. But not the head part."

"Oh. He bumped it when he first fell. And then a wine carafe conked him."

"That had to hurt."

"No doubt."

"So are you going to forgive me?" The question wasn't a slip-up. He'd been thinking it and waiting for an opening.

Dianna stared at him as if he'd just plucked a rabbit out of the air. "Forgive you for what . . . exactly?"

"I don't know. Maybe for everything since I first walked through your front door last Friday. I just get the impression that you've been upset with me since then, even before the Tamborello debacle, and I don't like that feeling. Seriously. If I've hurt you or pissed you off, then I'm sincerely sorry and I hate me, too."

She fought a chuckle and that heartened him. "I don't hate you. And it's not all that bad."

"But it is bad, right?"

She quirked her lips and then gestured as if helpless. "Yeah. But it's not you. It was . . . Friday night. You saw that. And the rest of the weekend was hard, too. It's like everything was going along so well, and then it all fell apart. Now I've got insurance companies to deal with, and poor, sweet Mr. Tamborello lost business. And the violinist. God, he cut his hand and maybe can't pursue his livelihood. I'm sure I'll have to make restitution for that somehow, and—" She stopped talking and cocked her head at Chris. "Why am I telling you all this?"

"Because I'm easy to talk to." The daunting thing was he wanted to fix everything for her that was wrong. Just charge in and slay all her dragons. And he had this big warm fuzzy feeling coming over him right now that made him want to reach over and hug her and reassure her. "So, keep going. I'm a good listener, too."

"No." She looked wary of him. "I think I've said too much already."

"No, actually you haven't said enough."

"What does that mean?"

"It means my weekend was every bit as rotten as yours. I had a hell of a time with Ronnie being ticked—"

"I thought you said there was no fight."

"There wasn't. But there was a lot of silence, if you get my drift."

Dianna grimaced. "Ooh. Never good. So put those two things together for me, Chris—her not talking to you and your being here today. What do you want me to do?"

"I don't know. I guess I want you to put together something quick that can come off in the next couple days." He'd had no idea he was thinking that until he said it. But now that he had, it sounded right. Just do it and do it quick. Get the scary thing over with.

Shock claimed Dianna's features. "Days? You want this in *days*? Why so quick?"

"Two birds with one stone. Apologize, propose, have the ring, get it over with, all that."

Some unreadable expression crossed her face. She wouldn't quite meet his gaze as she picked at a thread in her skirt and then smoothed the material over her legs. "I see. Well. The next couple of days. Just get it over with. All right."

"So you'll help me?"

"Sure. If that's what you want. I can . . . certainly help you get it over with."

"Why do you keep saying that? 'Get it over with'?"

"Because it sounds awful." The words spilled out of

her, catching Chris off guard. "I would hate for some guy to think he had to get it over with when he was thinking of me."

"But I wasn't thinking of you."

Some emotion flickered in her eyes and was gone. "That is *so* not the point. Veronica deserves better than that, Chris. Better than just getting it over with. And I cannot even believe I'm taking her side, as *nice* as she was to me. But you guys just don't get it, do you?"

Now it was "you guys." "Get what?"

"Romance and the time and thought put into the effort. That's the key. That's what we women want. We want to know you cared to take the time to sit down and think about us and to come up with something that shows you really know us and that we mean something to you. You know, like spend at least as much time and thought as you put into a football betting pool. But why is it never any different? I just don't get it. What is so hard about love that I have to have an entire business dedicated to getting two people together who are supposed to already love each other—"

"Whoa. Dianna. Hold up. Pull over to the side of the road a minute, okay?" Chris had a hand held out to her, as if he were the traffic cop and she were the traffic.

Breathing hard, impassioned by her subject, and looking confused or surprised at herself, she stared at him. "Ohmigod, I am so sorry."

"I'm not. In fact, I would have paid money to see that performance."

She laughed. "Well, in one sense, you already did. I mean, since you're a client."

"True. Add it to my tab. It was worth it." Chris could not believe how comfortable, or how forgiving, he was with her. Hell, he'd seen her maybe a total of two hours in his whole life, but already he felt as if she were his best friend, only a whole lot more than that. Somehow, that was unsettling. Not the notion of having a female as a friend, but the nagging thing at the back of his mind that said he was missing some big, obvious point that he really should get—

"I need to say something else."

Dianna's voice cut through Chris's reverie, bringing him back to the moment. Smiling, he shrugged. "Why not? It seems to be your day for that. Go ahead."

She looked askance at him, but carried on. "Well, it's nothing dire or soapboxy. It's just that we have a new policy here as of this morning. I sent around a memo."

"Sounds ominous."

She shook her head. "Not so very. Anyway, new policy. Because of last Friday night's debacle, and only in those cases where we suspect there might be a problem— like in Lenny's case where he's so, well, Lennyish— we're giving our clients the option of having us attend their actual proposals at no extra charge. You know, just be there to smooth over the rough patches. And discreetly, of course. And only if you agree."

Chris raised his eyebrows. "Only if I agree? So now it's me? Are you saying you think I need help to do this? That I'm like Lenny in some—or *any*—way?"

"Oh, God, no. Not at all like Lenny." Dianna kept shaking her head. "No. Don't be offended. We're telling all our clients of the new policy. Or maybe I should call it an offer. That's what it is, essentially, and you can certainly say no." She picked up his file from off the sofa cushion. "But before you decide, let's look at your case. Your lawyer—"

"My girlfriend."

Her gaze met and held his. "Right. Your girlfriend. She's pretty much a perfectionist, I'm guessing. And impatient. Expects top-level performance at all times. Wants excellent service and things to go smoothly."

Damn, that sounded cold . . . but true. "Yeah. She does. But who doesn't?"

Dianna nodded. "I suspected as much. So I think Melanie should be there when—"

"What? Wait a minute. Melanie? Miss Gone with the Wind? What's she got to do with this?"

"You're right. Not Melanie. So you'd prefer Paula?"

"Not without a shot of Valium, one for each of us. What's going on here? I thought I was *your* client. I signed a contract saying I was."

Dianna lowered her gaze to her lap. Chris watched her thunk-thunking her pen softly against his file. Dark waves of hair fell forward to frame her face. Though it totally was not germane to the moment, he couldn't help noticing that she had such delicate bone structure. Finally, she looked up at him, quietly asking, "Then you still want me?"

Those words, the way she said them . . . some primal thing rippled through Chris's body, leaving the hair standing up on his arms as his belly muscles tightened. Was she kidding? Did he still want her? Did people in hell want Popsicles? "Yes, I do want you," he managed to say, relieved to hear himself sound so rational. "In fact, I insist on it being you. If I'm going to pop the question, I want you there and no one else." Chris heard how that sounded. "Well, except for Ronnie, of course. She's pretty essential."

Again Dianna said nothing, but her gold eyes darkened with some emotion or thought. Absolutely mesmerizing, they were. Made Chris want to howl like a wolf. Hungrily, he watched her, wondering if the last forty-eight hours showed on his face. They'd been hell, and he'd been crazed until he could get here this afternoon to see her. All he wanted was for it to be okay between them. And all he knew, or was willing to admit to himself, was that it was important.

"Well, in that case, then," Dianna said, finally breaking the silence, "since you . . . *want* me to be there, we don't have a problem."

"Oh, hell, I've been had, haven't I? That was pretty slick, Dianna. Okay, so you got yourself invited along. Fine. But we still might have a problem."

Her expression gave nothing away. "How so?"

"Well, after last Friday night, and thanks to my not thinking, Veronica will recognize you."

Dianna shook her head. "No she won't because she won't see me."

She looked so "little girl" smug that Chris couldn't resist teasing her. "So I've got this all wrong? I'm picturing this cloak-and-dagger thing. Hat pulled down low over your face, the trench coat on, you hiding behind potted plants, sneaking around, spying on us. She might notice that. And here's more: Your just being there, and my knowing it, well . . . it might give me performance anxiety."

He'd meant to make her laugh and he had. Her face even turned red. "I promise not to give you . . . performance anxiety. And, *no,* I won't be hiding behind potted plants. But, still, she won't see me. I'll make sure of that. You just worry about you. Concentrate on how you want to"—she paused to inhale deeply and then exhale slowly before finishing—"propose to your girlfriend."

Now, that pause of hers was interesting. "You always have that much trouble with that word?" *Or is it just when you apply it to me?*

"No, of course not. I just had to . . . clear my throat, that's all."

So she wasn't going to rise to the bait. Damn. Not that he should even be out fishing. He had Veronica to think about. Yet his thoughts were consumed with Dianna. To make things worse, on the way over here, he'd heard on the radio that Lovin' Spoonful golden oldie about guys torn between two women and needing to make up their minds. The hell of it was, Chris assured himself, he'd thought he had.

"So, it occurred to me that I don't know a thing about you, Chris. And I really need to, if we're going to do this right."

"Then go out with me. Tonight. Be with me." *Shit.* It was out before he even knew he was thinking it.

Dianna's eyes widened. "Excuse me?"

Chris thought fast. "I just meant . . . it's so late already. Mrs. Windhorst said I was your last appointment. Let her go home, and we can do this interview thing somewhere else." That sounded good. "You know, in a little more laid-back location. Like that field trip thing. Maybe talk over our drinks or do an early supper. Put it on my tab. Totally about business. You can ride with me or take your own car and follow me. Then I'll tell you anything you want to know." He grinned, hoping it would seal the deal.

She shook her head. "Oh, I don't think that's a good idea at all. Your attorney girlfriend wouldn't like that."

Edgy excitement pushed Chris forward in his chair. He had to make her say yes, that was all he knew. Just the prospect of an evening with Dianna, no matter how innocent . . . well, he wanted it. "She won't know. She's in Boston today and tomorrow doing some legwork for a case she's been assigned."

Dianna sent him a penetrating stare. "I see. But what I meant was she wouldn't like us, as in 'me and you'— or you and anybody else, I'd bet—out on the town for any reason. It just smacks of, I don't know, cheating."

"Cheating? Oh, hell, no. Not like that. I'm talking business. A meeting between client and proposal planner." Chris sat back, trying to look sincere and as if he believed himself. "I *am* allowed to move freely about the city, you know, Dianna. Besides, we'd be doing it for Veronica's benefit."

Bemused skepticism laced Dianna's expression and her chuckle. "I would love to see you try to sell that one to her."

*Could this be harder?* "All right, look, if she finds out somehow, I'll just tell her what's up, ask her to marry me, and she can ruin her own surprise. But I'll still pay you. So, see? No risk."

When Dianna didn't say anything, Chris took it as a positive hesitation—she was at least thinking about it— and so employed his proven, surefire, hundred-watt,

broad, sexy grin. "Come on, Dianna, haven't you ever
heard that the customer is always right? Besides, the risk
here is mine, not yours. So what do you say? You up for
this? You wanna do it?"

*Do I wanna do it? Yeah. Like rabbits wanna do it.* That
darned Chris Adams. He'd made this adventure sound so
innocent and like so much fun. Could the man be more
persuasive? Not humanly possible. After all, here she was
at his place. Yes, *his* place. Very smooth of him, no? And,
apparently, where he was concerned, she was very will-
ingly led. If she didn't stop kidding herself, Dianna knew,
this could be big trouble.

Again she saw herself sending Mrs. Windhorst—along
with her very suspicious and disapproving expression—
home; heard her own babbled explanations to the woman
about a business dinner; saw herself locking up and then
following Chris's world-class Beemer—like a lamb to the
slaughter—right to his place. If she could forgive herself,
Dianna reasoned, it would be on the basis of her not
having known where they were headed until they got here.
And then, when he'd pulled up in front of this building,
she'd seen a neon sign for a really classy restaurant on
the first floor. What was there to suspect?

So here she was. Dianna looked around. A dark and
stormy Monday evening. The rain had finally come. But
who cared? She was in an honest-to-God penthouse apartment. So coolly elegant that it made her heart take a stag-
gered beat. Not one amenity had been overlooked. And
here she sat on his sofa. She ran her hand over the rich
fabric. *Nice.* Her jacket, which he'd helped her remove,
now lay folded over the sofa's arm. She'd kicked off her
shoes, too, when Chris had told her to make herself comfortable. But that was as far as she was going.

Oh, and she had a drink in her hand. Was this guy
suave, or what? Dinner, he'd informed her after a phone
call to the French Quarter—the exclusive restaurant on
the first floor—would be delivered to the door. Dianna

was so totally impressed that she was in danger of being swept away. And about this penthouse . . . she could do this, she told herself while looking around. Admiringly, she catalogued the furniture, noting that it was contemporary but done in soft earth tones. Several select pieces were set around the room in intimate little conversation groupings, one even around a two-sided fireplace. Was the other side in his bedroom?

*Don't go there.* Okay, not going there. Desperately she looked around, finally sighting on the wall of floor-to-ceiling windows in front of her that gave a panoramic view of Baltimore at its best. Now, this was nice. Viewed from this height and through the veil of the softening rain, the city appeared to have slipped into something more comfortable . . . an Impressionist painting, to be exact. Watery. Evocative. Alive.

Of course, the mood killers here, the splashes of cold water in the face, were the big questions. Things like, oh, did Veronica live here, too?

# CHAPTER 5

And were Veronica's clothes in the closets? Her toothbrush in the bathroom? Dianna continued torturing herself. Was the décor her taste? The music playing softly on the built-in stereo system—had she picked it out? And the flowers? The paintings? The bric-a-brac? Suddenly the absent attorney was everywhere.

And speaking of that hard-edged, possessive woman, Dianna wouldn't have been surprised to discover there were hidden cameras throughout the place, right now busily recording her every word and gesture. She could just see that tape being played back in court while she sat in the witness stand, red-faced with shame. Shame? What shame? She hadn't done anything wrong—

"What are you thinking about so hard, Dianna?"

Startled out of her thoughts, if not her skin, by the sound of Chris's voice, Dianna jumped, nearly spilling her wine. Steadying it, she put her free hand over her heart and looked up to see him rounding the other end of the sofa. "God, you startled me. I didn't hear your approach."

"Sorry. Didn't mean to scare you. Darned thick carpeting. Not my idea." He sat down on the sofa with her, but at a discreet distance. His expression was open, friendly, the perfect host. Leaning forward, his elbows resting on his knees, he took a sip from the squat crystal tumbler in his hand and then held it out toward her. "Rum and Coke. You want one?"

"No." She held up her goblet of white wine. "I'd better stick to this. I'm driving, you know. So, whose idea was it?"

His expression mirrored confusion. "For you to drive? Yours, I guess. Unlike you last Friday, I did offer you a ride tonight."

A self-deprecating grin claimed Dianna's lips. "All right, fine, you got me. And I should have taken you up on that ride, you know. I had a hard time keeping up with that machine of yours. But I meant the thick carpet. Whose idea was that?" His expression didn't clear. "Just now you said it wasn't *your* idea. So I was wondering if the place was already decorated when you bought it."

*Good save.*

"Oh." He sat back, crossing an ankle over the opposite knee. He switched his drink to his left hand and rested his other arm along the sofa's spine. Dianna spared only a glance at his fingers . . . long, supple, like a pianist's . . . and remembered this pose from her office last Friday. "The carpet, like everything else, was the decorator's idea," he said.

*The decorator! Not Veronica. God love the decorator.* Dianna wanted to jump up and cheer—a world-class college football cheer. Pom-poms. Short skirt. Lots of spirit. Megaphone: *Two, four, six, eight . . . who do we appreciate? The decorator! The decorator! Yah!* This would be followed by lots of tumbling and maybe even an attempt at doing splits. *Ha. Take that, Veronica Alexander.*

Chris was still talking. ". . . I have no clue about these things. I mean, what kind of doorknobs do I want? I told her the kind that open the door when you turn them, what else?"

Dianna took a sip of her wine and eyed Chris. "Her?"

"The decorator."

*Rah, rah, rah! Sis, boom, bah!* "What's her name?"

"Her name? I don't know. I forgot." His expression

somewhere between confused and bemused, Chris added, "But let me think a minute." He frowned, staring trance-like at the carpet. Then he focused on Dianna, pointing at her. "Got it. Jayne—with a *y*—Van Ling. Why?"

Dianna shrugged her shoulders. "I just like her style."

"You do?" Chris looked around his living room, frowning as if he'd never noticed it before. "So did Veronica. She worked with Jayne to get all this done. Dealing with the details would have made me nuts."

Dianna felt the corners of her mouth pulling down. *Darned, silly decorator. Couldn't even work on her own. How good could she be?* "Does, uh"—Dianna cleared her throat, striving now for cool and casual as she stared fixedly into her wine glass, much as if it were a crystal ball she was consulting—"does Veronica live here . . . by any chance? Already, I mean."

When Chris didn't say anything, Dianna forced herself to look over at him. His seriously contemplative expression said he was trying to divine what underlay her questions. "Is that important, whether she does or not?"

He spoke quietly. His dark eyes seemed to glitter in the low lighting as he raked his gaze over her. Though her mind whirred, looking for a safe way to answer him, Dianna felt certain her blood had stilled in her veins. She'd got herself into this corner. It was up to her to get herself out. She fell back on business. "It could be," she all but chirped. "In other words, say you wanted to propose right here. We'd have to work fast and discreetly to get everything in place before she came home that evening. Wouldn't want her to surprise us in the middle of set-up." *Or have her come waltzing in here right now because her trip was cut short.*

Chris nodded. "I see. Makes sense."

Dianna exhaled her relief. "So . . . does she?"

He chuckled. "You're relentless. No. She doesn't."

*Ta-rah-rah-boom-de-ay.* Dianna smiled broadly and sincerely.

"She does have a key, though."

*Hold the fireworks. Stop the marching band. Kill the grin.* "Oh. Of course. I would expect her to . . . I guess."

Chris apparently chose to ignore that as he pointed at her slender goblet. "You like the wine? Believe it or not, there's a wine cellar here, although it's not really a cellar at all. More like a big, temperature-controlled brick-lined room with wine racks. Go figure."

Dianna chuckled. "You sound as impressed as I am right now."

"I am. And I don't know the first thing about wine, which tells you the 'wine cellar' "—he said it so hoity-toity, as if he were embarrassed by his riches—"was not my idea. But ask me about beer. Beer, I know about."

Dianna grinned at him. "A total guy thing. Anybody who ever went to college knows about beer."

"And yet I never went to college."

Dianna pulled back, surprised. "Seriously? You never went to college?" She sipped at the really great wine he'd poured her, for someone who said he didn't know anything about wine.

"You mean all this stuff?" He gestured in a broad sweep of the living room. "How would a guy who never had any higher learning ever achieve all this?"

"No." Dianna felt chastised. "That would be totally snobbish of me. I didn't mean that at all." And yet she probably had. Her cheeks heated with her embarrassment. She could only hope the muted lighting hid her reaction. "Seriously, though. How'd you . . . *do* all this? Were you born with it?" *Oh, like that was better?* "Will you listen to me? I had no idea I was all 'Let them eat cake.' "

"It's okay, Marie Antoinette. Keep your head. But no, I wasn't born with all this. Just the hair color and these eyes. And the brains, apparently. But not the money. As to how . . . well, call it good timing. Knowing when to get in and when to get out. A lot of people lost their shirts, but I managed to sell mine and move on before the bottom fell out of the business."

"So-o I'm guessing, oh . . . the stock market?"

"Wrong. Bill Gates."

Dianna stared at him. "Bill Gates? You know him? Microsoft Bill Gates?"

"Not personally. But long story short, more than a few years back I invented and developed something vital he wanted and wanted bad. Really bad."

Excitement seized Dianna. "Ohmigod, you're a dot-com millionaire. I should have known."

"Really? How? Is there a computer chip embedded in my forehead?"

Very deadpan, she replied, "Yes, there is."

"Oh, damn. That's not supposed to show." Chris rubbed hard at his forehead.

Laughing, and careful of her wine, Dianna leaned over to grab his arm. An appreciative part of her brain registered that someone had been spending some time at the gym. His skin was warm and his arm muscled. "Stop it. I'm teasing."

Instantly serious, Chris looked from her hand on his arm to her face. He held her gaze. Naked desire radiated from his dark eyes. The man was two seconds away from kissing her and then some. Dianna's breath caught in anticipation, but her brain raised an accusation: So, one word from him, or one heated look, and you're ready to abandon your morals, your professional philosophy, *and* your Sunday-school upbringing?

*Yes. No!* Abruptly, Dianna sat back, thinking desperately how to lighten the moment. "I just mean, uh, wow, good for you. And this is really exciting for me, too."

"Really?" Chris sipped at his rum and Coke and watched her over the rim of his glass . . . watched her like a hawk, piercing gaze and all.

*Oh, God.* "Uh, sure." *Keep talking, Dianna.* "You know, you hear about dot-com millionaires all the time. Even read about them. But how many does the average person really know? I thought they—you—were like leprechauns. You know: little magical creatures of myth that everyone believes in but no one has ever seen. And now, here I am with an actual one."

Chris had sat through her paean to him with a bemused expression on his face. And with good reason, Dianna feared, hearing in her mind the echo of her words. She pasted a big self-mocking grin on her face and said, "Could I be more suave and sophisticated?"

Chris laughed. It made her feel good to realize that she could make him laugh. She'd bet Veronica couldn't make him laugh. She'd bet Veronica wasn't even funny. "Very suave and sophisticated. But what you're not is an average person. Not by a long shot."

Right then, something rang and something else buzzed. Dianna nearly jumped out of her skin. *Dear God, it's the alarm on the hidden cameras. The tapes need to be replaced.* She looked to Chris. He grinned at her. "Saved by the bells." He jumped up, drink and all. "Would you get the phone?" She nodded. "Great. Thanks. I'll get the door. It's probably our supper, and I'll need to sign for it."

*The phone. The door. Thank you, Jesus.* Weak with relief, yet ever cooperative, Dianna stood up, surprised to realize that her legs felt wobbly. Was that the effect of the wine? Or Chris's effect on her? Maybe both? *Not gonna think about that.* She set her wine glass on a coaster atop the coffee table and looked around as Chris headed for the double front doors of the penthouse. The phone rang again. Almost out of the room and into the wide hallway that led to the gallery foyer, he pointed to his right. "The phone is right over there on the bar. Just ask whoever it is to hold on a sec, okay?"

"Okay." Dianna's reply was a soft one full of trepidation. No one had to tell her exactly who was at the other end of that line. A very jealous attorney, no doubt. Nevertheless, she turned to the bar—the dark granite bar with the big, impressive saltwater aquarium backing it—and spotted the equally dark, effectively camouflaged telephone. Dianna walked stiff-legged over to it, eyeing it warily. On its next ring, she finally picked up the receiver, putting it to her ear. "Hello." No one said anything. "Uh, Mr. Christopher Adams's residence?"

The woman at the other end finally spoke. "Just who is this?"

"Uh . . . Dianna West?" she answered.

"You don't sound very sure of that, young lady. Don't you know your own name? Or did you make that up?"

"No, I didn't." Okay, so it wasn't Veronica Alexander. This was an older woman, by the sound of her voice. An older woman not too happy, for whatever reason, to hear Dianna's voice at the other end of her phone. "I am most definitely Dianna West."

She waited for the woman to identify herself.

"Where is my son?"

Dianna turned her eyes heavenward . . . or actually ceilingward . . . and mouthed a prayer of relief. *Oh, thank you, for letting it be his mother, and not his girlfriend.*

"Hello? Are you still there? Who are you? Understand, I'll call the police."

"No. Don't do that. I'm not a burglar or anything. I'm an invited guest. I swear." Dianna decided that this lady fell somewhere between Lenny's mother and her own in attitude and personality. Dianna remembered what Chris had said about his mother last Friday, about how she rode his back just fine. Apparently, she was going to ride Dianna's, too.

"You're an invited guest, you say? So, is there a dinner party going on?" Highly suspicious she was, too.

Dianna thought how best to answer that. Well, there was Chris. And her. And supper at the door. "In a way, yes."

"Why wasn't I invited?"

Dianna began to sweat—and to soundly curse Chris Adams for not answering his own phone and for not inviting his mother. How reasonable was that? "I couldn't say. It wasn't up to me to invite people."

"Veronica would have invited me. Is she there? Let me talk to her."

Now Dianna was ill. This *so* was not going to end well. "I can't. She's not here."

Oh, that was a deep, deep silence from the other end. "I see. So she wasn't invited, either?"

In her head, Dianna heard the theme music from the old *Dragnet* TV series her father always watched. Just the facts, ma'am. "No. Veronica was not invited."

"So you do at least know about Veronica?"

*Where in the hell is Chris? What'd he do—go to Paris to sign for that freakin' French food, for crying out loud?* "Yes, I know about Veronica. About as much as I want to." Ouch. Too late. It was out. Her eyes wide with guilt, Dianna clapped a hand over her mouth.

"I see, young lady. Well, Chris likes Veronica very much."

"I'm certain he does. She's a . . ." Dianna had to swallow hard to get the words out. "A lovely woman." *And so is Medusa, her sister.*

"So, who are you to my son, Miss West? If that's actually your real name."

"Ma'am, if it were possible right now, I could show you any number of photo IDs as proof that I am Dianna West."

"So you keep saying. Oh, wait. Hold on a minute. Someone is on my other line." With that, she clicked over, not giving Dianna time to respond.

So she stood there holding the receiver, thinking that if the phone had been a cordless one, she would have already gone in search of Chris. But it was just as well, she decided, that she was anchored here. For one thing, no way was she abandoning her post, only to have his mother maybe come back on the line before she could get Chris over here. What would the woman think? That Dianna had just wandered off like an idiot? Or that she was the burglar she'd said she wasn't and was even now ransacking the place? She could see his mother calling the police. *Oh, good. Let's have them show up. Maybe it will be that cop from last Friday night. Wouldn't he be happy? Or—*

*Stop it. Focus, Dianna. Something else is very wrong here. Think.* It was more a feeling than a physical thing that was wrong. Just something that nagged at the back of her mind. Dianna struggled to understand what exactly it was. Finally, she came up with it. Okay, first Veronica had jumped to that "intimate moment" conclusion last Friday. And now, here his own mother was pretty much accusing him of cheating, too. *So,* Dianna wondered, *is finding Chris in compromising situations the norm?*

She slumped, making a grumpy face. *No. Please. Come on, don't let it be true. Not him.* This *so* wasn't good. The women in his life, the very ones who knew him best, apparently didn't trust him to be faithful. How deeply disappointing was that? She'd thought he was different. He seemed like such a great guy. *But wait a minute.* This new thought pulled her upright with self-awareness. *I have no right to be upset. Chris Adams is my client, and nothing more. If he's a cheater and wants to ask his girlfriend—a barracuda woman who already knows how he is—to marry him, then fine. More power to them both. Not my concern.*

But it was, and she didn't mean professionally. No, the truth was she was very taken by him. Smitten. Infatuated. All of that. But beyond that, she realized she also just plain liked him. He was charming, he made her laugh, had nice manners, and was very helpful when called upon (i.e., Lenny). Was it too much to ask him to live up to all that? *I just don't want his personality to be a lie, to be a façade. And I don't want him to be the kind of man who cheats.*

*Unless it's with you?* her conscience asked quietly. *Well, yes,* Dianna admitted, caught off guard. Instantly appalled, she changed her answer. *No! Not with me. What an awful thing to think.* But was it? After all, when Chris had been in situations that had raised those suspicions in his girlfriend and now his mother, who exactly was the other woman he'd been with both times? Hello. "Oh, God. Me. *I'm* the other woman in his life."

Just then, Dianna heard those little clicks from the phone that meant the other party was coming back on the line. "I'm back. That was Myrtle Espinosa. She never shuts up. Say, you didn't hang up on me, did you, young lady?"

"No, ma'am. I wouldn't do that." See? It was a good thing she'd hung on.

"Well, at least you have good manners . . . for an intruder who doesn't know her own name."

Dianna gave up. This whole affair—more like a non-affair—was just silly. She resorted to her last line of defense: humorous resignation. "Thank you. I'll tell my mother you said so."

"You do that. Now, where were we? Oh, yes. You were about to answer my question about who you are to my son."

Dianna was ready for her now. "I'm a professional acquaintance."

"Oh, really?" The woman cheered up considerably. "Well, that's different, then. What's your profession?"

Dianna froze. Uh-oh. She couldn't say "proposal planner." That would give everything away. That he meant to ask Veronica to marry him was Chris's news, not hers, and she had no way of knowing if he'd divulged anything yet to his mother, despite his saying she rode his back. Maybe he hadn't meant over this specific situation—

"Hello?"

"Oh. Sorry. I'm here. I'm, uh, well, a professional woman, I guess you could say." Dianna made a face at her own answer. *A professional woman? What the hell is that?*

"You're a prostitute? I've been talking to a prostitute—"

"No! Not a prostitute. Not at all. That's not what—"

"I do not approve. And what is my son thinking, taking

advantage of a poor, downtrodden trollop like this? You should go to school, you know, and become a secretary or something else decent."

"But I am decent. And I did go to school—"

"Then why are you a hooker?"

That word coming out of Chris's mother's mouth was just so wrong. "I swear to God I am not a hooker." Dianna rubbed at her temple. Too many years of being kind and patient to her parents' elderly friends forestalled her being unkind and impatient now, even in the face of Mrs. Adams's . . . well, forthrightness. "Okay, look, Mrs. Adams—"

"Mrs. Eve."

"Excuse me?"

"I'm Mrs. Eve. I remarried, but then the poor soul died . . . not that it's any of your business. I just tell you that to clarify for you exactly who it is you're dealing with, young lady . . . and I use the term loosely in this instance."

Despite everything, Dianna suffered the crazy thought that if the woman hyphenated her last name she'd be Mrs. Adams-Eve. Too bizarre. Too unreal. And pretty darned funny, really. Dianna chuckled. "Look, I think I'll just let you hold on a minute for your son."

"Does he have his clothes on?"

Shock widened Dianna's eyes to approximately the size of dinner plates. "He'd better."

"Because I won't talk to him if he's naked."

"Neither will I."

"And where did you say Veronica is through all this?"

Dianne searched her memory. "Oh. Boston. She's doing some legwork."

"Don't you be crass with me, missy. Legwork, indeed. Veronica Alexander is a respected attorney."

"And I, Mrs. Eve, am not a—"

"Mrs. Eve? Oh, Christ." The phone was grabbed away from Dianna. Chris to the rescue. "Mom? What is going on?"

Evidently listening to his mother's reply or harangue

or whatever, he rolled his eyes at Dianna and mouthed *I'm sorry*. She grinned and shook her head, waving away his apology.

Sure, she could have been insulted and angry, but she'd sipped enough of that wine to be mellow. Besides, right now she was too happily tri-cornered by Chris's body in front of her, the bar at her side, and the wall at her back to care too much which little old lady verbally abused her. And he smelled so good . . . so earthy and warm and masculine. And he was such a man. Tall and muscled. Dianna stood there, grinning, gazing up at him, reveling in his nearness—and listening to him trying to reason with his mother.

"Hooker? There's no hook—You mean Dianna? Oh, God, tell me you didn't—" He made a face at Dianna, his expression an exaggeration of shock and embarrassment. Dianna could only grin up at him as she wondered what he looked like with his shirt off. "I say it, Mom," he continued, "because she isn't. She is *not*. 'A professional woman' doesn't necessarily mean—No, I'd know, wouldn't I?"

Chris pulled the handset away from his ear, covered the mouthpiece with his other hand, and said, "I cannot tell you how sorry I am about this. She's like a barking Pekingese when she gets started on something. Listen."

He put the receiver to Dianna's ear. Sure enough, Mrs. Eve's sermon continued unabated. Dianna pulled back, laughing, and held her hands up in defeat. "Hey, what can I say? You saw my mother in action last Friday night, remember?"

With the phone still held away from his ear, with his mother still yapping in that tinny way it sounds over the phone lines, Chris frowned as if trying to get a mental image of her mother. Suddenly, his expression cleared. "Ah. Got it. Looks a lot like my mother. Short. Big purse. Apple cheeks. Right?"

"Exactly. It's like a club they belong to, isn't it? They

all get to look like that after a while. Even Lenny's mother."

"Yeah, I saw her. She looked sane. But she's a nightmare."

"Yes, she is." Dianna pointed to the phone in Chris's hand. "Maybe you ought to say something to your mother."

"I don't think so." He held the phone out to her. "Maybe you'd like to?"

"No. She won't want to talk to me. I'm a hooker, remember?"

His expression that of a man mortified, Chris said, "I am so sorry. Damn. This is new, even for her." Then he smiled down at Dianna, his eyes warm, his closeness intoxicating. "Thanks for being such a good sport. Really. Veronica would have hit the roof."

Dianna shrugged. "Yeah, well, I'm not Veronica."

Chris roved his gaze over her face. "No, you're not. I'm very aware of that fact."

That look on his face . . . she knew that look. Dianna's breathing became stunted. *Oh, God, he's going to kiss me. And, oh, God, I'm going to let him.*

The phone in one hand, his other braced against the bar, Chris knew what he was doing, but at the moment he couldn't seem to muster much guilt or self-recriminations. He meant to kiss Dianna West. It was that simple. Yeah, that wrong. But also that simple. He lowered his head, angling ever closer to the sweet anticipation of her full lips, painted the color of strawberries. No doubt her kiss would taste of the wine she'd been sipping. Edgy anticipation seized Chris, tightening his belly muscles. Surely, as his lips molded themselves to hers, he'd also taste those strawberries. Sweet summertime—

"No." Dianna pulled back, shrinking away from him, her hands pushed against his chest. Chris jerked to a startled stop. His gaze met hers, and he saw Dianna's eyes. Dark gold, they looked wild as she shook her head no and hissed out her words. "Your mother, Chris. And Veronica. We can't. No. Don't. Please."

*Damn.* His breath left him in an exhalation of frustrated intentions. Even though he knew she was right—they really couldn't kiss—it took him more than a few mere seconds to hogtie his libido and engage his brain. Then, with sudden clarity, he saw the situation as it was. Christ Almighty, he actually had Dianna in a corner, wedged between the wall at her back, the bar at her side, and his body in front of her. *What the hell am I thinking?* He hadn't pulled antics like this since his smooth and suave yet pimply days in middle school.

"Dianna, sorry." He kept his voice down, too, because his mother's radar ears didn't miss a thing. "Let me get off the phone, and we can . . . talk, okay?" She raised her eyebrows suspiciously. "I mean it. Just talk. Business talk, I swear. And food. We have food. Lots of good, hot food. It's in the dining room. Go check it out." *Please don't leave. Just . . . don't leave.*

She shook her head, dashing his hopes. "No. I'm sorry, Chris, but I just can't do this. I can't stay. I was wrong to come here. And you were wrong to bring me here. But, believe me, I blame myself as much as I do you for this."

"Dianna, seriously." He was losing big time now. "There's no blame. It just happened. Or almost happened—"

"Let's don't lie, Chris. This didn't just happen. This has been looking for a place to happen since we first laid eyes on each other. We both know that."

Well, he sure as hell couldn't argue with that. Or tell her she was wrong. Defeated now, but a good loser—a lot of hard-hitting soccer had taught him that—Chris, still with the phone in his hand, shook his head, grinning apologetically. "All right. When you're right, you're right. If you want to go, I certainly won't stop you."

To prove it, he stepped aside, stretching the phone cord taut as he raised both hands in a hands-off gesture meant to reassure her. She immediately took him up on his offer, flitting by him as if she thought he'd reach out at the last minute and grab her back to him. Chris gripped the phone harder to keep from doing exactly that. Still physically agitated, he ran his other hand through his hair and exhaled a puff of breath.

With no other choice, tethered to the phone as he was, Chris silently watched Dianna walk stiffly over to the sofa. All right, so, yes, being male, he checked out her long legs and her cute butt. Again . . . wow. But the fun ended when she stepped into her shoes, grabbed up her short black jacket, and then her purse. Chris wanted to call out to her but couldn't or, more accurately, didn't think he should.

Dianna turned to face him. Chris didn't know what he expected to see in her expression. Maybe anger; or outrage; or a my-next-phone-call-will-be-to-NOW look. But none of that was there. Instead, and surprising him, he found regret in her eyes. Simple yet profound regret that said she too wished it could be different.

In seeming warp-speed time, Chris's gaze locked with hers. Barely daring to breathe, fearing it would break the spell between them, he stilled, slowly straightening up. He wanted her. And she wanted him. He couldn't look away from her, and she didn't walk away from him. So there it was. Pretty damned simple, huh? Tense with anticipation, with desire, Chris swallowed . . . and waited. The next move was Dianna's. And if it was the right one, the one he wanted her to make, then he was prepared to go all the way with whatever this thing was that was between them—

*Wait. This is crazy. Totally nuts.* Startled by his own conscience's belated awakening, Chris pulled back physically, abruptly. The spell was broken. Reality raised its ugly head. *What the hell am I doing? I've got a thing going on with Veronica. A very serious, heavy thing. And what the hell ever happened to such things as integrity? Suddenly I have the values of an alley cat?* Still, his gaze rested on another woman, Dianna West. And this moment remained one of those that he just somehow knew he would see for the rest of his life. It had that kind of dream-like quality, one fraught, unfortunately, with a busload of regret.

Dianna raised a hand in a slight wave to signal her good-bye.

Chris slumped, not so much visibly but emotionally. Then it was done. Over. Outta here. Dead in the water. Good-bye. Kaput. *Could this please just suck more? And while we're at it, could it also be harder?* Sure, he could call out to her. He could call her back, probably stop her. But what would be the point? So they could get it on hot and heavy tonight and have real regrets tomorrow? So he could feel like a heel and she could feel used? No. Wrong. Totally wrong. Things like honor had to mean something.

*Dammit.* With everything hammering at him like it was, with his heart and his head at war, Chris did the only thing he could. Totally aware that he still had the phone in his one hand and his mother on the other end of the line, no doubt with a thousand questions for him, Chris raised his hand to Dianna in a good-bye gesture of his own.

Across the way, standing in the dimmed lights and with the rain-washed image of Baltimore revealed behind her in the bank of picture windows, Dianna smiled softly. Hell, she didn't want to go any more than he wanted her to go. *Stay* was on his lips, but he couldn't speak it. He had no right to, not as long as Veronica was his reality. Chris exhaled, realizing his chest was tight with mixed and jangled emotions.

Abruptly, Dianna turned away from him, as if she'd had to force herself to do so. Yet she resolutely walked away, heading for the foyer. The thick carpet spared Chris the sound of her retreating footsteps.

The hallway swallowed her up, denying him the sight of her. He muttered a particularly spicy four-letter word that had, more than once, got his mouth washed out with soap when he'd been a little kid. At long last, and with nothing else to be done, Chris put the phone to his ear. "Mom? I'm sorry I kept you waiting, but—"

Stopping his words was the realization that all he heard was the flatlining dial tone. His mother had hung up on him. Just then, from another part of his penthouse, he heard the front door close. And Dianna was gone. *Great.* Unhappier than he knew he had a right to be, Chris hung up the phone and slowly walked over to the picture windows.

There he stood, feet spread apart, his arms folded over his chest. He stared out into the night, his gaze absently tracing the city's skyline. He'd thought he had it all with Veronica. They'd been going strong for years. Hell, he was about to ask her to marry him. And, yeah, he knew about temptation, about other women attracting him. He wasn't dead; he was in a committed relationship. Committed. That word meant, among other things, that he was to keep his distance from other women. And he'd done that successfully . . . until Dianna West came into his life.

Chris exhaled, wishing his doubts and all this upheaval could be as easily whooshed away as his breath was. After a while of thinking, *Veronica or Dianna, Veronica or Dianna,* it came to him that maybe he shouldn't be with either woman. Maybe he didn't know his own heart well enough right now to be any good to anyone. After all, something was causing this restlessness, something that he should probably explore. Too bad it couldn't be done in the Australian outback. But it wasn't that kind of exploring. Chris scratched irritably at his neck, wondering if all men went through this. Was he just getting the famous cold-feet syndrome? He shrugged. Maybe. Could be.

Then it became too much for him, all this indecision and soul-searching. Guys didn't do that. *Oh, hell, I don't know. But the Lovin' Spoonful are right. I have to make up my mind. And soon.*

# CHAPTER 6

So it was the next weekend. Sunday, to be exact. What a heck of a tedious week it had been, too, following all the emotions of Monday night. Lost in her melancholy thoughts, Dianna stood in her mother's kitchen, squishing her hands through a big bowl of ground beef in an effort to work the seasonings through. Soon her efforts would culminate in multiple patties suitable for grilling for the entire West family. But right now the messy, repetitious, mindless work served another purpose . . . it was soothing. A sigh escaped Dianna to prove it. *Could the last work week have crawled by slower than it did? God, so many long, long hours to get through. Actual snails had whizzed past, leaving time floundering in their dust.*

So, yes, obviously her mood sucked, she admitted. Still did. How bad did it suck? Well, she'd pretty much refused to subject herself to happy, starry-eyed people in love. Instead, and sparing them her mood, she'd closeted herself with the management aspects of her business and left the clients to Paula and Melanie. With her own emotions in such turmoil, she'd known she just couldn't stand to be around happy people who could be like gushy new parents telling you every tiny detail about their precious little darling—one of which you didn't have and desperately wanted. But still they expected you to be just as entranced as they were, only you weren't. Instead, you wanted to whack them over the head with their little bundle of joy's biggest toy rattle.

And that was how she felt right now about love and romance. *Love and romance. Ha. Neither of which I have. And why don't I? I'll tell you why,* she told herself, really working that ground beef over. *Because I'm the little-sister/best-friend girl. And I'm too busy with my business. Night and day and weekends. The paperwork alone could choke an ox. And then I have my family and my housework and laundry and all sorts of stupid chores. So when am I supposed to meet guys? Between midnight and three a.m.? Yeah, right. As if the choice ones—except for the good-looking vampires (and everyone knows they aren't monogamous)—are out and about at those hours.*

So, there it was—the sad truth that Dianna had to face. The only guys she knew right now were her clients. Yes, men who were already in love with someone else. For example, Chris Adams. Thus called forth, his smiling, handsome image assailed Dianna's consciousness, rendering her achy with wanting him and disgusted with herself for the same reason. The man was everything she'd ever dreamed of in her imaginings of what her Mr. Right would be like. Except for one small problem. *Mr. Perfectly Right for Me belongs to someone else.*

Dianna firmed her lips with determination. *Stop it right now. Just . . . don't. You can't keep thinking about him.* It wasn't that she wanted to or could even control it. He was just there in her mind every time she let her guard down. Dianna sternly shook her head, meaning to dislodge her mental image of him lowering his head to kiss her. But he wouldn't be banished. She saw him now as he'd been in her office on that first day they had met. God, he'd been so . . . and there it was again . . . everything she'd ever wanted.

Now she was mad. Needing a victim, she grabbed up a wad of the raw beef and treated it as if it had launched an unwarranted attack on her person. Spanking and smashing and smacking it into a patty, she puckered her face into an angry mask. *God, between Chris and Lenny— one I like too much and one I like not at all—I could be ruined both personally and professionally.* She quirked her mouth in self-mockery. *Well, there's something to look forward to, a reason to live.*

Dianna plopped the sorely abused patty onto the metal cookie sheet and yanked up another unsuspecting scoop of beef. About the only good thing she could say about the weekend, she decided, was she wasn't jumping with heated expectation every time the phone rang. He hadn't called all week at work—which explained her present mood—and he didn't have her home phone number. Unless he looked it up. She was in the book. But obviously he hadn't. So she didn't have to worry (hope, pray) when the phone rang at home that it might be him. And why should he call? She'd been the one to walk out on him and his expensive French dinner—as well as a warm, rainy evening meant for romance in that cozy cocoon of a penthouse of his.

*Wow.* Even now, as angry and frustrated as she was, the mere thought of him in that romantic setting affected Dianna's breathing. *Damn him. Why'd he have to happen to me?* She pinched and poked and nudged the meat she was working. *If some guy ever proposes to me, I want it to be just like that.* She could picture it . . . there she'd be, unsuspecting, yet all jittery with sexual tension. He'd be suave. Debonair. Suddenly go down on one knee in front of her. A huge diamond ring in his hand and offered up to her. Dianna exhaled softly, her breath making a "whew, you go, girl" sound.

"Dianna Joan, look at you. What are you doing to that poor meat, honey? I can't tell if you're trying to make sure it's dead or if you're meaning to resurrect the cow it came from."

Dianna snapped to, blinking, focusing her attention first on her mother and then on the abused meat in her hands. *Yikes.* It could use a coroner. "Oops. I guess I got lost in my thoughts."

"I'd say you did. You've been staring off into space and sighing a lot. Are you sick? You are. You're sick."

"I'm not sick, Mother. I just have a lot on my mind." *Stupid Chris Adams who won't get out of my head.*

"No. You're coming down with something. I just know it." Her mother dried her hands on her kitchen towel and said, to Dianna's horror, "Let me go get my thermometer."

Dianna tensed, ready for fight or flight. "Mom, no. I'm fine."

"Don't lie to me."

"I never would."

"Is that so? Remember that Halloween when you were twelve?"

"Are you serious?" Dianna stared at her mother, standing there, hands at her waist and across the kitchen. "You're reaching back fourteen years for this?"

"I am. You and that freckled little Jackie Snelling," her mother accused. "Don't tell me it wasn't you two who TP'ed a house and then lied to me about it."

How well Dianna remembered that fun night. She grinned to prove it. "Come on, Mom, you thought it was funny, too."

Her mother pulled herself up to her full five-foot-two-inch height. "I most certainly did not."

"Did, too. It was Lenny's house, and we TP'ed him because he'd smacked you with that water balloon instead of me."

An amused twinkle in her mother's eye gave her away. "The only reason I got soaked was because you ducked out of the way at the last minute. But my point was you lied to me."

"Well, of course I lied. I was twelve years old. You didn't really expect me to tell on myself, did you?"

"I most certainly did." With that said, and the thermometer apparently—and blessedly—forgotten, her mother turned away, taking up whatever the heck task she'd been doing before, and resorted to an injured discourse with herself. "I never thought I'd live to see the day when one of my own children would lie to me. You try to raise them right. Teach them right from wrong, but . . ."

Gently tuning her mother out, Dianna went back to her forced labor with the meat and her unhappy thoughts of Chris Adams. So maybe she'd lost a client . . . and the first guy in many moons to stir excitement in her. What would it have been like to kiss him? A shudder slipped over Dianna's skin, but she quickly stiffened her knees, adopting a pose of resistance. *Forget him, girlfriend. He's trouble for you. Concentrate on your life today.*

Okay, today. A beautiful Sunday afternoon in suburbia at the folks' house, with the scent of fresh-mown grass perfuming the warm air. Out front, in the wide, tree-lined street, neighborhood kids played and dogs barked. And in the middle of the comfortable block at the rambling brick home of the elder Wests, the whole family was over for this year's first once-a-month, spring-through-fall ritual, otherwise known as the big hamburger cookout in the backyard.

The window over the kitchen sink and the back door to the yard were thrown open to allow the fresh air inside. Screens on both kept out curious or incautious bugs. Stationed in the small yet tidy and airy kitchen, Dianna looked down at her handiwork to see she was nearing the end of her patty-making task. *Well, if the proposal business tanks,* she decided with a self-deprecating quirk of her mouth, *maybe I can be a short-order fry cook.*

"We work well together, don't we, sweetie?"

"That we do." Dianna smiled. Obviously her mother was over her martyr moment. "We *should* work well together. I've been your unpaid kitchen help since I was big enough to reach these counters."

Standing at the short end of the L-shape that was the kitchen counters, her mother grunted a chuckle. "Well, it was hardly a violation of the child labor laws. And I let you eat, didn't I? That's pay."

"Tommy and Edward didn't help and they got to eat."

"They were boys. They did the yard and the trash."

"Sometimes they did. But what about Karen and Vera? How come you don't let your daughters-in-law help in here?"

"They get in the way. They don't know where things are."

"They would if you'd let them help and showed them where things are."

"No. I just want us in here. The kitchen is too small, and I get nervous with too many people fluttering around me while I cook. Besides, Karen is pregnant with my first grandchild. She needs to rest. Let Vera entertain her."

As Dianna had no comeback to that, a pleasant silence descended over her and her mother. It was nice to be here, Dianna reflected. Sure, she loved her own place and her independence. But, God, this was home. Comforting. Steady. People who loved you and had to let you in. Just being together like this, whether slicing tomatoes or tearing lettuce apart or just leaning against a counter and talking to her mom, it was all good. Could they be more like the Cleavers? Dianna wondered, smiling. Or the opening shot in a Disney movie?

"Don't cut those tomatoes too thick, Dianna. Your father doesn't like them thick on his burger."

Dianna looked around, finding her mother now at the sink, her back to her daughter as she washed something. A surge of affection all but melted Dianna's heart. Could she love that gray-haired, aproned, and rounded little form of her mother's more? "I know about the tomatoes, Mom. I'm twenty-six, and I've been cutting them to Dad's specifications for about twenty of those."

Her mother remained focused on her chore. "I never gave you a sharp knife when you were six. And you say that every time I tell you about the tomatoes. I don't think that's necessary."

"Yes, Mother." It was as if she were six again. "So, anyway, I already sliced the tomatoes—"

"And the lettuce?"

"You did the lettuce." Dianna watched herself working with the beef. Her movements were now slower, more patient. "I'm almost done patting out the burgers."

"Good. Your father will send Edward in here any minute for them—if he doesn't blow himself up first lighting that gas grill."

Intending to defend her father, Dianna turned again to see her mother—and was struck momentarily speechless by the sight that greeted her. The woman was washing the plastic forks and knives she'd just taken from a newly opened box of plasticware. "Mom, what are you doing? And tell me I'm adopted."

"You are not. I have the stretch marks to prove it. I was forty-two and in labor for twelve hours." She got the martyr face again. "I nearly died bringing you into this world."

*Oh, dear God.* Dianna knew better than to comment on the twelve-hours-of-labor part. "Mom, you're washing plastic knives and forks. They're throwaway. And that's a new box."

"I know that. But we don't know who packed these, or what their hygiene was like. They could have sneezed right on them. Or not washed their hands after they went to the bathroom."

Disgusting. Dianna made a yuck face. "Gross. I'm not using them now."

"Well, they're not gross now, honey." She held them up. "I washed them."

Dianna playfully took her life into her own hands. "But did you wash *your* hands after you went to the bathroom?"

Her mother turned to her. An eyebrow was raised and her lips were pursed. Dianna laughed but quickly gave up her poor father, who rankled her mother more than her children did. "Anyway, Dad's not going to blow himself up. He knows what he's doing."

"He does not. Last October he poured all that lighter

fluid over those coals and lit them and burned himself good. Even singed his eyebrows. Remember?"

Dianna nodded. "I do. Vividly. Which is why he got a gas grill from his children last Christmas."

And yet her mother went on to tell her about last October. "Your father had that big square bandage on his forehead for three weeks. Looked like some kind of crazy person. Like a unicorn that had its horn cut off. People at church kept turning around to see. Morty Hufnagle, whom we are still not talking to, kept laughing, the old goat. Remember that?"

"Oh, yes." How could she forget the visit the entire, concerned West family paid to the emergency room? Dad had scared the hell out of them. And he could easily do it again. Just to reassure herself, Dianna looked out the kitchen window, sighting on her brother Edward's back. A tall, lanky guy with dark hair and an easygoing personality, dressed in khaki shorts and a knit golf shirt, he sipped from his beer and stood guard over Dad. It was a tough job, but somebody had to do it. Teach Edward to be the firstborn. He had the added task of not letting on to Dad that Mom had charged him with making sure his seventy-year-old father didn't maim or accidentally kill himself.

Dianna returned her attention to the last of the ground beef. But sudden laughter from outside pierced the quiet, causing her to look up again. From where she stood, she could just see through the screen door that afforded her a slivered view of the new wood deck that wrapped around the entire back of the house and up the two sides to the backyard fence. Mom had wanted it, so Dad had commissioned it, and then he'd stood by daily with handyman advice for the professional carpenters, much to their ha-ha delight.

"Is that Tommy laughing?" This was her mother. Given all the clacking Dianna was hearing, her mother had to be drying the plastic forks and knives en masse. "Is he teasing Karen again about her big stomach?"

"Probably." All Dianna could see through the doorway were portions of the people seated on the padded deck chairs: her other brother Tommy's hairy muscular legs; his wife Karen's very pregnant belly; and Edward's wife Vera's long red hair as she sat forward petting the family pooch. Dianna chuckled. Joe Cocker, the cocker spaniel. What had Edward been thinking—or smoking—when he'd laid that name on the poor pooch? But it had stuck and now Joe was a serious part of the family, only just shy of having his own place at the table.

Just being around her family, seeing them all together like this, brought home for Dianna exactly how much she had at stake in her business. Not only her parents' retirement fund, but also their trust and their belief in her. No way could she blow all that by giving in to what she might feel for Chris Adams. No way. She loved her family too much and wanted them to be proud of her. But how would they feel if she lost everything her parents had worked for all their lives? What would Edward think of her, given all his hard accounting work on her behalf? And Tommy, who called her his hero, his baby sister? And Vera and Karen who just thought the world—

"I'm thinking I should have your dad put some chicken on the grill, too."

Dianna turned to her mother. "Chicken? Why? We have all these burgers. And hot dogs and potato salad and deviled eggs and baked beans and cole slaw and macaroni salad and—"

"I invited some people over."

"You did?" Dianna stared at her mother. That pursed-lip expression of hers was never good. It meant she expected a fight. Suspicious, Dianna's hackles rose. "Who exactly, Mom? And please tell me it's the Gundersens."

Her mother raised her chin a proud and injured notch. "Not the Gundersens. They're not talking to us since last week at Tamborello's when Lenny ruined everyone's night and that poor little violinist cut his hand. Probably never play again—"

"Mother. He's fine. I talked to him this past week, and he said his doctor told him there's no reason he can't play again. And my insurance paid his bill, so he's good. I'm sorry about the Gundersens, but who exactly did you invite?"

"Delia Daschowitz and Lenny and Olivia."

Dianna slumped back against the counter, holding her hamburgery hands up in the sterile surgeon position. "Tell me you did not, Mother." Her mother said not a word. "You did, didn't you? What made you do that? We don't even like them. Well, except for Olivia. I'll bet Dad doesn't know."

"Well, no, he doesn't. Not yet. I want you to go out there and tell your father when you take him the burgers and the chicken."

"I don't think so. Edward is supposed to come get them. Let him tell Dad. I don't want to be the one who gets skewered with that sharp barbecue-fork-tong-thingie when Dad finds out."

"Oh, he wouldn't really do that. He's just teasing when he says that."

"Yeah, right. But, jeez, Mom, can't I even have a Lenny-free weekend? It's about to kill me getting him ready to propose to Olivia."

"Well, I just don't understand that. I mean, now that the pathetic thing knows Lenny is going to ask her, why doesn't he just do it?"

"His mother won't let him. She wants a big production for her only baby."

Joy West shook her head, disgust evident in her features. "That Delia just dotes on that grown boy. I'm surprised she didn't bronze it and put it on the mantel the first time Lenny made doody in the potty when he was two years old."

The horror. "Well, thanks, Mom. Lovely image. I'm no longer hungry."

"You'll eat. But don't you give me that 'all this business with Lenny' line and how it's about to kill you.

You're not the one with stitches and walking around on crutches, missy. I specifically asked you to help Lenny, not kill him."

"Yes, I know. Have I thanked you yet for that?"

Her mother puffed up like a pouter pigeon. "Such sarcasm. No wonder you're not married yet. And by the way, just who was that nice-looking young man who dragged you off from the policeman at Tamborello's? You never did say who he was. And I thought he was very rude, too, to just pull you along like he did."

Dianna firmed her lips together into a straight line. "So did I. But he wasn't . . . anybody, Mom. Just a man. A business thing."

"All right, fine, don't tell me. But speaking of your business, I thought that helping Lenny might be a nice way to mend fences between the families."

Dianna's answering snort could only be called unladylike. "Mend fences? As if, Mom. There's a reason why Dad had a six-foot wood fence put in twenty years ago between your property and theirs."

"That may be, but now there's something else."

Such a dramatic tone. Dianna's stomach muscles tensed. "Like what?"

Her mother carefully laid the germ-free plasticware down on the drain board and announced, in her bad-news voice, "You should know there's talk—and more than just talk—from the other side of that fence of, well, suing you, honey. I think they're serious, too. So I invited them over, hoping to smooth things over."

Dianna's brain froze and chilled her blood. She'd stopped listening after the word "suing." "Did you say 'suing' me? Did I hear you right? Lenny's going to *sue* me? And he's serious, not just blowing off steam?"

Her mother nodded. "He's serious."

Dianna lost it. "Sue me for what? I didn't do anything. I told the policeman that, too, at Tamborello's."

"I was there, honey, and I took up for you. You're my flesh and blood. But reckless endangerment, Lenny says.

And pain and suffering. And loss of affection. That's Olivia's part."

"Olivia's involved in this?"

"From what I was told. According to Delia, you should have known Lenny would get hurt because of his size."

"Oh, now it's Delia Daschowitz, too. This is just great." Dianna stormed around in tight little circles, trying not to hear herself in her mind urging Lenny repeatedly to get down on one knee. "I do not believe this. And it sounds as if Lenny has already talked to a lawyer. What am I going to do?"

What had she just been thinking about? Her family's respect for her and the money her folks had loaned her. Visions of all that going bye-bye danced in Dianna's head. *No. No way.* Really ticked now, she knew exactly what she was going to do. She stalked over to the sink, quickly washed her hands with antibacterial soap, and then dried them with a handy kitchen towel. "I'm not going to sit still for this, Mother. Lenny is *not* coming over here to eat the hamburgers I made with my very own hands. No. Instead, what that whiny little shit is going to get is—"

Her mother's gasp cut Dianna's threat short. "Such language from my only daughter. What would your father say?"

"He'd say I got it from him because that's Dad's nickname for Lenny. Personally, I call him 'the stupid nightmare jerk butthead creep next door.' " Dianna threw the towel down and stalked past her mother, heading off through the house. "I've had it with him, Mom. All my life that little—"

"Don't you say that again. And where do you think you're going?"

Under a head of steam now that had her walking stiff-legged and with her hands clenched into fists, Dianna exited the kitchen, entered the living room, and called out over her shoulder: "I'm going next door to do what I should have done years ago. I'm gonna kick Lenny's ass and really give him something to sue me over. And don't you tell Tommy and Edward to come interfere because I can do this myself."

From behind her, Dianna heard her mother say, "Oh, my God in heaven."

Ever the cooperative guest, Chris opened the solid-wood front door of the Daschowitz abode. Surprise! Dianna West, in all her radiant glory, stood there. Chris's happy heart all but leaped out of his chest. Apparently, upon seeing him here, Dianna had been struck speechless. Not a hard call to make because, although her mouth worked, no words issued forth.

Since she wasn't talking, Chris had the advantage of a good second or two to rake his appreciative gaze over her. Same dynamite face, figure, and brunette hair, of course. Same killer eyes. Same effect on his nerve endings. Today she looked very casual, very burbs, in her blue tank top, denim shorts, and slip-on leather sandals. Great legs, too, but then, he already knew that. He was thinking of that short skirt with the slit up the thigh from last Monday.

She still hadn't said anything. But she was lowering her fist, the one she'd presumably used to knock (an ungenerous person would have said pound) on the Daschowitz door. Chris grinned like a pirate. "Hi, Dianna. Surprised to see me here?"

"Surprised, Chris? You think I'm merely surprised? It's beyond that. How far, you ask? This far: If I'd been given a choice between two people I would *least* expect to *ever* see open *this* door, and my choices were between you and whoever the current mayor, or whatever they have there, of Auckland is, I would have said you, Chris."

Chris frowned. "Is there really such a place as Auckland?"

"Yes. It's in New Zealand. And what are you doing here?"

"I came to see how Lenny's doing."

"No you did not."

"Yes I did so."

Dianna's fisted hands were now at her waist. "Why?"

Chris adopted her Jolly Green Giant pose. "Because he was hurt. And he and I bonded after that day in your office."

"As if. Where's your car? It's hard to miss, and I didn't see it." She turned, scanning the street behind her. Chris looked with her. She faced him again. "I still don't see it."

"I parked in their driveway. It's on the other side of the house."

"I know where their driveway is. Here's the thing: You are not to be Lenny's friend. I won't allow it."

Secretly enjoying himself but wisely not letting on that he was, Chris crossed his arms over his chest and frowned. "You won't? Why not?"

"Because I don't want you to."

"I see. Did somebody die and leave you the boss of who can be friends and who can't?"

She looked him right in the eye, never wavering. "Yes. In fact, somebody did, and I say no."

"I didn't get that memo. Sorry."

"How did you find out where Lenny lives?"

"He told me."

"How'd he do that?"

"He called me."

"How'd he do that?"

Chris chuckled. "Well, Detective Columbo, I guess he looked my number up in the phone book first. And then he used a modern invention called 'the telephone' to call me. But I have a question for you: What are *you* doing over here?"

"My parents live next door."

"That's not the answer that goes with the question."

"You knew my folks were Lenny's neighbors. I told you that."

Chris nodded. "I remember that. Obviously you're working toward something here, Dianna, and I think I know what it is. So let me make it easy for you: My being here today has nothing to do with you." He was completely lying, but to admit to the truth meant too many complications. Apparently, Dianna's raised eyebrows and doubting look were to be his only answer. "Hey, come on, why can't the truth be that I like Lenny and I came by to see him?"

"Because nobody likes Lenny except Olivia and his mother."

"Now, that's not a very nice thing to say." Chris feigned being indignant. "Frankly, I'm surprised at you, Dianna."

"Not half as surprised as Lenny's going to be when I kick his ass. So get out of my way." She surged forward, trying to push past him to get inside the house.

"Hey, whoa, wait a minute." Alarmed, Chris grabbed her arms. A tiny but appreciative other part of his brain passed him the message that her arms felt warm, slim, and firm. "You're going to kick Lenny's ass because I'm here? You can't do that."

"I can. But, to use your words, this has nothing to do with you. I didn't even know you were here until you opened the door. So let go of me."

"Okay, I will. But let me tell you something first, all right?" He gave her his most sincere expression . . . she appraised it, him in general, and then shrugged her compliant reply. "Good. See, there's a pretty gruesome leg-wound bandage-change thing going on inside. And I don't think that a young woman like you, who possibly wishes to, one day, bear healthy children, should witness it. Seriously." He slowly shook his head, reaffirming, "Gruesome."

Dianna's grimace could only be called unappreciative. "I applaud your eloquence." She wriggled against his hold on her. "But step aside, please, sir."

"No. I'm sorry . . . uh, ma'am"—Chris frowned; what was with the "sirs" and the "ma'ams"?—"but on second thought I can't do that. Not until you tell me why you're going to kick Lenny's ass. Not that I think that would be hard. He's pretty beat up as it is."

"Not as beat up as he's going to be. Now let me in." She worked her shoulders against his grip, her actions a parody of a woman shimmying her breasts provocatively.

Chris totally noticed this, but still didn't give an inch. In fact, he continued to hold her, as well as his ground, because to see her so upset, well, it upset him, too. "I asked you what he did, Dianna."

"And I said it's none of your business."

"And yet I'm the one here on the inside, and you're not. So apparently I'm making it my business."

Dianna glared at him and poked her bottom lip out pugnaciously. "All right, fine, Mr. Buttinsky. It's not what he did. It's what he's going to do. My mother just told me that he's going to sue my business, Chris, because he hurt himself at Tamborello's." Tears sprang up in her eyes.

Chris's heart and bones melted at the sight of her unshed tears—and then hardened with anger at Lenny. He finally let go of her, turning first to view the interior of the Daschowitz abode, as if he could see Lenny there, before showing her his expression of outrage on her behalf. "Lenny's suing you? That little *shit*."

"Exactly." Her tears had dried up. She was back to plain angry. "I think I see what's going on here, Chris, even if you don't."

"Oh, really? And what would that be?"

"This: You were at my office when Lenny fell there. And then you were at the restaurant when Lenny fell again. And now Lenny wants to be your friend. See? He's trying to get you on his side, so you'll testify on his behalf."

"That's not very flattering for me or Lenny, Dianna. You really think Lenny is using me, and that's all there is to it?"

"I do. Well, maybe not *all* there is to it. I mean, you *are* likable."

"Not a glowing endorsement, but something. I'll take it."

"Stop it. You know what I mean. But this is exactly how Lenny works, so try not to feel bad. He does it to everyone."

"Then, hell, no wonder no one likes him."

"Agreed. But you certainly made it easy for him, didn't you?"

Chris frowned. He didn't like one bit how that sounded. "What are you accusing me of, Dianna?"

"If it weren't so important, Chris, I'd forget it. But since it is, I'll spell it out for you and risk totally embarrassing myself. Okay, here we go." She then proceeded to speak rapidly with no pauses for breath. "Are you and Veronica engaged yet? I mean, did you, on your own, ask her to marry you? I'm not worried about the contract or the money. But, see, I wouldn't know if you were or not since I haven't heard from you all week, not since Monday when you came to me and wanted something quick thrown together and then I went all soapboxy and we—"

"Dianna." Chris held a hand out, palm toward her. "I was there. I know what happened. But the answer is no. We're not engaged. I didn't ask her."

"Oh." She pulled back a bit, seemed to settle down more into her stance. "I didn't really think you had. And I thought that because you *are* here today, a Sunday afternoon, prime couple time, without Veronica—"

"How do you know I'm here without Veronica?" He couldn't resist.

Even as Dianna's eyes widened and her face turned red, her voice dropped to a whisper. "Ohmigod, she's not here, is she?"

"No. She's not here."

Dianna smacked his arm. "That was mean."

"Ouch. I know." Chris rubbed the offended spot.

Dianna eyed him now as if she couldn't decide whether to boil him up in a pot or behead him. "Well, the two of you not being together just makes my point, then."

"Which is?"

"Which is you came here today, without her, maybe hoping that I'd be around . . . that you'd see"—she looked everywhere but at him—"well, you know."

Fervently wanting to hear more along this line, Chris prodded her. "No, I don't know. But I am listening."

She firmed her lips together as if peeved at him. "Fine. You're just going to make me say it, aren't you? Okay, then I will. You came over here today knowing the possibility existed that I'd be around."

Okay, so that had been at the back of his mind. And it was wrong. Yada, yada. Still, he wasn't about to let her know she was right. "I did? You into reading minds now?"

"I don't have to read your mind. It's obvious. And here's how it happened: Lenny called you, pretty much dangling the possibility of me under your nose, and you came over here thinking you might see me. And that made it easy for Lenny."

Chris grinned. "I'd say that's a mighty high, flattering opinion you have of yourself there, Miss West."

"Oh, really? Am I wrong, though, Mr. Adams?"

He bit back a "no" answer. She wasn't wrong. But until this minute when he'd opened the door and seen her standing there, he'd actually convinced himself that the decision he'd made, after nearly a week of thinking, had been the right one and the final one. He'd believed he could come over here, could possibly see her, and be okay with that. But now, here he was face-to-face with her. And he was so wrong. Seeing her, being near her . . . well, his insides were as messed up as if someone had scrambled them. *Damn.*

"Are you not going to answer me?"

She looked so prissy and female. Chris chuckled. "How in the hell did you get to be so bossy? Oh, wait, you're the baby, aren't you? Two older brothers. Spoiled. And you're also relentless, like a dog with a bone."

Her lips twitched, whether in an effort to suppress anger or to keep from biting him, Chris couldn't say. "Thanks for the personality profile. And yet, I'm still waiting."

Chris leaned against the open door's jamb, crossed his arms, and upped the stakes. "Make that a *bulldog* with a bone."

"Whatever. So I'm guessing I'm right since you won't say. I am, aren't I? I'm right."

Chris had almost forgotten what their bone of contention was. "Do you always have to be right?"

"No. Only when I am."

"That makes no sense."

She pointed at him. "Neither does your being here to visit Lenny unless it's for the reasons I've already said."

Feeling a little put out, more with himself for being so transparent than with her for seeing that he was, Chris gestured wide with his hands. "Look, you might be right, okay? I don't know. It makes sense, I guess. But, still, we—Lenny and I—could be innocent, too."

She crossed her arms under her breasts. "Not."

Now it was just getting funny. "Look, Dianna, why don't you let me talk to Lenny first about this suing business before you pulverize him?"

"No. I'm over diplomacy. I need to smack him."

She was so damned riveting right now . . . angry, her color heightened, her gold eyes blazing. Chris wanted, in the worst—best—way, to grab her up and kiss the breath out of her. To hell with the consequences. Right now, he didn't give a damn for the implications or the complications. He just wanted her. It was that elemental and that basic. She made him hungry and in a way that food could not satisfy.

"Why are you looking at me like that?"

Chris blinked, striving for a more subtle expression than the Big Bad Wolf one. "Like what?"

"Like you want to . . . I don't know . . . do something."

*What the hell. Just say it.* "That's because I *do* want

to do something, Dianna. In fact, I've been standing here thinking about exactly that."

She pulled back to a safe distance, but gave herself away when she tipped her tongue out to lick her lips. He made her nervous. "Oh, you have, have you? And . . . how's Veronica, again?"

So she was going to pull out the big guns, huh? Chris shrugged. "She's fine. She's visiting some friends in Connecticut."

"I see." Dianna fluttered a hand up to toy with the tiny bow sewn to her very feminine tank top's scooped neckline. This quite fascinated Chris, as did his realization that if she didn't really like his attentions, all she had to do was turn and walk away. Yet she didn't.

"Why didn't you go?" she asked. "To Connecticut, I mean."

Chris tore his gaze away from that bow situated at her cleavage and met the very affecting molten gold of her eyes. "I wasn't invited."

"So, are you just not good company?"

He shrugged. "Not with the people she went to see."

"Oh. I guess I'm just surprised she'd go without you."

Chris bent a knee, shifting his weight to one foot. "You are? Why is that?"

Dianna shrugged. "It seems to me that two people who are madly in love should have some crazy yearning to be together at every possible moment. I'd think she wouldn't go if you didn't want to. Or you'd compromise and go for her sake. Something like that. At least, that's what I hear, anyway."

"Yeah, me, too. It's what happened for Rick Hampton. He has that kind of relationship with his wife."

Dianna perked up. "Oh, I remember him. Big, florid, cheerful. A really nice guy. We did a cruise-ship thing for him and his girlfriend."

"Right. I was his best man. And he's one happily married guy now."

"Oh, I'm so glad. That's really cool." Dianna surprised

him by suddenly looking shy or maybe unsure if she should ask something. She rubbed at her forehead and looked up at him from under her eyelashes.

Chris's heart thumped leadenly. "Go ahead. Say whatever it is you want."

She considered him another moment before speaking. "All right. I wanted to ask, well, what about *you*? Are you happy, Chris?"

"You don't mean am I happy for Rick, do you?"

Humor flared in her eyes. "No."

Now it was his turn not to know what to say. He shifted his weight, gestured vaguely, nodded. "Yeah. I guess. I mean, what's happy? What Ronnie and I have together works. It's casual. Easy come, easy go. What about you? How does it work for you?"

"How does what work for me?"

"Being in love. Have you ever been in love?"

Her face was steadily turning red. "All right, you know what?" she said. "This is the craziest conversation to be having on the Daschowitzes' front porch. Too bizarre."

It suddenly struck Chris that way, too. "I couldn't agree more. In fact, you're the first woman I've ever asked if she's been in love." He settled his fists at his waist. "I have no idea where this is coming from. Maybe I've been flipping through too many of my mother's women's magazines. Next thing you know I'll be taking those 'how to tell if he . . . well, she . . . cares' surveys. Somebody shoot me now."

"Before that happens, I'm going home." With no more warning than that, Dianna turned away, obviously intent on taking the shallow concrete steps down to the walkway and the lawn.

"Wait." He couldn't let her go, that was all Chris knew. She waited, as he'd asked, an expectant look on her face. "Aren't you forgetting something? Don't you still have to beat up Lenny?"

"No. I'm over that. For the moment, anyway. I mean, I know where he lives." She looked out at the street and then over to the house next door, her parents' house. Chris followed her gaze. "I can't believe my mother minded me and didn't send my brothers over here to get me. Or at least to referee." She spoke as if she were merely saying her thoughts out loud. Then she glanced Chris's way again. "Are you coming over for hamburgers?"

"I have no idea what you're talking about."

"The cookout at my parents' house. My mother invited Lenny and Olivia and Mrs. Daschowitz over."

Chris frowned. "Even knowing they intend to sue you?"

"Yes." The word was a drawn-out sigh. "She thought if we broke bread together, we might be able to smooth this over. Go figure."

Chris nodded. "Good strategy, I guess. But no, I won't be coming over. I wasn't invited."

"Chris, you've got to work on your personality, or you won't get invited anywhere except to Lenny's. But come on over. It might be fun to watch."

"So, are *you* inviting me, Dianna?"

Sunlight backlit her hair, glorifying its red highlights. "Yes. I guess I am."

Though his chest felt tight with emotion—she was so damned affecting—Chris smiled at her, but regret lay behind it. "Thanks. Tempting as it sounds, I don't think I'd better."

She cocked her head questioningly. "Why not? It's no big deal, really. Just my family and enough food to feed a small army."

Chris suspended thought and his desire to go. He'd made his decision, and he needed to stick with it. "Thanks all the same. But I don't think I'm ready to meet the family just yet."

# CHAPTER 7

"I have Mr. Adams on the phone, Miss West. He's requesting a luncheon business meeting with you today."

Dianna's heart did a pirouette of joy. *He called.* Suddenly Tuesday was a bright and sunshiny spring day . . . and not the bright and sunshiny total bummer of a spring day it had been a moment ago. Sitting behind her desk, having just made arrangements for a fifty-six-year-old widower who wanted to ask his newly found, former high school sweetheart to marry him, Dianna managed to stare intelligently—and to cover her joy with a frown—at Mrs. Windhorst. "Mr. Adams? A lunch meeting?"

"Yes. Mr. Christopher Adams. But a lunch *business* meeting."

"Business. Of course. What else?" Dianna looked at her watch, more as a stall tactic than anything else because she already knew what time it was. *Yep. Eleven-thirty.* Her stomach growled its vote, while her head told her that Mr. Christopher Adams should not be inviting women other than his intended fiancée to lunch. But her heart wasn't standing for any rationality on this point. Hey, back off, it warned, adding that Mrs. Windhorst had said he specifically asked for a *business* luncheon, hello—any number of which she usually accepted. Dianna brightened. *Hey, that's true.* Struggling to keep the excitement out of her voice, she soberly asked, "Did he say where?"

"Yes. Faidley's."

Oh, jeez, could he have chosen better to tempt her more? No. World's best crab cakes, in her opinion. Huge. Smooth. Jumbo lumps. Made by the owner herself. Total nirvana. But Dianna just couldn't. She really couldn't. If nothing else, think of the traffic and the crowds. "Is he serious? Downtown at Lexington Market?"

Mrs. Windhorst raised her impressively arched eyebrows in question. "Unless there's another one I don't know about?"

"No. There's only the one. But just hang on. Let me think about my workload a minute."

Sorting through files and papers on her desk, though not actually allotting her workload one jot of think-time, Dianna took a poll of her conscience. Okay, while Chris might couch this invitation as business and really mean it (though she doubted it), she wasn't certain of her own motivations. Meaning, could *she* accept solely on a business basis? Or was she hugely tempted to go for no other reason than she just wanted to see him again and revel in his handsomeness and the giddy way he made her feel, and then go away even more frustrated because she had no right to feel that way about a client and, after all, she was the one who had instituted the "no fraternizing with the clients" rule but still—

*Whoa, girl. Wait a minute.* Dianna focused on the patiently waiting Mrs. Windhorst. "No. Tell him I can't make it. Tell him I'm booked solid with appointments."

"Oh, dear. I'm afraid I can't do that. He already knows differently."

Disbelief had Dianna sitting back abruptly in her chair. "He does? How?"

Mrs. Windhorst's faded blue eyes clouded. "Because I told him."

"You *told* him?" Dianna narrowed her eyes, thinking, *Mr. Adams certainly has a way with my secretary, now doesn't he?* "Why would you tell him my schedule?"

The woman looked anxious to gain Dianna's understanding. "It's a matter of course, Miss West. In the performance of my job, I have to review your schedule, looking for time and availability, when clients, such as Mr. Adams, or prospective clients call for appointments. I did just that and commented to him that you were free from now until two-thirty and when did he wish to come in? That was when he suggested a lunch meeting. And he now remains on hold while I ask you if that's possible."

This speech was not remarkable for Mrs. Windhorst, so Dianna merely glanced at the office phone. Sure enough, a blinking red light on line three. She was tempted to pick it up herself and tell him no. But she didn't for fear the older woman, dressed in a two-piece lightweight pink suit, would reach over and smack her hand away. She was fiercely protective of what she perceived as her duties. "Exactly whose side are you on, Mrs. Windhorst?"

"I wasn't aware we'd chosen sides, Miss West."

She never won with this woman. Never. Dianna sat forward and fussed with rearranging manila files and notepads and pens and paper-clip holders atop her messy desk. "We haven't. Never mind."

"Did I do something wrong, Miss West?"

"No. Of course not."

"But you're obviously upset."

Dianna met the woman's gaze. "Yes. But more at myself than anything."

"I see." The older woman's neck was suddenly stained a deepening red of impending emotion. "However, rest assured," she said in a breaking voice, "that whatever your decision regarding this lunch, I will faithfully execute your wishes. My loyalty lies completely with you. I would never—"

"Okay, stop. Seriously. Whoa." Dianna had a hand to her temple. "No need for all that. We're fine here. Like I said, it's me, not you."

Mrs. Windhorst sniffed and nodded and raised her chin a proud notch. "I apologize for my outburst."

"No problem." Dianna quickly—before Mrs. Windhorst could get going again—began leafing through each file as if she were actually doing what she'd said; that is, making a mental assessment of the time required to deal with each one. But the truth was, she was hoping that Chris would get tired of being on terminal hold and would hang up and relieve her of having to make this decision.

"Excuse me for interrupting, Miss West, but might I pick up the phone line and tell Mr. Adams that we haven't forgotten him?"

"No! God, no!" Well, that had certainly been a shriek. Dianna cleared her throat. "I mean, uh, I won't be but another moment. Just hold on."

But almost immediately, Dianna quit stalling with the excuse of the pile of files on her desk. What was the point? She knew right from wrong. She could recognize the difference between what she wanted to do as opposed to what she needed to do. Decision made easy.

She opened her mouth to speak—and saw two heads (one shoe-polish black and the other Woody Woodpecker red) dart in from opposite sides of the open door to her office, and just as quickly dart back out of sight. Split-second timing. Totally startling. Of course, Mrs. Windhorst hadn't seen this because the door was behind her. But still . . . "Mrs. Windhorst, is something going on around here that I don't know about?"

The older woman's faded-blue eyes widened, yet she still managed to look guilty. "Going on? Why, no. I have no idea what you mean. What could possibly be going on? What made you think that?"

Hmm. Mrs. Windhorst babbling. Bobbing heads out in the foyer. Okay, something was definitely going on. Did it have anything to do with that patiently blinking red light on line three? One way to find out. Dianna purposely raised her voice, all the better to be heard, with her decision. "Tell Mr. Adams that I'm sorry, but I can't make it today. If he wants—"

"Aw, man, come on, Dianna. Go."

"Please? Faidley's sounds wonderful. Such dreamy food."

And suddenly her office was replete with employees. Paula and Melanie had popped in from their vantage points out in the foyer, and Mrs. Windhorst hadn't looked around in surprise. Studying them, Dianna leaned back in her chair and crossed her legs. "What in the world is going on here? Would someone please tell me?"

Staring at her, the three women remained silent. Then, as if at some cue undetected by Dianna, they suddenly huddled and put their heads together. What followed could only be described as a silent movie. Lots of gesturing and face-making but no hearable words. Dianna watched this fascinating display with raised eyebrows. Finally, the three women broke, faced Dianna, but flanked Paula, obviously their elected spokeswoman.

Attired in a multicolored, horizontally striped dress that just screamed Fashions by Dr. Seuss, Paula shrugged her shoulders. "No big deal. We want you to go because he invited us, too."

"What? He invited you, too?"

"Very good. Congratulations. You have just passed your hearing test." Totally deadpan. "Yes, he invited us. As in—" Paula jerked her thumbs first toward Melanie and Mrs. Windhorst and then poked herself in her chest with those bony digits. "Us. The three amigos. The Three Stooges. The Three Musketeers. He's paying, and we want to go. So you have to go."

Did this just reek of manipulation on Chris's part, or what? Suddenly stubborn, Dianna crossed her arms rigidly under her breasts. "No, actually, I *don't* have to go. If you want to go . . . then go." She raised her chin. "But I'm not going."

"Oh, gracious me, I do declare." Melanie abruptly put a pale, slender hand to her red, red lips and stared perfectly Shirley Temple wide-eyed at Dianna. She lowered her hand to her ample bosom, covered by a lacy, peach (Georgia peach) blouse, and said: "I for one certainly did not expect you to say that, Di." She turned her perplexed expression on her coworkers. "Whatever shall we do now?"

Paula eyed Melanie as she always did . . . much as if she wondered if the woman was for real. "Well, Scarlett, you might want to hold off on that case of the vapors you've got working there. Because what we're gonna do is go. Come on, ladies."

At her signal, they turned away, apparently intent on doing just that.

Dianna's jaw dropped open. She jerked forward in her chair and gripped the edge of her desk. "Hey, wait a minute. Didn't you hear what I said?"

That stopped her employees on their collective way to the door. As one, they turned to face their boss. Dianna felt suddenly childish, like the kid who'd just been told to play fair or take her toys and go home. But still, this was a point of pride—hers, to be exact. "I'm sorry, but as I said, I don't think we should go."

"No," Mrs. Windhorst corrected gently. "I believe you said *you* are not going, Miss West. And as Ms. Capland explained, Mr. Adams's invitation was clearly extended to all of us. And I assume—though I'm certain I'd find backing under the law for this—that we remain free to accept since our time is our own on our lunch breaks. And our afternoon schedules are agreeable with an extended lunch period."

Dianna joined Paula and Melanie in staring at the squarely built secretary who ran their professional lives. Paula was the first to recover. "Where in hell do you come up with shit like that, old girlfriend?"

Old girlfriend narrowed her eyes at her arch-nemesis. "I will not respond to your vulgarity, Ms. Capland."

While this exchange was happening, Dianna glared at the interminably blinking red light on line three that represented Chris Adams. So he'd gone behind her back and invited her employees, as well as herself, to lunch—all to insure that she'd have to say yes, now hadn't he? Obviously, he'd figured she'd say no. Well, his little tactic wasn't going to work. And yet, she wondered what he was up to and why he wanted this meeting.

Too bad she'd never know because she wasn't going. That decided, Dianna captured her employees' attention by announcing: "All right. Mrs. Windhorst is right. Your lunch break is your own time." Dianna raised her chin, showing how magnanimous she could be, even in the face of being supremely injured. You couldn't have Joy West as a mother and not learn a thing or two about drama. "However, I don't think this is a good idea at all, and for many reasons. But if you feel you absolutely must go, then I won't stop you."

Silence met this bravura performance. But it didn't last.

"Okay. Cool. Come on, girls." And the girls went, following on Paula's heels. That redheaded little stinker threw a careless wave her boss's way. " 'Bye, Di, see you after lunch. We'll probably be late getting back. And catch the phones, will you? We're taking the loquacious Mrs. Windhorst with us."

Dianna sat there, stunned, immobile, much as if her butt had been Super Glued to her chair. *They're going to go without me. But what about my great speech?* Apparently, when faced with the stiff competition of being treated at Faidley's, her eloquence held no sway. Dianna narrowed her eyes. *They won't really go.* And yet, the women filed out of the office and into the foyer. Dianna, who could no longer see them, given the positioning of her desk in her office, jammed her lips together into a puckered line and concentrated on the conversation and actions going on out of her sight.

"Oh, my goodness, I am so sorry, but I've forgotten my reticule." Archaic term for pocketbook or purse. How many times had Melanie told them?

"Well, go get it. Christ, Melanie, do you even know what century this is?" One downbeat of time passed before Paula added, "Jeez, I work with a bunch of freakin' lunatics." Then she called out: "Except for you, boss lady. Love *you*."

Dianna absolutely refused to respond in any way. She remained injured and disbelieving and in her office by herself. *They won't go. They're just teasing.*

"Hey," Paula called out again, this time to a more general audience who had apparently scattered, "in case anybody's wondering, I'm driving, and for the same reason I said before: you two are lunatics. Come on, Mrs. Windhorst, get a move on there, lady. Tell Mr. Gorgeous Adams that we three are heading out. Oh, and make sure you bring that whoopee cushion you sit on all the time. That's attractive."

"It is not a . . . a *whoopee* cushion, Ms. Capland. It is an orthopedic donut prescribed for me by my doctor because of an old fracture to my coccyx."

"Right. Whoopee cushion. But try not to say 'coccyx' in public, all right? It just sounds like something men need to keep covered with a pair of thick pants, if you know what I mean."

*They're bluffing. They won't leave me here.* Dianna remained convinced of this, even when the red light on line three went solid—indicating Mrs. Windhorst had picked it up—and then a moment later blinked out. A few seconds after that, the women evidently were congregated out in the tiled foyer. Dianne heard their milling footsteps, much like a restive herd of mares. Then the front door opened . . . three beats on the clock tick-tocked by . . . the door closed . . . and all was silent.

*They won't go without me.* Dianna pursed her lips. She drummed her fingers on her desktop. She looked around her office, waiting. *They'll come back.* More silence. They didn't come back. The pressure to peek out the picture window behind her, to see if they drove off, approached unbearable. But neither love nor money could have made her turn around and risk being seen by them in return. Dianna neatly folded her hands together in her lap . . .

and sat quietly. She sniffed. Raised her chin. Looked around—

And then totally lost it. "Hey, wait a minute! Wait for me!"

She ripped open the side drawer in her desk, grabbed up her purse and the office keys, jumped up, skirted her desk, and flew out of her office, into the foyer. There, she remembered she had to turn the office phones over to the answering service. Shrieking, she ran back into her office, picked up the phone, went through all the mumbo jumbo of doing that, hung up, and then ran again for the foyer. She flipped the OPEN sign over to CLOSED, jerked the door open, stepped outside into the wonderful spring air—

And stopped dead. There were her employees in Paula's big, red SUV, parked at the front curb, waiting for her. Totally embarrassed that they could read her so well—and yet very pleased that they hadn't abandoned her—Dianna wanted to die. Or maybe kill them. They might fuss at each other all day long, but they always stuck together. Sure, mostly to goad her. But at least they cared. Just look at them—how could she not love them? There was Melanie, laughing and hanging out the open window in the front passenger's seat, waving for Dianna to come on. On the other side of Melanie, in the driver's seat, Paula beeped the car horn repeatedly and waved. Mrs. Windhorst, of course, sat primly in the back seat, like a hostage, staring straight ahead.

Trying her best not to look like the joke was on her, and failing miserably as her grin kept getting away from her, Dianna nodded her "okay, so you got me" nod and chuckled. All in her own good time now, she closed the front door, locked it, and dropped the keys into her purse. Then, she turned around and ever so slowly strolled across the verandah . . . took the wide steps one at a careful time . . . and casually walked down the sidewalk—all of this to the accompaniment of Melanie's and Paula's feminine catcalls and wolfette whistling. Mrs. Windhorst continued to look pained and abducted.

\*     \*     \*

"I'm glad you could make it today."

Swallowing a big, unladylike bite of her crab cake, Dianna eyed her host, who stood to her left at the long communal bar at Faidley's. "Oh, as if." She grinned to show she knew she'd been had but could still be a good sport. "I wasn't given much choice in the matter."

"How so?" Like her, Chris was practically yelling, even though he was less than a foot away from her. Simply put, they were surrounded by a tide of jabbering humanity intent on the cacophonous conduct of market business. Furthermore, if one were to stray away from the bar, he or she would be swept away, never to be seen again in the tide of humanity that ebbed and flowed up and down the market's many enticing aisles.

"How so, you ask? Let's just say I was outnumbered. Four to one."

"Four?"

She laughed. "Stop trying to look so innocent. Yeah, four. My employees and you."

Despite the amused gleam in his eye, Chris said, "I admit to nothing."

"Why am I not surprised? So, anyway, Chris, why'd you call us all here today? You said it was business?"

"And it is."

"But not business we could conduct at the office, I take it?"

He shrugged. "Sure we could. But this is more fun."

"Agreed. So, Mr. Adams, what's your business?"

"Computers. And how come you don't have any in your office."

"Awk, the big no-no word." Dianna flapped her hands at Chris, trying to warn him off.

But the man didn't get it. "Computers—a no-no word? Why is that a—"

"Shhh." Acutely aware of her employees, who were to her right and ranged out along the bar's length, Dianna leaned in toward Chris. "Don't say that word out loud.

Are you just trying to totally undermine my office harmony?"

"Dianna, I have no idea what you're talking about. Why are compu—"

"Shhh." Giving up, she tugged him down to her level so she could whisper in his ear. Mistake. *Could the man smell better? No. Could he be more ruggedly handsome with that classic jaw and straight nose, and those deep-chocolate eyes? No. God, he just looks like he can bring home the bacon and fry it up in a pan*—Stop. Focus, Dianna. Deep breath, now whisper. "There are no computers because Mrs. Windhorst won't allow them. Melanie and Paula want them, and it's a big battle every time the subject comes up."

Chris pulled back, straightened up, stared at her, and then leaned in again toward her. "I'm not surprised. But are you serious? Mrs. Windhorst gets to not allow things?"

"Computers, she does. It's practically in her employment contract. See, I told her I had no interest in installing computers, which I didn't at the time, since we're mostly a phone business. You know, calling restaurants, florists, and the like. So I pretty much promised her that as long as she worked for me, I wouldn't force them on her."

"Then don't. Can't everyone else at your office have one?"

Dianna shook her head. "No. They would impact Mrs. Windhorst's job sooner or later. Appointments. Billing. Ordering supplies. All those things could be computerized, only she wouldn't know how to access the info."

"This is a tough one. Why doesn't she just learn?"

"I think she tried." Dianna shrugged. "Couldn't get the hang of it. And, look, Chris, you have to remember what it's like for someone who wasn't raised with computers at every desk. To them this is *Star Wars* stuff."

"Yeah, I guess I'm pushing too hard." He looked so disappointed. "So, she's afraid of the technology. I know a lot of people, well, *her age* are."

"That's pretty much it, really." Dianna found it was hard to concentrate on computers and technology while standing oh-so-close to the nicest, funniest, best-looking man she'd ever seen, one who set her nerve endings zinging, one she really, really liked and wanted to be around every day. *Damn. Not good.* Still, ever the female, Dianna figured that she had to be totally attractive right now, downing as she was—in a very messy fashion—a Faidley's masterpiece. She watched as Chris's gaze flitted from her face to her food and back to her face. That did it. She was a mess. She grabbed up a paper napkin and swiped it across her mouth.

"Do you mind my asking you all this, Dianna? I know your business's inner workings are really none of my business."

Since he'd just earned points for not commenting on the state of her face or the bar space in front of her, Dianna rushed to assure him. "No, it's okay. I don't mind. We're here to talk business, right? In fact, the lack o' computers is right now a sticking point. Our workload has grown to need a better information-storing system. And I now have the money to buy them. So ask me how many times a week my big brother accountant Edward tells me I need to get them." She waved a hand at Chris. "Rhetorical question. No need to ask."

"I gathered."

"Anyway, I'd override my promise to her, but here's the weird thing. If she quit, I'd be dead in the water. She's totally efficient. Really knows her stuff and the functions of the business world. She's also a real watchdog against wasteful practices, as she calls them. Edward adores her for that. And she has this filing system that only she understands. *And* she also orders the office supplies. You lose a pen, you answer to her. Nobody wants to do that."

"So she's made herself indispensable. And you're afraid of her."

"Exactly." Without thinking, Dianna sucked at all ten of her crab-cake-coated fingers and offered up her gaze to the equally delicious man at her side. "There's more if you want to hear it."

He shrugged those football shoulders of his, right now covered by a stark white T-shirt that revealed every rippling muscle underneath. Likewise his faded jeans . . . every muscle outlined. His expression droll, Chris said, "I wouldn't be able to sleep tonight if you didn't tell me."

"I'll take that as a yes." Dianna checked her watch. "And I have time, too. Good. Here's the thing: Have you ever had to hire an executive secretary?"

"Can't say that I have."

"Well, the competition is fierce."

Chris peered around Dianna, curiously eyeing the older woman. "So there was fierce competition for Mrs. Windhorst?"

Dianna shook her head and leaned in again toward the man. Head rush—the commingled scents of his body's heat, his aftershave, and the clean smell of his laundered T-shirt. "Hey, look at me. I don't want her to know we're talking about her." When she had Chris's attention, she continued. "And 'no' is the answer to that. There wasn't *any* competition for her, which is why I felt sorry for her and hired her. But she also felt sorry for me."

Chris appeared to be lost here. "You'll have to explain that."

"Okay. She was the only person to answer my ad in the paper. No surprise there because I couldn't afford top salary a year ago for someone with her qualifications. Still can't, but we're growing. So, anyway, to me, she was a godsend, and I was thrilled to get her."

"Ah. I think I'm seeing the picture now. She'd experienced a comedown. Not getting the big jobs and the big money. An age thing?"

Dianna weighed this, waggling her head and making a scrunched-up face that showed her ambivalence. "Yes and no. See, when the big company she worked for—this was years ago—went all computer, she was forced out because she couldn't catch on or keep up or something. So now she blames computers."

"That happens a lot." Chris grimaced and scratched at his jaw. "I almost feel responsible."

"You? Why? Oh, wait, I get it. You're the dot-com guy. So, anyway, she's a widow, no kids to fall back on, and no computer skills. She's always had to support herself. Before my job offer came along, she'd been forced to take drudge jobs. So she's pretty grateful to me. I think. But I know I'm grateful to her. End of story. And all that means the bottom line here is—"

"No computers. Shame. I still say that Internet thing, a Web presence, is your next step. I could do it all, Dianna. Set it up, do the heavy lifting, and even oversee it for you. You wouldn't have to do anything but approve the design."

"Chris, I would personally love that." And she meant it, too. Him every day there at her office? That didn't suck. But yes it did, too. Him every day there at the office? A bad thing. She'd just get more attached. And, too, there was that promise to Mrs. Windhorst not to put her out to pasture because of her fear of technology. "But you see my difficulties. Still, and again, thanks for the lunch. For all of us. That was nice."

"Yeah, I am a nice guy, aren't I?"

Dianna chuckled at his droll expression. "Who are you trying to convince?"

"Anyone who will listen." That killer sexy grin of his was unrepentant. "Still, I think we'd work great together, you and I."

Dianna arched her eyebrows—a fitting companion to her arch question. "Are we still talking business?"

He stared into her eyes, quirked up a corner of his mouth and stared at her. "Could be."

*Oh, God.* Dianna's hormones heard that. She inhaled deeply and held it a moment in an effort to restore calm to her feminine nether regions. "So, anyway, Chris, what's this really all about? You don't suddenly need the work, do you? Or are you just bored being a man of infinite means?"

"No to both. I'd do this for you for the sheer joy of it. And the love."

Dianna swallowed. He absolutely had to quit saying such provocative things. Light and chirpy was called for here. "Sorry. Get your own reasons. Those are mine. I work for the joy and the love."

"Exactly. That's what makes your business unique. You literally do it for love. Or because of other peoples' love for each other. That's fascinating to me, and I'd work for you for free. Hard to say no to a deal like that."

"Boy, no kidding." But she just couldn't give in. As attracted as she was to him on so many levels—the man was every bit as charming and witty and nice as he was good-looking and unavailable—she'd have her arm chewed off by the end of a week. And what was it about him, anyway? She wasn't inexperienced. She'd had her share of boyfriends and dates, et cetera, just nothing that had ever led to the altar. She hadn't worried unduly about that, really, because she was only twenty-six and had always told herself that surely the right man for her was just out there waiting to be found. And look—ta-da! Here he was. And he belonged to someone else. There was no hope, and life was cruel.

Dianna hid all this angst with a shake of her head no and used her fingers to pluck up the crab crumbs of her rotund eight-ounce cake. "I have to say no, Chris. No, no, no."

He looked disappointed. "You mean Mrs. Windhorst?"

*No, I mean you, big boy.* Afraid she'd blurt that out loud, Dianna popped the crabmeat into her mouth and chewed. She swallowed and nodded. "Her, for one thing. If I even suggested computers, she'd probably find some way to sue me. And one lawsuit at a time is enough for me. Remember Lenny?"

"Like I do the chicken pox I had as a kid. But Lenny's not going to sue you. I took care of that. Now, how about this: What if I offered to work one-on-one with Mrs. Windhorst until she got up to speed? Day in and day out. Just be there for her and explain things until she felt secure. I'll bet she didn't get that kind of help before. Besides, computers are a lot simpler now than they were years ago. She looks like a smart lady. I think with a little TLC and coaching, it wouldn't take her long to catch on—"

"Wait just a doggone minute." Dianna flapped a hand at Chris. "Go back to that Lenny thing. The part where you said he's not going to sue me, and you took care of it."

He chuckled. "Oh, you heard that? All right. After you left Sunday, I had a little talk with him and told him *I'd* be the one who'd kick his ass if he sued you. So, bottom line, he's over that. Unfortunately, he still wants to be your client."

She was so completely impressed with this man. Why couldn't he be hers? "My God, you've been out there, a knight in shining armor, slaying my dragons, haven't you?"

He shrugged off her glorifying him. "Not slaying, exactly. I pretty much just threatened to bitch-slap the dragon into behaving."

"The result's the same." She could not be more thrilled with this man, and that made her tongue loose. "I could just kiss you, Chris Adams, do you know that?"

He enthusiastically pushed away from the counter and spread his arms wide. "Hey, damsel no longer in distress because of my heroic actions, go ahead. I won't stop you."

Dammit, he just kept making her laugh and making her like him even more. "Quit it! And get back over here before you knock into someone or get dragged off." *By me to a dark cave somewhere.*

He was so adorable and attractive right now that in about one more second she would wrap herself, starfish-style, around his body and hold on forever. Probably not the smart thing to do right in the middle of the seafood section of Lexington Market. The people here were pretty much no-nonsense.

When Chris came back to the counter and rested his elbows on it, Dianna poked at his arm. "You didn't eat all of your crab cake. How can you let it just sit there? I could eat ten of these in a row."

"I thought you just had."

"Ha. I'd be dead now. But it'd be worth it." She popped another bite of the crabmeat into her mouth and closed her eyes, the better to savor the delicacy as she chewed. "God, that is divine."

"From where I'm standing, too."

His words, the sound of his voice, again sent the message straight to her erogenous zones, all of them. Dianna opened her eyes. Seeing the look on Chris's face, she pronounced herself glad that Paula, Melanie, and Mrs. Windhorst were not paying attention to anything or anyone other than their lunch. Because now it was time for Dianna to say some serious, not-business things to Chris. For example: "I shouldn't have said that about kissing you, Chris. And you can't keep saying things like what you just did to me. Very dangerous flirting territory. Not good."

Chris held her gaze a moment and then looked away from her, crossing his forearms atop the bar and gazing across the way. "I know. I keep telling myself that, too. But I can't seem to stop." He suddenly turned his powerfully affecting gaze her way. "Not where you're concerned, that is. I don't have this problem with other women. And, again, that's probably more than I should admit out loud to you, isn't it?"

"Yes. Exactly. Things like that. You can't do that. I can't do that." But she knew she could. Easily. Just swipe everything off this long bar, strip the man naked, throw him atop it, climb on, and have at him. *No!* With great difficulty, Dianna blinked that lusty image aside. There was too much else here at stake—her business, her family, the money, and his relationship with another woman—to give in wantonly to hormones. She needed to behave in a mature fashion. Do the right thing. Dianna winced at that. God, she hated being an adult. Self-sacrifice and honor and duty and other stupid and important things like that were turning out to be a lot harder to live up to than they sounded.

In the face of Chris's continuing silence and seeming introspection, Dianna added, "Okay, truth?"

He turned those troubled dark chocolate–brown eyes her way. "Sure. Why not?"

Dianna forced herself to ignore what her heart was telling her. Remember . . . noble. Mature. Adult. All of which sucked. *Come on, just one night, please?* No. She saw herself living with that aftermath . . . all that moping and whining and eating too much. Not a pretty picture. "What I mean, Chris, is yes there's something undeniable between us. We might as well acknowledge it. But we both know it's wrong, and we can't let it get the better of us."

Whew, there, she'd got it out. Still, the man remained silent. *Dammit,* Dianna fussed, *he could jump in and say he's broken it off with Veronica because he can't live without me.* But he didn't. And that told its own story, didn't it? Heartache. Dianna's chuckle was of the sad-clown variety. "Okay, this would be a good time for you to jump in here and tell me it won't happen again and you're totally in love with your prosecuting attorney, and how is she, anyway?"

"She's fine." A muscle twitched in his jaw.

Watching it, fascinated by it despite herself, Dianna commented, "That's all you ever say about Veronica."

"I didn't know you wanted to know more."

"I don't. Not really. But I think it's best if we keep talking about her." Dianna paused, trying to think of something nice to say about the woman, couldn't, and came up with: "So I guess she made it back from seeing her friends?"

"Yep."

"And how are you guys doing?"

"Fine."

"Okay, one-word answers. This is where I came in, when you said 'fine.' I've seen this movie from here. If you'll excuse me, I'm going to go out to the lobby and get some popcorn. You want anything?"

"Funny girl," he accused. "No, I don't want anything."

"You sure? A candy bar? Coke?"

He shook his head. "Be serious, will you?"

Dianna propped an elbow on the bar, turning fully to face Chris. "I've been nothing but serious. You're the one not saying anything."

A clear challenge. He opened his mouth to speak, but then closed it. Opened it again, closed it, lowered his gaze, just stood there mute. Dianna's breathing became stunted. Obviously the man was working up the nerve to say something momentous. Just in case it proved to be a tidal wave that could swamp her heart, Dianna ordered her defense mechanisms to start piling up emotional sandbags between her and this man who stood so close to her.

"Here's the thing." He spoke so suddenly that Dianna jumped. Chris put a hand out to her, but didn't actually touch her. "Sorry. Didn't mean to startle you. I just need to do this, to say it."

Dianna swallowed. "Go ahead."

He nodded. "I have an idea, one I want to run by you. It's pretty rough, but you're the expert and I'm sure you can build on it."

"I'm the expert?" That could only mean one thing—the proposal business. That hurt. A lot more than it should. She barely knew the man. Yet she felt as if she'd yearned for him all her life. But that was just too bad, huh? "All right. I'm listening." Dianna stiffened her knees and forced a mask of polite waiting to her face. "What's your idea?"

Leaning heavily into Faidley's communal bar, no longer looking at Dianna, Chris ran his thumb up and down the green-glass side of his empty beer bottle as if he'd been put on this earth to perform that specific task. "Like I said, I have this rough idea for what I want you to set up for me"—he turned his head until he was looking into Dianna's eyes—"when I ask Veronica to marry me."

She'd been expecting it, but still his words hit Dianna with the force of a slap that congealed the blood in her veins. Stupid, embarrassing tears sprang to her eyes. Blinking, feeling too hot, and clearing her suddenly clogged throat, she quickly picked up her paper napkin to wipe at her mouth and nose. She could only hope she didn't come off looking as emotional as she felt. "Oh, really? Well, good. That's great. Wonderful, in fact. I can't wait to hear it."

Unable to look away from him—cruel, cruel world— she laughed, sort of a sick little "ha-ha" that warned she was about to lose it. Her hand fisted tightly around the paper napkin she still held, fisted hard enough to dig her nails into her palm. With a quick, jerky gesture, she used her other hand to swipe her hair back behind her ears.

Chris put his hand on her arm. "Dianna, are you all right? I didn't mean to upset you."

She wrenched away from his hand on her arm. He did *not* get to touch her, did *not* get to show concern or try to comfort her. *"What makes you think you upset me?"*

Well, how about the fact that she'd yelled that and passing strangers had halted in their tracks, the better to stare fixedly at her? And even though her employees were behind her and she couldn't see them, Dianna felt the weight of their combined stares on her back. She swallowed and then spoke more calmly, quietly. "Why should the fact that you want to ask your girlfriend to marry you upset me, Chris? It doesn't, you know. I mean, I knew you were going to ask her. That's why you came to me— for help in doing just that. It's what I do, remember? I'm the expert at getting other people together."

She couldn't be here anymore. She couldn't be standing this close to him and hearing him say he wanted to ask this other woman to marry him. To Dianna, it felt as if he'd just admitted to cheating on her personally. And that was just silly. Pretty darned silly. She gathered up her purse and her employees and said, "Come on, everyone. Time to get back to work. Sorry, Chris, we have to go. But thank you for the lovely lunch."

"Dianna, wait. You don't even know what my idea is yet."

She managed a shaky but determined smile. "So fax it to me. I'll call you when I have something put together. Bye."

# CHAPTER 8

It was a scene at once familiar and comfortable, and yet one that left Chris feeling, well, somehow removed from it. He had to think why that would be, this sense of disconnection. After all, here he was at his own penthouse with his mother and Veronica. And the three of them were engaged in their normal routine: He and Ronnie took his mother out to supper once a week—Wednesday night this week, the day after Faidley's—and then the three of them came back here for coffee and dessert and catching up. That was where they were now, or were supposed to be. Coffee and dessert were done, but Veronica had closed herself off in his office to do some last-minute work. And his mother now occupied herself with worrying the fish in Chris's saltwater tank. All of this left him alone on the sofa with only his thoughts for company.

Pretty soon, Chris knew, he would take his mother home, while Ronnie cleaned up the kitchen. And then she would stay the night. Like he'd said, routine. Again, in his mind, he saw himself and Ronnie earlier when she'd come over before they'd gone for his mother. She'd brought her overnight bag along and a couple changes of clothes on hangers, which now hung in his bedroom closet. She'd used her key, opened the door, and called out, "Knock, knock," as she always did. And as he always did, he'd stepped out of his home office, gone to greet her, and they'd kissed. Pecked was more like it.

And that had been okay. A twinge of guilt suddenly tugged at Chris. Wasn't he supposed to be feeling this grand passion for Ronnie now that he'd made up his mind that she was the one? Where were the heat and the yearning and that whole primal passion thing you read so much about? Not going on here. Maybe it was because he'd known Ronnie for so long and was comfortable with her. Yeah, that had to be it.

Anyway, she'd come in earlier and had proceeded to bend his ear telling him all about her trying day. This defendant and that plaintiff and this rotten judge and that idiotic defense attorney and how busy she was and how she had to leave early tomorrow for court, so he wasn't to expect much from her tonight, please. Kiss, kiss. Then off she'd gone to change out of her power suit and into her slacks and a silk blouse. Chris shook his head, chuckling at his own expense. Apparently Ronnie wasn't feeling any grand passion for him, either.

But then again, she wasn't yet aware of his intention to ask her to marry him. Chris wondered if she would behave any differently once he'd asked her and she'd accepted. *Wait a minute. She will accept, right?* He frowned, thought about that, and finally convinced himself that of course she would. Why wouldn't she? Didn't they already behave like people who'd been married for years? Yeah, they did. So, okay, then this was the way it would be after they got married. Chris checked in with his emotions to see how he felt about that. Not bad. He'd lived with their easy way of dealing with each other for about four years now, so it was doable. Doable? Sounded like a business deal. Or maybe like he was settling.

Not liking that notion one bit, Chris slouched down on his sofa's comfortable cushions as he stared out the large windows at Baltimore's nighttime skyline. But that vague sense of dissatisfaction refused to go away, telling him his problem was he wasn't where he really wanted to be. And, worse, he wasn't with the one person he really wanted to be with—the person who, tears in her eyes, had all but fled from him yesterday at Faidley's.

Uncomfortable now in the extreme, Chris shifted his position on the sofa. *Man, I cannot keep this up. Maybe I'm lying to myself—*

"Honey, my grand-fish look a bit peaked. Did you call those people to come see about them?"

His feet up on the ottoman and a mug of coffee next to him on the end table, Chris leaned his head back on the sofa cushions and stretched his neck until he could see his mother. Dressed in a dark green polyester-looking pantsuit and lots of big jewelry, she stood over by the wet bar and faced the large saltwater tank. Her back to him, she had her hands at her slim waist. "The fish are fine, Mother. The guy came today and checked everything out. He said they're okay."

She made a tsking noise that served as notice that she, Mrs. Penelope Winthrop Adams Eve, widow of the late Harold Eve and the even later John Adams—not of the presidential Adamses, but you couldn't, and didn't dare, tell her otherwise—was not satisfied. "Hmph. What does he know?"

"Everything. It's his business."

"They said that in the seventies, too, about pet rocks, and that they were a business. They even said that young man who discovered them was an expert. But do you see those around anymore?"

Chris grinned. "Only every time I look at the ground. Those pesky rocks are everywhere, smiling up at me. Scary."

"Fine, you want to be smart. But these fish look peaked to me."

"You said the same thing about Veronica."

"Well, she does. She works too hard. Even now she's been at it in your office for the whole hour we've been here. She said she's working on a brief. Well, it doesn't seem very brief to me. Son, you need to marry her so she can quit work and have children. I need real grandbabies,

Chris, so I don't have to call these scaly things over here my grand-fish." She tapped at the aquarium glass with a fingernail and cooed to the startled fish.

"Careful. Don't let them hear you talking like that. They think you care." Chris tried to picture Veronica pregnant—and happy about it. He bit back a chuckle. No, he didn't think she'd be too amused. In fact, she'd probably try to figure out a way to have him, much like a male seahorse, carry the baby for those nine months.

"Don't be silly, Christopher." His mother was talking about his comment regarding the fish, of course. But it was a pretty good comment on his pregnancy thought, too. "They're fish," his mother reminded him. "They don't have feelings."

"So far as we know. But another thing, Mom, should Ronnie and I marry"—Chris suddenly realized that though this was the perfect opportunity to tell his mother of his proposal plans, he didn't want to, not yet—"and I'm not saying we will, but if we did—"

"Point taken, son. Go on."

Chris grinned. His mother was used to his procrastinating on this subject. "Anyway, I don't think she would want to quit. She went to school for a lot of years and worked hard to get where she is. She enjoys her career, and I wouldn't ask her to give it up." That sounded really noble, and he meant what he'd said. He respected Veronica tremendously. Only the whole truth was a little more complicated than that. Meaning, he couldn't picture the two of them, himself and Ronnie, being around each other all day, every day, without personalities and tempers wearing pretty darned thin in a hurry.

"All right, so she'll continue to work after the two of you—and I'm also speaking hypothetically—marry. Say you have children. Who will be staying home with my grandbabies?" Evidently this was pretty important to her because by the time she had her question out, his mother had rounded the end of the sofa and was now standing in front of Chris and blocking his view of Baltimore.

Chuckling, he met her gaze. "Okay, Mom, you're getting ahead of yourself. But to answer your question, I guess I'd be the one home with the kiddies."

Penelope Eve cupped her cheek with a hand. "Good Lord, I just knew it. My grandchildren will be as peaked as those poor fish. Or worse."

"Oh, come on, Mom, I hardly think I—"

"Honey, I love you dearly, but you can't keep a houseplant alive on your own. What are you going to do with real children?"

More amused than offended, Chris played along. "I don't know. How hard can it be, though? Feed and water them. Hose them down when they're dirty. Sit them near a window to get some sunlight on their little—"

"Never mind." His mother waved a dismissive hand at him. "I see what I have to do. Move in with you and help. No, wait. I don't want to give up my house and the Garden Club. And I have to write for the newsletter. Oh, dear, and there's the Annual Newcomers' Party." She sighed, defeated by her own full life. "I suppose you and Veronica will have to move in with me. It'll be easier. Save you coming all the way across town to get me every day and then taking me home at night."

She could drive just fine. And had a nice car to prove it, one he'd bought her, along with the matching house in historic Original Northwood, which was only about fifteen minutes away. Chris chuckled at his mother. "You've got it all worked out, haven't you? Here I am already married, a father, *and* Mr. Mom."

"Well, it's a better life than the one you have here by yourself like this."

"I like being here by myself." That wasn't totally true. He'd loved having Dianna West here. She fit nicely with the décor. And he meant that in the best possible way, a high compliment—like saying she belonged here. Fun, smart, easy to be around, yet sexy and exciting, no doubt about that. *A grand passion.* The phrase just popped into his mind, tensing him against the surprise of it.

His mother carried on unaware. "Well, you won't think being alone is so grand when you're a lonely, bitter, old man of eighty, if you don't get married and have a family."

"Damn. Sounds bleak."

"It could be. Now, move your feet over and let me sit on this ottoman. I want to ask you something that's got me worried."

Though instantly apprehensive, Chris complied, moving his feet over. He watched his mother delicately perch next to them. He had no idea what to expect. "You okay, Mom? What is it?"

She inhaled, exhaled, and then blurted, "You didn't order the crab cakes tonight, Chris. You always order the crab cakes."

Talk about coming right out of left field. Chris barely stopped himself from doing a double-take, but he did give in to a chuckle of affectionate disbelief. "You kill me, Mom. You're worried about me and crab cakes? Well, rest assured that I'm fine. I didn't order them this time because I had them yesterday for lunch at Faidley's."

His mother raised an eyebrow. "You went all the way down there in the middle of the day?"

"Faidley's isn't far from where I live. It's far from where *you* live."

She pursed her lips in that don't-you-take-that-tone-with-me-young-man way she had. "Maybe so. But what were you doing at Lexington Market? I thought you had to be here all the time for that global consulting thing you do on your computer."

Still amused, Chris raised his eyebrows. " 'All the time'? I love how you speak in absolutes. But I'm not chained to the computer, and yesterday was a business lunch."

"That sounds nice. Business with who?"

Chris stared at his mother. The woman honed in like a laser when she began questioning someone. Well, he'd certainly set himself up nicely, but no way was he men-tioning Dianna. *Got to lie. Note to self: Call Rick tomorrow and tell him he had lunch yesterday with me at Faidley's.* "Business with Rick Hampton."

A fond smile claimed his mother's face. "Oh, I like him. He's the one who just got married, isn't he?"

And they were back to that. "Yes."

"Now, what was it that was different about his wedding?" His mother tapped her cheek with a finger, as if this helped her think. Chris sat tensely by, unwilling to jog her memory. Suddenly his mother pointed at him. "No, wait, it wasn't the wedding. It was the way he proposed or something, wasn't it?"

*Keep your expression neutral. Give her no help.* "Yes."

"Well? What did he do? I forgot what it was."

Chris's frustrated exhalation of breath spoke volumes about how irritated he was with himself for not ordering the damned crab cakes tonight. All this aggravation over an entrée. "He used a proposal service, Mother."

"That's it," she cried. "What's it called, again?"

*No. Not giving that name up.* Wondering what lay behind her questioning, Chris cocked his head in curiosity. "Why is this important to you?"

"Honey, isn't it obvious? I think you ought to go there and get some help. You've been with Veronica for years now—and yet . . . nothing."

"I wouldn't say it was nothing." Chris heard the defensive tone in his voice. "We're committed. We're good together. And neither would I say we're going nowhere."

"Well, that's good to hear. At least you have a thought to your future. Mind, if you don't make something happen soon with Veronica, you're going to lose that girl. You'll look up one day, and she'll be gone."

Chris could only shake his head in wonder. "Why do you believe all of a sudden that I'm just drifting along?"

"It's not all of a sudden. I spend a lot of time thinking about you, you know. You are my son. My only child."

Chris nodded his head. "Acknowledged. Come on, Mom. What gives?"

His mother looked down at her lap, picked at her slacks a bit, and then settled her gaze on Chris. "I don't want to bring up painful memories, honey, but is it because of, well, Mary marrying Joe?"

Hurt and anger warred inside Chris, tightening his jaw. "Is *what* because of Mary and Joe?"

"Well, to use your words, your just drifting along like you are."

Chris exhaled sharply. "I said I'm *not* drifting. And Mary and Joe are not the cause of anything I do or don't do."

Chris's mother put a hand on his leg. "Son, I know that was a hard thing to get over, your fiancée marrying your best friend like that."

Hard? It'd been hell. Pure hell. Chris shifted about on the sofa, inadvertently dislodging his mother's hand from his leg. "That was nearly eight years ago. And I'm over it. I have been for a long time. Besides, Mary and Joe are happy, still together, and have three kids. So it worked out for the best."

"For them, maybe."

"For me, too, Mother. Let it go, okay?"

His mother's expression became the same one she wore when she'd sat bedside with him whenever he'd ever been sick as a kid. Total maternal concern. "I wish I could, son, and I want to respect your wishes, but I'm your mother so I get to take liberties. And I say that whole experience—your best girl and your best friend falling for each other and marrying—is holding you back. I think what they put you through has left you afraid to make that final leap in the love and marriage department. Now, you may call yourself happy with the way things are now, but you don't look happy to me. And you don't act happy."

"Well, hell, what do you want me to do, Mom? Perform some back flips? Run away and join the circus? Become a clown?"

Penelope Eve slumped. "Oh, now I've made you mad.

I didn't mean to." She tilted her head, smiling warmly. "I guess I just want to know you're okay. No, I *need* to know you are, or I can't be happy, son." She patted his leg. "You'll understand one day when you have children of your own." Her smile asked for his indulgence of her.

How could he stay mad? She was his mother. Chris reached out and took her hand, holding it. "It's okay, Mom. I love you. And I *am* happy, all right? I'm okay. Well, I'm working toward being okay."

Love shone from her eyes. "Oh, good. I won't press you anymore, but that's all I really wanted to know."

Well, he'd made her feel better. But Chris wasn't certain that he did. He didn't look or act happy? What was that about? He was a man in love, a man about to pop the question. But did that mean he was supposed to lose his mind and act stupid? Then he suddenly recalled how he'd behaved—lost his mind, acted stupid—when he'd successfully wrangled that second appointment with Dianna. What could that mean?

"Chris? Where are you?" His mother tapped at his leg. "You didn't even hear what I said to you, did you?"

He blinked back to the moment, shifting his weight atop the sofa cushions, as if that would help dislodge his introspective funk. "No, I guess I didn't. I'm sorry, what'd you say?"

"I said I hope Veronica doesn't inconveniently pop out of your study right now." Having said that, she leaned to one side and craned her neck to look beyond Chris and the sofa.

Chris resisted the urge to look behind him. "I think she's still working."

"I do, too, but I still want to make sure she isn't coming around the corner." Chris's mother—Pen, to her friends; an attractive woman with short gray hair and an indomitable spirit—suddenly directed her considerable maternal attention her son's way. Surprising Chris was that her dark eyes radiated censure. "I have to be honest.

I've been upset about something else and that's had me doing all this thinking."

"Here we go." Chris scrubbed his hands over his face and then smiled bleakly. "Go ahead. What is it?"

"Well, it's not something I can just blurt out, Christopher. It's embarrassing." She inhaled deeply and said, "But I guess I have to. I want to talk to you about that—" She leaned in toward him, whispering now. "That *prostitute* you had over here not too long ago."

"What?" Chris jackknifed to a sitting position, lifting his legs off the ottoman and putting his feet on the floor. "Mother, what the hell? A prostitute? What prostitute?"

"Don't act like you have no clue. I mean the one on the phone a little over a week ago. I talked to her myself."

Staring at his mother, Chris ran a hand over his mouth and thought back—and remembered. *Dianna.* They could not talk about her, not with Veronica close by—or at any other time, either. Chris kept his voice low but warned, "I thought we'd already dealt with that. I told you she wasn't a prostitute, for God's sake."

Penelope Eve raised her chin—a clear warning that she would not be put off. "That's what you said. But you never would tell me who she is and what she was doing here. What am I supposed to think?"

"Mom, look," Chris began, striving for firm and reasonable, "I'm all grown-up now. And I could just say this is none of your business—and it isn't. But, without going into details, I will tell you that everything was cool. Nothing bad." He sat back now, allowing himself to be insulted. "A prostitute? Come on, you know me better than that."

"I thought I did. No, I guess I do. At any rate, it's all very mysterious, you have to admit, so it's no wonder I'd think about it. The truth is, I can't get any straight answers from anyone. About the only thing I know is that woman said she knows Veronica. Is that true? Are they friends?"

To Chris's surprise, he found he didn't like his mother calling Dianna "that woman." But he could hardly correct her, not without raising more suspicions on her part. So what he said was: "Yes. They know each other. Sort of. At least, they've met." He was recalling Ronnie and Dianna's run-in at Tamborello's. "But they're not friends, Mother, and I'm not playing some twisted version here of Mary and Joe. I mean, I'm not seeing one friend and cheating on her with her best friend. So, come on, give me some credit here."

"I give you all sorts of credit, Chris. But I just wanted to be sure." His mother primly folded her hands together in her lap. "And I think I have some room to talk. After all, since the Mary and Joe thing, in your subsequent relationships, son, you haven't always been the most constant of men."

Okay, so he'd been with one woman, only to have his eye caught by another. When that had happened, he'd broken it off. He'd had women do the same thing to him. Such was modern romance. A life of serial monogamy. Something he was getting darned tired of. It was a different world now, and he wanted a lifetime commitment. "Hey, like I said, I'm all grown-up now, Mother. And I didn't care then like I do now—about those women, I mean. This one I care about."

"Are we still talking about Veronica?"

Chris sniffed, kept seeing Dianna's face in his mind, and had to blink to clear away her image. "Yes. Veronica. Definitely Veronica."

His mother firmed her lips together and raised her eyebrows. "So I'm just to trust that you have some innocent reason for having that woman over here at night without Veronica's knowledge?"

That did it. Chris snapped out an unthinking answer. "Quit calling her 'that woman.' She has a name."

"Oh? I see. Well, fine, then. Dianna West, it is."

"Dianna West? Who's Dianna West?" And this was Veronica, who'd obviously and very silently slipped up on them undetected.

Chris suffered an oh-shit moment. How much had she heard?

Intelligent, blond, perceptive, she stood by the end table closest to where Chris sat on the sofa. A questioning, perhaps suspicious, smile on her face, Veronica divided her gaze between Chris and his mother. "Anybody? Dianna West?"

The weekly Thursday-morning staff meeting of Popping the Question was now in order. Or as close to order as one could achieve when dealing with such personalities as Melanie, Paula, and Mrs. Windhorst. Dianna had made the executive decision to succumb to spring fever by convening outside on the elegantly decorated, wood-floored verandah. This had been met with cheers, followed by the women arranging themselves in a circle comprised of the floral-print padded chairs. In their midst squatted a rectangular, glass-topped wicker coffee table, atop which sat such diverse items as the women's coffee cups, muffins, notebooks, pens, and business cell phones.

The porch proved to be a very soothing location shaded by the wide overhanging eave, which sheltered the huge hanging baskets of ferns; three-tiered plant stands graced with tiny clay pots of spring daisies; assorted white wicker furniture; and little tables topped with decorative bric-a-brac. Not the usual corporate fare at all. But so what? This was her business, Dianna had decided, and she would conduct it however she felt best.

And right now, being outside on this warm, cloudless, blue-skied day, with its soothing breeze, was exactly what they all needed. But maybe especially Melanie did. She had flounced around all morning, looking troubled. Or maybe she was just more into her overwrought Southern-belle mode than usual. It was hard to tell with her.

Anyway, and this was Dianna's point, who cared who Chris Adams wanted to marry? It was no skin off her nose. Not with the trees greening, the flowers blooming, and the birds singing. No doubt, off in some green pastures somewhere, baby horses, cows, and lambs were being born. All in all, it was a good day to be alive . . . as long as she didn't think about Chris Adams and no one present asked her about him.

"Okay, so now we know when everyone's vacation days are scheduled for the next three months." Her smile benign, Dianna turned to her secretary for corroboration. "Before we move on, did you get all that, Mrs. Windhorst?"

"I did. And I will type it up, make copies, and distribute the schedule to everyone." She shifted her focus to Melanie and Paula. The two of them faced Dianna and Mrs. Windhorst across the intimate width of the table. The older woman peered at them over the top of her Ben Franklin reading glasses. "Please, ladies, try not to make changes after that point, as it only makes more work for me and is very confusing to your coworkers."

"Not to mention your boss," Dianna threw in, smiling pointedly at Paula to forestall her saying something provocative like how much easier their working lives would be if they came out of the medieval tower populated by electric typewriters and actually joined the space age of computers. When she got no argument, Dianna moved on. "All right, then. Now to the important stuff. Paula, tell us what you have working right now."

"Okey-dokey, boss lady." Much like a boneless cat, Paula uncurled herself from her chair and leaned forward, retrieving from the coffee table her schedule book. She settled back, pulled her pen out from behind her ear, adjusted her glasses on her nose, and leafed through a few pages. "Okay. Here we go." She ran a finger down the lines on the page. "Got a guy who's a sports nut, and luckily so's his girl. So I've set him up to pop the question this weekend on one of the promenades behind the outfield at Oriole Park."

"Oh, how sweet," Melanie chimed in, sounding more perfunctory than her usual titillated state.

"Nice choice," Mrs. Windhorst added. "Camden Yards is particularly lovely this time of year."

"Right." Paula tugged her blue-framed eyeglasses down and stared at her associates. "Lucky them, there's a home game this weekend, too. So they'll have that whole parking-lot ambiance going. Sweaty jocks and screaming fans. A stroll through the memorabilia shops while wearing your favorite team's jersey and eating barbecue. Nothing could be more romantic. But, hey, it's not my life."

Dianna cleared her throat, drawing her employees' attention her way, yet focusing on Paula in particular. No sense in allowing her to get started on a sports harangue. Athletics were too much like exercise to appeal to sedentary Paula. "Anyway," Dianna began, "I assume your client, at least, is happy and you got the proper permissions from the team?"

Paula's nod greeted Dianna's question. "All in place. Everything done. Everybody happy. Oh, and my little old man and his Bingo World honey got engaged last night, so . . . bingo for us! Our hundred-percent record is still in place." She flipped another page in her schedule book. "Okay, now here's one that's more like it. I've chartered the *Black-Eyed Susan*—you know, that new 1930s-style Art Deco yacht—for a private party thrown by an older guy who has invited all his and his lady friend's friends. It's her sixtieth birthday this weekend, so she'll be expecting a party anyway. I suggested that they all do this *Great Gatsby* thing and dress à la F. Scott and Zelda. He loved it. So, pretty darn cool, no? There'll even be champagne, a big band, dinner, the works."

"Oh, very good, Ms. Capland," Mrs. Windhorst said. "Outstanding."

"Glad you think so, old girlfriend." Paula winked at her, adding, "And with that"—she flipped her schedule book closed—"I am done here. That's me for the week. Except for some new clients coming in tomorrow." She propped a skinny elbow on her chair's arm, plunked her chin down on her palm and smiled broadly at Melanie.

"You're up, Miss O'Hara, ma'am. What's happening down on the plantation, my little honeysuckle?"

Dianna sat up, alert to Melanie's mood and ready to jump in if necessary. But Melanie totally ignored her associate. Dressed in some concoction that fell just shy of a ball gown with a full hoop skirt, she flipped back and forth through her schedule book, apparently looking for the correct page. "Now, let me see. Where am I? I do declare, things just tend to get away from me."

Batting her eyelashes now, Paula offered: "They do? You mean like your tiny little brain, for instance, sugar?"

Dianna exchanged a glance with Mrs. Windhorst, her being the one who had pointed out to Dianna that Melanie didn't seem herself—or whoever she thought she was—today. Dianna opened her mouth to tell Paula to knock it off, but Melanie was quicker.

"You poor thing, Paula. I just feel so sorry for you, honey. I truly do," she said, a white and pampered hand fluttering to her ample bosom. "Why, it must be awful to suffer from such a lack of breeding and manners." Her expression radiating sympathy, Melanie reached out to finger Paula's fuchsia-flowered sleeve. "But I'd like to help you. Why don't I put you in touch with a nice school of fashion and design? I think they can save you from continuing to look like a French fashion show runway-model horror, sweetie."

Totally not insulted, instead laughing and bright-eyed, Paula shifted in her chair until she was facing Dianna and Mrs. Windhorst. "Do you just love her or what? I'm saying, is she totally cool or is it just me?"

"No. It's not you," Dianna assured Paula, who truly did find Melanie a constant source of never-ending amusement and entertainment. "I don't know why she hasn't wrung your neck yet, but she is definitely cool."

Barely responding to this praise—not the first primp or smug look—Melanie focused again on her schedule book. "Now, let's see. Things I'm working on. Oh. Here we go. I just had a call this morning from that nice young man, Mr. Lansdon. He told me of his happy outcome. He asked his sweetheart last evening at the Ladew Topiary Gardens to marry him and got a yes answer. Isn't that darling?"

"Totally," Paula assured her. "In fact, I'm orgasmic, it's so darling."

Mrs. Windhorst sucked in an offended breath, and Dianna sat forward, ready to verbally smack Paula, but again Melanie beat her to the punch.

"Orgasmic. That's nice, honey. Good for you," she said, patting Paula's arm dismissively and continuing on. Using a finger to mark her place, she stared at the open page of her schedule book. "Oh, my. Oh, dear. I just don't know what to do."

Dianna frowned, not even certain that Melanie realized she was speaking aloud. "Are you okay, Mel? Is something wrong?"

Melanie shook her head no, but her expression crumpled as she covered her face with both hands. Not a sound issued from the woman, but her shoulders shook with emotion.

With her two other employees' eyes wide with concern and focused on her, Dianna immediately stood up and crossed the porch. Once at Melanie's side, she put a sympathetic hand on her shoulder. "Melanie? What is it?"

"Yeah, girlfriend," Paula said soothingly, sincerely, leaning over from her chair to rub Melanie's arm sympathetically. "So, what's wrong, huh? I was only kidding you. You know I wouldn't kid you if I didn't like you. Ask Mrs. Windhorst. I tease her all the time, and she thinks I hate her. But I don't."

"You don't?" This from the surprised-sounding Mrs. Windhorst.

Just then, Melanie raised her head, showing a face puffy and reddened with emotion. "It's not you, Paula." Her voice was hiccupy with tears. "I've been trying to hold back, but I just can't. I thought I could live with it. I thought I could put the experience behind me and pretend it never happened." She applied the back of her hand to her forehead and closed her eyes. "I hoped you'd never have to know, Di. But I find I can't keep it to myself. It's just too—"

"Blanche DuBois?" Paula supplied, her expression still one of puckered concern. "Tennessee Williams? *A Streetcar Named Desire*?"

Dianna made a sound of irritation. "Paula, please."

She of the French fashion show runway-model horror sat back. "What'd I do? I'm trying to help. She loves being these Southern heroines. You know, depending on the kindness of strangers and all that crap."

"I am nobody's heroine," Melanie wailed brokenheartedly—and loudly. "In fact, I am a villain of the worst sort. I have betrayed you all."

Dianna immediately squatted down beside the distraught woman's chair. She patted her employee's back, but directed her attention to her secretary. "Perhaps a cup of water, Mrs. Windhorst?"

The older woman nodded and got up, hurrying inside to comply. Dianna nodded for Paula to follow her. She did, muttering about Kleenex and Prozac for all this blubbering.

Finally alone with Melanie, Dianna tried to draw her out. "Come on, now, what's wrong? You know you can talk to me. What's all this talk about betraying us? How could *you* possibly betray us? You're everybody's sweetheart, Mel."

"Not anymore, Di." Melanie wrenched around in her chair and—surprise!—threw her arms around Dianna's neck in a very effective chokehold that had Dianna gasping and tugging on Melanie's locked arms. "You are the best of women, honey. I just love you, and I am so sorry. But you should fire me. Or have me locked up in an attic somewhere. I have committed the worst of all sins. I have engaged in a sexual indiscretion with a client."

# CHAPTER 9

It took a good two seconds for Melanie's words to completely sink into Dianna's consciousness and understanding. But when they did . . . "Oh, Melanie."

The ramifications hit Dianna's consciousness with the force of incoming meteorites. Still locked in Melanie's embrace, she felt hot and weak all over. But then she remembered that this *was* Melanie. "Melanie, honey?" she choked out. "Okay, let go of me, all right?"

Melanie relaxed her grip and Dianna slipped back but remained squatted next to the woman's chair. "Thank you. That's good." She rubbed her neck and smoothed her hair away from her too-hot face. "Now, I want you to look at me, and I want you to define 'indiscretion.' I know the dictionary meaning, but I mean as *you're* using it."

Before Melanie could explain, the front door opened and out trooped Mrs. Windhorst with a tiny cone-shaped paper cup of water. Right behind her came Paula with an industrial-sized wad of plucked-up tissues. Dianna forced herself to smile at Melanie. "Here we go. Have a sip of water and blow your nose, okay? You'll feel better."

"Thank you," Melanie said in a very watery voice. She took the offered water and the wad of tissues. "You all are too kind."

While she drank and then blew her nose, Paula and Mrs. Windhorst reseated themselves and turned questioning expressions Dianna's way. She gave a tiny shake of her head, coupled with a vague gesture, to convey that she didn't know yet what was up. The truth was Melanie's notion of a sexual indiscretion could be her hand accidentally brushing against a client's. Whereas Paula's would be total nudity and raunchy sex in a men's dressing room in Nordstrom's out at Towson Town Center. At noon. On a Saturday. During Christmas shopping season.

But once Melanie seemed to have better control, though her face remained pale and her makeup was smeared, Dianna took the initiative. "Melanie, are you comfortable talking in front of us all? Or would you prefer to speak to me in private?"

The New Jersey–bred Southern belle and benignly crazy rich young woman shook her head. "No. I feel it best to bare my soul in front of everyone. That way my shame can be bandied about only the one time, and there'll be no need later on for wondering or for gossip."

Dianna frowned at Melanie. "Well, I don't know about, uh, bandying or gossip, but go ahead whenever you're ready."

"All right." Melanie twisted a tissue in her hands. "It was Dr. Yakahama."

"What? That little Japanese man? The dentist?" This was the appalled Mrs. Windhorst. "What did he do, Melanie? Did he take a liberty with you? Now, do you all see? This is the very thing I worry about with you young women out alone with these men when you're scouting locations. There's a definite potential there for abuse—or worse."

"Thank you, Mrs. Windhorst," Dianna said evenly. "We're very aware of your concerns. I had the same ones, and that's why we have our clients fill out those forms that tell us all about them. It's also why we carry cell phones and check in regularly and only go to the sites during business hours. But I don't believe that's what has happened here."

"No?" Paula chimed in. "Then what did happen with the tooth-fairy guy?"

"We're still trying to find that out," Dianna said, smiling tightly. "So if we could let Melanie speak?" She watched as her employees sat back, apparently intending to keep their silence. Satisfied, Dianna settled her attention again on Melanie. "I think it's safe to say, Mel, that we recall Dr. Yakahama. Go on."

"Yes, ma'am." She lowered her gaze to watch herself wadding up the tissues she held. "As you've guessed, we were scouting the location late yesterday afternoon, Dr. Yakahama and I. I had suggested the National Museum of Dentistry."

"Hey, that's a public building," Paula cut in, her face lighting up with dawning respect. "You did it in public, didn't you, with tourists walking around? You go, girl. Tell me you did it up against some giant toothbrush or tube of toothpaste. That is *so* phallic."

Every bit as indignant as Mrs. Windhorst's gasp of outrage, Melanie puffed up impressively. "We most certainly did not. Why, the very idea."

"Paula," Dianna warned, standing up and returning to her chair. She sat down, saying, "Let her talk, please."

Grinning, Paula flopped back in her chair and crossed her arms under her breasts. "Yeah, go on, Melanie. I'd love to hear about a new use for dental floss or a Waterpik. Talk about getting drilled. This is so cool."

Mrs. Windhorst threw in: "Well, I think it's absolutely indecent, what you're suggesting, Ms. Capland."

"So do I," Dianna agreed. "And I don't think this is very easy for Melanie, so just chill, all right, both of you?" She glared; they quieted. "Go on, Mel."

"Thank you, Di." Melanie heaved a dramatic sigh. "Well, we'd already viewed the exhibit containing the thirty-two terrific teeth. And had an entertaining look at George Washington's not-so-wooden teeth. Then we went to the popular tooth jukebox—"

"No, no, no." Obviously Paula was in no mood for

anything but the most salient of details. "You're killing us here. Cut to the sex. We want to hear the part where you insert A into B and pump."

Mrs. Windhorst jumped up. "We most certainly do *not*, Ms. Capland. I find your prurient interest to be—"

"I know: more interesting than you care to admit." Paula's grin changed to an expression of surprise as she stared past Dianna and Mrs. Windhorst. "Uh-oh. Trouble on the horizon." Her pointing finger stabbed the air at a point approximately between Dianna and her secretary. "Ix-nay the ex-say talk, ladies and sister lunatics. Look who approacheth."

Dianna froze, her eyes wide. With her back to the street, she stared at the front door of her business. No way did she want to turn around. From what Paula had said, it could only be the vice squad coming up the walk behind her. Or Dr. Yakahama's girlfriend and her lawyer. Or maybe the legal people from the National Museum of Dentistry. A camera crew from *60 Minutes*. Jerry Springer. Or, even better, all of the preceding.

The suspense became too much for her. Dianna jumped up from her chair and turned in the direction Paula had pointed.

*Oh, no.* Weakness washed over Dianna. Her heart skipped a beat and then thumped against her ribs like a car's engine knocking badly. It was even worse than all those people she'd feared grouped into one lump. It was Chris Adams. He was the last thing—person—she needed to see right now. Or even ever, she suddenly decided. The man was a walking reminder to her of just how close she'd come to committing with him the same transgression that Melanie apparently had with Dr. Yakahama.

When her brain finally kicked in, Dianna quickly declared the staff meeting over, sent her employees inside—Paula and Mrs. Windhorst supporting Melanie—and then walked out in the sunshine to meet Chris. Heading him off, she signaled for him to step with her over to the small parking lot, where she and he now stood in the space between his parked car and hers. She leaned her hips against her car's front door; he leaned his against his car's front fender, a bit to her right. So they faced each other across a narrow, sun-warmed space. A gentle, playful breeze stirred Dianna's hair. She tugged its heavy weight behind her shoulders. "So, what can I do for you, Chris?"

Behind his aviator sunglasses, Chris's eyebrows shot up. "What can you *do* for me? Well, since you put it like that, I guess you can tell me why we're standing out here in the parking lot, instead of inside. Either I'm not welcome, or I got here at the tag end of a fire drill."

"I wish. Although it seems like one most days around here. But no, it was just an al fresco office meeting that went awry. And of course you're welcome here. You're a paying client."

With his eyes lost to her scrutiny, Dianna watched Chris's mouth. Not such an awful thing to have to do, not if one liked full sensual lips which had a tendency to curve up at the corners . . . like now, and somewhat ironically. "Oh, man. First, it's what can you do for me. And now I'm a paying client. I must really be circling the drain here."

"You're not. And it's not you, Chris. It's me."

Now his mouth became a firm, straight line. "When a woman says 'it's not you, it's me,' it's you. And don't tell me it isn't because I read that in one of my mother's women's magazines."

He was so droll. Despite her funk, Dianna couldn't resist teasing right back. She put a hand to her heart, feigning shock. "Your mother left one of our training manuals out for the enemy to find? The horror. Now I'll have to report her to the committee."

"Is that the same one that calls meetings in the women's powder rooms in restaurants? I'm guessing that's why you ladies go en masse."

"Oh, no. You know more than I thought. I suppose it can't hurt to tell you, then, that those meetings are where we train the young ones and where we compare notes on you guys and then change all the rules without telling you."

He nodded soberly. "I always suspected as much."

"And you were right. But it *really* is me this time, and I owe you an apology."

Frowning, Chris cocked his head at a comically questioning angle. "How so?"

Laughter forced its way past Dianna's present burden of worries. "You know what? You probably won't appreciate this, but you look just like Joe Cocker with your head tilted that way. I don't mean the singer. I mean my parents' dog."

Chris's frown increased as he leaned in toward her. "Your parents named their dog Joe Cocker?"

"God, no. They'd never heard of Joe Cocker. That was my brother Edward's doing."

"Ah. Edward. Let's see . . . that's the accountant brother, right?"

"I'm impressed. And you're right—Edward's the accountant. Oh, and by the way, I don't think you *really* look like the dog."

"Imagine my relief. So carrying this forward, I'm guessing the dog is a cocker spaniel?"

"Hey, you're good. Be glad he wasn't a springer spaniel."

"Ah. Edward would have named him Jerry?"

"Right. And who wants to live with that?"

"Not me. All that yelling and hitting." Grinning, Chris pulled back to his original posture . . . butt against his car, arms crossed over his chest, ankles crossed. "I think I missed a lot not having brothers and sisters."

"No, I don't think you did." So they'd slipped into the familiar and the chatty, Dianna realized. They always did somehow. The problem was she was very interested in Chris, very curious. She wanted to know what he thought, how he felt, what he was like. No way was this a healthy impulse. He wasn't hers and wasn't going to be, but, still, she did nothing to put them back on a business-only track.

"You would have hated the sharing and the teasing and the tattling."

"I don't mind teasing and tattling. I can do that. But it's the sharing that would get me. I'm more like 'what's mine is mine.' So, anyway, tell me why you owe me an apology."

"For Faidley's. The way I left. I was bad, I yelled, got emotional. Any of this coming back to you?"

"Yeah, I remember all that. But I don't think—"

"It was a business lunch, Chris. I shouldn't have behaved that way. And why are you being so easy on me?"

"You want me to be hard?"

*Chris? Hard?* Instant and naughty images popped into Dianna's lascivious mind, any number of which would get a Catholic schoolgirl's hand smacked soundly by a ruler-wielding nun. Dianna blinked and scratched absently at her temple and tucked her hair behind her ears . . . and looked everywhere but at him as she spoke. "You can't tell me you don't remember my sarcasm and my telling you to fax me? Totally uncalled for in a professional setting."

Dressed casually in black slacks and a gray oxford shirt open at the throat, he could have been a model in a new-car ad. So handsome and unconsciously sexy that he stunted Dianna's breathing—and her thinking. "All right, if you say so," he conceded. "So, go ahead, then. Apologize to me."

Incongruously, that caught Dianna wrong. He didn't have to look so smug about it. "I already did."

"Did not."

"Did."

"And yet I never heard 'I'm sorry' from you." He grinned, showing white and even teeth that Dianna would swear glinted when the sunlight hit them.

She crossed her arms under her breasts. "All right, Mr. Smarty Pants, I'm sorry. And you never did fax me."

"My fax machine is broken."

"Why don't I believe you? You're a computer whiz."

"Which is not necessarily the same thing as a fax whiz."

"Still, it's not really broken, is it?"

"No. Well, it wasn't until I hit it with a hammer."

"You did not."

"Did."

"Why?"

"So I could get out of the house."

"Are you going to tell me that your fax machine came to life, barred the front door threateningly, and you had to fight your way out?"

"Wow," he said, looking totally impressed with her. "It's like you were there."

Laughing, Dianna shook her head. "Stop it. And explain yourself."

He chuckled. "Yes, Miss Bossy, ma'am. Okay. It's simple. I'm talking about the pitfalls of this age of technology, even if I did help create it. I'm saying that if you're not careful, if you don't break something occasionally that forces you to leave the house, you'll never get to interact with real people."

"Be serious."

"I am. It's now possible to work and live in one room, be totally productive, and never leave. Never go outside. Never seek people out." Chris reached up to lower his sunglasses an inch or so down his nose. His dark brown eyes met her gaze and he said, pointedly, "Or never see anyone. Sometimes you just need to see someone, you know?"

He meant her. Thoroughly heated now, and in a way that had nothing to do with the spring day's warmth, Dianna swallowed. "I do know."

She also knew that they simply could not continue to stand this close and flirt like this. Very bad juju because, if they did, Dianna feared, she'd end up saying screw the consequences and set about checking out whose car, his or hers, had the most accommodating back seat. *Hello, Melanie and Dr. Tooth Fairy.* Splash-of-cold-water thought. Dianna exhaled and reverted to being business-like. "So, Chris, since you're here, I'm guessing you came out of your techno-cave because you needed to tend to something not, well, technical?"

"Precisely. I couldn't fax you—"

"Or e-mail me or phone me, I take it?"

"Could, but didn't want to. Wanted that face time. And that meant coming by in person and sans appointment to see you." He grinned like a pirate, much as if he'd just said something very clever that had made him proud.

"And that's another thing. Why *do* you keep coming back here?"

Chris raised an eyebrow. "I'm not feeling welcome again. Can't it just be because I like the company?"

"Well, if that's true"—she wanted terribly to believe that it was, but didn't dare—"then you must be the most forgiving person in the world. All you've seen so far is me at my worst and most bumbling. I'd think you'd run far away and never look back."

He shrugged those wonderfully broad shoulders of his that Dianna wanted to bite and kiss and knead under her hands. "Turns out I like bumbling."

Swept away by the moment, Dianna heard her idiotic self blurting out: "Then you really ought to love me."

Chris said nothing. He stuck his hands in his pants pockets and lowered his gaze to consider his shoes or the ground or whatever. This left Dianna hot with embarrassment from the forehead down and wanting to die right then and there. Maybe she could hurl herself into the path of oncoming traffic. Or throw herself off a cliff. Drown herself in a toilet. Eat too much cheesecake—

Chris raised his head, turning it in her direction. Though his eyes were still hidden behind his sunglasses, the set of his mouth and jaw adequately conveyed, *I wish to hell you hadn't said that.*

Dianna took her cue to speak. "I was only teasing, Chris, about you ought to"—big breath here—"love me. There's no reason why you should. You love Veronica."

He didn't say anything. "You do, right? Love Veronica, I mean." He still didn't say anything. *Damn man.* She reached over and smacked his forearm, causing him to blink and jump. "Help me out here, okay? Say something."

"All right." And then he did. "Sometimes I think you're right."

Dianna blinked. Could he be more vague? *Could he?* She suffered this mental image of herself really lighting into him, boy, with wind-milling arms and fists and just beating the living hell out of him until he quit torturing her. Just kick the man when he was down. *What am I right about?* she wanted to shriek at him. *Which freakin' part? About you loving Veronica? Or about you loving me?*

But of course she already knew the answer to that, didn't she? Dianna felt her heart do a belly flop right into the pool of her watery emotions. "Well, then, Chris"— she grinned so brightly, falsely, broadly, that her facial muscles ached—"I guess you're here today for purely professional reasons, right?"

He looked away from her for a seemingly interminable moment, and then swung his gaze back her way. "Right. I came to tell you in person that I'm ready for you to set up my romantic whatever-you-call-it with Veronica."

"Oh, really? Well, good. In person. Wonderful." Dianna nodded and smiled and somehow managed not to burst into tears. It just hurt like hell to realize he *had* been only flirting with her, and not even seriously, and she had no impact on him, not even now that he knew her. *Story of my life.* Still, what right did he have to look like he did, and smell so clean and citrusy like he did, and make her laugh like he did—and then go out and marry scary old Dr. Frankenlawyer?

Dianna rubbed at her forehead and directed her gaze to the general vicinity of Chris's car's hood. *Okay, I can stand here and suck, or I can behave professionally and salvage my pride and admit that I have been, for whatever unknown reason, cut from the herd of desirables—*

"Dianna?" Chris reached out and touched her arm.

Dianna wrenched away with a not-charming and spasmodic jerk. Embarrassed for herself, she used the motion to scratch at her head, which did not itch, and to talk really fast. "I'm fine. Just thinking about you and Veronica and what we might do. First, I need to know how soon you want to do it." That didn't sound right. "How soon you want to ask her to marry you, I mean. And where. Got any ideas? You said at Faidley's that you had an idea."

*Okay, could I sound more* Ally McBeal *neurotic and annoying?*

Chris was saying: "Yeah, I have an idea. But it's only sketchy. More of a feel to the thing than actual places and details."

"Of course. If you could visualize all that, you wouldn't need me, would you?" Her attempt at a laugh was a sick little watery bleat that did nothing for her self-esteem. *He doesn't need me at all.*

"No," Chris said quietly. "I guess I wouldn't."

With her arms crossed over her cotton blouse and under her breasts, Dianna lowered her gaze to watch herself ruining her favorite bone-colored pumps by toeing a bit of gravel, pushing it into a pile, and then smoothing it out. She absolutely could not look at Chris Adams at this moment. It wasn't fair. He excited her and made her hurt all in the same breath.

"Hey, are you all right, Dianna?"

She jerked her head up, wishing he'd take those damned shades off so she could see his eyes. "Yes. I'm fine. Never better." *I will fight this thing I feel for you, and I will beat it.* She cleared her throat subtly. "Anyway, this is a good thing. It's for the best. It's exactly what we need to do, you and I. Get you engaged. Yes, I like it."

"Well, I'm convinced." With his arms crossed, he watched her, still from behind those light-reflecting shades of his.

"Good." She was all business now—all cool, detached,

professional business. "I'm sorry if I'm off kilter. It's just that some"—she gestured vaguely back over her shoulder toward her place of business—"employee thing came up right before you got here."

"Something serious?" At long last, Chris removed his sunglasses, folding them and sticking them in his shirt pocket.

Dianna watched all this before looking into his melting-chocolate brown eyes. "Very serious."

"I'm sorry to hear it."

"Thanks." God, how the two of them had retreated. And how quickly. Dianna felt so defensive right now with him, like she physically had to hold him at arm's length.

"Can I do anything to help, Dianna?"

*Yes. You can make a permanent move to Antarctica so I don't ever have to see you again.* The man just did not know his boundaries. With that realization fueling her anger—something easier to feel than star-crossed yearning—Dianna inhaled deeply and exhaled slowly. "Are you just out looking for more dragons to bitch-slap, or what?"

He grinned. Totally James Dean. "If need be."

Denying she was affected, though her pulse throbbed hotly in a very private place not ever viewed in public, Dianna retorted, "Well, sorry, but you don't need to be."

"All right. Message received."

"Good. Oh, and by the way, once we get you engaged, I do think I want to talk to you about the computer proposition you had for me."

He perked up. "Hey, that's great. Really?" But then he looked suspicious. "After I'm engaged? Not before?"

"No. Not before."

"I see." He looked directly into her eyes, holding her gaze, somehow showing her a Technicolor world of regret and desire and what might have been . . . in a different time and place. But not here, and not now. Or ever.

"I was hoping you would see," she said quietly.

Chris exhaled and shook his head, no longer looking

directly at her. "Sure you don't want someone else to come in and set you up, Dianna?"

She chuckled . . . sadly and at her own expense. "No. You've already done a pretty good job of setting me up, Chris."

He swung his gaze back to hers. "Now, what does that mean? Damn, Dianna, why is trying to communicate with you so hard? It's like we're trapped in some Japanese film and need subtitles at about knee-level to spell out what we mean but aren't saying."

Dianna pressed her fingertips to her temples. "God, do not say 'Japan' to me right now."

"Now, see?" Chris's broad gesture was one of agitation. "That's exactly what I'm talking about. What's wrong with Japan?"

"Nothing. You wouldn't understand. And Japan has nothing to do with you. Could I be plainer? Here, let me say it again: It has nothing do with you." She was lying, and she knew it. It had everything to do with him. How well she knew that if Chris only crooked his finger at her, if he just gave her one sign, she'd be Melanie and he'd be Dr. Yakahama.

"All right, look," Chris was saying, "I'm not that vain guy who thinks everything is about him. I'm not. I just . . ." He looked away from her again, shook his head, exhaled, and then returned his attention to her. "Never mind. I should just walk away right now, shouldn't I?"

"Yes." Wasn't she the brave and noble heroine of high ideals and few words? Ha. Dianna sniffed and blinked, trying not to see herself prostrated on the ground and screaming and clinging to his ankles, should he actually try to walk away from her.

"Well, I'm not going to do it."

So he couldn't walk away from her, either. Dianna had no idea what to make of that. Feeling fatalistic, she smiled grimly. "Wow. You must really want that computer contract."

"Not me. I'm a man of infinite means, remember? I don't need to work."

"I do remember. Then . . . what? Some humanitarian impulse, maybe?"

"Now you're being a smart-ass."

"Sorry."

"And surly."

"Yes, I am."

"Why?"

"I don't know."

"I don't have to do your computers."

"I know. But I want you to." *After you're engaged. When you're safely and finally claimed. When I have it through my big, fat head that you're not ever going to want me, damn you.* How was that for subtitles?

"All right. Just tell me what changed your mind about the computers."

"The absurdity of not having them, actually."

"And Mrs. Windhorst?"

"She's why I want *you* to do it. She seems to have this thing with you—"

"Here we go. What do you mean, 'this thing'?"

"She likes you, or something. Gives you walk-in appointments. Always argues your side."

"She does? I have a side?"

"Yes, and yes. So I think she'll take the computer news better if you're to be the one to instruct her. Something tells me she'd like nothing better than to have you at her chairside for hours on end every day." Subtitle: *I know I would.*

Chris eyed her suspiciously, which made Dianna wonder if he was searching for the subtitle. "So you're just being a good boss, is that it?"

She shrugged, feigning nonchalance. "Yes. I'm vying for Boss of the Year."

"I hope you get it." He stood there staring at her, while in the background cars passed by in the street; bees buzzed around the flowers in the landscaping; and birds sang from the trees' branches. "I don't understand the part about my having to be engaged first."

"If not married."

"Damn. I've never had to go to such lengths to do something free for someone."

"I imagine you haven't." Dianna pushed away from her car. "Come on, let's go inside and we'll set up your dream scenario so you can ask the woman you love to marry you."

Chris grimaced. "Thanks. You infused that with all the joy of experimental surgery."

"Sorry. It's that employee thing I was telling you about," Dianna lied.

"Gotcha. So, you think it's safe to go inside right now?"

"Yeah. I'm sure they're okay. Well, relatively speaking." Dianna smiled. "I mean, you've met them." Dianna led off with Chris falling in at her side. As they walked, his hand periodically brushed against hers, sending her heart racing. Had anything ever been so bittersweet and so blasted hard before? "So, anyway," she said, striving for more control—over herself—"I'll see what I can set up for you. And how quickly we can get this thing going."

"I'm not in all that big a hurry, Dianna."

"I am."

"You are?"

"Oh, yes. I really want those computers."

# CHAPTER 10

Friday afternoon found Chris sitting in the comfort of his home office and surrounded by his favorite technology, which right now included loud but soothing music. He'd just signed off from the weekly online seminar he conducted for technogeeks like himself and now faced over two hundred e-mails he needed to answer but was avoiding. Just couldn't bring himself to delve into them. Instead, he sat and stared blankly at his computer's screen saver—a scrolling marquee he'd set up, a note to himself that admonished him to "Click here if you're a man, not a mouse."

Drumming his fingers on his workstation's desktop, he ignored everything in favor of a mental rehashing of the two fairly momentous (in terms of his life, anyway) telephone conversations he'd had today. He couldn't decide if they were as real as they felt. The first phone call had been from Dianna to tell him he was good to go on Saturday night—meaning she'd be there overseeing the details, everything was set up, and he could pop the question to Veronica. About a thousand emotions, all of them conflicting, had gone through his mind at her news and while he'd talked to her.

Chris didn't insult himself now by denying how his heart had flopped about in his chest like a landed trout at the sound of her voice and the certain prospect of seeing her again. Still, both he and Dianna had sounded, he admitted, as if they'd just been handed some really bad medical news that affected them both and was hard to accept. Totally unsettling.

She'd casually rung off, saying she'd definitely see him tomorrow night. And that had left him alone with the specter of phone call number two: calling Veronica. Okay, that was something he did every day but not like this, not with so much at stake. Suddenly everything—his whole life, the day outside—had looked different and felt different. Before he'd called her to ask her to play dress-up with him on Saturday night, Chris had first had to get himself past the required what-the-hell-have-I-done thing that came with an overwhelming urge to run screaming into the hills.

Then he'd realized he needed a smokescreen, some legitimate-sounding reason to give her for everything being so senior-prom formal and *Casablanca* romantic. He'd decided just to say he had some good news he wanted to share with her. Brilliant, no? Of course, there wasn't any good news to share. Well, not unless she considered his asking her to marry him good news. With that settled, it became all about "now or never." Chris had weighed those two options. Now. Or never. He'd come this far. It had to be "now." So, with his heart thumping with dread, or maybe it was anticipation, and his ears ringing, he'd made the call.

Frustratingly, and so "just like her," Veronica had balked, citing some law seminar she had to attend all day Saturday. She'd insisted she'd be brain-dead and good to no one by the end of the day. Then she'd gone on about how she wouldn't be staying with him this weekend because of that same seminar, which continued on Sunday. Teeth gritted and fighting flaring irritation with all her roadblocks—did he never come first with her?—Chris had reminded himself of his goal, and also that she had no idea what lay behind his invitation.

He'd ended up telling her that was fine—about not

staying over—and, hey, he understood (Understanding Guy, that was him). But his private impulse was to tell her to forget the whole thing. Just tell her to go on to her stupid seminar and he'd see her next week. But then it became about winning. A totally stubborn I-will-have-my-way-for-once thing. What scared him, though, was to realize how much he really *didn't* care if he saw her or not. Incongruously, that had spurred him on. Surely, he'd reasoned, that feeling was only the onset of the cold-feet/pulling-away thing that was a part of the commitment ritual.

And so he'd ignored the clanging bells at the back of his mind that said, *This is a huge mistake, man; you need to be listening to your heart,* and persisted with Ronnie. Finally, she'd caved and agreed to meet him for dinner after Saturday's seminar. But, really, that was all the time she could spare, and they'd have to make it an early night. With that, she'd rung off.

And now, here Chris sat, dangerously close to a just-fuck-it moment. Why the hell was he even trying? Ronnie didn't seem to give a damn if she saw him or not. Just like she didn't seem to give a damn whether or not they took their relationship to the next level. So, why did he? Fiddling with a stray paper clip that had wandered within his reach, Chris really wrestled with why he persisted in pursuing the woman. What had started him down this uncertain road to matrimony, anyway?

Oh, hell, who was he kidding? He knew. It was simple, really. He'd got tired of the way things were between him and Ronnie. They'd come to that sharp-edged point in their relationship that happens with every dating couple: the point where you either get married or you walk away. All he'd known was he hadn't been ready to walk away, or maybe was too comfortable to make the effort and have that scene. And certainly, back then, defined as a few weeks ago, no other prospects had loomed on the horizon. Chris made a sound of self-derision. *Right, buddy. Not too complimentary to either one of you.*

So, had they just got tired, or was it lazy? He couldn't speak for her, but he believed it was simple impatience on his part—and approaching the big 3-0. *Time to make some changes, man, take some risks.* All right, he could do that. Then, he had to ask himself: *What if Ronnie says no? Pretty much couldn't ignore that signal. And what will I do if she does?* He shrugged, telling himself he wouldn't know until he asked, would he?

But talk about guilt. Here was some: He hadn't felt impatient with Ronnie until the moment he'd looked into the gold-colored eyes of one Dianna West. Before he'd met her, he'd thought he knew what he was doing and that he felt good about it. Excited, even. But now? Well, it wasn't so simple. Ronnie was so much a part of his life. She was the landscape. The environment. And they'd been a couple for so long; and all his friends knew her; and everyone, including his mother, just expected them to get married. It was like an arranged marriage, a societal pressure thing. Like he was obligated to her. How crazy was that?

But if he didn't at least make the effort, he knew, there'd be at least two consequences. One, he'd have to hear that "fear of commitment" thing, have to have that *you're still scarred from Mary and Joe* conversation. And, two, he'd be the bad guy with everyone he and Ronnie knew. He'd then be outside that circle. He'd lose friends; they'd be forced to choose between him and her. And then they'd have to separate their stuff, all the things they'd bought together. *Damn, it'd be like getting a divorce, and we aren't even married.*

But Chris realized he didn't mind being the bad guy. He had been before. And could be again. But first he had to give Ronnie the chance to say yes or no. He owed her that much.

Frowning, Chris shook his head. *I owe her that? Man, that sounds like an obligation, a debt I have to pay. Where's the passion? The heat? The primal urge to merge? Not there.* So, proposing out of obligation? What the hell for? They weren't royalty. The fate of nations wasn't at risk. But, still, everything else aside, it kind of pissed him off, Chris admitted, to think how far *he'd* come in the commitment department, following all those years of trying to get past his former girlfriend marrying his former best friend, only to have Ronnie *not* meet him halfway now. And it stung a bit, in the what's-wrong-with-me department, to realize she wasn't pressing him for marriage and that she seemed happy to drift along as things were.

*Okay, it's not like I want the Nobel Prize for getting over an old hurt. It's just that, I mean, here I am ready to go, and thinking I have the right woman for me, and yet she's totally oblivious. So what am I—just some easy sex for her? The weekend lay? It's like I'm the mistress she keeps tucked away and sees only when it's convenient for her.*

That sucked. But too late. The die was definitely already cast. The show was on the road. The horse was hitched up to the cart. Scary. He tossed the paper clip across the room, telling himself that he hated talking to women. Two totally different languages, with theirs being much more complex and subtle. *Somebody ought to come up with a Man/Woman, Woman/Man language dictionary, like those Spanish/English, English/Spanish things. Talk about an Oprah best-seller.*

Hearing himself, Chris knew exactly what he had to do: He had to talk to a guy. *Rick.* Chris's eyes widened. *Oh, shit—Rick.* That "Yikes!" feeling jetted along his nerve endings as he remembered his mental note to himself from last Wednesday evening. He was supposed to call Rick. That was good. Rick was a guy's guy. Rick was a married guy. And Rick was a married guy whom Chris always talked to. They had a connection, like brothers.

Relieved to realize that he wasn't alone on Mars while all the women sat on Venus, Chris eagerly sat forward, lowered the volume on his music, and plucked up his cordless phone. He punched out the number to his best buddy's personal line at work. Three rings, and then a pickup.

"Rick Hampton here."

Instantly relieved, Chris sat back in his chair. "Hey, what are you doing, man? This is Chris."

"Yo, buddy. How's it hanging?"

"Pretty good. You?"

"Can't complain. What's up?"

Now, see? Right to the point. What was so hard about conversation? Guys did it just fine with each other. No muss, no fuss. No subtitles or subtexts. No html code required. Just pure, clean communcation. "You had lunch with me three days ago at Faidley's."

"I certainly did. Wait. Three days ago? That was . . . ?"

"Tuesday."

"Right. Okay. I love Faidley's. What'd I have?"

"Son, you had crab cakes. What else?"

"My bad. Beers?"

"Three."

"Sounds about right. Who paid?"

"I treated."

"Yeah, it was your turn. So, who're we ducking here?"

"My mother."

"Good idea." Silence. Then, "Is that it?"

"Yes. No." Chris inhaled, exhaled, and then made it official by saying it out loud. "Tomorrow evening I'm asking Ronnie to marry me."

"Hey, another good idea. You using Popping the Question?"

"Yeah."

"Good people, huh?"

"The best."

"Dianna?"

"Yeah. She's setting it up."

"Where?"

"The Palm."

"Excellent. She's nice looking, huh?"

"Who?"

"Keep up, man. Dianna West."

"Oh. Yeah. Very."

"The secretary's scary."

"She's afraid of computers."

"No shit? Why?"

"Got fired because of them."

"It happens."

"Yeah. I'm going to try to get her over it."

"If anyone can, it's you. So, congratulations, man."

"For what?"

"Getting engaged."

"Oh. Right. Well, hold that thought until she says yes."

"She will. You and Ronnie are good together."

Chris hesitated, then said: "You really think so?"

"I do. But you'd better, too. Got to be sure here, Chris."

"I am. I'm sure. We're good. How's Joanna?"

"Steaming along. Got a big promotion at work."

"Hey, great. She deserves it."

"That's what I said."

"And your folks?"

"Off to Colorado."

"Why?"

"Buffalo season."

"Lying bastard."

"No, seriously. They got an RV and want that John Denver 'Rocky Mountain High' thing, I guess, who knows?"

"Damn. Old geezers lose their reflexes, their hearing, and their eyesight, *then* they buy a four-ton house-on-wheels."

"You got it. Stay off the highways, dude. So, we done here?"

"Yeah. I think so."

"Okay. Hey, let me know how the thing with Ronnie goes, all right?"

"Sure. You'll be the first person I call. Hey, be my best man?"

"You bet. I got your back. See ya."

"See ya. Thanks again."

"No problem-o. Bye."

"Bye."

Chris hung up at the same time as Rick did. See? Mission accomplished. Couldn't be easier. Why did women have to make everything so hard? And why, all of a sudden, did there have to be more than one of them complicating his life?

"So, are you nervous?"

Chris stood, tense and irritable, in the wonderfully intimate, wood-paneled, low-lit private dining room of the Palm restaurant on Saturday evening. "I think I'm going to throw up."

"That's normal, but try not to, okay?" Dianna was fluffing some exotic flower arrangement that sat atop the white-clothed, round dining table and not looking at him. Totally in work mode. "It would put a definite damper on the romantic atmosphere."

"No doubt." Chris could not stop himself from hungrily watching every movement of Dianna's about the room as she, apparently oblivious to the torture he was going through, now fussed with arranging and rearranging the as yet unlit candles placed to either side of the flowers.

Outside the closed French doors to the room, which were directly at his back, he could hear people laughing and talking and carrying on as if this were an ordinary night. It wasn't. And it was all Dianna's fault. "Who knew you'd be this damned efficient and could get everything set up so fast, Dianna?"

A candlestick in each hand, she finally looked his way, did a double take, and raised her eyebrows. "Chris, I can see the whites of your eyes. Now, come away from those doors. It's too late to bolt for freedom."

"I'll be the judge of that."

"No, seriously." She set the candles down, cocked her head to eye them critically, and added: "Roman could come through the doors at any moment with a full tray. You wouldn't want him to knock into you and fling food everywhere, would you?"

"No, but why would he have a tray? I haven't ordered anything yet. And whoever heard of a guy named Roman, anyway? What kind of a name is that for a waiter?"

Dianna again gave him her full attention. With an eyebrow raised and her lips pursed, she looked like a reproving elementary-school teacher. "Chris, I am going to cut you some slack, based on your nerves. But be nice. Roman is Eastern European, and he's very good at his job."

So why was she defending Roman? She should be on *his* side. "He may be, but I'll never know. I can't understand a word he says. I'll spend all evening saying 'What?' or order the trout and he hears lamb. I hate lamb. Who eats lambs anyway? That's sick."

Now Dianna sighed, sending him the same harassed-mother look his own mother had worn all his teenage years. "Chris, if you keep up in this vein, you're going to end up having to breathe into a paper bag."

Chris frowned his eyebrows down over his nose. "I wanted to go to the Brass Elephant. I like Italian."

"And I told you I checked and they were booked. Some big private party."

"So you just called here and they were available?"

She cocked a hip and clamped a hand to her waist. "Nothing is that easy. Lenny and Olivia were supposed to have this room tonight. But Olivia got a head cold and they had to cancel."

"Somehow I just knew this was all Lenny and Olivia's fault."

"Anyway," Dianna said pointedly, "I simply substituted you and Veronica."

"You're telling me that I have the same taste as Lenny Daschowitz?"

"No. Only the same room. Everything was upgraded

for you. And you will be fine because the people here are every bit as wonderful as their award-winning cuisine."

"You sound like a promotional brochure."

She narrowed her eyes at him. "You know what? Even if you can't, *I'm* going to stick to the point."

"Which is?" Chris suddenly had no idea why he was picking this fight with Dianna, but he couldn't seem to stop himself.

"Everyone here has worked very hard to pull this together and see that this evening goes well for you. Everyone."

Seeing the appeal in her eyes, and feeling its effect on his mood—could he *be* a bigger shit right now?—Chris relented. "I know they have, and you have. Look, I'm sorry, Dianna. I really am. I'm just saying this didn't have to take place this weekend. I needed time to get used to the idea, really. That's all I'm saying." He rubbed agitatedly at his forehead. "Hell, I should have just done something simple like pop the question at McDonald's."

Finally, a smile from Dianna. "Somehow, Chris, I don't see Veronica at McDonald's. Picture this: You give her the ring and the kid behind the counter asks her if she wants fries with that. Not a pretty picture."

"You got that right. But I'm just shook here. Needed more time."

"So you said. Only, I couldn't wait, Chris. I needed to do this now."

Something about the way she said that had Chris frowning. "Why?"

Dianna started to speak, closed her mouth, stared silently at him, and then looked down and away, fiddling with the tablecloth, straightening wrinkles that weren't there. "Because I have other clients to focus on. And because I want those computers," she said quietly.

"That's not what you were going to say." Even as he said it, Chris knew he shouldn't be prodding this conversation along—not here, and not tonight. But he couldn't seem to help himself. There was so much left unsaid between the two of them; so much that suddenly seemed urgent to say. "Come on, Dianna, talk to me."

She abandoned her fluffing of the table's accoutrements and faced him directly. "There's nothing to talk about. Look where you are and what you're getting ready to do. End of story."

"Maybe."

A look of disbelief had her raising her eyebrows. "Maybe?"

"Yeah. Maybe."

"Chris, the Mona Lisa is less enigmatic than you are right now."

"I don't know about enigmatic, but I am hungry. You want to cut for McDonald's with me? That sounded kind of good. I'm thinking a Big Mac."

Dianna pursed her lips. "I will personally kill you if you even think about leaving here right now. Look, you're just nervous. It's normal. Maybe you'd feel better if we did a run-through."

"A run-through?"

"A rehearsal of sorts. Do you have the ring?"

"The ring."

Apparently he hadn't exuded certainty with his response because Dianna crossed the small room with quick, stiff strides and clutched at his arm, turning imploring eyes up at him. "Tell me you have the ring."

"Okay. I have the ring. I do. I have it." She let go of him, and Chris patted himself down, now faking a panic. "Oh, shit. The ring." Dianna's expression fell. Laughing, Chris said, "Just kidding." He patted his chest, indicating the inside pocket of his suit coat. "Right here."

"Chris, that was not funny. If you had any idea how many times my clients have forgotten to bring the ring." Dianna consulted her watch, a slim, gold, feminine thing. A fleeting expression of pain, maybe, crossed her face and was gone. She looked at Chris. "Ten minutes before nine. Veronica should be here soon."

She said it like "my life will then be over." Or was he

imagining it? He didn't know. He couldn't sort the wheat from the chaff of other people's emotions tonight. Not with his own in such turmoil. In fact, right now his heart threatened to pound right out of his chest—just explode through his skin like that thing in *Alien* that got after Sigourney Weaver. "Did you have to tell me the time? I thought you were trying to calm me down, Dianna. Knowing that the moment is nearly at hand doesn't calm me down—"

"Chris." She clutched his arms and really gripped them tight. "Look at me. Breathe."

Hard to do, especially with her almost hugged up against him, but he tried. He did, nodding and indicating that he was better now. "All right. Under control here. It's all good. Besides, Ronnie won't be here on time. She's always late."

"Not a problem. We're not on anyone's time clock here. Well, I mean you do have to vacate at closing time."

"When's that?"

"Midnight."

"We won't be here that long."

"How can you be so sure?"

"Ronnie has an early day tomorrow. A law seminar."

Dianna looked totally appalled. "She's calling it an early night on the very evening you ask her to marry you?"

"It was already scheduled. But she doesn't know I'm going to ask her, remember. And, let's face it, she might say no. Like I said, an early night."

"Chris, every man I've ever represented has thought his girlfriend would say no." She sounded so downhearted. "Now, let's look at you." She eyed him critically, much as she had the room . . . so calm and collected . . . and then he saw her throat working and heard the hitch in her breathing. "So. You're fine. Wonderful, in fact. You look great."

"Thanks. But I hate wearing a suit. Against the techno-geek code."

Dianna raised her head until her gaze met his. She smiled, sort of a wounded-fawn smile. Chris clenched his hands into fists to keep from pulling her to him and holding her close and stroking her hair. It wasn't a lack of courage, he knew, that kept him from doing that very thing. Instead, it was the realization that tonight didn't belong to him and Dianna. It belonged to Ronnie. He owed her this moment. One entanglement with a female at a time. That was the rule. Chris fussed around in his new suit, tugging on the jacket, pulling at his tie. "Have I said yet that I hate wearing a suit?"

"Yes. And I said you look great in it." Her smile now was more a teasing, friendly one. But she quickly lowered her gaze away from his eyes and pointed to his chest. "I especially love this thin pinstripe. Very dashing."

"I hate it."

"You said that."

"Good. So what do I do now?"

"Well. Okay." She folded her hands together and looked around at all the arrangements. Then she focused on him. "Let's do a trial run. We'll get that big question and all the nerves that go with it out of the way."

"What question? What are you talking about?"

"Chris." Dianna turned her face up to him, her golden eyes liquid with meaning. "Popping the question. Asking the woman you love to marry you."

He nodded. "All right. Dianna, will you marry me?" The words were out even before he knew he was thinking them. What the hell was going on here?

Suddenly the air crackled with awareness and electricity. Staring into Dianna's surprise-rounded eyes, Chris felt the hairs on his arms stand up. He fully expected the crystal sconces hung on the walls to pop and shatter, so thick was the atmosphere with desire and anticipation as he held Dianna's gaze. His mouth dry, Chris swallowed, certain he could actually feel his blood coursing through his veins. "So, Dianna, what do you say? Will you marry me?"

He noticed that she had to inhale through her slightly opened mouth, a mouth he very much wanted to kiss. "That's not funny," she said. "You're here to ask Veronica. Not me."

Talk about bursting a balloon with a pin. Prick. Pop. The moment was over. The air cleared; Chris's blood cooled. "Right. I'm sorry, Dianna. I don't know what all that was about. I wasn't trying to be funny. It just . . . came out."

"It's okay. Really. No big deal." As if she were looking for something she'd mislaid in the room, she cut her gaze here and there. "Uh, why don't you go ahead and be seated? And I'll . . ." Her voice trailed off. She set herself in resolute motion, heading for the closed French doors to the room. "I'll just go have Roman bring you a drink. What would you like? I seem to remember rum and Coke."

"Dianna. Stop." He put a hand out to her, but of course she was already out of range. "Have a drink with me."

She turned to look back at him. Her expression said she'd closed herself off to him. "Sorry. I'm on the clock."

"But it's my clock. And I'm asking you to have a drink with me."

She tensed. "On second thought, maybe you shouldn't have a drink."

"On second thought, I think I need one. I'm about to pass out." He wasn't, but he thought it would get her attention.

It did. "Don't you even think about it, mister." She stalked back over to him and clasped his arm. "Think good, positive thoughts."

Now he had her where he wanted her—in front of him and touching him. "You mean like Veronica saying yes?"

Something indefinable flickered in Dianna's eyes, darkening them. "Okay."

Damn her. She wasn't going to allow this thing between them. But what the hell did he expect her to do? As she'd just said, he was here to ask Veronica to marry him. So what did he expect Dianna to do? Orchestrate some big emotional end-of-the-movie scene where she confessed her love for him and he ran away with her? Hardly. "So," he began, mad for some reason he didn't want to explore, couldn't afford to explore. "Thinking good thoughts. Veronica saying yes. Visualizing it. Seeing it happen."

"You're not taking this seriously, Chris."

"Believe me, I am. Very seriously."

Nodding, acting as if she didn't want to be in his way, Dianna stepped back, away from him, and crossed her arms under her breasts. She looked great, Chris decided, standing there in a sleeveless slim black dress that ended above her knees. She'd pinned her dark hair up off her neck. Very Audrey Hepburn slender and graceful.

*Warning: I can't keep doing this.* Knowing the truth of that, and going for light banter, Chris wagged a finger up and down Dianna's figure. "So, is this your disguise? It's not very good, if it is. I'd certainly notice you. In fact, I already have."

"That's because I'm standing in front of you. And it's not a disguise. I never said I'd be in a disguise."

"Veronica will notice you."

"Only if I'm standing here in this room with the two of you. Which I most definitely won't be doing."

"Why not? You could hide behind that big fake potted palm over there." He pointed to one in a corner of the room.

Dianna's gaze followed his pointing finger. "A great idea. Why didn't I think of that?"

He was doing it again, admiring her profile, watching her, wanting her and wanting to say *Stop this speeding, out-of-control train.* "Dianna," Chris heard himself say. She met his gaze. "Veronica is due here at any minute. Tell me, if she came through that door right now and saw us like this, what could we say was going on?"

Shaking her head, Dianna opened her mouth to speak, but then closed it. Blinking, looking somehow emotional, she stared up at him, her eyes rounded gold disks, like molten precious metal. "I don't know."

Though he knew all the reasons why not, why he shouldn't, Chris suddenly felt he had to push her, had to get a response from her. It was that important. "Okay, you don't know. Well, here's something else, Dianna. What if she does say no? What would that mean for you and me?"

She looked genuinely perplexed by that. Not a good sign. As if she'd never even considered them a him and a her. "Me and you? There is no me and you, Chris. This is about business. You're my client. That's all there is to it."

Despite her denial, which he didn't believe, Chris was on fire, full of that passion he kept saying he didn't feel. "Do you really believe that, Dianna? That's all there is between us—a professional relationship? And that's it?"

"I don't know." She'd raised her voice and looked scared or uncertain. "Why are you doing this, Chris? Why now? Why tonight?"

"Because after tonight, it can't be said, Dianna. It's now or never."

She hugged herself, sending him a beseeching look that made him feel like a jerk for taking this tack. "Veronica is not going to turn you down, Chris. I can't imagine *any* woman turning you down."

"Thanks. Yet, she very well could."

"So, is this a pride thing? If it is, I'll be so disappointed in you."

"It's not pride. I'm just being realistic."

"About what? Trying to steel your heart against the possibility of her saying no? Is that it?"

Chris shrugged. "Not as much as you'd think."

"Because if it is, I see this all the time."

"You're not listening to me, Dianna. And, no, not this you don't."

Frowning, Dianna studied his face. "You're serious, aren't you? Okay, then tell me how what you're feeling is different."

"Here's the thing, and it's hard for me to admit. See, I just don't know"—*since I met you*—"if I'm hoping more for a yes or a no from her tonight. I don't know which one will upset me more."

Dianna's eyebrows arched upward. "Oh, Chris, then what are we doing here? Why did you have me set this up?" She shook a finger at him. "And before you think of it, let me say up front that my concern here has nothing to do with money or keeping my business's one-hundred-percent track record intact."

"I knew that, Dianna." No sense kidding himself. He wanted to hear her say she was concerned about him.

Dianna roved her gaze over his face. "My concern here is totally for you. And quit smiling like that. Just let me point one thing out to you: If you're not sure of Veronica's feelings for you, or your feelings for her, all you have to do, Chris, is not ask her tonight."

"What, and chicken out?" Go back to the way he and Ronnie had been before he got this crazy idea to ask her to marry him? Go back to the uncertainty and the vague dissatisfaction? Have nothing reconciled? Then throw in what he felt, could feel, or thought he might feel, for Dianna? No, thanks. "Major ulcer" was written all over that. "And put myself through this again at some later date? No."

"I swear, you are such a guy, Chris." She didn't mean it in a nice way. "This—tonight, here, all of this—is the rest of your life. It's not about chickening out. It's about, well, love. And getting it right. The face on the pillow next to yours every morning. The important stuff."

"I know all that, believe me. Why do you think I'm acting like a jackass? I have no clue if I'm doing the right thing. I thought I knew. But now I don't and I think I'll take that drink now."

"What?" He'd caught her off guard. "Oh. The drink. All right. I'll go get it and bring it to you." Dianna made as if to hurry off again.

"No." This time Chris succeeded in snagging her before she got away. Her bare arm felt warm and firm in his grip. He turned her to face him, clasping her now by both arms. "I want to go to the bar, and I want *you* to have a drink with me."

"We've been over this, Chris. I can't. I have to go check on . . . things."

"There are no things left to check on. We both know that."

She stood quietly in front of him and lowered her gaze to about the level of his tie tack. But she didn't pull away. Their pose could only be called intimate. He wanted nothing more than to lean down and kiss her forehead right at her hairline. It looked so tantalizingly sweet and innocent—

With a bang, the double French doors to the room suddenly opened inward. Everything happened at once. Chris's breath caught, Dianna gasped, he let go of her, and they both turned to see—

Roman the European standing there. If he'd noticed anything untoward about their intimate pose and guilty breaking apart, he gave no hint of it. He did, though, speak in heavily accented English, looking from Dianna to Chris and back as he spouted an entire paragraph of words that Chris stood no chance of fathoming. Then Dianna said, "Okay. Thank you," and Roman nodded and bowed and backed out of the private dining room, closing the doors after him.

Alone again with Dianna, Chris looked to her. "What the hell did he say?"

Her expression unreadable, Dianna fisted her hands at her hips and stared up at Chris. "Oh, he said a lot, but the bottom line is we have a little more time than we thought." Dianna smiled up at him. "So, sailor, wanna buy me a drink in the bar?"

# CHAPTER 11

Dianna stirred what was left of her rum and Coke and looked over at Chris. He sat next to her on a bar stool pulled up to the long, polished wood bar. People were everywhere. Crowding, jostling. Cheerful. It was, after all, a beautiful spring Saturday night. She and Chris had been lucky to find two seats together. Well, "found" wasn't the right word. Holding firmly on to her arm, Chris had muscled them in when a couple they were standing behind had been called to their table. And now he and she sat very close. It was the only way to hear each other.

"So, Chris, tell me this," she said, striving for conversational and girl-pal when all her nasty-girl hormones wanted to do was take a big bite out of him, he was so close and smelled so good. "What *did* you say to Veronica about tonight? I mean, here you are all dressed up. She'll notice that. And this *is* the Palm. That has 'special occasion' written all over it."

Chris hoisted his own rum and Coke, finished it off, and then sort of chuckled and grunted. "I told her we needed to play dress-up because I had good news to share with her."

Dianna nodded. "Appropriately vague. That was good. So you'll tell her the good news was her saying yes to your proposal?"

"Maybe. We may never know."

"Oh, I think we will." Dianna couldn't believe how tight her facial muscles felt around her smile. Could she be any more conflicted? On the one hand, the guy was her client and needed a bit of bolstering right now. But on the other, he felt like so much more than a client and she really didn't like priming him for Veronica—or any other woman, she felt certain.

"She might not show at all." Chris took a long pull on his drink and glanced toward the entrance to the bar.

Poor guy. Dianna gently gripped his arm, intending a show of support and reassurance. "She'll show up, Chris."

He turned to her, slowly raking his smoldering dark-eyed gaze up and down her body. "What if I don't care if she does or not?"

"Don't say things like that." Dianna withdrew her hand and swallowed, feeling a need to moisten her lips with the tip of her tongue. She could feel a gently pulsing throb at the base of her throat that told her she wanted this man, and she wanted him bad.

"Why not?"

"Because there's no reason for us—especially you—to be here if you truly feel that way." Dianna leaned in toward him, filling her vision with the planes and angles of his handsome face. "Do you? And I mean *really,* not just a guy thing because she's late. Remember, she did call."

Chris chuckled. "So what are you—her agent?"

"No, but I sound like one, don't I?" Dianna sat back. "I guess I just want to be certain you're all right. I worry."

"You sound like my mother."

"Sorry. That can't be fun for you. But how is she? Does she still think I'm a hooker?"

Chris raised his drink to his lips and, looking at her over the rim of the glass, took a big swallow. "It's come up."

"Great." Dianna waited, giving him an expectant look, but Chris didn't take the bait. Instead, he watched her watching him, essentially. She couldn't look away, couldn't think of a word to say. He didn't seem prone to conversation, either. She had no idea what he could be thinking right now. None.

But, beyond that, how could this be so intimate in such a crowded, noisy bar? People reaching around them, calling out their drink orders, crowding up against their backs, talking too loud, glasses clinking, money exchanging hands. And yet, the people and the noise around them existed only as backdrop to the sensual web that she and Chris were weaving between them as his gaze held hers riveted to his face.

Dianna noted the small details about him. The way his hair fell neatly over his forehead. The squareness of his jaw. Those high cheekbones. The fine wings of his eyebrows and the deep set of his dark eyes. She knew better than to allow this to draw out upon itself. But she couldn't seem to stop. Still, she had only two words for herself: Melanie. Dr. Yakahama. Look what had happened there— they'd gone all the way in the big dentist's chair in the museum. *But the sign had said "interactive,"* Melanie had wailed.

Just then, Chris blinked and straightened up on his bar stool. "I think I've been stood up."

Brought rudely back to the moment by his abrupt movement, Dianna made a show of checking her watch. "Not yet. Veronica told you she'd be thirty minutes late. It hasn't been thirty minutes."

"It's been longer than that. And no, she didn't tell me. She told Roman she'd be thirty minutes late. She didn't ask to talk to me."

He didn't sound hurt or whiny. He sounded mad. Dianna exhaled a sigh for having to continue to be Veronica's advocate, when in reality she wanted to take the woman's man from her and never let him out of her sight. "But it's still the same thing."

"Right. The seminar, Dianna, was supposed to be over at seven. It's now nine-thirty and no Veronica."

"Now, Chris, you heard Roman as well as I did. Veronica said the seminar was running late and they were on a break and she had to go right back in. And surely she had to go home after that and change clothes, Chris. Maybe she got a run in her nylons and didn't have another pair and had to go buy some and—"

"You women really stick together, don't you?"

He didn't look happy about that, either. Maybe he wanted her to be on his side. Dianna sobered appropriately. "All right. So, what are you implying, Chris? Do you think she's, what, seeing someone else?"

He shrugged his shoulders, smiling at her as if he were trying to convince himself he didn't care if she was. "I don't know. Could be. How would I know?"

Dianna shrugged. "There'd be signs, right? Not like big, printed ones, or billboards or anything . . . although those would be helpful. But, still, signs."

Chris nodded. "Probably. What do you think they'd be, those signs? That she'd break dates? Maybe show up late? Always be distracted or start fights? Not want to stay over? No interest in the, uh, bedroom, to put it delicately?"

Dianna felt the embarrassed heat traveling up from her neck to her face and called herself grateful for the bar's low lighting. "Those would all work."

He nodded. "Yes, they would. And they do."

Uh-oh. Dianna sniffed, more of a delaying tactic than anything else, and toyed with the glass tumbler that held her drink. "I'm guessing that list wasn't just off the top of your head."

"Good guess. You're right. It wasn't."

As much as she wanted a chance with this man, she didn't want it this way. By default or on the rebound. She felt pretty good about herself to realize that, though he was perfect for her in every way, it was still more important to her that he be happy than that he be with her. *God, I'm the noble heroine again.* Dianna swung her gaze to Chris's face and looked into his eyes. She saw a challenge there. And hurt and disappointment. The man needed handling with emotional kid gloves. Dammit. Given the way she felt about him, or could come to feel about him, she was not the woman to do that. But then again, it was her job.

So, taking that stupid bull by the horns, Dianna sat up perky and chirpy. "All right, what we're going to do here, Chris, is not jump to conclusions, okay? We're going to give Veronica the benefit of the doubt. We're going to go with the nylon thing and keep in mind that she doesn't know that tonight is special. She could be telling the truth. The seminar ran late. It happens. Come on, I bet that years from now you'll both laugh about this, about how it almost didn't come off."

"Yeah. Ha-ha."

How was this for irony? Here she was, trying to cheer up a guy whose proposal effort had hit a snag—a guy she no more wanted engaged than she did the man in the moon. And here she was defending a woman she didn't even like and didn't want engaged to this guy who was sitting next to her and was upset because his girlfriend was late, when less than an hour ago he hadn't even been certain he wanted to ask her, or if he wanted her to say yes if he did.

*Hello. The definition of "conflicted."* Dianna took a big, fat swig of the hard liquor in front of her. It burned all the way down her throat. Whew. This stuff was a lot stiffer than she was used to drinking. But it sure did taste good. "So, Chris," she began again. "Are you going to go down on one knee when you ask Veronica to marry you?"

"If I ask her. And if the down-on-one-knee mood strikes me."

"It will, and you will. It really is more romantic."

"Tell that to Lenny."

"Touché. But just because it didn't work for him doesn't mean it won't work for you."

Chris shook his head. "You know, on second thought, I don't see me down on one knee. Too *Romeo and Juliet.* Too hearts and flowers. Veronica would probably laugh her head off. So, no, I won't go down on one knee."

Dianna gripped his arm, feeling the fine fabric of his suit under her fingers. "All right, Chris, this is not my business, what I'm about to say. But I'm going to take a big chance and just say it."

"Go ahead. I'm listening."

Dianna inhaled deeply and exhaled slowly. "You don't seem even to *like* Veronica. When you talk about her, you seem only to resent her."

Chris stared at her. Didn't say a word. Just stared at her. Feeling like a tiny cocktail sausage that had been found floating in the big punch bowl, Dianna pulled her hand back to her lap. "My two cents. And if there was a big, invisible line here I shouldn't have stepped over, then you'll have to tell me."

Chris shook his head. "No. That's okay. Really. You just stopped me because I had no idea I came across like that. Or that she did, I guess. Or we did." He frowned his concern. "So I sound like I resent her? That's an interesting choice of words."

Dianna's stomach started to hurt. "Maybe it's too strong a word. I'm sure she's a very nice woman."

"Come on, don't back off now. Give me an example."

"No. I can't. I don't want to. I don't know one."

He chuckled. "Sure you do. And I'm not mad. Seriously."

"You are. You're mad, and I'm so sorry." She held up her rum and Coke. "It's this drink. I told you I wasn't used to such strong liquor."

"It's not that strong. Just tell me what you meant a minute ago when you said I seem as if I don't like Veronica. Obviously I said something to make you think that. What was it?"

Well, she had been the one to start them down this road. "All right," Dianna announced. "For one thing, she doesn't sound like a nice person, even though I just said she did. I mean, the things you say about her when you're telling me how she might respond or what she might say.

Things like that. That she'd laugh at you when you're proposing to her. That's not nice. It's cruel. See? She just sounds, well, mean. And I'm fired, aren't I?"

Chris grinned and shook his head. "No, you're not. And you're also right. I used to call it her sense of humor, but she is sharp and cutting sometimes. But then, who isn't?"

"I'm not." The words were out before she knew she was going to say them. Her eyes wide, Dianna picked up her drink again. "I tell you, it's the liquor talking."

Chris gently took the glass tumbler from her and set it on the bar. "Maybe these *are* too strong for you. You ought to go easy since you've got to drive yourself home."

"So do you."

"Not me. I've got a limousine waiting tonight, remember?"

"Oh, yes. You're proposing. From your chair. Not down on one knee."

"You sound disappointed."

She shrugged. "Well, it's your proposal. Not mine, or how I'd want mine."

"Really?" He sat up straighter, suggesting she'd piqued his interest. "So, what about you? Would you go down on one knee?"

"I hadn't really thought about it. That's the guy's place."

He chuckled. "Boy, some things just never change, do they? But, come on, you've thought about it a lot. You have to have. It's what you do."

Dianna grinned broadly. "Okay, I have."

Laughing, giving her a mock jab to the shoulder—a tender, gentle one, for which he deserved points—Chris teased, "I knew it. Tell me."

Suddenly Dianna felt shy and overly warm in a way that had nothing to do with the liquor flowing through her veins or the press of bodies around them. This was Chris and this conversation was exciting. No one had ever asked her before what she dreamed of or how she saw it happening for her. She thought back to that night in Chris's penthouse and how she'd envisioned him proposing to her in that seductively romantic setting. Well, she could hardly tell him that, now could she? No. What she needed was a smokescreen.

That decided, Dianna sat up and fisted her hands together, resting them in her lap. "So. Me. Okay. If I was the one asking, I'd go down on one knee . . . if the guy was right."

"If the guy was right?" Chris grinned at her, roving his gaze over her face and then her figure. "Tell me about the right guy for you. What's he like?"

Maybe it was the rum and Coke; maybe it was Saturday night fever; or maybe it was having Chris all to herself again, much like she had at his penthouse, but whatever it was, Dianna went into vamp mode and boldly looked him up and down. "My ideal guy would have to be tall, dark, and handsome."

With dancing lights in his dark eyes, Chris grinned. "With you so far. *I'm* tall, dark, and handsome."

"Are you? I hadn't noticed." She'd managed to say that with a straight face before going on to describe him to himself. "Anyway, he'd also be filthy rich. That's a must."

Chris nodded. "Agreed. I am, of course, filthy rich."

"So you keep saying." She ducked her head regally. "We'll see when you get the bill, Mr. Adams. But, anyway, we're not talking about you. So, he'd also have to own a penthouse."

"Check. Goes without saying."

"And be older than me."

"A must. Could he be, say, twenty-eight?"

She knew from the forms he'd filled out that Chris was twenty-eight, but she pretended to consider that. "Hmm." Then she promptly and pompously rejected it. "Only two years older than me? No. That's not good."

"Well, what do you want—someone's grandpa?"

"If he has all of the above, sure."

Chris shook his head. "Women. So fickle. Okay, go on."

"Thank you. Let's see. Oh, he'd have to have a good sense of humor."

"I have a good sense of humor."

"And I keep telling you that you're not applying for the position, Mr. Adams." Still, she leaned in toward him now, propping an elbow on the bar and looking right into his eyes. Who was this sexy, flirty woman? a part of her mind that hadn't drunk the rum and Coke wanted to know. "However, in all fairness to you, and keeping an open mind here, tell me a joke."

"Okay. Let me think." He did, frowning and working his mouth. Then he brightened again. "Got it. Well, it's not a joke. It's more of a limerick."

Dianna popped out of vamp mode, clapping her hand against his mouth. "No. Don't you dare, Chris Adams. Never mind. I will take your word for the sense of humor."

Laughing under her hand, Chris kissed her palm. The surprise and shock of it dazed Dianna. He pulled her hand away, only to hold on to it. "But I want to tell you. It's a classic. Here we go." He cleared his throat and proceeded loudly. "There once was a girl from Nantucket—"

"No!" Laughing, shrieking, embarrassed, Dianna clapped her free hand over Chris's mouth. "Don't you even think about finishing that."

Chris grabbed her other hand away from his mouth. And again he held on to it. Now they were holding hands and facing each other and staring into each other's eyes. Quietly, totally, raptly. Absorbed in each other—

"Am I interrupting something? Or can anyone join this barroom game of pat-a-cake?"

Talk about flash-frozen while melting at the same time. Moving only her eyes, sliding them to the right and relying on peripheral vision, Dianna suffered a just-shoot-me-now moment. No last cigarette or blindfold necessary. Just ready, aim, fire. It would be a mercy because . . .

Oh, yes. Veronica Alexander, blond attorney dressed in a slinky black cocktail dress, and smiling like a pit viper, now stood in the space between the two bar stools occupied by Chris and Dianna. She divided her gaze between Chris, the man with whom she enjoyed a committed relationship, and his . . . Dianna cringed . . . friend who just happened to be a girl, maybe? Apparently knowing she owned this moment, the attorney turned first to Chris, lightly kissing his cheek. "Hi, honey, sorry I'm late. I tore my nylons."

A functioning part of Dianna's mind brayed triumphantly: *Now, what did I say not ten minutes ago?*

And Chris, Mr. Suave and Debonair, acting as if he weren't still holding Dianna's hands and hadn't just been caught dallying red-handed—*ha-ha!* Dianna feared she was going to lose it—said testily, "Late, Ronnie? You're not just late. You were supposed to be here over an hour ago."

The prosecuting attorney for the state was unmoved. "I told you. Unavoidable."

Then, her eyes glittering, her teeth bared in a deadly smile, she rounded on Dianna. "Hello."

"Hello. And this isn't what you think."

"Don't tell me what I think."

"And yet, it really isn't. In fact, you're going to laugh when you find out."

"Am I?" She half-turned to Chris, somehow not breaking eye contact with Dianna, either. "Introduce me to your little friend, Chris. I think it's time we met, don't you? And I'll assume she's not the good news you told me you had for me, because you, of all people, would know I wouldn't want a woman of my own. And I don't do threesomes."

Dianna felt herself shrinking. Oh, there was no way this was going to end without bloodshed.

"Knock it off, Ronnie. I mean it. It's like she said: You don't know what's going on here."

"Then tell me what is, Chris. I come in to find you

sitting here at the bar and laughing and having a great time with this woman. And you're holding her hands."

*Yikes.* Dianna tugged fiercely against Chris's grip on her. He let go of her and Dianna dropped her guilt-ridden hands to her lap. "So, Chris, you know what? She's got a point here. Why don't you just introduce us?"

Chris raised his eyebrows. "You sure?"

Dianna nodded over and over. "Under the circumstances, Chris, and with everything else that is supposed to transpire this evening, yes, I'm sure."

"Yeah, I guess you're right." But first he stood and drew some folded money out of his pants pocket and signaled to the bartender, instantly getting the man's attention. "The tab, please. Need to settle up." Then he turned to the waiting women. "Dianna West, I'd like you to meet Veronica Alexander. Veronica, Dianna."

"Dianna West?" The attorney flared up at Chris like the hideous dragon queen/stepmother in *Snow White.* All scary green scales and red eyes and slashing tail now, she pointed at Dianna. "*This* is Dianna West? The *prostitute* you and your mother were talking about the other night?"

Heads turned, conversations stopped, the bartender fled after taking Chris's money.

And Dianna's heart all but flew out of her mouth. "I'm *not* a prostitute, and I also told his mother I'm not—"

"Knock it off, Ronnie. Right now." Chris's angry frown rivaled that of any self-respecting bulldog. "I told you she's not a prostitute."

Dianna yelped. "Hey, could we say 'prostitute' more, please? And louder? I don't think the people in that back corner over there heard you."

Both Veronica and Chris ignored her, continuing their argument unabated.

"Oh, she isn't a prostitute?" Veronica challenged, searching Chris's face. Dianna did, too. The man was implacable. Gave nothing away. So the attorney turned to Dianna and held a pale, slim, long-fingered, French-manicured hand out to her. "At long last we meet. How do you do?"

Dianna stared at the woman's hand and fought a whimper. Surely it would be cold and reptilian. But there wasn't a thing she could do except clasp the other woman's hand—warm, dry, soft—and mind her manners. "Nice to meet you."

"Oh, do you really think so?" She was smiling and so chatty.

"No. Probably not." Eeyore, that sad little blue donkey in the Winnie-the-Pooh books, could not have sounded more desultory. "In fact," Dianna added, "I suspect you're going to make my life a living hell before this is all over, aren't you?"

"Oh, yes," Veronica Alexander assured her, still smiling brightly. "You can count on that, Miss West. And to prove it, let's start now. If you're not a prostitute, then what are you?"

Dianna opened her mouth to tell the blond woman exactly who the hell she was, by God, but Chris chose right then to intervene. He gripped Veronica Alexander's arm, much as he had Dianna's when he'd escorted her into the bar, and pulled her to his side. The attorney's eyes flashed but before she could say or do anything, Chris addressed Dianna. "If you'll excuse us?"

Pretty damned hot under the collar now, Dianna nodded regally. "Of course. Please. Go. Enjoy your evening." And because she felt diminished sitting there, and also because she couldn't resist, and because she knew it was innocent—though it certainly wouldn't sound so right now—Dianna added, "Call me when you get home, Chris. I'll be waiting with bated breath to hear how this turns out." She winked at him. "Oh, and I'll send you my bill for services rendered."

Chris rolled his eyes, as in "I'm a dead man," and tugged his hissing girlfriend along behind him as he threaded their way through the crowd, which finally closed around them and hid them from Dianna's sight.

She sat there. Conspicuously alone. Well, now what? What was she supposed to do? Hang around? Wait for some big, fun moment when Veronica came gliding back in with Chris's ring on her finger and hugged her and told her how wrong she'd been and, oh, how wonderful all this was? Of course, that was what she was supposed to do: wait here for that moment. But . . .

*Barf. I don't think so.* Dianna looked around her and accidentally made eye contact with a couple of guys standing close by who were staring speculatively at her. She sized them up . . . your basic slick and polished little yuppie types . . . and glared at them. "What the hell are *you* looking at? Like you've never seen a prostitute before."

It was the end of a busy Monday at Popping the Question and Dianna found herself the sole focus of Paula's wildly agog attention. Her employee sat with her arms crossed and a hip perched atop Dianna's desk. "Don't tell me you said that to those yuppies about being a prostitute, Dianna. I *know* you didn't."

Dianna grinned evilly. "And yet I did."

Staring bright-eyed at Dianna over the top of her blue glasses, Paula said, "Pretty damn cool, boss lady. I didn't know you had it in you."

High praise, indeed, coming from their resident high priestess of cool. Feeling pretty good about herself, Dianna shrugged. "They deserved it. They were staring."

"Hope they don't see all the press coverage next month and the *People* thing. They'll go around telling everyone you're a hooker."

Dianna cringed. "Yikes. I didn't think about that."

"No. You wouldn't. So what'd they do? The yuppie snots, I mean."

"I don't know. Ran home to mama, I guess. Anyway, they left me alone."

"Well, I guess they did. And our Mr. Adams and his paramour?"

Dianna lowered her gaze and contemplated her blotter. "I don't know. Never heard from him."

"But I thought you were going to hang out until the deed was done."

Dianna looked up, meeting Paula's very direct gaze. "I was supposed to, but I just couldn't."

Paula eyed Dianna speculatively. "Why not?"

Totally self-conscious now, Dianna chuckled. "Please don't be shy, Paula. Just ask away."

"Okay. Again, why didn't you stay? Come on, talk to me. Are you maybe feeling something more than you should, boss lady? It happens."

Dianna frowned at her employee. "Of course not, don't be ridiculous. He's just another client." *All right, deep breath. Enough protesting. Giving yourself away.* "Anyway, I left because there was really no place for me to hang out, and everyone was staring. Remember, they thought I was a hooker."

"Not everyone. The people who work there know who you really are."

"True. But why's this so important to you?"

"Because I think you care about this guy."

Dianna's yelped response was immediate. "I do not. At least, not any more than I do any other client. I care only that he has a happy outcome."

"Right. He's just another client. Then why's your face so red, huh?" Paula's expression mingled amusement and concern, but she didn't wait for Dianna to answer. "So, Mr. Razzle-Dazzle got to you. Interesting. But more to the point, chief, you still don't know if he popped the question and got a yes or a no."

Dianna had recovered enough to be droll. "Your point being, Paula?"

"Our track record. It's at stake here. 'We're number one,' and all that."

"Yes, I know. And I'm not worried." Dianna firmly clasped her hands together atop her desk to prove it. "He'll call."

"Maybe they're still holed up somewhere and, you know, celebrating."

Dianna refused to allow that image to take hold in her mind's eye. Too . . . hurtful, somehow. "I doubt it," she said, struggling for neutrality in her voice. "Chris's girlfriend is a prosecuting attorney. She's at work, trust me."

"So, you don't like her much, do you?"

Sudden impatience with Paula's too, too pointed questions—questions that cut too damn close to the bone today—seized Dianna. "You know what, Paula? Don't you have something else you need to be doing?"

Unfazed, her redheaded employee who viewed the world through a filter of amused and detached cynicism shook her head no. "Uh-uh. I'm done for the day. Well, except for messing with your head."

Despite herself, Dianna chuckled at the woman's benign brashness. "Great. Then how about if I call it done and say we're through here?"

"Suit yourself. But come on, you know you can talk to me. I'm all discretion. And I *do* have more than a paycheck here at P the Q that I care about, you know, boss-lady dearest."

Touched, Dianna realized this was as close as Paula would probably ever come to saying she actually cared. In light of Paula's bending, Dianna decided she could do the same. Besides, she really could use another perspective on this Chris Adams issue. "All right, Paula. Let's talk."

"Yes! I won!" Paula fisted her hand triumphantly and settled herself more securely onto her precarious perch. "I am all ears, my friend. Dish at will."

"Okay. So the whole thing was just this huge bust."

Paula nodded sagely. "That's because it was tainted with Lenny. That was his restaurant, his private room, yada-yada."

"I know. I wanted quick, and that was quick. I won't make that mistake again. Not with Lenny, either. For his and Olivia's next time, I'm sending them out to Fort Mc-Henry."

"Ah. Rockets' red glare and all that. Hey, the fort survived a whole war and, now, tourists. Lenny probably can't hurt much that's out there."

"Or get hurt." Then Dianna heard herself blurt her uppermost fear: "Is it just me, Paula, or is everything suddenly falling apart? I mean businesswise."

"It's just you. You're being tested. The annoying gods have found you and are just messing with your head."

"Well, great. How long does that go on, do you suppose?"

Paula shrugged her narrow shoulders, which were covered with a black lace shawl over a white peasant blouse. "Until they get bored or you give up. So, what are you going to do about Melanie and her dentist?"

That was abrupt—and probably the real reason Paula was in here. Dianna scratched at her forehead, as though her gesture would bring an answer to the fore. "I don't know. This is really hard. I told her I'd talk to her tomorrow. I've always said that doing what she did would be grounds for instant dismissal."

Paula nodded. "Understood. Protecting your business's rep and the fear of all the legal shit that could come down if the tooth fairy's girlfriend sues us. The accusation of fraud. Et cetera. I get all that. And yet? There's more, right?"

"Isn't there always? I don't know, Paula, this is a real mess. Adult stuff." Dianna slumped dejectedly. "I'm the boss here and I have a clearly stated policy, but I just can't bring myself to fire her. And I shouldn't even be sharing this with you, either."

"Hey, it's cool. We all know what's up. But, anyway, your problem is you're too nice. No killer instinct."

"Oh, and what about you? Could you fire Melanie?"

Paula picked up and fiddled with a pen. "I'm not the boss."

"If you were."

She met Dianna's waiting gaze. "No. I wouldn't."

"Why not?"

"You looking for reasons not to?"

"Yes."

Paula grinned. "Okay. I wouldn't fire her because she could never get another job anywhere and so she'd starve to death and then you'd burn in hell for that."

That left Dianna blinking. "Succinct, as always—and definitely something to look forward to. But you're wrong. Melanie wouldn't starve. She doesn't really need to work. She has more money than God."

Paula frowned. "God has money?"

"Focus, Paula."

"Okay. You're telling me that Melanie is a rich bitch?"

"Well, rich, yes. Bitch, no."

"So, why's she work if she's loaded?"

"It's probably the only thing that keeps her family from committing her. And, too, everybody has to be somewhere."

"True. She never told me she has all this money."

"Gee, I wonder why." Dianna's tone blended humor and sarcasm, which was, as always, lost on Paula.

"Beats me," she said sincerely. "It's not like I'd take advantage of her. So, it's like, what, family money or something?"

"Of course. Where would Melanie get money on her own? And it's very old family money." Dianna was silent a moment, considering Paula. "And now that you know?"

Paula tossed the pen back on Dianna's desk and stood up. "Hey, I've got to protect that girl from herself and other people who might try to rook her out of her vast wealth. So me and Mel are now new best friends."

"No, Paula. Down, girl. Sit."

Too late. Paula was already leaving Dianna's office as she called out: "Hey, Mel, wait for me, girlfriend! I know just the thing to cheer you up—a big shopping spree." She was now out in the hallway. "We'll start at Towson Town Center, where I saw this totally killer sweater I've been dying to have. Get your reticule. I'm driving."

Dianna cupped her face in her hands. "Forgive me. I have just done a very bad thing." But she'd had to for her own survival. Paula was like a terrier—a very smart one, too—when she got on the scent of something. And the last thing Dianna needed was for her to nose around her feelings for Chris, which were pretty raw right now.

Dianna leaned her head back against her chair's padded head cushion and stared at the light fixture overhead. So Chris was—most likely—engaged now. Consequently, whatever she felt for him was now totally irrelevant. Time to send him a bill. He was no longer one of the fishes in the sea. Instead, the man had been caught up in the marital net, gutted, cut up, and canned, like so much tuna.

Dianna abruptly sat forward, making a face at her comparison. "Gross. Where did all that come from?"

Just then, Mrs. Windhorst stepped into the doorway of Dianna's office. "Line two, Miss West. It's Dr. Yakahama."

Her secretary's voice radiated censure and disapproval and all things negative. Dianna's stomach muscles contracted. "Melanie's dentist?"

"In a manner of speaking, yes."

Dianna eyed the guiltily blinking line two. Just the man she wanted to talk to. How dare he compromise one of her employees—a woman she thought of as a friend? And how dare he compromise Popping the Question? Wait. There was more: How dare he cause her to realize just how close she'd come to doing the same thing with Chris Adams? Dianna looked up at Mrs. Windhorst. "Is Melanie still here? Perhaps she should be here for this."

"No, I'm afraid she isn't. Miss O'Hara and her reticule have already been dragged out the door by Ms. Capland."

"Well, at least they're out doing their part to help the economy. Thanks, Mrs. Windhorst. Why don't you go ahead and leave? I'll take care of this and then lock up."

"Yes, ma'am." But she didn't leave. And she didn't look happy.

Dianna got that sinking feeling in her stomach. "What is it, Mrs. Windhorst? Are you all right?"

"No." A sudden high color stained the older woman's face and neck and she looked as if she were about to cry.

Dianna could only stare at her secretary of the bouffant hairdo and paisley shirtwaist dresses and wonder if Paula was right about the annoying gods. Because surely today was some cosmic joke wherein the wheels came off her life. Dianna slowly came to her feet. "What's wrong? Did something happen?"

"Yes. And I'm afraid I must give you my two-week notice."

"Two-week notice?" Dianna stiffened her knees against the shock. "Tell me we're talking about your vacation time."

"I'm afraid not. I mean . . . I'm quitting." The woman adopted an heroic pose of the injured worker. She could have been cast in bronze. "Once again I find I'm being forced out by computers."

A hot and cold weakness turned Dianna's bones to water. Computers, huh? That could only mean one person (Chris) and one thing (he was engaged now, and so could start on the computer thing for her office). And yet, this wasn't how it was supposed to happen. Dianna tented her fingers atop her desk and leaned her weight into them. "Computers?" Could her voice be higher or sound more guilty? She cleared her throat and tried again. "Why, whatever do you mean?"

"I think you know, Miss West. Please do not further offend me by pretending you don't."

That stung. "Yet I would like you to clarify."

"If you wish. Mr. Christopher Adams called me today, and we had quite the conversation."

# CHAPTER 12

Madder than she'd ever been in her entire life and hating Mondays with a passion, with a vengeance, Dianna drove furiously, madly, recklessly, across Baltimore. She had it all worked out. Once she got to Chris Adams's penthouse, she would calmly ask the security guy to ring Chris and then he'd tell her to go on up and she would, and then Chris would let her in—and then she would kill him. It was as simple as that. Maybe she'd drown him in his marine tank. Or throw him off his own balcony. Or hit him repeatedly over the head with one of those especially fine pieces of sculpture he had sitting around the place.

And then, following that, she would be prosecuted by the late Chris Adams's girlfriend—whoops. Sorry. His bereaved fiancée. Whatever. And then, after a fair trial, she would spend the rest of her life in prison. Seemed like a good trade-off.

So, with her bright future mapped out for herself, Dianna knew she first had to make it alive through this Monday-afternoon rush-hour traffic. Why the city had to declare rush hour at the same time of day when everyone was trying to get home was beyond her. The mobs of cars forced her to drive like Batgirl through Gotham. Horn honking, tires squealing. Lane changes. Cussing. Gestures. It all helped.

It also got her stopped by the police. And so, of course,

here she was, caught on the radar and pulled over to the side of the road. Near to tears and embarrassed, she sat there with cars whizzing by and with her hands shaking and her heart pounding. Behind her, the long arm of the law—in this instance a big uniformed officer—sat in his patrol car with the glaring, throbbing lights. He had yet to approach her. She knew what he was doing. He was checking her license number and her for wants or warrants. Dianna hadn't watched all those hours of *America's Most Wanted* without learning something of police procedure.

As she dug through her purse for her wallet and then in her car's glove box for her proof of insurance, she intoned, "OhGodohGodohGodohGod." One big long word. Then her chant changed. "Mom is going to kill me. Oh, shit, *Tommy* is going to kill me. No. Wait. Tommy. He's a cop. I'll mention Tommy. It pays to have a cop in the family. Thank you, Tommy."

A tap on Dianna's driver's-side window made her cry out. She jerked around. It was the policeman's crotch. Hey, this was a big guy. No. Change that to a tall guy. Tall. Not big, that other porno way. Well, maybe he was. He could be. She had no way of knowing. Yet all she could see of him was his zipper and hips and thighs. Of course, he had pants on, too. It wasn't like the guy was some kind of pervert—*Stop it*. Dianna's brain finally kicked in, telling her to lower the window's glass. "Yes. So he can talk to me."

She hit the little electric button and heard the soft whirring—but nothing happened, i.e., the window didn't go down. But, and this was strange, the sounds of the traffic were suddenly a lot louder. *What the hell?*

Then the tall policeman did the oddest thing. He twisted to his right and leaned down and peered in the back—hello!—rolled-down window. She'd hit the wrong button. What a goof. "Sorry, Officer, sir. I guess I'm just nervous."

"Yes, ma'am."

Dianna couldn't tell too much about how he looked—whether he might be nice or more like "Book 'im, Danno"—because he had on a hard, wide-brimmed hat and his face was in shadow. He also wore those same kind of silvered sunglasses that Chris Adams wore.

"I need to see your driver's license and proof of insurance."

"Yes. I've got them right here." She twisted in her seat, handing them to him over her left shoulder. "Here you go. Everything's in order."

He didn't say anything. Just took the paperwork and straightened up. No doubt he was . . . making a list and checking it twice? Then, at the exact moment Dianna's fear foamed up into a horrible need to confess every wrong deed she'd ever committed, the officer leaned down again to peer at her from the back window. "You know why I stopped you, Ms. West?"

And then, there was no stopping her. "I'm hoping it's because maybe my taillight's out. Well, not *my* taillight. That would be silly because I don't *have* a tail, much less a light on it, so how could it be out, right? Or even a heart light. Like *ET*. Some people would tell you I don't even have a heart light, but they'd be wrong. I do. I have a heart light. And I donate regularly to police charities. You're my heroes."

"Ma'am, are you all right? On any medicines I should know about?"

"No. I'm fine. And I haven't been drinking. Or taking drugs. I don't do that. Well, the occasional drink. Socially. But if I have a drink, I certainly don't drive. That would be just plain wrong. Why do you ask?"

"I stopped you because you were speeding."

"Oh. That was going to be my next guess."

"Yes, ma'am. But you were also engaged in some other, more serious violations, as well. Excessive lane changes. Not signaling. Tailgating. But after that speech, I'm going to have to ask you to step out of the car and submit to a field sobriety test. Do you agree to do that?"

"Of course. But remember, I haven't had time to study. Ha-ha."

"Yes, ma'am."

Dianna got out of the car, submitted, evidently passed, and was allowed to get back in her car. Whereupon the nice policeman peeked at her again through the lowered rear window and continued with his lecture. "I could run you in to jail for all your infractions"—Dianna's breath caught and her heart pounded—"but since your record is clean and I think you're just nervous, I'm going to write you a ticket. A pretty big ticket, though. And I'm also going to recommend that you go to traffic school."

No, no, no, no, no, Dianna wanted to shriek but wisely didn't. Instead she smiled for the officer. "Traffic school. Good. I was always good in school. And thank you for not taking me to jail. Oh, can you put on my ticket there that I was wearing my seat belt? That counts for something, right?"

"Yes, ma'am. Now, do you suppose I could get you to roll down that front window, please?"

"Oh. Of course." Though her hands were still shaking, she managed to work the correct button and get the driver's window lowered. "There. Much better, huh?"

"Yes, ma'am." The big policeman leaned to his left this time, now peering at her through the front and open window. Then he pointed at her. "Hey, wait a minute. It's starting to come back to me now."

That didn't sound good. "Uh, what is, Officer?"

"Where I know you from. Have we met before?"

Oh, this was what she needed: a cop on the make during a traffic stop. "I don't know. I don't think so." Still, given all the traffic-fine trouble she was in, she considered flirting with him. *Well, I don't know, big boy, we might have met before. But I think I'd remember a big, handsome, strapping man like you.* Or maybe *Is that a gun in your pocket or are you just glad to see me?* Totally discarded that route. For one thing, she wasn't good at Mae West impressions. And for another, he did have a gun.

"Yeah," he persisted. "I do know you. I've seen you before. Somewhere recently." He turned her driver's license over and over, looking at it as if for clues. "West. Dianna West. Hey, you got a brother or something named Tommy who's a cop?"

*I love you, Tommy. I am getting you the biggest Christmas gift ever this year.* Big grin, lots of charm. "Why, yes I do. Tommy's my brother. You know him?"

"Oh, yeah, I know Tommy. You don't recognize me?" The policeman removed his silvered shades. "You're the lady from Tamborello's. The one with the wacky business for guys to ask their girlfriends to marry them, aren't you?"

Well, she didn't know about wacky, but . . . "Yes, I am!" And then she remembered him. No, no, no, no. Despite the sinking feeling in her stomach, she cheerily said, "Oh, hey, you're the cop who hates Tommy, aren't you? The West-family-hating policeman. Of course." Tommy would get no present from his sister this year. She offered the big policeman her hand to shake. "Nice to see you again. How are you?"

He shook her hand readily enough. "I'm good. And you?"

"Oh, fine. You know, zipping around here and there. Busy."

"Yeah, I saw that. Listen, you got a business card or something? See, I've got this girlfriend. And we, well, we're getting kind of serious—"

"Say no more." Dianna rooted through her purse until she located her calling-card holder. She extracted one and handed it to him. "Here. Call me any time. And congratulations."

"Thanks. I'll do that." He tucked the card in his shirt pocket and smiled down at her. Dianna dared to believe she'd catch a break. "Just let me write this ticket out and you can be on your way, Miss West."

No break today for her. She slumped down in her seat. "Yeah. Thanks. Take your time, Officer. I'm in no hurry."

\*     \*     \*

Chris held down the button on his security intercom. "Yeah, Steve, what is it?"

Stephen Row—the building's blond, muscled, and friendly security guard extraordinaire—said, "Sorry to bother you, Mr. Adams, but are you expecting anyone this evening? There's a lady here asking for you, and I don't have her on my list."

Chris frowned. Couldn't be Mom or Ronnie. They had their own electronic passkeys, so they'd zip by Steve, pretty much. Then who could this be? A face with dark hair and golden eyes popped into Chris's mind. He grinned. Like he didn't know who this was. "So, what's this lady's name, Steve?"

"She says she's Dianna West, and I should know her because she's been here before. But I don't remember her, Mr. Adams."

"No reason why you should. It was couple weeks ago. That rainy Friday night, and I had you wave her car through."

"That explains it."

Chris chuckled, knowing he was in for a bumpy evening. Scary how exciting that felt. "So, is she mad, or what?"

"I'd go with mad, Mr. Adams. In fact, she says she's here to kill you."

Chris had to smile to himself, thinking how calm and matter-of-fact Steve was about this, well, death threat. "Wouldn't be the first woman who wanted to. So, sounds interesting. Let her come up."

"You sure? She sounds pretty serious about killing you."

"Trust me, Steve, she has every reason to be."

"All right. It's your neck, Mr. Adams. I'll let her in. Oh, and have a nice evening. Call me if you need backup."

"I'll do that. Thanks, Steve." With that, Chris took his

finger off the intercom button and stepped away from the panel.

Grinning, excited, his blood thrumming through his veins, he turned and leaned against the wall behind him. He crossed his arms over his chest and, in his mind, calculated and visualized, in real time, how long it would take her to find a visitor's parking space. Okay, getting out of her car; walking to the express elevator that went only to his penthouse; okay, she's there, now pressing the call button and waiting for the doors to open; getting in and riding up to the penthouse . . . Chris hummed a tuneless ditty, giving the express elevator time to levitate itself here; now waiting for the elevator doors to open; taking the few steps required to cross the narrow hall, standing in front of my beautifully carved and polished double wood doors . . . Chris paused . . . *And right about now—*

The buzzer to his double front doors sounded. Grinning, triumphant, Chris punched the air with his fist. "Bam! Am I good or what?"

Proud of himself, he pushed away from the wall and stepped over to the doors. But before he opened them, he ran a hand through his hair, tugged at his knit shirt, messed with the waist on his jeans, settling everything around. Ready now, he plastered a big smile on his face and opened the doors . . . and there she stood. Chris felt his heart take a joyful leap. "Well, hello, Dianna—"

"I almost got in a fight with your security guy. He takes his job seriously, doesn't he?" Totally pissed, in a frowning brew of black temper, Dianna blew past him.

Chris watched her go . . . very appreciative of the nice bounce of her backside. "Nice to see you, too. And I mean that."

"You won't for long, mister." In one hand, she clutched her purse tightly by its straps. And in her other, she had wadded up some kind of form. She stalked back over to him and shoved the paper into his hands. "You have to pay that. I'm certainly not going to."

He spared the official-looking document only a cursory

glance before closing the door behind him. "So, what is it—my bill?"

No answer. He turned around to see he was alone. Dianna had stormed off across the tiled gallery entryway—he'd heard that part—but apparently she'd proceeded down the narrow carpeted hall that led to the living room. "Come in, Dianna," he said, grinning.

"No, it's not your stupid bill," she yelled back. "And would you please come here?"

Chris chuckled softly before yelling back to her: "Depends. Do you have a gun?"

"Lucky for you, no."

"Good. Are you going to hit me with something heavy?"

"I might."

"Then I don't think I'm going to come in there." He grinned, waiting for her to explode. It didn't take long.

"Who knew you were such a chicken?"

"I am not," he called out.

"You are so. I'm one woman, Chris, and you're twice my size."

"True. But ask me nicely."

A shriek of frustrated rage came from the living room. "I am so going to kill you."

"I don't think that falls under the category of nice."

Silence met this. Then, "All right, fine. Will you *please* come here?"

"Sure," he said amiably. "I'm on my way." He walked the hall's length and stepped into the raised space that contained the dining room/kitchen/wet bar. This area overlooked the long living room with its wall of lightly tinted windows. Outside, the late-May evening was going down softly. "And here I am. Hi, Dianna. Nice to see you."

"Oh, shut up. Your bill will be a lot bigger and longer than that." She pointed to the form he held. "What you have there in your hands, my friend, is a speeding ticket I just got."

"Ouch. That had to hurt."

"Worse than you think. Remember the policeman who was at Tamborello's when Lenny capsized? The one who was questioning me when you grabbed my arm? Big guy, big gun? Well, this was the same guy. He rotated his duty to traffic cop, he told me. Lucky me, right? And he still hates my stupid brother Tommy. So, not only did I not get a break for being a policeman's family member, *but* he really socked it to me on fines. And then—and *then* he asked me for my *business card* because he wants to ask his girlfriend to marry him. Can you *believe* that?"

Absolutely mesmerized by her, Chris was barely aware of what she was saying. He knew this was important and he should be listening, but, damn, she had no idea of the picture she made just now. Her color high, her chestnut hair as wild as her eyes, which were suffused with piercing points of light, she reminded Chris of some untamed avenging goddess. She was magnificent. Passion personified.

He knew he was grinning stupidly at her—and that would probably only make her madder—but he couldn't help himself. *Wow. Look at her.* She stood flat-footed in his living room, her purse nowhere in sight, her hands clamped to her waist . . . like some pirate on her ship's main deck. However, she'd obviously come straight here from work in the real world, given the early evening time and the way she was dressed—like a successful executive in a tailored two-piece olive-toned suit.

"Chris, look at me and not my breasts. The girls won't talk to you."

Caught, and embarrassed, Chris gave his head a subtle shake, as if that would take the froth out of his suddenly carbonated hormones. "I am listening."

Dianna's arched eyebrows said she clearly didn't believe him. "Oh, really? Then what did I just say?"

*Oh, hell.* The ticket still in his hand, Chris stared at it a moment. He then gave himself away by rubbing the back of his neck with his free hand as he unhappily sought her gaze. "Uh, something about breasts and the girls not talking to me?"

"God! *Men*." Dianna actually stomped her foot. She pointed to the thing he held. "I was talking about the ticket. I am giving it to you, and you have to pay it."

"Oh, that's right. But, again, why do I have to pay it?"

"Because it's your fault I got it, that's why."

"How's it my fault, Dianna? I don't know—"

"You sure as hell do." She advanced two steps on him.

Chris stiffened his knees against the crazy urge to back up. "I sure as hell do not."

"Oh, right. Two words, Chris." She held up two fingers. "One is 'Mrs.' " She bent a finger down. "And the other is 'Windhorst.' " She bent her second finger down. "Any of this coming back to you now?"

"Not really. I know the lady, of course. But in relation to this ticket, I haven't got a clue."

"You talked to her today. Now put two and two together."

*Oops.* Obviously his phone call had garnered results, but not good ones. "So, you want a drink?"

She did a double-take. "Do I— No, I don't— Wait. Yes I do. Rum and Coke. Make it a double."

"Whoa. You sure you don't want to start slow, like with maybe a white-wine spritzer?"

She made a face. "Total sissy drink. No. I want a double rum and Coke."

Chris stared at her. "I've created a monster. But . . . yes, ma'am." He put the speeding ticket on the formal dining room table and headed for the bar. "Kick your shoes off—and don't throw them at me. Then come over here and talk to me while I mix up our magic potion."

"Forget that. I'm staying right here, and I'm keeping my shoes on. I don't feel like being nice and friendly and chatty with you right now. I'm mad at you."

"Amply demonstrated." Chris turned around to see Dianna had her arms crossed over her chest. "So you didn't come over here to talk. What did you come over

for, then—to give me this ticket and drink my liquor? Or
are you here to place blame and maybe assign damages—"

"All right, all right, I get it." She stalked toward him,
signaling for him to precede her. "Go on. I'm right behind
you."

"And that's the part that worries me." Chris punched
his fists to his waist and raised an eyebrow. "You don't
have a knife, do you?"

She stopped and held up both of her hands, palms toward him. "Do you *see* a knife, Chris?"

He grinned at that opening. "No. But I think I should
frisk you just to be sure."

"Ha. You wish."

"Actually, I do. But since it ain't gonna happen, come
on over here and tell your favorite bartender what's
wrong."

Managing to look like someone had just licked the
stripes off her candy cane, she nodded and followed him.
Chris went behind the bar and spoke to the denizens of
his marine tank. "Behave, guys. We have a lady here."

"Do you always talk to your fish?" She squinted, looking again. "And starfish and squid or whatever that thing
is?"

"Not always. Just sometimes. They're not great con-
versationalists."

"I guess not." She perched herself atop one of the tall
stools that fronted the granite-topped bar. Her elbows on
the bar, she cupped her chin in her fisted hands and stared
at him. "You need to get out more, Chris."

"Maybe." Amused, aroused, just totally fucking happy
that she was here, Chris said: "So, what's up, doc?"

Dianna exhaled a huge sigh. "It's Monday. That's
what's wrong. God, everything just blew up."

He pulled out the makings of two Cuba Libres. Bacardi
Light. Coke. Wedges of lime. Crystal tumblers. "Such
as?"

"Do you believe things come in threes, Chris?"

Filling the tumblers with ice from the compact refrigerator under the bar, he nodded his agreement. "Seems like it sometimes. What's your three?"

"I got that speeding ticket—"

"Which I *will* pay, by the way." Picking up a shot glass, he measured the rum into each tumbler.

"No. You don't have to do that. I was just mad."

Chris opened a Coke and poured it back and forth between the two glasses. He looked up, met her always-entrancing eyes. "So you're not mad now?"

She shrugged, her slender shoulders bouncing her thick, shining dark hair. She flipped it back over her shoulders. "It's hard to stay mad at your bartender."

Topping the drinks with a wedge of lime each, Chris grinned. "I know. Smart of me, huh? So, the speeding ticket is the first thing in your three. What's the second thing?"

"Dr. Yakahama called."

Frowning, Chris placed her drink in front of her, telling her: "It's not a double, by the way. So who's this doctor? What'd you say his name was?"

"Yakahama. He's a dentist, and one of Melanie's clients."

"I see. So what'd he want?"

She sipped at her drink—her eyes instantly rounded and she coughed behind a hand. "God, that's strong."

"And you wanted a double." He tasted his own drink. "Good stuff. So, Dr. Yakahama and Scarlett?"

"Had sex in the National Museum of Dentistry."

Chris thunked his drink down atop the bar. "You're shitting me."

"Wish I was. But they did it right there in that big oversized dentist's chair in one of the displays."

"Damn, they'll let you do that? I have to get to that museum."

"Shut up. The dentist was a client, Chris."

She looked so miserable that Chris sobered. "I think I see where you're going with this. That's a big no-no, right? Professional reputation. Potential lawsuits. Et cetera."

"Exactly. Fortunately, their . . . indiscretion went undetected, the hour being late and the chair being in a pretty secluded part of the museum. So at least the people there won't be suing. But the rest of it? I cannot believe it. The implications alone. If we start seducing the attractive men who come in—" She stopped herself to stare meaningfully at him.

Totally taking her meaning, Chris raised his drink to his lips without giving up eye contact with her and swallowed back a swig. "I see your point. And I have to confess that I hadn't thought about that. But you're right. You boff some guy and then take payment from him for, uh, professional services rendered, then that would pretty much make your business a house of ill repute, right?"

Dianna desultorily raised her glass to him. "Hi. Nice to meet you. I'm a madam. Not that your mother and Veronica don't already think that or worse about me."

Chris waved that away. "They don't know anything. Go on." He couldn't believe they were having this intimate conversation. And it was intimate. Like a loving couple at home after work, telling each other about their day. Very sexy, somehow. "So, Dianna, what are you going to do about Melanie?"

She exhaled. "Well, I was going to fire her."

"You were? But you didn't?"

"No."

"That's good. I like Melanie. She's, well, eccentric, but she seems like a good soul."

"She is. Completely harmless." Dianna frowned. "Or so I thought before this museum thing. Anyway, I didn't fire her. Dr. Yakahama saved me from having to do that."

"Yikes. He didn't fall on his sword or anything noble like that, did he?"

"No, but I was about ready to tell him to go ahead. Still, he made it okay."

"Meaning?"

Grinning, shaking her head, Dianna said, "Get this: He told me that he didn't ever have a girlfriend he wanted to propose to. Can you believe that?"

Surprised, Chris drew back. "What the hell?"

"Exactly. Apparently, he attends the same church as Melanie does. And they'd met there at some functions. Just superficial stuff and only occasionally. So, anyway, he fell for her but was too shy to speak directly to her about his feelings. So he made up this lie about having a girlfriend."

"Get outta here."

"I'm serious." And yet she was still clearly amused. "So, anyway, as you know, he and Melanie hit it off at the museum."

Chris nodded. "Understatement of the year."

"Totally. Long story short, he called me today after Melanie left to confess and apologize. And get this: He wants me to help him make it right with her. Can you believe that?"

Chris thought about it. "Yeah. In some sick, romantic way. But you're not sure you should? Am I right?"

Dianna shrugged again and took a pretty good-sized swig of her drink without apparent aftereffects. "Yes. What do you think I should do?"

She cared what he thought. More warmed by that realization than he cared to admit, Chris adopted a contemplative pose . . . arms crossed, frown on his face. "Well, I guess you could talk to Melanie and see how she feels about the guy and then go from there. Just tell her he called. If she's still interested, then I don't see any harm in your brokering their next meeting. After that, it would be up to them how it went."

Dianna grinned. "See? I knew I came to the right bar. You're pretty smart, you know. That's exactly what I was thinking I'd do."

"Then, good for me. Okay, so we dealt with number two. What's number three in your cluster of disasters that happen all at once?"

She wrinkled her nose, and Chris was won over. Could she be cuter? Hell, he'd already had to put a slab of granite—the bar—between them to keep from sweeping her up in his arms and kissing the hell out of her . . . for starters. "Out with it, Dianna. You've come this far."

"Well, okay. Number three is why I'm so mad at you. Or was. I don't think I am now. Anyway . . ." Dianna heaved a heavy sigh. "Mrs. Windhorst came in at closing time to give me two weeks' notice that she's quitting."

Surprised and upset, Chris stood up straighter. "What? Why?"

"Computers. She said you called and talked to her about computers. I don't know what you said—"

"Nothing that should have upset her. It was just off-the-cuff things to lay some groundwork, get her thinking about them."

Dianna laughed. "Well, it worked. She definitely thought about them and apparently decided that she was going to be replaced by R2-D2 or some such thing. Still, that was the absolute last thing I needed today."

"I guess." Chris reached across the bar to give her arm a reassuring squeeze. It always surprised him how slender and fragile her bones felt. "Hey, I'm sorry. I should have let you bring up the subject with her."

Dianna nodded. "That would have been nice. But, anyway, there's more fun stuff if you want to hear it."

"Are you kidding? Let's have it."

"Okay. In a word: Paula."

"Well, you did say fun," Chris said, his tone wry. "What's she done, I shudder to ask?"

"Nothing . . . maybe. Well, she could have by now, I don't know." Dianna companionably crossed her arms atop the bar and leaned in toward Chris, who couldn't have been happier with her proximity. "What I mean is she just found out that Melanie has 'old family' money. A ton of it. And is like the richest under-twenty-fiver on the whole Eastern seaboard."

Dumbfounded, Chris stared at Dianna. "Melanie? *Our*

Melanie? The one I know? Scarlett O'Hara Melanie?"

"One and the same. Lots and lots of old-family money."

Chris made a helpless gesture. "Hell, I don't even know where to go with that."

"Paula sure as heck did. She dragged Melanie off to Towson Town Center. I'm sure the economy will soon feel the good effects of that little outing. So I was dealing with that when Mrs. Windhorst came in to tell me that she had Dr. Yakahama on hold, and he wanted to talk to me. Then she lays that on me about quitting. Which brings me to my mad dash to come here and strangle you, which is when I got the ticket. So. Three things."

"Damn. That's some afternoon, all right, you poor kid." In his mind, Chris was already trying to think up ways of keeping her here longer, even though he knew all the reasons why he shouldn't. "Maybe it's over now, Dianna. Maybe things will be good from here."

"I don't think so because we—you and I—still have some unfinished business between us to discuss."

"We're not back to you killing me, are we?"

She waved that away. "No. I'm over that." Then she switched emotional gears, sobering and lowering her gaze to her rum and Coke in front of her. She ran her fingertip around the glass's rim. Chris felt the dull thudding of his heart as he awaited her. She started off with "I'm talking about, well, last Saturday night and you and Veronica—"

"The answer is 'I don't think so.' "

Dianna jerked her head up. Her amazing gold-colored eyes looked like twin moons. "Really? You don't think so?"

Chris shrugged. "I don't think so. It doesn't look good. But she's going to think about it."

"Think about it? She has to think about it? Chris, you've been together for years. How can she not *know*?"

That old defensiveness came back. "Hey, I owe her that much. And precisely because of all those years and what we've had. But in my book, right now, I think it's toast."

Dianna's deepening frown produced two tiny, vertical lines between her eyebrows. "I'm sorry to hear that . . . if you are."

Chris shrugged. "I don't know what I am. But what choice do I have? I can't force an answer from her. And if I have to, then what does that tell me?"

"I see your point. Kind of a tough spot." Dianna looked away from him, concentrating on a painting that hung on the far wall.

All Chris could do was watch and wait her out. A fine tension, like that of a drawn bow, thrummed throughout his body. The truth was, he wasn't any happier about the state of his love life than Dianna was, and for two cents, or just one sign from her, he would tell—

"So, you actually did ask her? You went through the whole thing? 'Will you marry me?' All that?"

This was the last thing he wanted to talk about. But, given that it was literally her business . . . "No. Not really. I never asked her. In fact, we had a pretty big fight. Turns out that private room was a very good idea. By the way, I tipped Roman the European Waiter very generously. He earned his money that night."

Dianna made a sympathetic face. "Poor guy. And, Chris, I'm so sorry it happened like it did. It was like one big disaster that shouldn't have happened. A comedy of errors, or something."

He nodded. "That's pretty much what it was."

"Still, what's she got to think about, if you didn't ask her?"

"Just let me tell you how it went down. She was carrying on about you and who were you."

Dianna sat up and grinned. "She was jealous of me?"

"Women. You don't have to look so happy. But yes, she was. So I just told her. No point in keeping a secret now, right? So, she didn't believe me. Pissed me off. I pulled the ring out to prove to her what Saturday was all about. And—big finish here—she snatched the ring from me and told me she'd think about it for a week, and not to call her, she'd call me. And then she left."

Looking amused and appalled, Dianna clapped a hand over her mouth and stared at Chris. After a few seconds, she lowered it and said: "Chris, that's almost funny, if it weren't so painful. What a scene."

"It was that. And it all took less than fifteen minutes. Probably seemed more like three hours to Roman. He kept popping in and running out."

"Well, at least he has a story to tell. Oh, I should have stayed."

It was Chris's turn to lean in over the bar between them. "Yeah, why did you leave? As it turned out, you could have shared a limousine ride with me. And supper. That's twice I've had supper ordered with you around and it never got eaten."

Dianna raised her eyebrows. "Do I actually have to call you Dr. Yakahama to get you to understand why that couldn't happen?"

Feeling sour, Chris stood up and finished off his drink. He plunked the tumbler on the granite bar. "No, I guess not."

"Anyway, there didn't seem any point in staying last Saturday. I was mad. You two were mad. I was at the bar alone, and then these two guys there . . . Well, don't get me started on them."

"What two guys? What'd they do?" Surprising Chris was the sudden burst of jealousy and fear and protectiveness toward Dianna that welled up in his chest. He'd kill the sons of bitches if they'd so much as—

"Nothing. Calm down. They didn't do anything." She'd reached across the bar to lay her hand on his arm. She so rarely touched him. Chris's breath caught . . . and his libido perked its ears up alertly. "They were just staring," Dianna assured him. "You know what they had to think after hearing all that prostitute talk."

"I know exactly what they thought. What did they look like?"

"Your standard yuppie larvae. Why? What are you going to do—go find them and beat them up, Mr. Dragon Slapper? Forget them, Chris. They don't matter." She sat back, taking her warm, soft hand with her.

Chris wished he'd put his hand over hers to hold it there on his arm. Sure, it was probably all in his mind, but he seemed to burn where she'd touched him. But after hearing her Melanie story and knowing what was at stake for Dianna, and with him still being technically a client, he could do nothing. God, he hated this. He'd never felt so impotent before in his whole life. It wasn't a feeling he liked at all.

"So, Dianna," he said, scrubbing a hand over his jaw, "you said those guys at the bar don't matter. And you're right. But what does, then?"

# CHAPTER 13

Chris's question took Dianna by surprise. *What mattered?* She stared at him, feeling that old melting giddiness chugging right along in her tummy. That feeling always assailed her when she just thought about Mr. Christopher Adams, darn him. He was staring at her, waiting. She swallowed and was surprised to realize that doing so hurt, as if maybe there were a lump there. Time for a stall tactic. "Hold on just a minute, okay?"

"You all right?"

*No, Chris, damn you, I'm not okay! I haven't been okay since the day you walked through my front door.* But what she said was, "Sure. I'm fine. Just a frog in my throat. And you know what? Where did we get that saying? A frog in your throat? That's stupid. You'd choke to death. Or freak out so bad you'd have a heart attack and die." *Shut up. You're babbling.*

Chris frowned. "You sure you're okay, Dianna?"

Coughing, clearing her throat, she nodded and waved and finally said, "That's what the policeman said. But, yeah, I'm fine. Just great."

Feeling too hot all over, she picked up her rum and Coke, drained that puppy—oh, how it burned all the way down—and eyed Chris right back. How could she answer him? *What does matter?* he'd asked. What could she say and still be true to herself? How to answer without being totally self-serving, too? "So, bartender," she began, still hedging, "how about another one of these?"

Giving her a disapproving-parent look, Chris shook his head no. "I don't think so. Not if you're going to drive."

She plunked her crystal tumbler down onto the granite surface of the bar. "Oh, really? Then maybe I won't drive. Maybe I'll take a cab. Or have you take me home. Or maybe I'll just stay here."

His dark eyes glowed like hot coals. "You can if you want."

"I was teasing." Actually, she hadn't been. And yes, she knew all the reasons why saying suggestive things like that were taboo here, but, damn, sometimes, if you wanted life to be worth living, you just had to throw caution to the wind. Or let it hit the fan.

"Well, don't. Just tell me what's really going on here."

"What do you mean?"

"I mean you could've called me with all this. You didn't have to come over here."

"Yes I did. I was that mad. But not anymore. I mean, look at us: Here we are, two friends having a drink together."

"Bullshit. What's really wrong?"

"Nothing," she said, fearing her heart was in her eyes. If it was, she knew what it would communicate: *I have all these feelings for you. And you keep giving me hints that you have them for me, as well. What am I supposed to do with all that? You have Veronica and your sense of honor with regard to her, which I really admire about you. And I have my business and professional and personal integrity—and quite possibly my heart—on the line here. So, dammit, where does all that leave us?*

"Oh, the famous female 'nothing,' " Chris was saying. "Sorry. Not falling for that."

Puckering her mouth over her conflicted feelings, Dianna pushed her glass toward him. "Here. Make me another of these." She saw he meant to protest, but cut him off. "No. Those are my terms. A drink for a confession."

Chris eyed her like she was the enemy. "A confession, huh?" He picked up her glass. "All right. But you're not driving after this one. And those are *my* terms. Nobody leaves my bar and drives."

She shrugged. "Whatever you say. Awfully nice of you to be so concerned."

"I am concerned. This isn't like you, Dianna."

"What isn't?"

"The way you're acting. It's like you're depressed."

"I think I have every reason to be, don't you?" She gestured for him not to speak. "No, don't answer that. Anyway, how would you know what is and isn't like me?"

His chocolate-brown eyes gleamed. "That's easy. I know you."

"Do not."

While he talked, he prepared her new drink and his. "Do. And what I don't know, I can guess."

"You can?" Dianna's arch tone of voice matched her raised eyebrow. "Am I that transparent?"

Chris handed her a refreshed rum and Coke and then sipped at his own, eyeing her over the rim of his glass. "No. I just spend a lot of my time thinking about you and the way you act and the things you say."

Oh, now this was fraught with possibilities. How well her happy little beating heart knew that. "You do? Why do you do that?"

Chris didn't say a word. He didn't have to. He merely held her gaze, allowing his seriously sexy and intent expression to speak volumes for him.

Her breathing suddenly stunted, but with every intention of meeting his seductive challenge by being cool and sophisticated right back at him, Dianna took a sip of her beverage . . . and frowned. She peered suspiciously into the smoky depths of her glass and then up at her bartender. "Hey, this is watered down."

"No it isn't. You're just getting used to the liquor. Come on, you got your drink. Talk to me. That's the deal."

"Oh, all right." She set her drink down and leaned forward, crossing her arms atop the bar. On his side of the bar, Chris did the same thing. Now only about three inches of air and space separated their noses. For some reason, with that pleasant buzz in her ears and the liquor humming through her veins, their sudden closeness was funny to Dianna. "I feel like I ought to say something like 'Hi, sailor, you come here often?'"

Chris chuckled. "And if you did, I'd have to say 'Every day. I own the place.' So, tell me, lovely lady of the golden eyes"—he reached out to oh-so-tenderly tuck a lock of her hair behind her ear—"what's really on your mind?"

A delicious shiver slipped over Dianna, setting the fine hairs on her arms on edge. Could he *be* more wonderful and sexy—and unavailable? "All right. Here goes. But you have to accept right up front that this is the liquor talking. I wouldn't be saying any of this if I were stone-cold sober."

He nodded. "You've only had one drink, but accepted."

"Good." She schooled her features into thoughtful seriousness. "Okay, Chris, well, you know how relationships just sometimes reach that point where you either have to act or it just doesn't happen?"

Chuckling, nodding, he said: "Vividly, trust me."

"Well, you and I are there."

She'd obviously surprised him with that. He stood up, pulling away from her, looking wary. "I thought you meant me and Veronica. You meant you and me? We have a relationship?"

*Uh-oh.* Instant embarrassment brought its attendant heat and thudding pulse with it. Dianna covered by sitting up and talking rapidly, no breaths taken. "Okay, maybe not a relationship, but *something*, right? I'm talking about all these undercurrents and the flirting and the looks that pass between us. You can't tell me I'm imagining those things, or even that I'm alone in this. Seriously. Because if you are, my male-signal sensors are way off, and I am right now the most mortified woman on the face of planet Earth, Chris."

Grinning, he raked his appreciative gaze over her face and body, which only served to make Dianna warmer. "Don't be all that because I'm most definitely not saying you're wrong."

"Then, those things are there?" She dared to hope, despite knowing that down that road lay heartache.

"Most definitely there," Chris told her, nodding. "But we both know it's not that simple."

"And now you're talking about Veronica, right?"

Again he nodded. "Yes, but not just her. I mean your business and my being a client. That whole Dr. Yakahama and Melanie thing, too. I don't want that to be us—a big problem that we can't get past."

Why did he have to choose now to be so darned good and noble and moral? What was that all about? And yet, could she like him more for being those things? Dianna wanted to groan. "Listen to you. You are such a gentleman, Chris. And that is so rare. You just take care of everybody. I totally admire you."

She'd embarrassed him. He lowered his gaze and shook his head in denial. "Damn, you make me sound so . . . Victorian. Or boring."

"Neither one, really. You're . . ." *Perfect for me, darn it. I want you, and I'd fight for you if you'd just give me one sign.* "Well, you're what we in the business call a nice guy."

Chris's expression blended bemusement and shy disbelief. "Thanks. But I hardly think I'm a nice guy. And you wouldn't, either, if you could read my mind right now." He held up a cautioning hand. "Never mind. Don't go there. The real issue here is what, for us, is the right thing to do . . . if anything."

Dianna's big balloon of hope burst. What did "if any-thing" mean? He wasn't sure? *Well, how could he be?* she argued right back. *We've never actually done anything together or been anything except planner/client to one an-other.* Again, how could they? Hello, big stumbling blocks between them. "So," she said, resignation pepper-ing her words, "you have thought about this, like you said."

"I have. But I still don't have the answers."

Room to hope. Dianna began mentally blowing up an-other, even bigger balloon. Smiling, she stared at him while, on the inside, she assessed the warmth and the depth of her feelings for him—and made her decision. "Chris, I think you do know the answers. I know them, too. I think, like me, you just don't want to, well, make the right decision, the hard one, and then act on it."

"Okay, this is getting a little oblique. Tell me what you mean. Straight up."

"I mean there are two answers here: the easy one and the hard one."

He crossed his arms over his chest, looking dubious. "Still not with you."

"Okay. The easy answer is where we just go for it, where we act on what we feel, saying to hell with anyone else's feelings or the consequences and the morals—"

"You call that easy? It's not. It's shitty."

"Exactly. And, hence, our dilemma. If we act on what we feel, then we hurt a lot of people."

"Gotcha. Or we walk away and hurt ourselves, right?"

"Bingo."

"Damn, that sucks."

"Royally."

Chris steepled his fingers, rested them against his lips, and stared at her. Then he lowered his hands to grip the edge of the bar. "All right, here's the thing. Everything you just said? Accepted. No argument. *But* the bigger problem is"—now he hesitated, looking shy and uncer-tain—"and I know it's wrong, but I don't want to let go of this ... thing that's between us." His eyes darkened with knowledge of himself. "Not so noble now, huh? Not the gentleman at all."

"Oh, Chris." Looking into his eyes, Dianna wanted to cry. Some instinctual thing inside her heart told her that if they acted on what they felt for each other before everything else standing in their path was cleared away, then they would not end up together ... because they wouldn't respect each other.

"I have to tell you," Chris continued, much as if he hadn't heard her speak his name, "that the funny thing is I keep hearing in my head that Lovin' Spoonful song about this guy who thinks he's got his mind made up and then gets distracted by another woman and ends up not knowing what to do. All he knows is he needs to make up his mind."

Though that struck her wrong, and she didn't really know why, Dianna nodded. "I've heard that song before on the oldies station. It's cute."

"Until you find yourself living it."

Okay, now she got it. He was coming off sounding fickle, like his head was turned too easily. But hadn't his mother and girlfriend alluded to that already? Then shouldn't she be wary, too? "So that's where your head is now? You're just distracted?"

He held her gaze. "More than distracted, Dianna. Conflicted."

Her heart thumped with longing, yet her head warned her to proceed with caution ... not that she was listening. "So who's this other woman who has you conflicted?"

"Come on, Dianna. You know."

All flirty now, she feigned surprise and coupled it with a knowing grin. "Do you mean me? Well, I'd say I'm sorry to be a problem to you, Chris, but I'm not. So if I said I was, I'd be lying."

Shaking his head, like the joke was on him, Chris said, "I am in over my head here. But as long as you're being honest, tell me if I'm a problem for you. Tell me if I'm someone you can't walk away from."

Thoroughly warmed, Dianna felt a blush claim her features. "All right, I admit it. You are."

Chris exhaled, shifting his weight as he ran a hand through his hair. "So, what in the hell do we do about it, Dianna? This thing between us that we haven't even named or acted on? What the hell do we do?"

She was suddenly sober and felt way too close to the raw truth to be comfortable. "I don't know."

But sitting there and watching him unhappily mess with the trappings of the bar, moving a bottle here, wiping the counter there, she had to admit to herself that she did know. Chris needed to kiss off Veronica. He needed to end it with her, but for the right reason. Not because he was fickle or flighty—how could she trust or respect that?—but because he didn't feel what he should for the woman he was with. Only then could he walk away with a clean conscience, something Dianna knew would be of importance to a man like Chris Adams. It was important to her, too. So, it was that simple and that hard. Yet smart guy that he was, why hadn't he realized any of this? Or had he? Time to find out. "Chris?" He looked up, meeting her gaze. "Can I ask you something?"

"Sure. That's what we're here for, evidently." His grin softened his words.

"Evidently. Why *did* you agree to give Veronica a week to think about it?"

"And that's the hell of it. I didn't. She tossed that out as she went out the door. I never got to reply. But I know where you're going with this. I could call her and tell her to forget it. Just end it. But she won't take my calls or see me. I've tried. And she's got the ring. So, in one way, the ball's in her court. I don't want to do this over the phone and I'm not about to show up at court or her law office for this. That isn't kosher."

"That's true. Who needs that scene? But, still, what would you say to her if you could see her right now?"

Dianna hoped like hell that Chris understood exactly how important his answer was to this question—and to them, or the possibility of there being a them.

"It's hard to say. We've been together for four years, so I don't know, Dianna. I'd want to do it right. I mean, what I feel, what I'm going through now, isn't her fault. She shouldn't have to pay for it."

"Good answer." *So freakin' . . . noble, dammit.* On any other guy this would look wimpy, but not on Chris. The man was a chivalrous knight in shining armor. Well, whoever said she wanted one of those? Couldn't he instead be the good-looking, swashbuckling, and marauding yet basically good-hearted and monogamous pirate bent on ravishing only her for the rest of time? Talk about delicious and shivery. And who said women didn't know what they want? "If it were me, I guess I'd want you to be that considerate."

Thoroughly demoralized now, Dianna admitted she was getting nowhere fast—and maybe that was how it needed to be. She should just get up and go home. Because here she sat . . . Jezebel, the possible other woman, the temptress—

Chris's chuckle captured her attention. "Hey, before you put me up there on the Perfect Guy pedestal, you need to ask me one more question."

Dianna's emotions quickened. "I do? What is it?"

"Ask me how I feel about Veronica's answer, no matter which way she jumps."

"What do you mean?" Quivery excitement filled her. "Are you saying your mind's made up about her without even knowing what her answer will be?"

"Pretty much." Now he was thinking and grinning like that pirate as he dried a bar glass.

"Whoa. And what is your decision?"

He just grinned and stared at her and dried that glass.

Dianna wanted to bop him with a pillow. "You stinker. You're not going to tell me, are you?"

He shook his head. "I think I owe Veronica the courtesy of her being the first to know, don't you?"

Great. The knight again. "No. Oh, okay, yes. But this is so unfair, Chris. Seriously. This is only Monday, and her week started Saturday."

"Can't stand suspense?"

"No, I never could. Just tell me this: Will I like your decision or not?"

Again, the pirate grin. "You talking business-wise or personally? Can't have it both ways."

He was right. Yes or no, it didn't matter. She'd lose in one arena . . . and win in the other. Dianna clapped her hands to her face and spoke through her fingers. "I hate this. I really, really hate this."

"Look at me, Dianna."

Reluctantly, she lowered her hands to her lap and stared plaintively at him. She knew she was giving away too much of herself but couldn't help it. "What?"

Chris looked embarrassed. "Okay, first, I'm very flattered that you, well, care so much. And, second, I don't think she'll take a whole week."

Dianna's heart flopped hopefully, or maybe it was hopelessly, around in her chest. "You don't?"

"No. She won't need a whole week to throw the ring back in my face."

"Are you serious? That is not going to happen. She'd have to be nuts. Does she not know how fabulous you are? How lucky she is?" Dianna was giddy with emotion. "Has she never seen you? I mean, look at you, for crying out loud. What's to think about? You're gorgeous. Any woman in her right mind, and I include myself, would bleed to have you ask me to marry you—I mean *her* to marry me— No, *you*—"

Dianna cut herself off and sat there, her heart thumping like a tom-tom. She clapped a hand over her mouth and felt the hot sting of embarrassed tears at the backs of her eyes.

Chris's dark eyes, if it was possible, were even darker, black now at their centers. "Is that the liquor talking?"

Dianna saw the desire in his eyes, saw the want and the holding back he was doing. She believed she could actually reach out and touch his need for her. Her breathing slowed. He did care . . . and so did she. Maybe, after all, tonight was about boldness. "No," she said quietly. "It's not the liquor. I know what I said. And I know what I want to do, what I want to have happen."

Chris exhaled and scrubbed a hand over his jaw, much as if he were feeling for whiskers. "I know. But this can't happen, Dianna. Not like this."

The air seemed to have thickened with the sweet scent of seduction. Dianna breathed it in, willing herself to be a siren for once in her life. "You're telling me no, Chris?" Was that low, husky voice really hers? "After everything I've said, you're telling me no?"

"Yes. I am. For your own good."

Dianna raised her chin a proud notch. "What does that mean—for my own good? Who are you to tell me what's good for me or not?"

"If we're talking about me, then I am."

He certainly had her there. But then again, he had her already in every way, if he only knew it. "Well, too bad, I reject your rejection. So there."

"You can't reject my rejection. That's not how it works."

"Is too." Dianna belted back a big swig of her drink, put the glass down, and then slid sensuously off the stool she'd been sitting on. "Watch this."

She kicked off her shoes and proceeded to undress, starting with unbuttoning her suit jacket.

"What the hell?" Chris reached across the bar, trying to grab for her.

She took a neat step back that put her out of his range . . . and unbuttoned another button.

Though Chris looked beside himself, Dianna realized he also couldn't, or simply chose not to, look away from what her hands were doing. "Come on, Dianna," he called out, sounding desperately close to losing his own control, "think about this. This can't happen."

"Not if you won't cooperate, it can't." She undid the third button and shimmied out of her jacket, lightly tossing it to the carpet. Now clad in her lacy bra and her short skirt, she struck a pose worthy of a Victoria's Secret model and blew him a kiss.

His face suffused with red, Chris pointed at her. "Stop that, Dianna. Stop it right now."

She grinned, the vamp. "Why don't you come out from behind that bar, big boy, and make me?"

Finally, at long last, Chris's hands were on her body. Dianna felt certain she would faint from joy and desire. Oh, he'd come out from behind the bar, all right. But it hadn't been to make her put her jacket back on. Instead, he'd stalked over to her, wrapped her in his embrace, and seared her very soul with his kiss. She'd opened up to him like a Georgia O'Keeffe flower. A thrill had leaped through Diana, leaving her with the certain knowledge that this kiss, from this man, was the one she'd waited for all her life.

She'd wanted to tell him that, but he'd given her no opportunity. Apparently as on fire for her as she was for him, Chris had, without saying a word to her, swept her up into his arms and carried her to his bedroom.

And that was where they were now, rolling around naked on his big, king-sized bed. Their clothes lay everywhere, much as if the people who'd been wearing them had somehow vacated them when they were beamed up to the mother ship. And the wonderfully thick and rich earth-tone bedcovers were tossed back to the bed's foot. The pillows were flung here and there. The draperies were askew. The closet doors hung off their hinges. A couple windows were broken. Flower vases were smashed. Water was everywhere. And time had stopped on a big wall clock . . .

Or at least it seemed that it should be that way.

With Chris stretched out full-length atop her, with his wonderful, heated weight holding her captive, with his muscled hardness contrasting with her firm feminine softness, she had her hands fisted in his hair and was kissing him in such a way that mimicked the act of love. Her tongue jousted with his, plunging and plundering his mouth, just as his did hers. She matched him with every gasp and whisper and sound he made. He pushed his hips against hers; she raised her hips to meet him, communicating her need to him.

She would hold nothing back with this man. This was love. And this was war. She had only this one chance to make him hers. She didn't know how she knew it, but somehow, on some primal level, she knew the rightness of what they were doing and she knew the inevitable nature of this loving act between them. It had been fated from the moment they'd met. And everyone knew there was no sense in fighting Fate.

Chris finally broke their kiss, leaving Dianna gasping. "My God, Chris. I just knew it would be like this. I could pass out."

"Try not to. But I'll take it as a compliment if you do." He buried his face in her neck, planting biting kisses up and down its column. Dianna arched her back, raising her head to better expose her soft flesh to Chris's questing mouth. Then, suddenly, he held still, his mouth against her skin. She felt his tongue touching her, and then he pulled back slightly, whispering, "I can feel your pulse, Dianna, against my lips. Your every heartbeat."

Could he say more sensual things? Could he?

"Oh, Chris." Her skin afire, her eyes closed, and her breathing ragged, Dianna rode the tide of want and need and desire for this man that racked her body. With her arms tucked up under his, with him holding his weight off her by bracing his elbows against the mattress under them, Dianna roved her hands over Chris's broad back and down his slim waist and around his firm buttocks. He was heaven. He was a Greek god. He was the prototype for Man. He was—

—sliding down her body, kissing his way as he went. He bit and nipped at her collarbone, leaving her whimpering, and then lowered himself down her, nuzzling and seeking, until he found what he evidently wanted . . . the underside of her breast. "God, I love it here. So warm. You are so beautiful, Dianna. Just made for love."

"Oh, Chris." She didn't seem capable of saying more. He left her breathless. She writhed and twisted under him, alternately urging him on and yet not wanting it ever to end.

Chris slowly made his sensual way across her breast until he'd captured in his mouth her tender, sensitive nipple with its already tight and peaked little bud. And then he gave it his full attention and drove her wild flicking his tongue against it, circling it, suckling it—

Awash with desire, Dianna cupped his jaw in her hands and pulled him away. "Chris, if you keep that up, I will die."

He grinned. "We're all going to die someday, Dianna."

"No. I mean right now, in your bed. I will die."

He was unmoved—and grinning like a satyr. "And yet you still have one more to go. I can't let it think I play favorites, can I?"

"Oh, God. No, I don't guess you can." A jet of desire, like a heat-seeking missile, rocketed through Dianna, centering itself between her legs. If he hadn't been atop her, pressing her into the mattress, she would have writhed and squirmed. She was so ready for this guy; everything else was just frosting on the cake . . . topped with chocolate whipped cream. And a cherry. Well, too late for that whole cherry thing. But still—

Dianna gasped. Chris had captured and was now sweetly torturing her other breast. This was the one that was hot-wired directly to her Pleasure Dome. And, to prove it, Dianna heard a sound come out of her that she'd never made before. Somewhere between a growl and a shout with a tiny bit of bark thrown in for good measure.

Chris's head popped up. A lock of his black, black hair had fallen endearingly over his forehead. Wide-eyed herself, Dianna met his gaze. "That sound. Was that you?" he wanted to know.

As mortified as she was mystified, Dianna toughed it out with a sprinkling of bravado. "Well, who else? But, yeah, pretty scary, huh?"

"Pretty damned." But a lopsided Elvis Presley grin claimed his kiss-swollen lips. "Sick bastard that I am, I think I like it."

Dianna chuckled at him. "Good. Because there's plenty more where that came from, buddy. Especially if you keep doing what it was you were doing."

He raised his eyebrows. "Really? I wonder what sound you'll make if I do this." With no warning, he slid farther down her body. That alone was wonderful enough, yet Dianna held her breath. What could he be up to now—

"Mmm. An inny." He swirled his tongue around her navel, dipping into it, teasing it and then kissing it much like he had her mouth.

Okay, now that was just decadent. Especially when he moved left and right to nip at her pelvic bones and trace kisses across her seriously rippling belly muscles. Limp now, giving herself over to Chris's worshipful ministrations to her body, Dianna closed her eyes and went to a place beyond making sounds. Her limbs lethargic, she felt certain she floated on a sensual ocean of desire not yet fulfilled. How could anything be better than this?

As if he'd heard her thoughts, Chris showed her what could be better than this. He slid down her until he cupped her bottom in his hands . . . and then he lifted her to his mouth. Gasping, making a rattling sound at the back of her throat, Dianna tensed, went rigid, and clutched at handfuls of the sheet under her. She moaned, she writhed, she pushed herself against his mouth. Chris held her tightly to him and proved he knew exactly what he was doing and that he knew exactly where that loving little nub was.

Almost out of her mind with pleasure, Dianna tossed her head and held on and then felt the tightening, the coiling, the centering of her entire being on where Chris touched her. "Oh, God," she moaned. "Oh, Chris. Oh, Chris. Oh-oh-oh, here. Here it is. Oh, Chris."

And she was right, too: There it was. Her orgasmic contractions—intense, fiery, rippling—she felt certain, were registering right now on a Richter scale somewhere out in Utah. Dianna shook and shook with them, and still Chris held her to him. She rode the wave as long as she could, as long as she dared, but then, at a fever-pitch of sensation, she pulled away, whimpering, panting, begging for mercy. Gentleman that he was, Chris released her and kissed her as he lifted himself up and over her again. Dianna tried to hold him to her, but he resisted. "Hold on a minute, honey. I'm not, uh, dressed for the occasion yet, so to speak."

"Ah. Be my guest." Dianna grinned up at him, loving him for being so considerate and responsible. To her, his using protection was another way of showing his respect for her.

Winking at her, Chris rolled off her, opened a bedside-table drawer, pulled out a condom, sat up and did that whole necessary thing. Dianna busied herself with running her hand wonderingly over the broad musculature of the man's back. God, he was beautiful. So warm and firm under her touch. When Chris turned to her again and joined her on the bed, she snaked her arms around his neck and pulled him down to her. "Come here, you."

She then kissed him with all the strength and desire she had left which, judging by Chris's muffled gasps and throaty moans, turned out to be a whole lot.

Without breaking their kiss, Chris positioned himself between her legs. And suddenly Dianna knew that nothing and no one who'd come before had ever felt this right. Every fiber in her being shouted: "Girlfriend, this man is the one!" Then, as if it were the most natural thing in the world between them, as if they'd been doing this all their adult lives together, Chris entered her in one smooth, slick motion that filled Dianna completely and had her sighing into his mouth. Chris broke their kiss and dragged in a ragged, gasping breath. "Dianna, you're so—"

He didn't say anything else but let his thrusts into her speak for him. Totally in a joyous state that had to be somewhere pretty high up there on the Zen scale, Dianna wrapped her legs around Chris's hips, fully opening herself to him. Each powerful thrust of his hips, over and over, and at its peak, found her Happy Woman's Secret Place and had Dianna revving up again. Oh, baby . . .

It seemed to go on forever, this impassioned wrestling. And then, just when she thought she'd die and melt and be nothing but a grinning puddle of former womanhood, the match ended in a tumultuous tie when Dianna felt Chris's erection thicken even more and her bud tightened again and the heat started and Chris made a hoarse sound and his strokes came faster and faster and harder and harder and she gasped and clutched at him and he held her tight, held her tight, held her, held her until she made a certain sound at the back of her throat and raked her fingernails over his back and then just wantonly dug them into the man's skin and they both—

Achieved Nirvana at the same moment. The breath left her body. She became one giant Gumby exposed-nerve of sensation. Who the hell knew that Nirvana meant a screaming nuclear explosion with mushrooming clouds and a crescendo of orchestral music (*1812 Overture*, possibly) and lots of sweaty clenches and biting a guy's shoulder like she was some kind of lioness in heat, huh? Who knew that? Not her. Not ever before. But there it was.

And now, done, spent, all out, down for the count, the man collapsed atop her in a slick sweat of tangled limbs and gasping breathing. And Dianna couldn't have been happier. It was wonderful. He was wonderful. Being with him was like coming home. This was like coming home.

And then she heard a noise, one outside the bedroom that she knew was real because Chris tensed at the same moment she did when she heard it. He raised his head, and still lying atop her, pretty much stuck to her by the cooling sweat of the loving sheen that coated their bodies, locked his wide-eyed, oh-shit gaze with hers.

That sound . . . a somewhat distant door? A door . . . like say, the front door to the penthouse . . . slammed closed and a woman who sounded uncomfortably like Dr. Frankenlawyer called out, "Chris, honey? Surprise! Are you here? Hello, babe. Where are you? I have good news. I'm sorry I was such an ass last Saturday and I love you and my answer is yes, honey. I'm so happy and I couldn't wait any longer to tell—"

There was a reason for that stab of silence, Dianna knew. And she believed that Chris too had thought of what lay behind it at the same moment she had because the man lowered his head until his forehead touched hers and he whispered, "Oh, no."

Her arms still around his neck, their bodies still one, Dianna nodded. "Oh, yes. My jacket. In plain sight. On the floor by the bar."

Chris raised his head, looked down at her, kissed the tip of her nose, and whispered, "We are so screwed here."

"In more ways than one," Dianna agreed, smiling fatalistically.

"What the hell?" came the keening feminine cry. "This is a *woman's*—Whose jacket is this?" And then, a little angrier and a lot closer: "Chris? Where are you? What the hell is going on here?"

# CHAPTER 14

Tuesday morning, Dianna thought about calling in sick to work. Then she remembered that she owned the business and had to go in. Great. A full day scheduled with three new clients, two other half-planned events that needed pulling together before next weekend, and, as if all that weren't enough, an appointment with Edward the accountant brother about . . . oh, who knew or cared, some financial business thing that he always said was important. And it was. And she did care. She just didn't want to see him today.

He'd take one look at her and he'd explode and then the big snitch would go tell Mom. And that would mean yelling and tears and freakin' hell to pay. And Mom would call Tommy, who'd come rushing over, policeman gun and all, ready to press some charges and kill someone.

While that last part sounded pretty okay to Dianna right now, she just didn't think she was up to dealing with all that drama today. Dear God, there would be no end to it. So, no, she hadn't wanted to come in to work today. She just didn't feel like it, and she just didn't feel like it because she had the great-grandmother of all black eyes. So why would she want to have to listen to her employees? Or have to explain it to her clients? *Whoopee. What a fun day.*

But, anyway, here she was at work an hour early so

she could gather her thoughts; figure out what to say to Mrs. Windhorst so she wouldn't quit; think of how to handle Dr. Yakahama's confession and how to broach it with Melanie; hopefully catch Edward on the phone when he got to his office and reschedule her appointment with him; and, finally, she meant to test explanations, otherwise known as outright lies, for her shiner and see how believable they sounded, and then choose one to stick with as her story—all before everyone arrived at work.

So, no, she wasn't stressed at all. Just another day at the beach. Anyway, while standing in the powder room to the private salon at the back of the first floor—the scene of the first Lenny/Chris debacle—Dianna peered into a large, oval, decorative mirror, and cautiously applied gobs of foundation to the steadily bruising, already swollen, really painful big, fat lump of swollen flesh around her half-closed left eye.

"Like this is helping," she fussed wretchedly. "I don't know which is worse—the black eye or the sad cover-up job. Who knew lawyers could hit that hard? Damn. Ouch. Okay, enough. You know what? Forget it."

She capped the bottle of foundation and set it on the narrow table positioned below the mirror. She pulled two or three tissues out of the box and wiped her makeup-smeared fingers clean. Then she surveyed her handiwork, looking this way and that at her poor, abused face. How to explain it?

"I ran into a door," she said, testing it out loud. Then she shook her head. "No. That's the oldest one in the book. No one believes that one." She sighed, thought a minute, and brightened as she came up with another candidate: "It was the funniest thing. I was coming around the corner outside my condo and my neighbor was walking his dog and came around the other way and we ran smack into each other. Ha-ha-ha. Who knew his head was that hard?"

Dianna quirked her mouth. "No. Not only is the truth stranger than fiction, as Mom always told me when she caught me lying, but it's also shorter. Got to remember shorter." She exhaled, sighed, thought again. "I was mugged."

That was short. And would require huge explanations and would garner sympathy she didn't deserve. Then she'd have to explain why she still had her purse, her credit cards, her driver's license, and why she hadn't called the police, or if she had and if Tommy knew. And, then, no doubt, he'd drop by and wouldn't know what the heck everyone was talking about when they fell on him about his baby sister being mugged and—

"Morning, boss lady."

Startled, Dianna turned toward the doorway. There, a shoulder leaned against the doorjamb, dressed like Cyndi Lauper in her heyday, or maybe it was Madonna, stood Paula. She immediately straightened up, her mouth a perfect O. "Whoa! Holy *shit*! What happened to *you*?"

Dianna slumped, near to tears. "So the makeup didn't hide it?"

Paula strolled into the room, stopping in front of Dianna and grasping her boss's chin to gently turn her head this way and that. "Not if we're talking about this shiner. Wow. What'd you do—get caught in the wrong person's bed?"

Stunned, Dianna burst into tears and threw herself into Paula's arms.

That old saying from somewhere in literature, Chris reflected, was true: "Hell hath no fury like a woman scorned." Or, in this case, like a woman who only thought she had been. But he hadn't been able to make that point yet because in front of him, and having just arrived on this fine Tuesday morning, was a woman essentially screaming "scorned" at him, only she was using many, many more words than that to make her various points.

Though Chris was letting Ronnie have her say and do her venting while she tore through his bedroom and cleaned all of her things out, it didn't mean he had to like what she had to say. It also didn't mean he wasn't hacked off at her for attacking Dianna like she had, because he was. With all his emotions roiling and his temper barely in check, Chris stood with his arms folded across his chest, his shoulder leaned against his bedroom door, and his jaw clenched as tightly as a sprung bear trap.

Watching Ronnie now, Chris realized that Dianna had been right when she'd pointed out to him that he didn't really seem to like Ronnie in the way you do friends you hang out with. Ronnie didn't invite liking or easy intimacy. It was all work with her—all one-sided, and on the part of others. He had to believe, then, that even had he never met Dianna, he would have been true enough to himself to realize that. So there it was—he and Ronnie would have had this parting of ways at some point. In fact, going to Popping the Question had been for him, Chris now knew, a way of pushing that very point.

He simply hadn't counted on Dianna West. But there she'd been, and now here he was. No way could he have married Ronnie after meeting Dianna. No way. All of this meant that now he had to, figuratively speaking, put his house in order—once Ronnie got through literally trashing it. Not that he was going to stop her. Let her have her moment. Hey, maybe he owed it to her. He was mature enough to look at things through her eyes. She comes over, ready to say "I do" . . . and he's in bed with Dianna. That had made its own quiet statement, now hadn't it?

Still, he had never intended for his relationship with Ronnie to end like this. They'd meant something to each other once, and he respected that—or thought he had until he lost his mind when Dianna started taking her clothes off. But even before that had happened, he'd already decided to tell Ronnie it was over. In a much more civilized way, certainly—and with his clothes on. But this way was a lot quicker, more surgical, he wryly admitted. Okay, sure, he felt like a heel on one level. If nothing else, apparently Ronnie had still thought she was in a relationship with him. She hadn't been, only she didn't know it yet. And yes, he would have been glad to tell her that if she would have taken his calls. And no, he shouldn't have slept with Dianna until Ronnie knew, but things hadn't played out like that. And for that, he was sorry.

But the one thing he wasn't sorry for was what had happened between him and Dianna. Making love to her had been the most right thing he'd ever done in his life. And he would love to tell her that, too, only she currently was not talking to him. Chris scrubbed a hand over his jaw. Man, this was crazy. And it was his own fault. He accepted that. He'd say it again: He hadn't meant for it to happen this way, but it had, and so now he'd deal with it. One woman at a time.

The woman currently here was ripping and tearing her clothes off the hangers in his walk-in closet and tossing through a chest of drawers looking for her things. On his bed was her open valise into which she was throwing a growing pile of her belongings. Perfume. Hair dryer. Makeup. Bras. Pictures. Jeans. Alarm clock. Laptop computer. Cosmetics. Slips. Everything. And she wasn't doing it silently, either.

"I have never been so humiliated in my whole life, Chris," Veronica was letting him know, her voice somewhere between cold and sobbing. "I will never forgive you. How could I be expected to? I have to say I cannot believe it of you. I really can't. I had no idea. None. Why should I? You ask me to marry you and then two days later you're in bed with that—that *woman*?"

Chris worked his jaw, feeling the muscles jump and his teeth clench. "Don't call her 'that woman,' Ronnie."

"You're going to defend her? Even now?"

"She doesn't need defending. But let's tell the truth here. I never actually asked you to marry me."

Ronnie waved her curling iron at him. "Are you going to stand there and split hairs like this? Was that not your intention last Saturday night to ask me to marry you?"

"Yes, it was." *Madam Attorney.*

"Well, thank you for that much. Then you do know how hurt I am, right?"

Actually, he wasn't sure if she was at all. Pissed, he could buy. Telling herself she was hurt, okay. But really hurting, like you would if this were someone you truly cared about? No. Still, for the sake of the argument, he quietly replied, "I think I do."

"No you don't. Four years, Chris. I've given you four years of my life. Four." She slam-dunked the curling iron into the valise on the bed and then stood there, her hands clamped to her waist. "I feel like such an idiot for not knowing. I mean, how could I not?"

"Before yesterday, there was nothing to know, Ronnie."

"Oh, really? I caught you with her twice before that."

"No, you didn't. There was nothing to catch. The first time was a fluke. She was there with another client. And the second time she was there for me."

Ronnie's eyes narrowed shrewishly. "Wasn't she, though?"

"Sarcasm is not attractive on you, Ronnie."

"Forgive me if I don't care."

"Fine. Are you about done here?" All Chris could think about was how devastated he'd be if this were Dianna wanting to leave him for any reason at all. But it was Ronnie . . . and he pretty much didn't care. He just wanted the damned scene over with and her gone. Very illuminating.

"Oh, I'm sorry. Am I boring you, Chris?"

"Everything but." He really shouldn't be provoking her like this, he knew that, but he was suddenly tired of her tantrum. He'd done all the explaining he was going to do; he'd said he was sorry he'd hurt her; and he'd tried to be patient and let her get it out of her system. But this was enough.

Ronnie had been staring at him, but now her Nordic features hardened into an angry mask. "I could sue her, you know."

Though his stomach muscles clenched, Chris gave nothing away as he ran a hand through his hair. "Come on, Ronnie, I told you I'd already decided to break it off with you before I . . . well, before. You don't want to sue her. It's me you're mad at. And I understand why you are. It shouldn't have happened the way it did. It's all on me. Just leave Dianna out of this."

Fire flashed from her eyes. "Don't tell me who I can sue and who I can't, Chris. I'm the attorney here, not you. And the truth is anybody can sue anybody at any time for any reason and make their lives a pure living hell."

"Your specialty. So, what would you sue her for, exactly?"

Smugly triumphant now, she said, "It's really pretty simple. She owns a business, the express purpose of which is to facilitate proposals, right?"

"Right." It was as though someone had turned on a bright light and, in its harsh glare, he was seeing Ronnie for the first time as she truly was. How could he have ever thought he loved this woman?

"And now, by her own willful behavior, she has compromised a client and destroyed a relationship—"

"Bullshit. I don't feel the least bit compromised, and our relationship—mine and yours—was all but over. Admit it: That's the truth."

"The truth is I had an engagement ring from you and an implied proposal. But truth isn't even the issue here, Chris. It's what the law is. And under the law, she's guilty of fraud—or will be when my lawyer is done. He'll probably want to toss in alienation of affection, too. So, see? We entangle her time and money and shut her business down in a heartbeat. She'll lose everything."

Though his blood ran cold, Chris quietly said, "No, she won't. She'll still have me, Veronica."

Veronica softly applauded him. "Oh, nicely said, Chris. You have a very high opinion of yourself. Let's see how comforted and warmed your little friend is by that when it's all over."

Chris exhaled. "Look, why don't you just sue me? I'm the one you're mad at."

"True. I could. But suing her will hurt *you* more."

A cold calm settled over Chris. He eyed his former lover very levelly. "That's what this is all about, isn't it, hurting me back?"

She laughed. "Now you're catching on."

Chris knew he had to think quickly, had to see if he could talk Ronnie out of this. He went with the one thing he knew would push her buttons: her vanity. "So you want to expose all this in public? You want me to stand up in court and say I never really asked you to marry me? That you assumed I was going to? Because I didn't ask you, Ronnie. You and I both know it. I don't want it to be this way, but I'll go there if you do. So think about *your* reputation here."

She pulled herself up to a proud and injured posture, blond hair perfect, eyes wide and round. "My reputation? I didn't do anything wrong."

"It won't matter, and you know it. You always told me about how people talk, Ronnie, about how it's a small legal community. In fact, you've been one of the chief ones to hit your colleagues when they're down. So don't think they'll cut you any slack. They'll talk, and they'll laugh. And this will get tremendous airtime on TV and in the newspapers. Your boss won't be happy. And, yeah, you'll be compromised professionally. Is that what you want?"

She rolled her eyes and laughed, but Chris felt certain he saw some hesitation in her expression, as if what he'd just said had made her think. "So now *you're* going to tell me what I want and don't want, Chris? I think you've lost that privilege."

Chris pressed his advantage while he had one. "For God's sake, what are you—some wronged soap opera diva? Christ, Ronnie, last night just *happened*. We didn't plan it, and no one was trying to humiliate you or hurt you. That's not what it was about. And today, whether you'd come over last night or not, you and I would still be having this conversation because you and I are over. I think we have been for a while, too, if you'd only admit it. But since you won't, you have the opportunity to behave with some dignity. Just get your things and walk away. Why can't you do that?"

He saw Ronnie's chin tremble, yet he wasn't certain he believed that any honest emotion lay behind it. "Because I choose not to, Chris, that's why. I'm hurting and someone is going to pay."

Chris had thought they were making some progress. But if Ronnie wanted it like that, then fine. "You do remember Dianna's eye, don't you? You hit her pretty hard. So, before you go talking about suing somebody, let's talk about assault and battery."

She waved a hand in a dismissive gesture. "Easily explained. I was overwrought, emotional. A jury would be sympathetic. Oh, and let's not forget, Chris," Ronnie continued as she stalked into his walk-in closet and began shoving his shoes aside as she presumably looked for pairs of hers—shoes she knew damn well she didn't have here. "I could bring your Miss West up on charges of running an escort service. I could have her business investigated and see if this has happened before. If she's done this before—"

"She hasn't 'done this' before, Ronnie. And let me tell you, you're skating on some pretty thin ice. Pretty damned thin. You can come in here and trash my place all under the guise of looking for your things, and I'll take that. And you can diss me all you want. But I won't listen to you insult Dianna."

Ronnie stalked out of the closet to confront him. Dangling from her hand was a pair of red strappy sandals that Chris had no idea had been in there. "Do not defend her to me. Not today. Maybe Polly Pureheart hasn't seduced her clients before, but if anybody who works for her has, well, what they're doing out there at Popping the Question is called prostitution."

Chris's gut tightened. Melanie and Dr. Yakahama and the dentist's chair at the museum were all he could think about. *Holy shit.* Even though it had turned out not to involve a third party, what could Ronnie make of that? One hell of a lot, probably. And beyond that, if his memory served, the advertising and publicity for Popping the Question that would hit the stands and the airwaves in about two weeks' time. *Oh, man.* The last thing Dianna needed was for this thing to make the news at the same time.

Feeling helpless, Chris watched Ronnie tossing her shoes on top of her messy pile. Standing in profile to him, she suddenly turned to look at him. Though blond and beautiful and very familiar to him physically, she still was a complete stranger as far as Chris's heart was concerned. It was the oddest thing to him, when he compared this to how he felt about Dianna. He'd known her less than a month and yet already felt as if he'd known her all his life.

"You don't have anything else to say for yourself, Chris?"

With his arms crossed over his chest, he shrugged his shoulders. "Only that I can't believe you're going to do this and ruin three lives."

"Three lives, Chris? No. Only two." With that, and a self-satisfied smile, Ronnie pulled her gaze away from his. "I'll be perfectly fine."

All Chris could do was feel sick at heart and watch as she flopped the lid over on her luggage, smashed it down, and zipped it. She then tugged it off the bed and set it on the floor on its wheels. Releasing the catch for the long handle, she smoothly pulled it out. Only when she was poised to walk out of his penthouse and his life did she turn back to him. "Good-bye, Chris. I'll see you and your little friend in court. And soon."

By about lunchtime Tuesday, Dianna had her various crises sorted into some kind of prioritized order. She'd changed her appointment with Edward to the end of next week. *Ought not to be so bruised by then that makeup can't cover it.* And, on Paula's advice—once she'd told her a true but abbreviated version, sans details of the love-making, of last evening's rumble—Dianna had decided on the "I walked into a wall" story for her other employees and any curious new clients. Then she'd reassured Paula that she didn't have to worry about her new best friend Melanie because she, Dianna, had good news for her. And finally, after all that, Dianna had simply gone to work on her day's tasks. She'd even managed to school herself not to jump every time Mrs. Windhorst told her she had a call. None of them had been Chris.

Dianna could only imagine what he was going through with Veronica Alexander. She didn't envy him that scene. However, her greatest fear was that maybe Chris wouldn't end it with the lawyer, that maybe Dianna would be the loser. Again. As always. The little friend who was easy to talk to—and apparently just plain easy. *No. Stop that. It wasn't like that and you know it. Focus on today and the job. Just get through the day. He will call. He will.*

Dianna smiled. *Everything will be fine.* Of course, that was precisely the point where, again, the caca hit the fan—and again in the form of the redoubtable Mrs. Windhorst. The woman stood in the doorway to Dianna's office, waiting for her attention. Just like yesterday afternoon. Dianna barely stifled a whimper. No wonder they killed the messenger. It was beginning to sound like a good idea. "Yes, Mrs. Windhorst?"

"If you have a moment, Miss West?"

Dianna would have smiled at her secretary, but her face (her own) hurt too much to move the muscles involved. "I have all the time in the world for you," she said cheerily, hopefully. "What's up? Something good, I hope?"

Maybe not. The older woman, dressed today in a flowered shirtwaist dress that did nothing for her stalwart figure, stood there hesitantly and held a sheet of letterhead in her hand. "I have prepared my letter of intent to leave after a suitable two-week notice and it requires your signature."

It took Dianna a moment to cut through the rhetoric before she got the message: Mrs. Windhorst was quitting. *No.* Dianna swallowed back the primal scream and her fervent desire to beat her forehead against her desktop. Instead, she tightly folded her hands together atop said desk and calmly, sincerely said: "Tough patooties. I refuse to sign it. I also refuse to let you give your notice. So there." *Nanny-boo-boo.*

Mrs. Windhorst looked suitably thunderstruck. "But . . . you can't do that."

"Can. And I just did. Look, I'm your boss, and I'm telling you to tear that letter up. You're not quitting. And you're not being replaced by some computer. That's just silly. A machine could not replace you, Mrs. Windhorst. You're extremely valuable to me, and I like having you here. In fact, I'm going to give you a raise to prove it." Feeling pretty darned good and adult here—well, except for that nanny-boo-boo and the patootie thing—Dianna added, "So, is there anything else?"

The older woman didn't seem able to comprehend what had just happened. She divided her attention between the letter in her hand and Dianna. "But you don't understand, Miss West. This letter—"

"Old news. Tear it up."

"I don't really see how I can. Mr. Adams—"

"Should not have said anything to you about computers. Yes, he and I have talked about installing them. We need them, Mrs. Windhorst. But that doesn't mean you have to leave."

"But I don't understand the technology—"

"No one does, except for people like Mr. Adams. But think about it, you probably don't understand what makes a car run, but you can drive one, right?"

"No. I take the bus."

*Damn.* "Okay, bad example. How about your dishwasher?"

"I don't have one. I do my dishes by hand."

"VCR?" Dianna was desperate for a viable technological example, but the older woman kept shaking her head no. "How about a TV? You have a TV, right? And a washer and dryer, I'll bet? I don't think you're out at some creek beating your clothes against a rock—"

"Of course I have a TV and a washer and dryer."

"Aha!" Dianna pointed at her secretary. "How do those work? Do you know all the technology behind them? No, of course you don't. But you can use them. You've mastered them, haven't you? It'll be the same with computers, I promise you."

Mrs. Windhorst shook her head sadly. "No, it won't. I've tried in the past, and I just couldn't understand it all. It's so . . . humiliating." She held her letter of resignation out to Dianna. "You promised me no computers. And now we're to have them. Therefore, I have to leave your employment."

Mrs. Windhorst crossed Dianna's office and placed the letter on her desk. Defeat ate at Dianna's heart as she eyed the offending document. "All right, look. Here's what we'll do. I'll keep this for now." She tapped the letter. "But we won't enact it, okay? All I'm asking you for is a chance. Let Mr. Adams help you. And if you truly can't get the hang of a computer, then you don't have to have one on your desk."

"But everyone else will have one, correct? And you'll want to put the files and the billing on the computer, won't you?"

This whole scene was making Dianna's injured face throb. It was tough being the boss. "Yes."

"Therefore, I'll be obsolete. I won't have access to my own job."

Well, she was right there. Still, Dianna tried one more time. "Mrs. Windhorst, I think you can do this. You're one smart woman, and I respect you." Dianna attempted a shameless, pleading smile but couldn't produce much more than a grimace of pain. "One month. Just give me a month. Mr. Adams will be here every day with you to help you. That's part of my deal with him. You like Mr. Adams, don't you? Think of him here all the time with you. Pretty cool, right? But if, after that time, you're still convinced you can't learn to use a computer, then we'll do this." She held up the letter. "What do you say?"

Nothing, right off. But then, a tiny smile cracked the corners of her secretary's mouth. "Mr. Adams will be here with me? Every day? Well . . . all right, then." She put on a brave face. "I'll try."

"Yah!" Dianna actually cheered—and totally wanted to scream from the smarting around her eye and cheek. She gently cupped her offended flesh in her hand. "That's the spirit. Good for you." *And for me. One disaster averted.* She put the letter of resignation aside and, acting all business-as-usual, asked, "What's next on the agenda?"

Looking more cheered, Mrs. Windhorst said, "Miss O'Hara wishes to speak with you. Shall I send her in?"

"Yes. Excellent." A perfect opportunity to avert a second disaster. "Send her in."

Mrs. Windhorst nodded and exited Dianna's office. Hearing her secretary talking to Melanie out in the foyer and telling her she could come in now, Dianna quickly opened a drawer to her desk and stuck the letter of resignation inside it. She'd won that one. No more talk today of resignations, thank God.

Just then, Melanie entered. The woman was wearing chiffon and silk. Pink chiffon and silk. Her chin was trembling and her eyes were red and puffy, as if she'd been crying, but she held her head high. "Thank you for seeing me, Di. I know I don't deserve your time or your attention."

Dianna had to grit her teeth for patience. *Cannot do Blanche DuBois today.* "Melanie, it's okay. Really."

"You're very kind." In Melanie's hand was a document she held out to Dianna. "I hate very much having to do this because I love working here. But I've wronged you and my coworkers and I've compromised your business.

I must do the right thing and tender my resignation—"

"No! No you're not, dammit. Uh-uh. No way. Not gonna happen." Dianna jumped up and rounded her desk and pounced on the startled Melanie and her stupid letter, yanking it from her employee's hand and proceeding to tear it into tiny shreds and allowing them to sprinkle the carpet. "No! Do you hear me? N-O. I have had it. No one is resigning. Not today. Not ever." Dianna's heart pounded and her head hurt. She felt too hot and way out of control.

Melanie wasn't in much better shape. She backed up in total shock and fear, yet Dianna advanced on her and kept tearing up the letter, which was now down to postage-stamp-sized pieces. "You're not quitting. You're not leaving. Dr. Yakahama called me late yesterday. He has no girlfriend, Melanie. He likes you—"

"What?" Melanie finally stopped her retreat. "He has no girlfriend he wants to marry? Then, why—"

"Because he wants *you,* Melanie. Which is pretty obvious by now. He was too shy to say anything to you—although not too shy, I have to say, to engage in public sex—but the truth is he's very sorry and I was supposed to put this gently to you, but I don't feel like dancing all around this. So get over yourself. Nothing here is compromised—not if you care about Dr. Yakahama. Do you?"

Melanie was doing some rapid eye-blinking and pretty good blushing. "I . . . I think I do."

"Well, good, Melanie, under the circumstances. So go call him and tell him and then get back to work, do you hear me?"

"Yes, ma'am, I do." Grinning broadly, apparently brimming with happiness, Melanie shrieked her joy and grabbed Dianna in a bear hug. "Oh, Dianna, I am so very happy this has all worked out. Thank you so much." She planted two or three big lipstick kisses on Dianna's un-injured cheek. "I will call Dr. Yakahama—well, I guess I can call him by his first name now, can't I?" Still holding Dianna a squawking hostage in her embrace, Melanie giggled. "Just think, he did all that and paid that deposit and met with me just because he likes me. Oh, this is so wonderful . . . me and Harold."

Dianna struggled and finally freed herself from Melanie's joyous grip. "I'm going to hate myself, but who's Harold?"

Melanie stared at Dianna as if she were the nutty one. "Honey, haven't you been paying attention? Harold is Dr. Yakahama, of course."

"His name's Harold?" Dianna held up a hand to forestall any explanation that might be forthcoming. "No. Never mind. Come on, now"—she herded Melanie to the office's door, which stood open to the foyer—"back to work. Everything is fine."

"Oh, Dianna, I just love you. And you must be careful, honey, and take better care of yourself. No more walking into walls."

A guiding hand on Melanie's back, Dianna escorted her frothy employee to the foyer. "Excellent advice. I'll try to remember that. Off you go, now." She gently shoved Melanie along her way. The woman went happy and trilling and floating down the hall to her office. Dianna exhaled, shook her head, made a move to go back into her office, had another thought, and turned to face the hall. "Paula?" she called out a little too loudly for her swollen facial nerves. "Ouch," she whimpered.

Paula zipped out of her office, auburn eyebrows raised in question. In her hand was the world's largest chocolate-chip cookie, on which she'd obviously been munching. "You bellowed, boss lady?"

"A word of warning: Don't you even come in to my office today or any other day to tell me you're resigning because if you do, I'll tear your head off and beat you with it until you die, understood?"

A couple of doors down the hall from Dianna, and eyeing her boss, Paula calmly took a bite of her treat, chewed it, and then swallowed. She rubbed at her nose and nodded. "Sure. That's cool. Understood. No resigning; keep head."

"Good. Just so you understand."

She nodded again. "How's the eye, Ali?"

"Hurts like hell. Especially when I yell."

"And yet you can still rhyme." Paula started up the hall toward Dianna. As she came, she looked left and right, giving the impression she was trying to ascertain if they were essentially alone. When she stopped in front of Dianna, who had her back to the front door, Paula adjusted her blue-framed eyeglasses on her nose and said, "He call yet?"

To her utter consternation, tears sprang to Dianna's eyes. "No."

Paula shrugged. "Doesn't mean anything."

"What if he . . ." She couldn't get the words out. Inhale, exhale, just say it. "What if he doesn't call, Paula? What if he doesn't even break up with *her*?"

"Then you should tear his head off and beat him with it until he dies. Pretty effective corporate policy, if you ask me, so it will probably work in the private-life sector, too." Smiling, she took a bite of her cookie, chewed, and just stood there in front of Dianna, watching her.

Dianna's heart warmed, and the stupid tears threatened. "You know what, Paula? I like you. I really do."

Paula nodded. "Most people do. I'm pretty cool."

"Well, just so you know."

"Yeah." Then, "Hey," her multiply-pierced employee said, using what was left of her cookie as a pointer as she shook it at Dianna. "What happens if, instead of wanting to resign, someone asks for a raise?"

Her expression sober, Dianna said: "That someone would be hanged from the front porch."

"Whoa." Paula gave a subtle quirking of one side of her mouth and pivoted around. "I'll just hang out with Melanie instead. She's rich. Anyway, I don't think we're going to get much work done this afternoon."

"Oh, really? And why is that?"

" 'Cause if you'll whirl around real quick, boss lady, you'll see Mr. Chris Adams himself coming up the steps outside. Looks like he's got lunch with him. Just in time, too. I'm starved."

# CHAPTER 15

Totally frustrated and a bit bewildered, Chris eyed Dianna as she sat across from him—as far away from him as she could get—at the big, round table and quietly ate. Damn, it just broke his heart to look at that black eye of hers. And yet, could this be more awkward? Dianna was very subdued, would hardly look at him or talk to him. But maybe that was because they weren't alone in the surprisingly modern and well-equipped break room on the second floor of Popping the Question.

To Chris's right sat the giddy Melanie O'Hara, who was full of talk of Harold-this and Harold-that. Whoever the hell Harold was. What had happened to the Japanese dentist? But if Melanie was happy . . . hey, okay. She was the only one who was, though. On Melanie's other side sat Paula, who alternately ate and sent him withering glares. On Chris's left was Mrs. Windhorst, who acted as if she'd been recently dipped in a cesspool. And across the table, isolated from them all by an empty chair to either side of her, sat Dianna.

It'd been a hell of a morning with Veronica, and now it looked like it would be a hell of an afternoon with Dianna. *Damn.* Chris exhaled and concentrated on his lunch, which was beginning to taste like ashes.

"This is very good food, Mr. Adams," Mrs. Windhorst said, breaking into Melanie's long-running Harold harangue. "Thank you for bringing it to us. How nice of you."

Grateful for the innocuous opening that had nothing to do with black eyes or computers or Harold, Chris smiled at her. "You're welcome. Glad you're enjoying it. It's from the French Quarter." He looked at Dianna, who only briefly met his eyes. "I owed your boss a meal from there."

"That's not all you owe her, Buck-o."

"Paula. Please."

Chris looked from Paula to Dianna. Obviously she'd told her employee something, at least, of what had happened yesterday. While he certainly didn't begrudge Dianna a confidante, Chris figured the last thing he needed was Paula on a warpath with his name on it. He didn't think he'd like to see his scalp hanging from her belt.

"Oh, the French Quarter," Mrs. Windhorst said a bit loudly. "I've never been there. I've heard it's a bit pricey."

Chris turned to Mrs. Windhorst. "It can be, I guess. But it's worth it. You ought to go sometime. I eat there a lot because it's in the lobby of the building where I live. And I don't cook."

"Could have used some snails," Paula threw in, moving her crepes around on her plate. "I like snails. Or escargots, I should say, at these prices."

" 'Escargots' is snails?" Melanie looked a little green. "I didn't know that."

Ignoring her comment, Chris looked over her to Paula. "Sorry about the snails, Paula. Or the escargots. I'll remember for next time."

She captured and held his attention—not hard to do since she held a knife fisted in her hand. "There're a lot of things you need to remember for the next time, mister."

"Paula," Dianna warned. "Please. That's quite enough."

And that was when Chris had had enough of this tension and innuendo. He flopped his paper napkin on the table beside his plate and pushed his chair back, standing. The women all stopped eating and watched him. "Dianna, do you think I could speak with you in private, please?"

"Of course." She mimicked his actions . . . napkin, chair, standing. "Please," she said to her employees. "Take your time. Enjoy." Then to Chris, she said, "Shall we?" and gestured toward the open door to the break room.

"We shall."

Then, much like soldiers marching in lockstep, Chris followed Dianna out of the door and down a short hall that led toward the front of the Victorian house. The old wood floors creaked and groaned under their weight. Chris had no idea where Dianna was leading him, but he knew he'd follow her anywhere. And right now, all he wanted was to be alone with her. At the end of the hall was a landing that had three doors set around it. Probably what had originally been bedrooms. Dianna turned left into one.

To Chris's surprise, it was a pleasantly furnished sitting room done in earth tones and with the look of Ethan Allen about it. Clean lines, high quality, restful colors. Select pieces of furniture. Very comfortable and tasteful. Despite everything not said between him and Dianna, Chris led off with: "Hey, I like this room. Now, this is more like it."

Dianna turned to him, looking surprised and maybe pleased despite herself. "Really? I did this myself."

At least she was talking to him. "Nice. So all that Victorian stuff downstairs isn't you?"

"No. Hardly. I couldn't live with that clutter. That's just for effect. I think I told you that." Looking suddenly thoughtful, she swept the room with her gaze. "I like it in here the best of all the rooms. I come up here sometimes when things downstairs get to be too much for me, or if I just need a different perspective."

"We can all use that sometimes." Now that he was alone with her, and neither one of them had sat down,

Chris didn't know quite where to begin. Or maybe he did. "Dianna?"

She settled her gaze on him. That swollen black eye blotched with makeup tore at Chris's heart and made him ache for her. After a moment, she said: "Yes?"

Chris fisted his hands against the urge to pull her into his embrace and hold her close and kiss her forehead and protect her from the world. Her manner and her expression were too forbidding at the moment to allow for such an intimacy, so he kept his distance. "What's wrong? I mean with you today. With us. Me and you. I don't know what's going on. You're not acting like yourself."

"Well, Chris, for one thing I have the great-grandfather of all black eyes right now and it's giving me a killer headache, you know. Talking hurts. Smiling hurts. Chewing hurts. And there's no yelling allowed. I found that out."

"Who were you yelling at?"

"Melanie, mostly." She settled herself on the plump cushions of the window seat that overlooked the busy road outside.

Her positioning left Chris no choice but to stand in front of her and cross his arms over his chest. "I can't imagine having to yell at Melanie."

"I know. It's like kicking a puppy. But I did—yell, not kick. Anyway, she thought she was going to resign over Harold."

"And who is this Harold? What happened to her dentist?"

"He's Harold."

"Well, that explains that."

"Yeah. Harold Yakahama. Who knew? And then there was Mrs. Windhorst before her who was going to resign over computers."

"Ouch. That's where I come in, right?"

"I guess. I mean, I don't know." Dianna lowered her gaze to her lap. She crossed her legs and picked at something on her tan slacks. "The deal was you couldn't start all that until you were engaged or married."

"I remember. But you didn't say to who."

Dianna raised her head to look into his eyes. Chris saw the question in them. "Dianna, Veronica is no longer a part of my life. She's cleaned out and gone."

Dianna blinked her one eye. The other one was swollen closed. "Oh. I'm sorry."

Chris shrugged. "I'm not. And I'd think you'd know that."

"I don't really know much of anything, Chris. Not when it comes to us. It's hard for me to even think there is an us."

"And yet I'm hoping there is." She was pulling away. A highly motivated impulse had Chris stepping over to Dianna where he squatted on his haunches in front of her. He took her hands in his, feeling their warmth and small-ness, and raised his head so he could see her face. "I'm sorry about your eye, kiddo. That was a shitty thing Ron-nie did. I had no idea she was capable of such an act. Or even that she'd go for you like that. If anybody is at fault here, it's me."

"How so? You were struggling to get into your pants."

"No kidding I was. Totally off balance, one foot in, one foot out, when she jumps on the bed right on top of you. I didn't think I'd ever see anything like that outside a pro wrestling ring."

Dianna shrugged, looking brave and bruised. "Still, you did okay. You did some tag-team stuff. You pulled her off me and made her back off. And, you know, I even understand her. She was defending her territory, her man."

Chris snorted his opinion of that. "Her pride is more like it."

"Maybe." Dianna's mouth turned down at the corners. "I'm pretty mad at myself for not putting up a better fight, though. I mean, I have two older brothers, remember, one of them a cop who's taught me some moves. She wouldn't have got me with that sucker punch if I hadn't been so, well, naked."

Chris chuckled. "It's okay, champ. You don't have to beat anybody up for me to be proud of you. Besides, what could you do, tangled up like that in the sheet with a crazy woman on top of you? Damn."

Dianna shrugged and looked at his hands holding hers. "Chris, I am so embarrassed. And mortified. I have never been involved in something like this. I can't believe I have a black eye. I had to change an appointment set for today with Edward. Ohmigod, if he saw this? And Tommy? Please."

"I figure they'd come after me. And I'd deserve every bit of it, too, for not taking better care of their baby sister. So what *did* you tell everybody had happened?"

She quirked her mouth. "I told them I walked into a wall. Original, huh? But not Paula. She was too quick for me. She knows."

"I gathered that at lunch."

Dianna raised her head and nodded at him. "If I were you I wouldn't turn my back on her for a while."

"Duly noted." Reluctantly, Chris let go of Dianna's hands and stood up. He stepped to one side of her and looked out the window without actually focusing on the view. He hooked his thumbs in his jeans' front pockets and shifted his weight to one leg. *Here we go. Might as well find out now as later.* "So, what do we do from here, Dianna? I wouldn't have to be a genius to see that you're maybe having some second thoughts or regrets."

"No, Chris, I'm not. Not really."

His heart lurched. "Not really? Now, there's a ringing endorsement."

"I'm sorry. It's all I can do right now. My face hurts. And I'm embarrassed. And confused. And I'm having to lie and duck people. And I guess I'm mad at me and some at you. But most of all, I feel so bad for you—"

"Me? Why?"

"Seriously? **You** just had a four-year relationship break up."

"It was dead long before you came on the scene,

Dianna. And I'm not unhappy about it being over, so why are you?"

"I guess I'm just waiting for reaction to settle in."

"Reaction?"

"Chris, no matter what else you say, we both know you cared enough about Veronica Alexander—Ouch." She cupped her hand to her face. "Just saying her name makes my face throb. Anyway, we both know you were prepared to ask her to marry you."

"Yeah, but not for the right reason. I think it was more of a test of my own feelings for her, to see if I could or would. I pretty much knew all along that she would say no."

"And yet she didn't."

"Yeah, how about that? But it turns out I essentially took it back, didn't I? Ring and all."

"She gave you the ring back?"

"Threw it back at me is more like it. I've already returned it to the jeweler."

"So, was this morning pretty unpleasant for you?"

"No. A root canal is pretty unpleasant. This morning was a bitch."

"Yikes. What happened?"

Chris eyed Dianna, suddenly knowing the rightness of this crazy thing that had just popped into his head. It was like this sudden big blazing revelation. Like seeing the aurora borealis. "Before I tell you, can I ask you something?"

Dianna shrugged and looked taken aback. "Sure. I guess. What is it?"

Chris didn't move from where he stood. "Will you marry me, Dianna?"

Hers was a totally autonomic response. Dianna smacked Chris's rock-hard thigh, hurting only her hand, and cried out, "No, you big jerk. What is wrong with you, Chris? You can't ask me to marry you."

"Why can't I?" He gripped her by her arms and pulled her to her feet. "I want to marry you, Dianna."

"Chris, this is insane. Do you just do this—go around asking women to marry you?"

"No. You're the only woman I've ever asked to marry me."

"And Veronica would be . . . ?"

"I didn't ask her."

"You were going to."

"Maybe. I'm not sure if I actually would have. No, that's not true. In the end, I wasn't going to ask her."

"Still. You can't just ask me the same day you blow her off."

"If only it had been that easy. But why can't I ask you? This isn't as spur of the moment as it sounds. I've thought a lot about it lately. And I know what I feel for you."

"No you don't. How can you?" Overwhelmed and weak-kneed with surprise and emotion, Dianna wasn't sure her legs would hold her up if Chris let go of her. "Chris, I'm telling you that you can't just walk into my place of business and disrupt my whole life and say you want to ask some other woman to marry you and then come on to me and have me over to your place and then have a big fight with your girlfriend and make love to me and she beats me up and then you bring your fine French food here and want to work with us to put computers in and then ask *me* to marry you, Chris. No. You can't do that."

"Again, I say: why not? I'm not convinced yet."

Dianna stomped her foot. "Chris, I could just do I-don't-know-what to you. I really could. You big jerk."

"You've said that before."

"And I mean it. No. This is all wrong. All wrong."

"Oh, that's right. The down-on-one-knee thing." He let go of Dianna and started to drop to one knee.

"No! Don't!" She tried desperately yet futilely to stop him. Too late. The man was on one knee in front of her.

She was so mad at him she could have pushed him over—
and thought seriously about doing just that.

Chris took her hand in his and repeated his question.
"Dianna, will you—Wait. What's your middle name?"

"Joan. But that's not relevant—"

"Dianna Joan West, I am down on one knee in front
of you. Will you marry me?"

"God, no."

"Why not? What's wrong this time?"

"Chris, if you knew how much like Lenny Daschowitz
you are right now, you'd be insulted."

"I already am, just hearing his name in the same sentence with mine."

"I swear to God, get up."

"I can't. Swear to God."

"Don't be funny. I'm serious."

"So am I. I can't get up because you haven't answered
me yet."

Dianna tsked her impatience. "I did, too. I said no.
Now, get up."

"You're turning me down?"

"Twice. I already did."

"You better think about it. I won't ask again. I'm serious."

Dianna looked down at the man on bended knee in
front of her. He was magnificent. She met those dark,
melting-chocolate eyes of his and saw earnestness and raw
emotion in them. He *was* serious. So why was she saying
no to him? He was everything she'd ever wanted. She
knew somewhere in her heart that if he were a poor beg-
gar, she'd live happily with him in that cardboard box
under a bridge that she'd suggested to Lenny for him and
Olivia. But this wasn't right. Not like this. It was too
quick. Too soon.

And he'd never said he loved her. And she wasn't sure
if she would believe him if he did. Only a few days ago
he'd thought he loved another woman. And what was the
rush on his part? Did he just not know how to be alone?

She couldn't help thinking about his own mother's suspicions regarding him and cheating, and Veronica's, too. Well, okay, they'd both been right, but she certainly couldn't judge him because—how well she bore the mark of this—she was the other woman he'd been with. All she could think, and maybe unfairly, was if he'd do that to Veronica, wouldn't he do it to her, too?

"Okay, Dianna, honey, maybe I wasn't specific enough. When I said think about it, I meant today, while we're young. I don't mean to rush you but, see, I've counted to one hundred, and my whole leg is going to sleep."

Dianna closed her eyes . . . well, her eye. Tears wanted to squeeze out past her eyelids. Her heart was breaking, if only he knew it. She opened her eyes, looked down at him, and cupped his strong, smoothly shaven cheek and jaw. "Chris, my answer hasn't changed. I'm sorry. It's still no. You might think you're serious and that you know your heart right now, but I just don't see how you can."

His expression suddenly haggard, like someone had let the air out of him, Chris nodded slowly and then rested his forehead against her hand. To Dianna, they resembled a picture she'd seen of a young queen bestowing a knighthood on a handsome courtier. She fought hard not to complete that picture by resting her other hand on his black hair. This was killing her, this rejecting him. She knew this man's moves, his particular masculine scent, the sounds he made in bed, the way he laughed, what his temper was like. She knew what he liked to drink, how he lived, where he lived. But she didn't know his heart— not really, not where she was concerned.

"All right," Chris said into the quiet that had settled over them. He let go of her hand and smoothly rose to his feet, though he did stomp his foot and wiggle his leg, thus verifying that it had gone to sleep. "Can't be much more clear than that."

Dianna put a hand out to touch him but pulled it back. "I'm sorry, Chris."

"No. Don't be. You were right to say no."

"I was? Why?"

"For all the reasons you said. But don't expect me to stand here and tell you even more reasons why you should reject me. And even though you didn't ask, my decision—the one I wouldn't tell you last evening—was to tell Veronica, no matter her decision, that I didn't want to marry her. Not that it matters now, but I just wanted that said."

Dianna lowered her gaze away from his. "I'm so sorry, Chris. It's not that I don't care. I do. I really do—"

"Dianna. Stop before you get to the part where you think of me as a friend and nothing more—"

"I wasn't going to say that. Besides, that's my line. And my life."

"Only because you want it to be."

"That's not fair."

"All right, maybe it isn't. I'm sorry. Anyway, we might have a bigger problem." Clearly upset now, his jaw set in a rigid line, Chris moved away from her, pacing around the room and rubbing his forehead.

Dianna's heart sank. "A bigger problem? Such as . . . ?"

He stopped and turned to face her. "Veronica is talking lawsuit."

The word sent a cold chill, like a knife's blade, down Dianna's spine. She sat down abruptly on the window seat cushions behind her. "A lawsuit? What'd she do—hurt her hand when she hit me?"

Chris's chuckle was fatalistic. "That's good. But no. Much more serious charges. Alienation of affection, fraud, and anything else she can come up with on short notice."

"This is awful, Chris. Just awful. What am I going to do?"

"Look, I don't want you to worry about it right now. I don't think she'll really go through with it. She's just pissed. Doing that 'woman scorned' thing. I think, in time, she'll settle down and get over it. I sure as hell gave her plenty of reasons why she didn't want to go down that road—"

"Okay, stop. That's enough for now." Dianna felt certain her throat was closing. "Chris, this cannot be happening. Why is all this happening? I'm a nice person. I try to do the right thing. I mean, sure, yesterday evening was wrong—"

"Don't say that." Again, Chris hunkered down in front of Dianna, on his haunches, balancing his weight on the balls of his feet. "Please don't say what we did was wrong." He took her hands in his, rubbing them with his thumbs. "Dianna, being with you, even though it ended like it did, was the most right thing that I've ever done. Don't tell me I'm alone in this."

Completely overwrought, afraid she was going to lose it, Dianna shook her head. "You're not, Chris. I'm sorry. I'm just such a mess today. Yesterday, what we had, what happened between us—pre-Veronica—was beautiful, Chris. In and of itself, it was. But that's as far as I can go with it in my head right now. It's everything else that's wrong."

Tears welled up, and she began to cry.

"Oh, no, honey, don't." Chris immediately gathered her into his arms, holding her, kissing her uninjured cheek, her hair, rubbing her back. "Come on, baby, don't cry. You're breaking my heart. We can beat this thing, OK? We can. I'll talk to Ronnie and get her to drop everything."

"No," Dianna sobbed, angry and adamant, her voice muffled with her face pressed to his shoulder. "I don't want you around her. She's mean and evil and I hate her."

Chris made a surprised chuckling sound. "Okay, bad idea. I don't have to do that. We'll just wait and see what happens."

"No we won't. I'm going to kick her ass. I hate her."

"Point taken. Don't blame you for feeling that way. But I don't think that would be a good thing—"

"Chris, I want to go home."

"You want to go home?"

Dianna nodded. She hadn't realized she was going to say that, but now that she had, she knew that was exactly what she needed to do. She raised her head and clutched at his arm. "Will you just take me home, please? I can't be here today. I can't. Look at me—I'm falling apart. I'm talking about kicking a lawyer's ass, for God's sake. And everyone except Paula wanted to quit today. And I can't even let my family see me. I can't talk to clients. I don't care if they want to get married or not. And then you come here and ask *me* to marry you. And how stupid am I? I say no."

Dianna stopped and stared at Chris for a long moment. Then, solemnly, she said, "You have to take me home. I don't even think I can drive."

"Of course I'll take you home. You shouldn't have come in today, anyway." He stood up, helping Dianna do the same. "Come on, I'll take you right now."

"First I have to tell Mrs. Windhorst and Paula and Melanie. They'll have to cover things for me today."

"Sure. Whatever you want to do. I'm all yours."

"Don't say that, please." Dianna distractedly rubbed her forehead. "Will you stay with me, Chris? I'm sorry to ask you and I'm usually stronger than this, but will you please just stay with me? If only for a while? I feel as though I need someone with me who knows everything that's gone on, so I don't have to explain myself—"

"Hey. You don't even have to ask, Dianna." Chris pulled her to him and held her tightly, kissing her forehead. "Of course I'll stay with you. For as long as you want me."

# CHAPTER 16

So they'd already done that "Hey, I really like your place; oh please, it's nothing like yours; it doesn't have to be, I like it anyway, and maybe better" thing. And Chris, quite the gentleman, had sat in the living room and politely waited while she changed out of her work clothes and into her comfort clothes.

That meant her "Caffeine Junkie" pajamas. Here she was now, sipping at her mug of herbal tea, contentedly ensconced on her big, comfortable sofa. Plump pillows supported her back, and her favorite cotton throw covered her from the waist down. All of this was Chris's doing. He'd even retrieved her raggedy teddy bear from its place of honor on its miniature rocking chair by her fireplace and handed it to her. Totally embarrassed, Dianna had nevertheless tucked it against her side and tried to act as though she didn't do this every evening . . . keep her teddy bear with her, that is.

For his part, Chris now sat at the other end of the sofa from her, somehow commanding it with his hand stretched out along the sofa's spine and his legs spread, his feet flat on the carpet. In his other hand he held his mug of herbal tea, which he hoisted to her. "This is good. I've never tried it before."

Dianna grinned at him. "No, I imagine you haven't. Guys tend to run the other way from such things. But I'm glad you like it, even if you did turn your nose up at the idea."

Chris raised an eyebrow at her. "I was obligated to do so. Herbal tea is not macho. Real men don't drink herbal tea. Or eat quiche. Gross." With that, he took another sip of his tea.

"Too bad. I make a mean quiche."

Chris shrugged. "Well, if it's mean, that might be allowed."

"Allowed? So what is there—a manual or something?"

"Hell, yeah." He said this very soberly, very seriously. "You ladies have yours, we guys have ours. In fact, Dave Barry wrote it a few years back."

"I had no idea."

Again he shrugged. "That's because you're not a guy."

As she watched him, Dianna's heart just melted. Could he be nicer or funnier? She didn't see how. Or more warm and tender toward her? What a great guy he was. So rare. A genuinely nice man. Her heart as thoroughly warmed by his calming presence as was her tummy from the tea he'd made them, Dianna said, "Chris, thanks for staying. I mean it. You've been so, well—and at the risk of insulting you—nice."

Sure enough, he made a face of mock disgust. "Great. Now I'm nice. And apparently I drink herbal tea. This keeps up and I won't be allowed in sports bars anywhere."

"You go to sports bars?"

"Sure. Sometimes." He raised an eyebrow. "Something wrong with sports bars?"

"No." She looked down at her tea and then met his waiting gaze. "I just couldn't picture Her Nastiness going there with you."

"She didn't. You don't take girls to sports bars."

"Meaning she wouldn't go."

Chris shook his head no. "Wouldn't set foot in one."

"So did you go by yourself, then?"

He chuckled. "No, Dianna. I have friends, you know. Remember Rick Hampton?"

She brightened. "Oh, yes, I like him. How's he doing?"

"Good. Still happily married. He thinks you're really nice-looking."

"What? He said that?"

"He did. Not too many days ago, too."

"Oh, how sweet of him. So, who are some of your other friends?"

"Is this some sort of interrogation?"

"Actually, yes. I'm trying to get to know you. I mean, you did ask me to marry you and all."

"Yet you said no. I told you I'm not asking you again. But, anyway, my other friends. There's Mike Talbot and Jack Kaplan."

"What do they do?"

"Mike's an investment banker. Not married. And Jack's big into computers, like me. Works high up for a huge company. He's married. They have a baby. A little girl."

"They sound like nice people, your friends."

"They are. All good people. Now tell me about your friends."

Dianna shrugged. "I don't have any, not anymore, not since starting my business."

"What's that got to do with it? Jealousy?"

"No. We just sort of drifted apart. I guess it was the time constraints. There's only so much of that, and I didn't have time for girlfriend things like I used to. And then there's my family—" She rolled her eyes. "Besides Mom, Dad, my brothers and their wives, I have hundreds, it seems, of aunts, uncles, and cousins, all of whom live around Baltimore. We're very close, which means time happily given to them, but still . . . time."

Chris nodded. "Gotcha. What about Melanie and Paula and Mrs. Windhorst?"

Dianna grimaced. "Not so easy to answer. Surprisingly enough, if any one of them, I'd say Paula. But they're all employees whom I like and respect, yet I don't see them outside of work. For their part, it's kind of hard to be friends with someone who can fire you."

"Yeah. That lonely-at-the-top thing." Chris took a sip of his tea. "So, anyway, are they for real?"

Dianna chuckled. "I get that a lot. But yes, they are. A totally eclectic threesome, right?"

"I'll say. I thought everyone was in costume except you that first day. It's interesting to me that you're so, well, normal, and the rest of them aren't."

"Really? Are you trying to figure out what that says about me?"

"Exactly."

"And what have you come up with?"

"You like eccentrics."

"I prefer to think of them as originals."

Chris nodded. "That's good. I like that. You're fostering originality. I guess that's what it takes to be so creative."

"Exactly. And we create from scratch every day. They might be messes otherwise, but they're extremely effective in their jobs. So what in the world were you doing with someone like Veronica, anyway?"

Chris shook his head as if he'd just been slapped. "Whoa. Big shift in topic. Where'd that come from?"

Dianna shrugged. "Me being nosy. So, how'd you two crazy kids meet?"

Chris's expression hardened. "That's a long story, Dianna."

She felt the bloom of a guilty blush spread across her cheeks. "I'm sorry, Chris. I shouldn't have asked. It's been a rough few days, hasn't it?"

Nodding, exhaling his breath with a whoosh, and mindful of his tea, he shifted his weight about on the cushions as he performed a sort of abbreviated stretch. "Oh, yeah. Rough. Sorry I snapped at you like that." He settled into position and sent Dianna a considering gaze. "Oh, what the hell, I'll tell you."

"You don't have to."

"Nah. It's okay. I want to. Basically, she was a friend of a friend. Well, my old girlfriend. My first love." Chris grinned, waggling his eyebrows and acting like it was all too silly.

But Dianna saw through that. His first love. "And I'm guessing your first love didn't end all too well?"

He shook his head, his expression neutral. But Dianna saw a deep shadow in his eyes. "No, it didn't end well. Not for me. My girlfriend Mary married my best friend Joe."

Dianna grimaced at the hideousness of that. "Oh, God, Chris. That sucks. You poor thing."

He shook his head, quirking his mouth like no big deal. "Nah. I've let all that go. It was a long time ago." He settled his gaze on her. "They're still together, got some kids."

"Well, good for them. But if you tell me you're big friends with them now, then I'm submitting your name for the Nicest Guy in America award. Or the Most Forgiving."

Chris's frown made two little vertical lines appear between his eyebrows. "Why do you keep trying to ruin my reputation as a tough guy?"

"Oh, please. It could only enhance your rep. Women love tough but compassionate guys. Sort of a blend of knights in shining armor and marauding pirates. But it doesn't hurt to be nice-looking or rich. All that and we're talking a major religious experience."

As if amazed, though not in a good way, Chris stared at her. "You women are scary, you know that?"

Dianna batted at him, totally missing him by many inches. "We are not." She sat back. "So Dr. Frankenlawyer was a friend of this Mary chick's? What'd she do, come on the scene to comfort you?"

"I guess. She was just what I needed at the time."

"Really? I'm not sure I want to hear this, but how so?"

"She didn't make demands on me. Didn't expect me to . . . Hell, I don't know, Dianna. I'm not good at talking like this. We're like girlfriends here, you and me."

"Well, if you're my girlfriend, Chris, and we've, uh, slept together, then you know what that makes us, don't you?"

He sat up straight. "Hey, now we're getting interesting. This is more like it."

Chuckling and shaking her head at his antics, Dianna said, "Never mind. I shouldn't have pointed that out, you naughty man. So, we were talking about Ronnie the Scary." Dianna sobered. "How was she ever what you needed, Chris? I just don't see it. She's mean and cold and totally not engaged emotionally. She just seems so distant. And so self-contained."

"Bingo." Chris slumped back against the sofa's cushions and turned his head to look at Dianna. "Everything you just said is why she was what I needed then. She made no demands on my heart or my head when neither of them were in a good place."

"Okay, that I can understand. Makes sense. So I'm guessing, or hoping, you're all better now?"

He roved his smoldering dark-eyed gaze over her face. "Yeah. Since you, Dianna, I'm all better."

Deeply touched, and yet undone somehow, Dianna closed her eyes and rubbed at her temple. The man could heal her with a word, a touch, or a single look, that much was clear. All right, then, what was this hesitation she felt, this drawing away on her part? Dianna struggled to understand—and then it came to her: If only she could get over her fear that what she felt for him, and what he obviously felt for her, was just too much too soon, something so hot that it inevitably would cool down . . . and leave her devastated.

"Maybe I shouldn't have said that."

Dianna opened her eyes, directing her gaze to Chris's handsome face, the taut, masculine angles and planes of which never failed to make her heart beat faster. "Please don't take it back. What you said is beautiful, and I cherish it."

"Then why did it make you unhappy?" Looking unhappy himself, he set his mug on the end table and turned his head to look into her eyes. "Can you tell me why, Dianna? Because I don't know what to do."

Tears pricked at her eyes. "I know, and I'm sorry, Chris. I really am. I don't know what to make of me, either, except to say I'm just not hitting on all pistons today."

He smiled his sympathy. "You poor kid. Of course you're not. I shouldn't be pushing you. I mean, look at that eye. How's it feeling?"

Dianna cupped her hand to her left eye. "Better since the ice pack and the Advil. Thanks for taking such good care of me."

Nodding, Chris held her gaze. "You're welcome. And despite what I just said about not pushing you, I'm going to do it again. Here goes. I'd take care of you forever, Dianna, if you'd let me."

The undercurrents of deep emotion ran swift and treacherous. Dianna swallowed and lowered her gaze. "I know you would. And that means a lot to me, Chris, it really does—"

"But don't push it today, right?"

She forced a smile for him. "Right. There's just . . . too much that's happened too quickly. I haven't had time to sort it all out and see how I feel. Well, except for this now-famous eye. And it hurts."

"I imagine a lot of things do."

"They do, but they're not fatal."

"Imagine my relief."

"And mine." Tucked into her end of her sofa, and knowing he was watching her do it, Dianna gazed longingly at Chris. She couldn't take her eyes off him. So handsome. There was just something about him, something elemental or primal that called to her on a cell-deep level. Just looking at this man caused a pleasurable response in her body and made her pulse race. She wanted nothing more than to crawl into his lap and curl up like a cat atop him.

Just then, Chris put his head back against the sofa's cushions. "I'm beat, Dianna. I'm just going to close my eyes for a minute, okay?"

"Sure. Of course. Go ahead." She was a bit taken aback by that, but then she remembered all the emotional upheaval he'd been through today, too. Could she be more selfish or self-centered? *And there I was, all "Take me home. Wah. I'm so upset. I can't cope." What a jerk.*

Her mouth puckering in concern for him, Dianna drank in Chris's profile. For the first time she noticed that he hadn't shaved today. For some reason, the sight of those grown-up-man whiskers made him look young and vulnerable. She studied his face, noting the dark eyebrows, the high cheekbones, and the generous mouth. His strong jaw; the bobbing of his Adam's apple as he swallowed. Dianna fairly hummed with wanting to touch him. But . . . the poor man, his face in repose, looked dead tired. He even had bluish-purple circles under his eyes and the corners of his mouth had turned down.

Feeling suddenly protective of him, Dianna took a sip of her tea, more so she could swallow her yearning than anything else. Why had she told this kind, handsome, funny man no when he'd asked her to marry him today? *Oh, come on, you know why.* Yes, she did. Earlier, at her office, the moment he'd chosen hadn't been right. She'd felt then that she didn't know him and his heart—much less her own—in the ways that mattered. But now, after talking to him like this and being with him, she'd changed her mind. He was the one she wanted for all time.

*Then do something about it.* Dianna blinked, all but looking around to see who'd spoken. Then she realized the order had come from within her own heart and mind. And now, this same urgent something assailed her senses, telling her she'd better act on this feeling right now, this minute. Dianna's heart pounded with a brew of fear and anticipation—and hope: Screwing up her courage, taking a deep breath, she quietly called out his name. "Chris?"

He didn't answer. Frowning, though bemused, Dianna cocked her head and really stared at him, listening now and watching him. His breathing was deep and regular. His body—his magnificent body, which she knew intimately; oh wow, just the thought, the memory of his hands on her body had that secret little place deep inside her quickening—was totally relaxed. *Down, girl.* Smiling at him, doting and adoring, Dianna realized he'd gone to sleep.

Just then the air-conditioning clicked and whooshed on, providing a soothing backdrop of white noise much like a gentle breeze. Dianna blinked and blinked and yawned. *A nap. Yes. A nap. I'll talk to him later when we're both rested.* She put her mug down on the coffee table in front of her . . . and took her blanket and her teddy bear with her as she scooted down to Chris's end of the sofa. She laid her head on his firm, jeans-covered thigh and curled up. So sleepy, and so content she could purr, Dianna closed her eyes.

Like a king on his throne—his posture slouched, his knees apart, his arms resting along the armrests and his hands gripping the ends of them, Chris sat in the big overstuffed chair placed catty-corner to the sofa where Dianna still slept. He stared at her, thinking he should probably leave. He shouldn't be here like this, just watching her. And yet he hadn't left. Why? It was simple. Because there was nowhere else on earth he'd rather be. And no one else he'd rather be with. He checked his watch. She'd been asleep about two hours.

Chris grinned warmly. He'd been surprised to wake up—surprised, first, to realize that he *had* gone to sleep— but surprised to find her sleeping with her head on his leg. She'd had to do that willfully. He liked that she had, too. That was a first step, her coming to him. Well, maybe it was the second step, the first one being her asking him to bring her home and to stay here with her. He'd been pretty stupid earlier today to go down on one knee and ask her to marry him. He made a face at his own expense. *What a creep, man. Your girlfriend had just beat her up, remember? And that's another thing: You pretty much had a whole other girlfriend not twenty-four hours ago. So what was Dianna supposed to think—easy come, easy go? Shit, Chris, you weren't thinking with the right head, son.*

He accepted that now. But it didn't mean he didn't know his heart. And right now, just looking at Dianna's injured face broke his heart. How could he have seen that coming? Ronnie had never been violent before. Hell, half the time, he hadn't thought she cared enough about him to work up a good temper. But obviously she did because she had. Or did she? Chris frowned. What the hell was up with her, anyway?

Maybe it was that trial-lawyer thing with her, that not liking to lose. Sure, she'd walked in on a shocking scene, from her point of view, but still . . . to jump on Dianna and punch her like that. Total disbelief. Way over the top. And he wasn't buying her *I'm overwhelmed with love and want to marry you* routine. That didn't ring true. To his ears, her voice had held the note of some frantic emotion. He didn't know how better to put it. All he knew was . . . it hadn't rung true and something else was up.

Chris shook his head, thinking, *Forget Ronnie, man.* But he knew he couldn't afford to, not right now. He had to get her to see reason and drop her talk of a lawsuit that would ruin Dianna professionally and, he suspected, personally. She had values. Morals. That girl-next-door quality. There was just a goodness about her, a caring for people—even people like Lenny and his girlfriend and Melanie and Paula and Mrs. Windhorst—that he admired. Dianna was a gatherer of people. He liked that, too.

And he'd be damned if he'd let Ronnie ruin that about her. No way in hell, either, would he stand for her dragging his and Dianna's relationship through the mud and the tabloids. No way. Whatever fragile peace he and

Dianna had come to this afternoon he didn't want washed away in the shame and embarrassment of a public trial with tabloid news coverage. If that happened, then forever after, Dianna would associate him with it, and nothing would tear them apart quicker.

Again Chris heard Ronnie saying how she could hurt him worse by hurting Dianna.

"Son of a bitch," Chris intoned barely above a whisper. Feeling like he'd just been stomped on, he exhaled and shook his head, then scrubbed his hand over his face. *What the hell am I going to do? Not be with Dianna so Ronnie will back off? Just let her win?* He shook his head, feeling stubbornness set in. But some instinct told him to fight that "cornered" mentality and to think of Dianna. *All right, so Ronnie wins. So what? This isn't about winning. This is about what's best for Dianna. And she's already told you no when you asked her to marry you. Pay attention.*

He knew what he needed to do, dammit. He needed to walk away. Do the right thing. Freakin' knight in shining armor.

*Problem: I can't walk away from Dianna.* This was at once a troublesome and an uplifting first for Chris. Always before in his life, with the women he'd been involved with, he'd known he could walk away and be okay. He'd lived through what Mary had done to him. There'd been other women. Casual stuff. And, hell, even with Ronnie and after four years of togetherness, he had no urge to mourn. *Nothing there to mourn.*

Always before, the knowledge that he could walk away without too much hurt and hassle had made him feel safe and whole. But now, with Dianna West, he wasn't safe or whole. Far from it. Instead, he'd break and shatter if she walked away from him. He didn't know how he knew that this early on in their, well, whatever they had together. But know it he did. And it scared the hell out of him in the same breath as the realization made him want to whoop for joy.

His heart overflowing with a sudden whoosh of love, Chris grinned at Dianna's sleeping form, all curled up like a little kid and holding her teddy bear. Maybe one day in the far, far future, he'd tell her about the ragged end of his baby blanket that he still had—okay, it was hidden in the back part of a bottom drawer somewhere, all right? And he wasn't even sure which drawer. It wasn't like he slept with it or anything, for crying out loud.

"Chris, what are you frowning so about?"

He jumped. "Oh, you're awake. Nothing. I wasn't frowning about anything."

Her head resting on a pillow he'd slowly and carefully substituted for his thigh when he'd awakened earlier, she looked relaxed and content, and somehow totally sexy as she called his bluff. "Were too frowning. And now you sound guilty about something."

"Well, I'm not." He met her gaze and held it in a challenge—then totally caved: "I still have a piece of my baby blanket that I keep in a drawer somewhere. At the back of a bottom drawer. I don't know exactly where. And I don't sleep with it or anything. I just . . . have it. I like it. It's mine."

She chuckled. "And no one is going to take it from you, either. I like you better for having it, Chris. Thank you for sharing." She sobered. "Just don't touch my teddy bear."

He held his hands up, palms toward her. "Hey. I wouldn't think of it."

"Good." She patted the pillow under her head. "I liked you better as a pillow than I do this one, too."

"Great. I guess I need to spend more time at the gym if I'm that soft."

"Oh, as if. I just meant you're more . . . comforting. And warm."

Something in him quickened. "Want me to come back over there?"

"Yes, but no. Meaning, I should get up." She struggled

to sit up, and Chris catapulted himself to his feet and went to help her. "Thank you. What time is it?"

She was sitting up now and arranging her pajama top. Her actions molded the stretchy material to her breasts. Chris swallowed, his gaze riveted to her wonderfully full and feminine attributes.

"Chris? The time?"

He met her amused and knowing gaze. "Time. Right." He retreated to his designated end of the sofa and sat down heavily. "Okay." He glanced at his watch. "It's a little after five."

"Are you serious?" Dianna cried. "You should have awakened me."

"Why? You needed your rest. And besides I've only been awake for about ten minutes myself."

"You poor thing. I feel so bad for you, Chris. You had it rougher than I did last evening and then again this morning."

Though warmed and pleased by her concern for him, Chris toughed it out. "I'm all right, but how does your eye feel now? Any better?"

Using only her fingertips, Dianna gingerly probed the swollen and bruised flesh around her eye and made a face. "Ouch. My eye, to answer your question, feels like someone hit me really hard with her fist."

"And that's because someone did."

"And I thought it was all a dream."

"Not unless you include me in it because here I am."

Yawning and grinning at the same time, she ran her hands through her hair to straighten it out. Very provocative, those thick, dark, shining waves. "Talk about my dream guy, huh?"

Chris put his heart and soul into his answering grin. "I could be that guy."

She nodded as though unmoved, but said: "You could." Then she looked around her living room as if she'd never seen it before. "So, anyway, I'm amazed that

I'm this casual. Here I am in my pajamas and sleeping . . . with you right here."

"Did you think I might steal the silver?"

She shook her head. "No. There isn't any."

"Yeah, I know. I looked." A big teasing grin followed that. "But it's not so hard to understand, Dianna. I mean, about my being here and you sleeping. We have been, well, intimate, as they say. At least now I know how you look in the morning when you first wake up."

"And how is that?" She raised her eyebrows, evidently daring him to say the wrong thing—or maybe it was the right thing.

"Great. You look great."

"You are such a liar, but thanks. Anyway, I guess we got that awkwardness out of the way, didn't we?"

"Yes. And seeing each other naked. Did that already, too." He seasoned that remark with a big-bad-wolf grin.

Dianna arched an eyebrow. "Moving along, Mr. Adams."

Chris loved this teasing, sexy banter between them. It spoke of an easy intimacy he'd not experienced before to this degree with anyone else. "Okay, moving along in our consideration of awkward relationship moments already experienced. Oh, got another one. I've asked you to marry me and you said no, so I don't have to do that again."

She cocked her head in question. "You're really not ever going to ask me again? Really? Ever?"

Chris schooled his features into a solemn seriousness. "No, I'm not. One per customer."

"Well, fine, then. All that's left is moving in together and having children, right?"

"Right. Except for our mothers."

"Our mothers?"

"Yeah. Do you think yours will like mine? If they don't, our lives will be miserable. I ask you because you know yours, obviously, and you've had the misfortune of talking to mine. So what do you think?"

Dianna grimaced and slouched down into the sofa's

cushions. "Oh, Chris, I'm afraid they'll love each other. Wouldn't that be awful?"

"A total disaster. They'll compare notes."

"It won't be pretty. And you'd already know that if you'd come over to my parents' house the other weekend for hamburgers when I invited you."

"The one where your cop brother was?"

She laughed. "Are you afraid of Tommy?"

"Yes. And Edward."

"The man's an accountant."

"There's a reason why they say they're *crunching* numbers. They use a nutcracker to do that."

"Listen to you. Anyway, back to our moms. About the only difference between them is my mother knows I'm not a prostitute."

"Man." Embarrassed, Chris rubbed a hand over his jaw. "My mother's got that into her head and there's no shaking it. Hey, I have an idea. I always take her to supper on Wednesdays—"

"My mother would say you're a good son."

"Well, score a point for me. So why don't you go with me tomorrow night and meet my mother?"

"No. Can't do that."

"Why not?"

"Lots of reasons. One being she doesn't know that you and Veronica broke up yet. Maybe you ought to attend to that little detail before you spring me on her."

"Good point."

"I know. When I talked to her on the phone, she went into great detail about how much she liked Veronica and about how you two were a serious item and were about to be married soon."

"I never told her that. But she had this whole opera composed about how I should marry Ronnie and make grandbabies."

"Well, that ought to be a fun dinner tomorrow . . . which brings me to the other reason why I won't be accompanying you. This shiner of mine. Your mother will be certain I got it in a drug bust or in a hooker deal gone bad."

"A hooker deal gone bad?"

"I don't know what they're called when it turns out bad."

"I should be glad for that."

"You're very funny, Mr. Chris Adams." Dianna suddenly cocked her head. "Hey, what's your middle name?"

"Where'd that come from?"

"You know mine. I don't know yours. Just trying to even the score."

"All right. It's Allen. A-L-L-E-N."

"So, Christopher Allen Adams."

"Yes?"

"Nothing. Just testing it."

"I see. And how does it play?"

Dianna nodded. "I like it." She got up off the sofa. "Will you excuse me? I have to go to the little girls' room."

"Sure." Chris came halfway up and put a hand out to her. "Be careful about moving around on your own. Your perceptions will be off with that eye like that."

"Whoa." She stood there, swaying, her hand on the sofa's arm. "You have had a black eye before, haven't you?"

"More than one." She started to walk away, and he called out to her back, "Hey, you hungry yet? I could fix something."

She stopped and slowly turned around. "Well, that's sweet. But I distinctly remember you saying more than once that you can't cook."

"I can't. Maybe I should have said I could break something, then."

"In that case, no, I'm fine." She turned away again.

Chris grinned at the baggy seat in her loose pajama bottoms. "A can of soup, maybe? I can open soup. And use a microwave oven. Okay, I can't. But I can call someone who knows how."

She just waved a hand at him without stopping or turning around. "Shut up. Don't make me laugh. It makes my face hurt, and I have to pee." After a few more shuffling steps, she said, "Those two things are *not* connected." Before she went around the corner, she turned to him, her eyes wide, imploring. "Chris, thanks for staying. I appreciate it more than you know. But I know it's late, so if you want to get home, I'll understand."

He feigned horror. "You're not going to send me out in this rush-hour traffic, are you?"

"Not if you don't want to go. I just didn't, well, want to keep you."

"Why not? What's wrong with me?" Chris crossed his arms over his chest. "I'm housebroken."

She chuckled. "Could you *be* cuter? I just meant if you had somewhere else you need to be. You've already gone above and beyond the call of duty with me, but I—"

"Uh-oh. The big brush-off is coming."

"Will you stop that?" She shook her head at him, as if she were thinking, *Men.* "Never mind. Just give me a minute, okay? If the phone rings, answer it."

"Yeah, right."

"Seriously. It could be about business."

"It won't be. It'll be your mother or one of your brothers."

"Or it could be my father. He likes to blow things up."

Chris started to feel sick. "You mean like out of proportion?"

"No. I mean like *ka-boom*."

"Well, all kinds of good news here. We'll just pray it doesn't ring then, won't we? And you don't lock the bathroom door, missy." She raised her uninjured eyebrow at him. "In case you fall. Or pass out."

"I thought for a minute I had a Peeping Tom on my hands."

"Hey, I'm off probation for that. I was framed. But I am still facing charges on the axe-murder thing."

She grinned at him. "Shut up." And then disappeared down the hallway.

A moment later, Chris heard a door close. He relaxed. She'd safely made it to the john. Satisfied with how this afternoon was going and how witty and warm and funny Dianna was and how full of himself he was, Chris grinned at the living room at large and then sighted on the sacred teddy bear sitting at the other end of the sofa from him. "Hey, buddy, if this keeps going this well, you and I could be sharing living space—"

The telephone rang. Chris's feeling of good will fled. "Oh, shit. How'd she know it would ring?" He stared stupidly at the ringing apparatus just sitting there on the end table at Dianna's end of the sofa with the teddy bear. "Get that, will you?" he asked the teddy bear. Stubbornly, it wouldn't. Chris grimaced at it. "Traitor."

By the third ring, he had the handset plucked up. He punched the talk button. Knowing somehow that there was no way this was going to end well, he put the handset to his ear and said, "Hello. Dianna West's residence."

# CHAPTER 17

"Chris, exactly what did my mother say? Word for word." Dianna was now dressed in jeans and a blue V-necked Victoria's Secret T-shirt. Also wearing dark, dark sunglasses against the spring evening's lowering yet very bright sunlight, she sat seat-belted in the front passenger's seat of Chris's big killer Beemer. And they were on their way to the hospital. It was like being in a space capsule or something. Not one outside sound penetrated the interior. Or vice versa, which was a good thing because rush-hour traffic made Dianna cuss.

And right now, rush-hour traffic was all but standing still. In fact, snails . . . escargots, should any of them chance to be French . . . were whizzing past. Or so it seemed. "Can't we go any faster? Go around those people, Chris. You have a BMW, for God's sake. Drive like it, man."

Without taking his eyes off the road, Chris reached over and gently, reassuringly, squeezed Dianna's hand. "Hey, calm down. It's okay. You're not the one having the baby. Karen is, and she's already at the hospital."

"I know, but this is so scary and so exciting. Tommy is probably scared to death. God, Chris, I am going to be an aunt. Hurry! Pass that nine-thousand-year-old man in that Dodge. I think he's dead at the wheel or something. He's going about three damn miles per hour."

"Dianna," Chris said, still maddeningly calm, "pretend I'm Greyhound, okay, and leave the driving to me. You might not realize it, but we're going sixty-five right now. And I think I'm beginning to understand that ticket you got yesterday."

"You're paying for that."

"I said I would." He withdrew his hand from hers and put it back on the leather-wrapped steering wheel.

"And that's another thing. Why *are* you so calm, dammit? I find that to be a very annoying trait right now, Chris. I really do. My sister-in-law is going to have a baby, and I need to get there."

"And we will, but safely."

She very hotly crossed her arms. "You sound like some highway patrolman or somebody's grandpa."

His eyes hidden behind those silvered sunglasses of his, Chris spared her a glance. His mouth was unsmiling. "Speaking of annoying traits, Dianna . . ." He left it unfinished.

"Oh, I know, I'm sorry. But I think you don't want to get there fast because you think my brothers—no, my whole family—is going to kill you when they see this black eye, don't you?"

"And there's another annoying habit. Predicting my violent death. Wow. Two annoying habits revealed in as many minutes."

"Three if you count cussing and yelling while driving or even riding in heavy traffic."

"Three it is, then. By the way, you're never driving our children anywhere."

"We're not going to have any."

"You don't want to have children?"

"Yes, I want to have children."

"Just not with me?"

Whimpering, Dianna leaned her forehead against Chris's muscled bicep. "I can't do this right now, Chris, okay?"

He gave her leg an affectionate squeeze. "All right.

Sorry. Bad timing. So, I was going to say I've never seen this side of you before, but then I realized that's not true because I've seen all sides of you, having seen you naked—Ouch." She'd sat up and hit his arm. "Don't hit the driver, ma'am. Very dangerous."

"*Anyway,* which side of me haven't you seen before? And we'd better be talking personality here."

"We are. The side where you yell and cuss and hit and insult. Is that from having older brothers?"

"Yes. And I'll be sure to tell them you said so."

"Great. At least we'll be at a hospital. That's got to be a good place to be if you're going to get your ass kicked."

"Ha-ha. And, anyway, thanks for thinking I'm obnoxious and bossy."

A grin creased the corners of Chris's mouth. "Your words. Not mine. But maybe those reasons are why you're not married yet."

She hit his arm again.

"Did we not just talk about hitting the driver? I'd hate to have to pull over and put you out at the side of the road." He turned a full smile on her now. "And I will not refund the cost of your ticket, lady."

Grinning now, too, and fearing she was totally smitten with this guy—no, knowing she was—and knowing she was behaving badly and Chris was exhibiting the patience of a saint with her, Dianna again apologized. "Sorry. But what *did* my mother say? You never told me. I mean, when you answered the phone."

" 'Who is this?' "

"What?" Dianna looked all around. "Who's who?"

Chris laughed. "You sound like an owl. I was just repeating for you what your mother said. She said, 'Who is this?' "

"Oh, I get it. Sorry. But she said it like that?"

"Pretty much."

"Ooh, Chris, look!" She grabbed his shirtsleeve. "That other lane's open now, and it's moving faster. Go, go, go."

Using his turn signal, Chris went, went, went, smoothly moving his muscle machine into the next lane's flow of traffic. "Happy now?"

"Yes." Dianna let go of him and slumped back against her leather seatback. "What else did she say?"

"Well, first I said I was me. Or Chris Adams. For some reason, that seemed to satisfy her. Have you told her about me?"

"No."

"My feelings aren't hurt." He was so droll.

"Oh, come on, there was nothing to tell until last night." Dianna's tone of voice was a plea for understanding. "But I don't even want to tell her now."

"Again, my feelings are not hurt."

"Chris. Look at me." Dianna pulled her sunglasses off and pointed to her shiner.

He glanced over at her. "All right, point taken. So then she said, 'Where's Dianna? I called her work and they said she went home sick.' Not wanting to get into that with her since I didn't know yet what you had or hadn't told her about last night and us, I went with a literal answer and simply said you were on the pot."

Dianna grabbed his arm and squeezed hard. "Do not *ever* say 'pot' to my mother in the same sentence as my name."

"Yeah, I found that out. College?"

"Undergraduate. It was the biggest mess. Anyway . . . ?"

"Anyway, she said that I was to tell you that Karen's water broke."

"Well, you had to love that, and on an empty stomach. You poor man."

"I thought at first it might be some kind of code."

"It is. It means 'baby on the way.' "

"I found that out, too. Then she said—all in one breath; let me see if I can do it—to tell you that she didn't think you were all that sick . . . though how she could know that, I don't know . . . and then she said I was to tell you to hurry and get to the hospital and no, wait, on second thought, what was I doing that was so important anyway and I was to drive you so she could be sure you would arrive alive."

Dianna's grin was sickly. "She's ridden with me before."

"As a sort of punishment?"

"Yes. She was mad at my father this one time and wouldn't ride with him, and she won't drive herself—"

"My mother, either."

"A pain in the ass, no? Anyway, by the time she got there, her blood pressure was way up and she had to be put on medicine and she blames me for giving her hypertension. So every time she refills her medicine, whatever Medicare doesn't pay, she sends me a bill for the amount."

"That's one tough woman. We have to make certain, Dianna, that she never meets my mother. If they get together and start comparing notes, do you realize what could happen?"

"I shudder to think."

"Exactly. So what I don't get in all this is why your mother didn't even question who I was and what I was doing at your place and answering the phone. For all she knew, I could have been a burglar or some—"

"Be glad you didn't have that conversation. I know my mother. She'd say you couldn't be a burglar because you'd already given her your name and a burglar wouldn't do that. Or even answer the phone. Ta-da." Dianna sat back smugly, happily crossing her arms and wiggling her sandaled feet.

Chris laughed. "You must be feeling better, Dianna. You're awfully talkative now and pretty animated. That Advil help?"

"Sure. But not as much as the Percodan I took when I was in the bathroom."

The BMW swerved and Chris yelled. "What the hell?

You took Percodan? What are you doing taking Percodan? How many?"

"One. Calm down, Chris. It's legal. And I'm not driving, and I haven't been drinking. It's my prescription I got when I had my appendectomy two years ago."

"Two *years* ago? You took *old* Percodan?"

"What are you—my pharmacist? It's not expired by much. And I really do feel better." She grinned at him.

"Oh, this is rich. I show up, a stranger, at the hospital with you for a blessed event. And you're stoned and have a black eye. Your family is going to love me."

"Good," Dianna giggled, leaning over to hold on to his arm and rest her head against him. "Because I sure do."

Fourth floor of the hospital. Maternity ward. Looked like stepping into a Mother Goose book with all the appliquéd lambs and flowers and little babies that decorated the walls. That was supposed to be soothing, right? Well, it wasn't. In fact, the very notion that he was in the alien environment of a birthing center gave Chris emotional hives. He could only imagine the fear a man would go through knowing his wife was in the throes of giving birth and he was about to be a father. Scary and exciting stuff.

"Now, who are you again?"

Obviously, he wasn't as invisible as he'd tried to make himself by merely being quiet. Chris closed the *Modern Maternity* magazine he'd been idly turning the pages of— *who knew that maternity clothes were now so stylish?*— and smiled at Dianna's mother, who sat next to him. "I'm Chris Adams, Mrs. West. We spoke on the phone."

"I know that. I'm not senile."

"No, of course not. I didn't mean to imply—"

"I want to know what you are to my daughter."

Now, there was a tricky question. "Right now, I'm her ... friend. And her chauffeur."

"Right now?"

"Well, we could be working together soon, too. Computers." And that was as far as he was going with this gray-haired, apple-cheeked little woman who eyed him as if he'd sprung up in a musty patch of dank earth in some swamp somewhere.

"Oh, computers, you say?" This came from Dianna's father—the man who liked to blow things up, as Chris recalled. The harmless-looking old guy peeked around his wife and smiled at Chris. "Hate the things, myself. Just a lot of noise and trouble. Nothing good about them at all."

Chris just smiled and smiled. "Yes, sir. A lot of people think that."

"You know, when televisions came along, nobody thought much of them, either. Thought they were just a passing fancy. Telephones, too. And automobiles. Airplanes, the same thing."

So that pretty much put them back at the turn of the twentieth century. Still smiling, though it now hurt, Chris simply nodded his head, fearing that Mr. West was going to discount every invention all the way back to the wheel. "So, Mr. West," he said brightly, looking past Mrs. West and acutely aware of her continuing close scrutiny of every pore in his face. "How do you feel about becoming a grandfather?"

"Oh, fine. Good. Good. Karen's a strong girl, ought to be fine. You know, back in my day, women just dropped the babies and went back to work in the fields the same day."

And that got him his wife's attention—much to Chris's heated relief. "I never worked in a field a day in my life. And all three of your children were born in hospitals, Mel. What's wrong with you?"

"Joy, I was just telling the boy about how things were—"

"Well, no one gives a hoot. He can read a history book if he wants to know about—"

"Mom, Dad? Not now, okay?" This was Edward, a tall, lanky guy who eyed Chris with a distressing solemnity and who sat across from him and the older Wests, next to his wife, a pretty redhead named Vera. She sat stiff and excited on the lime-green vinyl seats, her eyes bright with expectancy. Edward was holding her hand tightly. Chris suspected he did so to keep her from yet again flitting down the hall to the nurses' station to see how her sister-in-law was doing. Though Edward's remarks were directed to his parents, his gaze bored into Chris. "We wouldn't want to give Chris here the wrong impression about our family."

"Chris here" wondered if he should make for an exit. *I didn't hit her,* he wanted to say to Dianna's brother. But he wisely didn't. Instead, he forced a smile and did say, "No problem." . . . Whatever the hell that meant in this context.

Yes, they'd seen Dianna and her eye. And yes, they weren't happy with him or her or the official "I walked into a wall" story. And no, they weren't happy to meet him. And yes, they were doing nothing to hide that fact. Could this be more awkward? Well, yes, it could be, because it was: Dianna was currently not present to lend moral support. She'd gone off with Tommy—the expectant father/cop brother who, blessedly, was in surgery scrubs and so did not have his gun with him—to see Karen in the labor room. Only two family members at a time could go back.

In a sweat, Chris didn't know if he wished that the elder Wests would go next, or if the Edward Wests would go. All he knew was he wanted Dianna to come back—and now.

"So, Chris, what do you do for a living?" Edward West asked, leaving off the implied *besides beating up on women*.

Sliding a glance the way of the senior Mr. West, Chris said, "Computers. I work with computers."

"In what capacity?"

God, how he hated accountants. "Global consulting on new technology. That sort of thing."

"That pay much?" This was Mr. Mel West, the elder

statesman of Dianna's family. He still peered around his
wife, who had renewed her consideration of every one of
Chris's facial features.

Chris managed a bleak smile for Dianna's parents.
"Uh, yes, sir, it can."

Mr. West did not think much of that. "Need to get
yourself a real job, son. You go to college?"

"No."

"Should get yourself an education and make something
of yourself. How old are you now?"

Okay, this was going well. "I'm twenty-eight, sir."

Mr. West nodded. "Not too late. A good technical college, something like that. Take some classes. Get ahead."

"Uh, yes, sir, I'll take that under consideration."

"Well, see that you do. You know, my daughter has a
master's degree. And Edward here is a CPA. And Tommy
has a degree in criminology. Could have gone with the
FBI, if he'd wanted to."

Chris smiled. "I'm sure you're very proud of them all."

Just then, Dianna came around the corner, grinning stupidly. "Hi, everybody. Karen's . . . somewhere. What are
you all doing here?"

A thrill of joy leaped through Chris. Had he been eight
years old, he knew, he would have burst into relieved tears
and run to her, throwing his arms around her waist and
begging her never to leave him alone again with her family. But since he was the stated twenty-eight years of age,
all he did was stand, as did her parents and brother and
sister-in-law, and smile. And stare.

And *that* was when Tommy—crew-cut, muscled,
shorter than his brother, Edward, and his face hot with
anger—came around the corner right behind Dianna and
grabbed his sister's arm. "Dianna, wait a minute." He held
her at his side and sighted on Chris. "What the hell's
wrong with my sister?"

Alarm flitted through Chris. He swept his gaze over
the policeman's muscled person . . . still looking for that
gun. "Nothing. I think she's perfect."

"Bullshit. She's loopy as hell is what she is. Look at her."

Everyone did. Tommy was right. She looked loopy as hell. "She took a Percodan."

"Oh, my God in heaven," cried Dianna's mother. "She's allergic to that. It makes her hallucinate. She got some when she had her appendix removed. I told her to throw that stuff out."

Tommy's expression became that of a rabid bulldog. "You gave my sister drugs?"

*Enough. Game over.* Chris got pissed and lost it. "Hell *no,* I did not give your sister drugs. Only Advil. Two of them. But then she took the Percodan in the privacy of her own bathroom and from an old prescription of hers. I didn't even know she had done that until we were halfway here. And, while we're on the subject, I did *not* hit her and I have never in my life hit any woman. So everybody can just knock that shit off right now, okay? And *no,* I don't need to go to college or a technical school because I was a multimillionaire before I was twenty-five because of an invention of mine that Bill Gates bought. And I live in a penthouse and drive a BMW. And what's more, I'm a really nice guy who comes from a nice family, I'm a regular-guy sports fan, and I give a lot of money to charity and I support my mother—and, dammit, I just happen to be in love with your daughter." He took a breath. "Or sister, as the case may be." Feeling way too hot, Chris sighted on Vera the redhead. "Sister-in-law, in your case."

After taking a breath, Chris once again addressed the astonished, staring assemblage of Dianna's immediate family here for a joyous occasion that had nothing to do with him. "Any questions?"

And there were. There were many of them. From all quarters.

"Bill Gates? You know Bill Gates?" Mel West.

"You're a millionaire?" Joy West.

"If you're all that great, how come I've never heard of you?" Edward.

"You're in love with Dianna?" Vera.

"So, what *did* happen to her eye?" Tommy.

Chris stood there blinking and thinking, *Can of worms*, for some reason. In his mind's eye, he saw fat worms wriggling out of this huge tin can—

"I think maybe I'd better get something to eat." And that was Dianna.

So, of course, that put Chris, his expression grim, in the hospital's basement cafeteria with a grinning, hallucinating Dianna in tow. Bombarding his senses were the commingled scents of the food and of industrial-strength cleaners and the steamy humidity of the hot-water warmers under the metal trays of the selections. Chris could only imagine how all of this was affecting Dianna's already addled senses. The setup of the place was confusing even for someone like himself who wasn't drugged out. Holding on to Dianna's arm so she didn't float off like a helium balloon, Chris stood back and looked around to get his bearings. A huge stack of trays here. Two lines. One for hot food. One for soups, salads, and sandwiches.

Everything smelled pretty good. Chris's stomach growled to prove it. Okay, drinks and condiments were nowhere to be seen. A huge salad bar ran down the middle of the aisle. Two cash registers at the end of it. Medical types dressed in all colors of surgical garb, some with lab coats and beepers, swirled by Chris and Dianna. Obviously familiar with the setup and in a hurry, they offered only a cursory "Excuse me" as they rushed around.

Damn. It was like high tide and he and Dianna were trapped in a fierce whirlpool. "So, what do you want to eat, Dianna?"

"Coffee."

"Which is not a food. And . . . no, you're awake enough as it is. Let's not add caffeine to the mix, okay?"

She grinned up at him. "You're very handsome, you know."

She'd made him grin. Chris exhaled. She might be hallucinating, but she was still cute as hell and saying everything he wanted to hear. Too bad it didn't count since she probably would not remember any of this. "Thank you. But let's get you something hot to eat, okay? Some protein and carbs."

Dianna wrinkled her nose at that. "Sounds fattening."

"You hardly need to worry about that."

"Good. Then I want chicken and dumplings."

Chris blinked. What were the odds of there being chicken and dumplings here tonight? Then he realized Dianna was reading the posted menu for the day on a big dry-mark board. And, sure enough, right there was listed chicken and dumplings. *Thank you, Jesus.*

"All right, come on, let's wade in." Chris gently shook an admonitory finger at her. "You stay with me, okay?"

"Okay. I'll stay with you always."

This was torture. "Good. Ready?"

"As I'll ever be. Look at that fountain. Isn't it beautiful?"

*Fountain. Fountain.* Chris looked around. Found it. On the wall. A mural of an outdoor scene of what looked like Greek ruins. In the foreground was a fountain. "Yeah. Nice. Come on, let's get some food into you. You'll feel better."

She frowned up at him. "I feel fine now."

"Of course you do. You're high." With that, he grabbed a tray, set it on the metal rails that ran the length of the hot food selections, got two sets of napkin-wrapped silverware, and ordered their meals. Got the drinks—finally found those on the other side of the salad bar—and paid the nice, elderly black lady at the register. That done, and balancing a full, unwieldly tray in one hand while holding on to Dianna with his other, Chris guided them safely to a table way in the back of the crowded room by a wall of windows that looked out onto the pleasing scene of a bricked courtyard planted with flowers and having a gurgling-stream effect.

More than one table of medical employees stopped eating and stared at Dianna's black eye and then at Chris as they passed by. Only by gritting his teeth and refusing to make eye contact had he resisted the urge to say that her eye was not his fault. And yet, obliquely, it was. How well he knew that and how well he knew that the gnawing in his stomach was as much from guilt as it was from hunger and worrying about Dianna.

*Damn.* It was a good thing for Ronnie that she wasn't here because Chris couldn't say for sure what he'd do if he saw her.

Waiting on Dianna now, hand and foot—and realizing that he took pleasure in doing so and wasn't the least bit impatient or put out about it—Chris got her seated and her food arranged in front of her. Napkin across her lap, fork in her right hand, everything salted and peppered for her. Only then did he sit down and arrange his own plate and drink and silverware. "You got everything you need, Dianna?"

She smiled sweetly at him. "Yes. You're here, aren't you?"

God, he wanted to believe these things she was saying. Chris's heart actually lurched with his need to believe her, yet he firmed his lips together. Did she mean it? Did she have any idea what she was saying? He decided to test her. "Dianna, honey, where are we?"

"Where are we?" she repeated. Then, frowning and looking befuddled—and totally little-girl adorable—Dianna made a slow sweeping visual pass of the noisy cafeteria. When she was done with that, her gaze again rested on Chris. Her pupils were so dilated that her eyes appeared black and only ringed with their usual gold color. "My guess is a cafeteria. In a hospital. Right?"

"Right. And why are we here?"

She looked at the food in front of her and then raised her head to look at Chris. "To eat?"

That got a chuckle out of him. *Okay, be more specific.* "Yes, to eat. But what are we doing here at the hospital, Dianna?"

She grinned widely and warmly. "We're having a baby."

Chris waffled, thinking he could go either way with that answer. "Sort of. Not us, actually, but ... ?" He waited for her to fill in a name.

"Tommy."

"That's good. Close. Not literally Tommy, but who?"

A frown flitted across her features and then cleared. "Karen. Can I eat now?"

Chris laughed, picking up his fork. "Sure. You can eat now."

Reality came back to Dianna with a rush. Pop! Zow!— and here she was. She gasped, breathing in deeply, holding it, unable to exhale yet, and clutching at a yucky little round table's edge. Finally her lungs allowed her to exhale. "Ohmigod, Chris."

He was sitting across from her. "Hey, you're back!"

"Back from where? Where am I? Wait. I know. Karen. Baby. Hospital."

"Yeah. Exactly. And this is obviously the cafeteria."

She pointed at him. "Chicken and dumplings, right?"

"Very good. You were a good girl and cleaned your plate."

Dianna gave a start. "Oh, Chris, the baby. Did I miss the baby?"

He held out a placating hand to her. "No. There's no baby yet. Edward said he'd come get us if anything happened. And he hasn't yet, so you didn't miss anything. More importantly, how are you feeling now?"

"Wait. I'll check." Dianna turned her attention inward to her body, paying attention to its signals. Everything seemed in order. "Good," she told him. "I'm okay." Then she frowned. "Percodan, right?"

"Right. And we will be flushing that as soon as you

get back home." A troubled expression claimed his fea
tures. "Why in God's name did you take something you'r
allergic to, Dianna? You scared the hell out of everyone.

She felt just awful about that. "I'm so sorry. I knov
it's crazy, but I forget which painkiller it is that I'm al
lergic to. I hardly ever take anything and things accu
mulate in the medicine chest and I don't clean it out, ther
when I need something, I've forgotten which one of then
it was—"

"Okay. Fair enough. We'll just clean that cabinet ou
and write down somewhere what you can and cannot take
okay?"

She smiled. "Okay. You're a nice man, Chris Adams."

"So you've been saying."

"I have?" Embarrassed for herself, Dianna raised
hand to cover her face. "What have I been saying?"

Chris chuckled at her discomfiture. "Let's just say I'n
very flattered. But, hey, don't beat yourself up." His darl
eyes warmed. "I've missed you."

Dianna frowned. "You keep saying that. How long wa:
I gone?"

"About two or three hours, total. Here in the cafeteri:
about an hour. Long enough for it to pretty much clea
out."

She looked around. He was right. There weren't more
than five or six tables, besides theirs, that were occupied
"Wow. This place is pretty bleak."

Chris shrugged. "Not bad as hospitals go."

Dianna looked at the all-but-licked-clean plate in fron
of her. "So I guess the food's pretty good."

"You seemed to think so. You ate yours and part o
mine."

Dianna sat back in her chair. "I am totally appalled a
myself. You poor man." Then, that "poor man" thing re
minded her . . . "My family, Chris. How'd they trea
you?"

Grinning, he pushed his chair back, away from the ta
ble, and crossed his legs, an ankle atop the opposite knee.

and crossed his arms over his broad chest. Totally sensual and powerful. "Let's just say they were polite, then curious, then pissed, and finally pretty amazed with me."

"That doesn't sound good. Except the amazed part."

He shrugged. "Not 'good' amazed, but I'm a big boy. They'll come around."

*They'll come around.* That meant he intended to be around. Suddenly flooded with emotion for this strong, handsome, smart man who made her laugh and made her yearn and want and need and be better than she actually was, Dianna leaned forward over the wobbly table, shoving her dinner plate back and crossing her arms atop the table. "You know what, Chris Adams?"

"No. What?"

"I think I might love you."

She'd surprised him with that, she could tell. His eyebrows went up and he sat up straight. But then he shrugged, looking unaffected and waving away her declaration. "Sorry. Old news. You already said that."

Dianna's eyes rounded. "I did? While I was under the influence?"

"Yeah."

"Well, that doesn't mean I don't mean it, you know."

He grinned, reaching across the table for her hand. "That's nice to know. And you know what else? I think I might love you, too."

Warmed to her very soul, overjoyed, Dianna reached out to Chris across the cluttered table in this most unlikely of locations and grasped his hand. The instant he touched her, she felt the electric shock of joy and the sheer rightness of this moment and this man—

Then she heard a voice. A familiar one. A mean one. Off to her left. Then a laugh. His hand still in hers, Chris froze, gripping her hand hard. Dianna's involuntary response had been the same. She looked into Chris's eyes, saw the recognition in his face . . . and saw a muscle tic in his jaw. Dianna wrenched her hand out of his and stood up abruptly, forcing her molded plastic chair to scrape back loudly in the almost empty seating area.

"Dianna, don't." Chris was getting up out of his chair

"Oh, but I am."

"Let me handle this."

"No. I owe her. And I'm going to kick her ass."

# CHAPTER 18

Dianna immediately set out to do just that. With Chris hot on her heels, but with her closer to her intended victim, she stalked around the tables and toward the cash registers—and toward Veronica Alexander . . . who was making all lovey-dovey with some sharp-looking, tanned, buttoned-down blond man in a white lab coat—a doctor, no doubt—who was paying for two cups of coffee.

The man was of no consequence, and so would be allowed to live. Having dismissed him, Dianna riveted her gaze on the object of her anger. What with her back to the room and her looking adoringly up at the doctor-god, Veronica hadn't spied her yet. And that was fine with Dianna. The element of surprise was a proven military tactic; everyone knew that. And she meant to take full advantage of the maneuver. God, she was so boiling mad she could just snatch this blond woman bald-headed.

Just as the doctor finished his transaction with the cashier, an elderly black lady whom Dianna dimly remembered, she stepped up in front of Frankenlawyer and her sweetie—still only one step ahead of Chris—and got in their startled faces when they turned and found her standing there. Dianna crossed her arms and shifted her weight to one foot. "Evening."

Immediately, Chris grabbed her arm and tried to pull her back. "Dianna."

"You need something else, baby?" the cashier asked Chris.

"Maybe a squadron of marines, ma'am. I'll let you know."

The cashier, sitting on a stool behind her counter, just nodded. "All right, y'all go on ahead, then, with your business. Don't mind me. I'm here until closing."

Hearing this exchange as background noise, and ignoring Chris's pressure on her arm, Dianna directed all her anger at the startled blond attorney, with whom she now stood toe to toe. "I hope that guy you're clinging to is a plastic surgeon, honey," Dianna said pleasantly, "because you're going to need one in about two seconds."

The doctor sucked in a big breath. "What is this? What's going on?"

"Lord above," the full-figured cashier intoned. "Annie's going to be mad she took her break and missed this." Dianna just stared at the woman, who explained, "Annie's the other cashier. She was sitting right there when you checked out. And you look better now, honey. You didn't look too good when you came through the line with your young man. But you're good now."

Dianna nodded. "Thanks." And then held a hand up as if to block the doctor. "Hold on a minute and you'll find out what's going on here." Next she turned to her nemesis. "Why don't you tell him, Veronica, what's going on here?"

"Yeah. Tell him, honey." This was the cashier again, whose name tag proclaimed her to be Merle. So, Merle crossed her arms and added, "We all want to know what's up. And don't look at me like that. There's nobody behind you in line, girl. We got time."

With great satisfaction, Dianna watched color stain Veronica's cheeks. Her chin aquiver—no doubt with anger and you've-been-caught-sister embarrassment—she flicked her gaze from Dianna to Chris and then back to Dianna. "What are you doing here? Are you spying on me?"

"Don't flatter yourself, Veronica." That was Chris. Dianna looked up at him and saw him dividing his gaze between his former lover and her apparent new lover. Dianna wondered just *how* new, though—and so did Chris, apparently. "Who's your little friend?" he asked, doing Dianna's heart a world of good. "Aren't you going to introduce us?"

"Fine." Veronica's eyes narrowed to slits. Obviously, she'd recovered. "You want an introduction? I'll give you one. No reason now why not." Without looking away from Chris, she raised her right hand to indicate the doctor. "Anthony, I'd like you to meet Chris Adams"—she pointed at Chris—"and Chris, I'd like you to meet Dr. Anthony Boatman." She indicated the doctor, who raised the tray he held in both hands as if to indicate that he would shake Chris's hand but his hands weren't free.

"No need, Doctor," Chris assured him, his face a hardened mask. "I can sympathize with just how full your hands are." He looked right at Veronica.

"Lord," Merle cut in, fanning herself. "This is better than my stories on the TV." She turned to Dianna. "Who're you, baby?"

Really liking this woman, Dianna shook Merle's hand. "Hi. I'm Dianna. The other woman."

"The other woman? Child, you don't look like the other woman. You're just a baby."

"And yet I am." Dianna quirked her mouth, purposely talking directly to Merle and ignoring Veronica, her doctor boyfriend, and even Chris. "Well, it's kind of a long story, Merle, but Chris here"—she pointed to him—"thought he wanted to marry Veronica"—she pointed to her—"so he came to my business, which is called Popping the Question—"

"What kind of a business is it?"

"I help bachelors come up with romantic scenarios to ask their girlfriends to marry them."

"Seriously?" Merle smacked playfully at Dianna's arm. "That's wonderful. My boy has a girlfriend I want him to marry. You got a card or something you can give me, honey?"

Dianna patted herself down. "No, sorry. My purse is upstairs. My sister-in-law is going to have a baby."

"Oh, that's nice. Congratulations. Hey, you in the book? I'll look you up and have my boy call. His name is Ronald. He's a good boy. Got a nice girlfriend, too."

"Sure. That would be great. Tell him to ask for me. Dianna West."

"Dianna, can we—"

She turned to Chris. "Hold on. I'm almost done here." She turned back to Merle. "So, anyway—"

"How'd you get that eye, baby? What happened with that?"

And there it was, what she wanted to talk about. "Thanks for asking. *She* did it." Dianna pointed to Veronica.

Dr. Boatman sucked in a breath. "Veronica? You hit this woman?"

Looking spitting mad, the corners of her eyes and her mouth twitching, Veronica ignored her little friend and turned on Dianna. "I will not be humiliated like this in public. You will step aside and allow us to pass, or I will—"

"You'll what?" Dianna interrupted. "Hit me again in front of all these witnesses?"

"All right, this is enough," Chris said, tugging Dianna back to his side. "We're done here. And I think you are, too, Veronica. If you're smart, you'll drop all your talk of a lawsuit. Because I think your Dr. Boatman here explains a lot of things that you or he won't want brought up in a court of law. Your weekend trips. The overnight things. Your being tired and so overworked. It's all clear to me now. And things are starting to make a lot of sense."

"Now, wait just a damn minute here," Dr. Boatman said. "I'm a married man. How dare you suggest I have anything going on with Miss Alexander?"

Her expression stricken, Veronica blanched and jerked

her head up to look at her doctor companion. "Tony! How dare you deny me—"

"Baby, that's a wedding ring on Dr. Boatman's finger." Merle was right on target and talking to Veronica. "Of course he's going to deny you. You leave them married men alone, girl. Ain't nothing but trouble that you don't need." She held a placating hand out to Dr. Boatman. "No offense."

Dr. Boatman looked pretty ill right then. He stared at the cups of coffee on his tray. Dianna could almost feel sorry for him and for Veronica because they just seemed pathetic, and she really didn't want to hit the woman anymore. She probably wouldn't have anyway.

"Just one thing, Veronica," Chris said, grabbing their attention again. "Why the big scene in my apartment? Here you were all but living with me for the past four years—"

"What?" Dr. Boatman apparently had been lied to, also. "You were still with him? You said you'd broken it off with your . . . lover over six months ago."

"Oh, now, wait a minute, Dr. Boatman," Merle interrupted. "You don't get to go all betrayal on us. You're married."

"One more word out of you and I'll have your job," Dr. Boatman threatened the cashier.

Chris pushed forward. "Don't you go threatening this woman. You want to pick on someone, you pick on—"

"Hold on, son. I can take care of this." Merle pulled Chris back and eyed Dr. Boatman. "You want my job? Is that it? Well, you can have it, but you won't like it. And don't you forget that I know your business. Now, you just stand there and be quiet. Or you go on off and drink your coffee. But you let these people straighten out their lives, you hear me?"

The doctor slammed the tray down on the metal rails, turned on his heel, and stormed off.

"Tony!" Veronica called out, but he didn't turn around.

"You better leave Tony alone, honey," was Merle's

advice. "He's too mad to talk to right now. Besides, you've got some explaining to do here."

Veronica narrowed her eyes at Merle. "Excuse me, but do you know who I am?"

Merle crossed her arms and looked Veronica up and down. "I think I do, girl. You're some cheating, little two-faced Barbie, that's who you are." The cashier turned to Chris. "Go on, honey. You were saying?"

To Dianna's surprise, Chris chuckled and put his arm around her shoulders and hugged her to his side. She wrapped her arm around his waist, feeling much calmer and very much happier. Chris addressed Merle first. "I like you, Merle. You're pretty damned cool. If Dr. Boatman makes good on his threat, and you ever need a job, look me up. Or better yet, just call Dianna. She'll know how to reach me."

Then he faced Veronica. "Why the scene, Veronica? That's all I want to know. If you had something going on with this other guy and wanted to be with him, why didn't you just tell me? And why'd you come over to my place saying yes and wanting to marry me? What was that all about?"

Veronica's expression closed. "I don't owe you any explanations, Chris. Not after finding you in bed with *her*."

Dianna stiffened. Chris tightened his grip on her, but kept talking to Veronica. "All right, fine, I'll talk. I think you were playing both ends against the middle. And I know you don't like to lose. So maybe you thought you were losing your doctor and came running back to me so you wouldn't be humiliated. Is that it? Were you stringing me along until your doctor left his wife—"

"Leave his wife? He's not about to leave his wife," Merle cried. "Honey, his wife's the money." She focused on Veronica. "He didn't tell you that part, did he? Shoot, it's her daddy that has his name on everything around here. Dr. Boatman's not going to leave on your account. And I'm sorry to tell you, but you're not the first one, either. Don't look at me like that. I sit here every day and I see everything that goes on, and I'm telling you the truth."

But Veronica was having none of it. "This is none of your business, and I have had about all I'm going to take from you, do you hear me?"

Apparently not afraid of anybody or anything, Merle came off her bench. "Hey, don't you let your mouth write a check your butt can't cash, Blondie. Because I'll mop this floor up with your narrow ass."

"Oh, my God." Dianna gasped and pulled away from Chris. He freed himself from her, too. And they both stepped in.

Apparently alarmed, Veronica made a sudden move as if to turn around, but her hip hit the tray that her doctor/lover had clanked onto the rails. The darned thing up-ended in Merle's direction, splattering the hot liquid all over her. In frozen horror, Dianna, along with Chris and Veronica, watched a dark stain spread down the stunned woman's white uniform. Gasps and comments from all around them reminded Dianna that they weren't alone. There were kitchen workers standing around. And there had been other customers in the dining room, too. No doubt, with this brouhaha escalating, no one had left.

Merle recovered and cried out, holding the front of her uniform away from her body. Chris grabbed the cashier and quickly herded her back to a tall, skinny woman wearing an apron and a hair net. "Get her out of her uniform. Help her. All of you. Make sure she isn't burned."

Several employees rushed forward to help take Merle away. The poor woman was crying and shouting. Chris put an arm around her and went with them. "I'll be right back, Dianna."

She heard him, but completely outraged and incredulous, Dianna stepped up to Veronica. "It's a good thing for you that was an accident, and we all saw that it was. But how could you be so careless? She's got to be seventy years old."

Veronica's arrogant sneer marred her blond good looks. "Like you said, it was clearly an accident. But if the woman hadn't got up off her stool to stick her nose in where it wasn't any of her business, she wouldn't have been in the line of fire."

"That's all you have to say? Could you *be* less apologetic or compassionate, Veronica? What is wrong with you?"

"There is nothing wrong with me." Veronica wagged a finger in Dianna's face. "And I will not stand here and be lectured by you, do you hear me?"

Dianna slapped Veronica's pointing finger away. "Listen up, Veronica, I don't know what your problem is, but your wheels are coming off. How can you act like this and have the responsible job you do? You're a nightmare."

"And you're a saint, is that it?"

"No, I'm no saint. We both know that. But I'm not an asshole, either. And I'm not mean-spirited. Again, what is your problem? How in God's name could Chris have ever been with a woman like you?"

"You don't know anything about Chris."

"I know everything I need to know. Except you. I don't see you with him. You couldn't have always been like this, or he wouldn't have been with you. So what's changed, Veronica? What's different? You lose your job? The doctor get you pregnant, what? You got some kind of hormonal imbalance going here?"

"Nothing's wrong with me. I am who I am."

"So, now you're Popeye?" A more rational part of Dianna's brain was telling her to be the heroine and walk away. But another part of her brain was telling her not to turn her back on this woman. And the other part just wanted to have her moment.

Veronica made a scoffing little chuckle that really insulted Dianna. "Oh, please. Is that the best you can do? By the way, nice eye you've got working there. You are no worthy opponent for me. The only thing I find hard to believe is that I could lose him to you."

Dianna fought hard not to respond to that and to just get said what was important to her to say. "So Chris was right. It is about winning to you. And about your doctor not leaving his wife. It was all about pride and never about love with you, was it? That is so pathetic. I feel sorry for you, Veronica. I thought I hated you, but all I feel is sorry for you."

Veronica's face twisted into an ugly Halloween mask, and she grabbed the front of Dianna's T-shirt. "I don't want your pity."

Stunned, Dianna's heart thumped-thumped-thumped. But more calmly than she would have believed she was capable of being, she said, "Take your hands off me, Veronica. Right now. Or I'll finish what you only started yesterday. And make no mistake, I'll kick your ass."

*You'll kick her ass?* The sweet, well-behaved-girl side of Dianna's brain was shrieking at her. *What do you mean you'll kick her ass? Who do you think you are—Xena, Warrior Princess? Wonder Woman? Batwoman? The queen of the Amazons? Have you lost your mind? You've never hit anyone in your whole life except for Lenny and Edward and Tommy. And, yes, that mean girl in seventh grade; what was her name? The one in gym class. Amy Something. She kept hitting you in the stomach with the volleyball.*

To Dianna's surprise . . . and yes, disappointment . . . Veronica let go of her and very mockingly straightened her T-shirt. "Sorry. I'd hate to muss such expensive material."

Dianna couldn't react fast enough. Her ears were buzzing, the adrenaline was pumping . . . and she just stood there. Slowly, she realized that, from behind her, she was hearing Chris's voice. "You're lucky, Veronica. Merle wasn't burned. Just scared. I can't believe you were so careless. Or that you obviously couldn't care less now how she is. How can you be that way? Look, I don't know if you're just in over your head or what, but you need help. Professional help. But for right now, you're done here. Just say good-bye and go on about your business."

She arched an eyebrow at Chris. "I don't take orders from you."

Chris exhaled. "Fine. Don't. But *we're* leaving. Come on, Dianna." He took her arm. "I just saw Edward out in the hall. It's time."

Excited now, Dianna forgot all about Veronica, turning her back on the woman and going with Chris. "The baby? It's time for the baby?"

"Chris?"

He stopped and turned around to Veronica. Since his arm was around Dianna, she turned with him. "What is it? We're in kind of a hurry here."

"I just wanted to say that you won't be all that hard to forget."

Chris exhaled as if impatient. "Whatever."

"And you never satisfied me in bed."

"For Christ's sake." He looked down at Dianna. "Do you believe this?"

"No. I really don't, Chris. I know better, remember. But will you excuse me a moment, honey?" She pulled away from him.

"Hey, what are you going to do?"

She dusted her hands off and flexed her fingers. "Something I should have done before now." She stepped up to Veronica. "You shouldn't insult my man like that, Veronica. Now, normally, I'm not a violent person—"

"Oh, shit. Dianna, don't—"

She didn't. Veronica did first. The attorney stepped up to Dianna, apparently meaning to deliver an open-handed smack to her face; otherwise known as a bitch slap.

No way was Dianna taking another blow to her eye. Thus highly motivated, and scared to death yet adrenaline-pumped, she proved quicker—quicker even than Chris who made a (too late) diving leap for her. As if she were Jackie Chan, Dianna blocked the woman's blow with her left arm and, with her right hand fisted, punched the nasty little blonde solidly hard and high on her cheek, right beside her eye—just like Tommy had taught her.

It was late Tuesday night before Dianna made it home. Very late. Chris drove her, of course. And then he insisted on slowly walking her up the inside stairs to her door. She didn't argue because she was so tired that she didn't trust her legs to carry her on their own.

They were now outside her locked door in the long, carpeted, quiet, well-lit hallway. Dead on her feet, Dianna handed Chris her purse. "Here. See if you can find my keys. I'm no good with this cast yet."

"Okay. And how does your hand feel?"

"Like I broke my knuckle. I can't believe this." She leaned back against the wall and rolled her head loosely until she could see Chris fumbling around in her purse. "Who knew the person doing the hitting got hurt, too?"

"Guys know that. Why do you have all this stuff in here?" He held up a wad of tissues and frowned at her, a questioning expression on his face.

"In case there's no toilet paper in the ladies' room."

"Oh." He kept sorting through the contents, doing more holding up of things and examining them in the light than he was looking for keys. "Anyway, the hospital security people were pretty cool about not arresting you or Veronica."

"They could have arrested her, for all I care."

"I agree. But it was an accident—I mean Merle. And she wasn't burned and didn't want to report it. Still, I don't think Veronica will be talking lawsuit anymore. She's pretty much shown her motivations here." Chris eyed the third tube of lipstick he'd pulled out of her bag and said, "I'm thinking of asking Merle if she'd like to come be my housekeeper and cook. What do you think?"

"I think you could use a cook. But what makes you think she's a good cook?"

"I was talking to her while you were getting X rays. Cooking came up."

"You're not just thinking about it. You already hired her, didn't you, Chris?"

"Yes. She's nice. I like her. She starts next Monday."

"You're an old softie, you know that?"

"Yeah. Besides, she'll make my mother crazy, so it'll be worth it."

"As long as it makes your mother crazy. Chris, can you not find a simple set of keys, honey? I'm dead on my feet. My face hurts, and my hand is killing me. I just want to get to bed and forget this whole day."

"It's not over yet."

"Oh, God. What do you mean? It's nearly midnight. I became an aunt today and—"

"What a beautiful little girl, too. Margaret. Maggie. Wow. A whole new life. What an experience. You know, your dad even forgot himself and hugged me, he was so excited. And Tommy looked every inch the proud papa, too. Well, once he got over his notion to beat the crap out of me."

"*I'm* going to beat the crap out of you if you don't find those keys, Chris."

"Okay, okay, hold on, champ. I think I got them here. Yep. Here they are." He came up with them, holding them up for her to see. "But first I want to ask you something."

"Chris, I swear to God if you ask me to marry you—"

"What would you say if I did?"

Dianna stared balefully at him. The damned man could not have looked more handsome—*how do guys do that? It's midnight; they've been through the same hell you have, and they still look like Prince Charming*—or more endearing standing there with his hands and arms full of her purse and its contents. "I would say no, Chris."

"Why?"

"*Why?* Are you serious? Look at me. I look like Quasimodo here. Or like I lost a fight with a junkyard dog.

My new Victoria's Secret T-shirt is all wadded up. I have no idea what my hair looks like. My jeans are trashed from this little fiberglass-cast episode. The whole side of my face is swollen and bruised. I can't see out of my right eye. And I broke my freakin' hand defending *your* honor."

He stuffed everything back in her purse, except the keys. "Not to argue, but you actually were defending my prowess in the bedroom."

"Whatever, Mr. Stud Muffin. Would you just please unlock my door and go home?"

"Sure. If that's what you want." She showed him which key was to her door. He stuck it in the lock and said, "So let me get this straight. A woman doesn't want to be asked by her guy to marry him if she's not looking her best, right?"

"I cannot believe I have to do this tonight. But no, not always and not all women. It's just that it's such a memorable moment in a woman's life. She wants to always remember what she was wearing. Where they were. Like that."

"Oh, so location is important, too."

"I have a whole business that says it is."

"I see. I guess I hadn't realized all that about location and how you look."

"And the ring is pretty necessary, too. And flowers. You'll catch on more when you're there every day and working with Mrs. Windhorst. She'll fill you in."

"I'm sure she will. So how do you want it to be for you, Dianna? Some soft night in Hawaii? Atop the Eiffel Tower in Paris? At the Taj Mahal?"

"Oh, hardly. I guess I want sincerity. And constancy. Someone who's always there. Someone who understands me. Who laughs at my jokes and knows me really well and yet still likes me. And someone who loves me so much that he'd die rather than walk away from me."

Chris held up his hand in the air.

"What are you doing?"

"I'd like to apply for that job."

"Chris, it is so late, honey. And I'm so tired."

"All right. You're right. One more question. Do you love me in all those ways you just said, Dianna?"

Dianna was certain she was going to cry. "Yes, Chris. I do. I love you in all those ways."

"You do? You could see yourself living with me for the rest of your life?"

"Chris, that's another question, and you said one. But, yes, I could. And you're just taking advantage of me being so tired. Not fair."

"Maybe not. But I have to press my advantage while I have it. Is my face the one you want to see every morning when you wake up?"

"Yes, dammit. Are you happy now?"

"Not completely. Why won't you marry me?"

"You haven't actually asked me yet, you know. Not tonight, anyway."

He still hadn't turned that key in the lock, either. "Oh. Will you marry me, Dianna?"

"No. And only this afternoon at my office, you said you wouldn't ask me ever again, remember?"

"Yeah. But a lot has changed since then."

"Like what?"

"Like I can't live without you."

"You're just afraid to take on Merle alone."

At long last, he turned the key in the lock. "That's true." And opened the door. "Okay, here you are, all safe and sound." He ran his gaze over her and winced. "Well, safe, anyway."

"Thanks. Good night, Chris."

"You aren't going to invite me in?"

"No. I can't think tonight, Chris. I'm dead tired. I just want to go to bed." She stepped inside and pushed against his chest. "Good night. Go home." She took her keys from him and closed the door, locking it from the inside.

No more than one second passed before there was a knock on her door. "I'm going to kill him," she muttered. She looked out the peephole. There was Chris, that nut, grinning like an idiot and holding her purse up for her to see. "Oh, for God's sake." She opened the door and snatched the purse from him. "Thank you. Go home." She impolitely closed the door in the man's face again and locked it.

She stood there, listening. Another two or three seconds went by. He didn't knock. She looked out the peephole. No one was in the hall. Okay, so she was a bit disappointed that he'd given up so easily. And pretty jazzed that he kept asking her to marry him. She smiled, thinking of how much she loved him and how she would probably say yes before long because she knew him so much better this evening than she had this morning and, God, how she loved him. He was so the right man for her. That one in a million—

A knock on the door startled her. She chuckled. *All right, you stinker.* She looked out the peephole. Nothing but hallway. Her smile faded. She didn't know what to do. Oh, come on, it had to be Chris. But what was he doing? Hiding to one side of the door? Yes, that sounded just like him.

Dianna turned the deadbolt and eased the door open. And what she saw there made her burst out laughing. She quickly clapped a hand over her mouth to keep from disturbing her neighbors. "Chris Adams, what are you doing?"

The man was down on one knee in her hallway. In one hand he held a velvet ring box out to her. "I just remembered I had this in the glove compartment. I bought it this morning for you."

Dianna leaned a shoulder against the doorjamb. "And the flowers, Chris? You have roots and dirt and all. Where did you get them? Do not tell me you pulled them out of Mrs. Blodgett's planter."

"I don't know Mrs. Blodgett, but is hers the door right before the outside door and if you stick your foot in the doorway so the security door doesn't close and then lean

way over to the planter there, you can pluck flowers up
and still get back inside?"

"Yes." Dianna thought she was going to cry from sheer
happiness and love for this nutty, intelligent, witty guy
she could not bear to spend one more day apart from.

"Then these are hers. Well, yours now. So, okay, I'm
down on one knee. I've got the ring. Go ahead, open the
box. It's gorgeous. And here are the flowers. If you hurry
we can probably replant them and she'll never know." He
grinned.

"Ask me."

"No. You always say no."

"Go ahead. Ask me."

"I don't want to."

"Why not?"

"You'll say no."

"Chris, I've been saying no all day."

"Oh, by the way, I forgot to tell you something that
your mother told me this evening when you were getting
your cast put on."

"Oh, God. What?"

"Lenny and Olivia eloped and ran away to Florida, and
his mother is going ape-shit. Well, your mother didn't
actually say 'ape-shit,' but it was the same thing."

Dianna stood there with her mouth open. "Are you
serious? Lenny finally grew some balls?"

"Or Olivia did. Apparently she got a call from her old
employer offering her a huge raise to go down South and
work. So she threatened Lenny with leaving him. And he
bit and went with her. I understand that Lenny's mother
is inconsolable."

"She'll get over it, the old harridan. Or fly down there
and live with them."

"Your mother is hoping that's what will happen."

"Cool. New neighbors. Finally."

"And your track record stays at a hundred percent."

"That's right. I forgot about that."

"No, wait. It won't. I'm a client, too. I have a contract

with your place of business. And I'm asking."

"So . . . ask."

"You want to see the ring first?"

"No. Ask."

"Okay, but you better say yes." He took a deep breath, exhaled, and said, "Dianna Joan West, I love you with all my heart and all my soul. Everything I have, I give to you. I cannot live without you. And I don't even want to try. I don't think I've known you for even a month, but what is time to the heart? I knew the first moment I looked into your eyes that I would love you. Will you do me the honor of marrying me?"

Very seriously, very soberly, Dianna considered him down there on one knee.

"Dianna? My foot is numb."

"Shh. I'm thinking."

"What's there to think about, for crying out loud? If you say no, I'm just going to ask you tomorrow. And every day after that for the rest of our lives until I'm too old even to talk."

"Well, that sounds kind of bleak."

"I know. So?"

She smiled. "Yes."

He looked suspicious. "Yes what?"

"Yes, I'll marry you."

"You will? You're saying yes? You're actually saying yes?"

A door down the way opened and a little old man with wispy hair and a bony chest popped out into the hall and yelled, "She said yes, already. I heard her. Maury Jacobson heard her. Flo Mendicott heard her. My dog heard her. Give her the damn ring and kiss her, you jerk, so we can all get back to sleep." He drew his head back in and slammed the door.

Chris looked up at Dianna. "Who was that?"

"Mr. Hartz. He's cranky."

"We can't live here."

"We'll live at your place, but I'm redecorating."

"Fine. So, you want the ring?"

"Sure." She took it, opened it, damn near lost her breath, it was that big and that beautiful. "Nice," she gulped out.

"Thanks. And the flowers?"

"No. We have to replant those."

"Oh, right. Can I get up now?"

"Yeah, I guess. Want me to hold the flowers while you do?"

"Can you, please? That'd be good." She took them; he stood up. "Want me to place the ring on your finger now?"

"Okay."

He took it out of the box and slipped it on her finger and stood there with her, staring lingeringly at it with her. "Sure you're not disappointed, Dianna? I mean, this wasn't elaborate or wildly romantic or—"

"It was all of those things, Chris. But not as much as it's getting ready to be, big boy." Startling Chris, she tossed the ruined flowers onto the hallway carpet. "We'll buy Mrs. Blodgett more tomorrow."

With that, she grabbed him by his shirt and pulled him into her condo. The door slammed after them.

And thus began their happily-ever-after.

And that was also how it was that Popping the Question's track record remained at one hundred percent.

ONLY THE MIRACLE OF LOVE COULD
SET HER FREE . . .

# Captive Angel

## CHERYL ANNE PORTER

Jack Daltry came back to his father's ranch to
mend fences between them. Instead, he finds his
father dead, and a feisty, beautiful woman claiming
his dad gave her the Circle D ranch. Now a stand-
off begins between a man eaten up with anger
and a defiant beauty with emotions locked behind
a wall of self-control. But when a ruthless killer
comes after them both, Jack finds a woman of
passion and courage beside him . . . and the
chance for redemption if he can show Angel the
transforming power of love.

AVAILABLE WHEREVER BOOKS ARE SOLD
FROM ST. MARTIN'S PAPERBACKS

C ANG 12/00

*1/09*

# WELCOME TO TEMPTATION

**THE SENSATIONAL *NEW YORK TIMES* BESTSELLER**

# Jennifer Crusie

Sophie Dempsey is content living a quiet life filming wedding videos until an assignment brings her to Temptation, Ohio. From the moment she drives into town, she gets a bad feeling; Sophie is from the wrong side of the tracks and everything in Temptation is a little too right. And when she has a run-in with the town's unnervingly sexy mayor, Phineas Tucker, making a little movie turns out to be more than a little dangerous.

As events spiral out of control, Sophie and Phin find themselves falling deeper and deeper in trouble . . . and in love.

"Bright, funny, sexy, and wise." —*Kirkus Reviews*

"Crusie charms with her brisk, edgy style . . . a romantic comedy that adds luster to the genre, this effervescent tale will please readers."
—*Publishers Weekly* (starred review)

**AVAILABLE WHEREVER BOOKS ARE SOLD FROM
ST. MARTIN'S PAPERBACKS**